SHOW STOPPER

Scholastic Children's Books
An imprint of Scholastic Ltd
Euston House, 24 Eversholt Street, London, NW1 1DB, UK
Registered office: Westfield Road, Southam, Warwickshire, CV47 0RA
SCHOLASTIC and associated logos are trademarks and/or
registered trademarks of Scholastic Inc.

First published in the UK by Scholastic Ltd, 2017

ISBN 978 1407 17967 4

A CIP catalogue record for this book
is available from the British Library.

Printed by CPI Group (UK) Ltd, Croydon, CR0 4YY
Papers used by Scholastic Children's Books are made
from wood grown in sustainable forests.

1 3 5 7 9 10 8 6 4 2

www.scholastic.co.uk

SHOW STOPPER

HAYLEY BARKER

SCHOLASTIC

For Mark

Prologue

HOSHIKO

The cries of the audience pound in my head as I stand, poised, above them. I'm a hundred feet off the ground but, if I try, I can make out individual faces in the sea of bodies below me.

I begin swinging. Backwards and forwards, backwards and forwards. Gaining momentum, gaining pace, becoming rhythmic: backwards and forwards, backwards and forwards.

There is only me now; only the arc and the fall. If I let go too soon I won't reach the wire; too late and I'll loop right over it.

Just as I am perfectly level, I pull my legs inward and upward, on to the wire. I crouch there, both feet gripping, as the twanging vibrations ease. My breathing gradually steadies. I'm in control once more, back in my element. Time to give them what they want.

Balancing easily, I lift one leg off the wire, higher and higher, leaning my body forward until the line of my legs is completely vertical, like a giant letter T. I stay poised for a moment or two and then somersault, again and again and again, feet landing back on the wire each time.

I look down at the cheering throng below then lower myself down so that I'm sitting, legs split, resting on the wire either side of me before I grip on to it and let myself spiral, above and below, faster and faster and faster, whirling the crowd into a frenzy. Eventually, when their screams feel like they could raise the roof, I stop and pull myself up on the wire again. Time for the highlight of my little show.

Reaching over to the wings, I am handed a stool. I raise it aloft, my feet curling round the wire as I balance, feeling my way back to the middle of the tightrope. There's a tense silence as the audience holds its breath.

I rest two of the stool's legs on the wire. I mustn't rush it, it's all about balance now. Balance and instinct. I climb on to the stool, sitting on it. Legs crossed, arms thrown out wide. Finally, I curl my legs in and straighten myself, so that I'm standing on the stool. I elevate one leg, rise up on to the point of my toes and spin. Round and round, high above the world, defying gravity. Defying the odds they've given me yet again. The band strikes up, a grandiose crescendo of celebration. Fireworks explode all around me, cascading down like stars. Far below in the arena, a band of gymnasts in white tumble and leap while I, the pinnacle, the centre point, reign supreme.

It's then, out of the corner of my eye, that I see Silvio watching from the platform. He looks furious. Why? My blood runs cold as I realize.

He wanted me to fall.

He's concealed from below by the great curtains billowing either side of the platform.

I'm the only one who can see him.

Our eyes meet as he reaches out one hand and clasps hold of the tightrope. Grinning wickedly, he jerks it back and forth, sending his message of execution down the wire.

I can't maintain my balance and I fall, hearing the collective gasp of the audience as I plummet head first to the ground.

BEN

I can't take my eyes off her, hanging there. She must be one hundred feet up, but I can see the expression on her face so clearly. She doesn't look frightened; she looks angry. Why?

Without warning, she swings. The spotlights catch on the sparkles in her costume as she pendulums back and forth. A human glitter ball, casting patterns over the arena. Her long black hair is alive and dancing, the light reflecting off its glossy waves. Springing on to the wire, she's so agile she takes my breath away.

Around me, they're all caught up in the excitement. Mother, Father, Francis, even the bodyguards, actually jumping up and down in their glee, so hard that I feel the box shuddering beneath my feet.

I look back at the girl, now flitting effortlessly across the wire. She starts to dance up there, as if she's not on a wire at all. She's up on one leg, and then down, spiralling, a blur of light and motion.

Someone hands her a stool. I can't believe my eyes when she somehow balances its legs on the wire and sits on it. If this was on TV, I wouldn't believe it; I'd think it was all a fix, just down to clever camera work. She's sitting on a stool. A stool on a tightrope.

She rises upward. Surely she's not going to? She is. She stands on it. This can't be real. How is she doing it?

She spins on one foot, whirling round and round and round. Everyone's on their feet now, stamping and clapping: a thunderous applause.

She's not smiling though. Her dark eyebrows are arched disdainfully and she's so close I can see the blaze in her eyes as she spins, lashes lowered, glaring down at the crowd.

I stop cheering.

I've never seen anyone like her before. I can't stop staring at her face. I see her eyes shift to the side. See them widen in horror. See her slip backwards. See her falling…

BEN

The Cirque coming is all anyone's been talking about for weeks. As soon as the adverts appear online and in the papers, there's a buzz of excitement in the air, so electric you feel you could touch it. It's been over ten years since it was last in London and I was too young then, really, to care that much when Mother and Father said we couldn't go. I remember afterwards how the older kids at school couldn't stop talking about it in the playground, and we all gathered around to listen. There was a big crowd of us, straining forward to try and catch their words. I must have only been five or six, but I can still hear them now.

"It's magic," one boy said. "Not fake magic, but real magic. It must be, the things they can do in there!"

And there was a girl, her eyes glowing when she joined in. "It's like a dream," she said. "It's like a fairy story."

The day it's due to arrive, it seems like every kid in the whole school is heading over to the fields straight after the bell to watch it turn up. I have this ridiculous fantasy in my head that I'll be able go too, but as soon as I turn to Stanley, my bodyguard, lingering discreetly at the back of the classroom, his mouth tightens and he shakes his head. I know exactly what he means: *Don't even think about it.*

I ask my twin brother, Francis, about the circus in the car on the way home from school.

"Are you annoyed that we can't go and watch the circus coming?"

He looks at me like I'm mad.

"Why would I want to watch that? Why would anyone want to watch a load of Dreg scum coming into town?"

I don't know what to say. I just shrug and stare out of the window.

Once home, I don't even go into the kitchen to ask our servant Priya for a snack. I head upstairs straight away, right up to the library at the top of the house. You can see for miles around up here and all the way down into the city below. The main road into town snakes away to the left. That's where the circus will head in from.

I can see the other kids, dozens of them, all perched on the fence posts which line the fields. I've got a far better view from up here but I'd rather be down there, with them, huddled up for warmth, legs dangling down on the fence, exhaling smoky puffs of cold air every time we laugh.

It looks much more fun where they are. It looks like freedom.

Nothing happens for ages and then four huge lorries come winding their way up the hill.

Six Dregs and a guard jump out of each one and the Dregs begin assembling great iron fences, cordoning off four fields. They work quickly and efficiently and before long the fields have vanished from the view of everyone down there at eye level.

It makes it all seem even more mysterious and secretive. If you want to see into the Cirque, you pay your money like everyone else. There aren't any free viewings, not unless you're way up here, and there aren't many people whose status makes them important enough to live as high above ground as us.

Once they've finished, the men jump back into the lorries and drive away, leaving all the kids staring at the miles of iron fences.

The Cirque must be absolutely massive if it's going to take up all that space.

Everything goes quiet again after that. Some of the kids get bored and wander off home for tea, but they're replaced by others, and then they return again, and still there's no sign of the Cirque itself.

I don't go downstairs at dinner time so Priya sends my food upstairs on a little tray. I don't eat much though; I'm too busy craning my neck out of the window.

Finally, twinkling and shining its way up the hill, I see it.

The procession.

None of the kids can see it at first, and then, as it makes its way over the crest of the hill, they're all suddenly up on their feet, standing on the fence posts, jostling for position.

Six white horses all dotted with fairy lights trot along at the front; on their backs stand girls and boys in illuminated, spangled costumes. They spring up in the air, tumbling again and again and landing, incredibly, on their two feet.

After them comes a gleaming Palomino horse, much bigger than the others. You can sense its restrained energy in the way it moves: legs rising high as it trots, neck arching forward.

There's a man standing on its back, all dressed up in a funny little suit, with a monkey on his shoulder. He's carrying a big box and he tosses handfuls of sweets from it to the kids, who are all jumping up and down, crying out to him desperately with outstretched hands.

After him come dozens of pretty little pastel-coloured wagons, huge trailers of equipment, and then even bigger trucks – which must house the Dregs and the rest of the animals, I suppose.

Last of all is a huge open trailer, lit up with hundreds of multicoloured lights. It's full of people – the performers – all waving to the crowd of children. Clowns are juggling balls, more acrobats are tumbling and there are two fire-eaters devouring angry tongues of flame.

Way above them, there's a girl, a tightrope walker, somersaulting and spiralling.

A bright white spotlight follows her as she darts and weaves through the inky sky.

The wire she's on stretches between two high poles, connected across the dozens of carriages. She twists and turns along the whole length of the procession, fluid like water.

Lasers dance all around her, and fireworks soar up into the sky, framing her in golden stars.

Her image is projected as dozens and dozens of holograms way up into the air, so that everywhere you look replicas of her arch and tumble and somersault, lighting up the darkness.

People must be able to see her for miles.

One of the images is right outside the window, inches below my head. She looks up suddenly and I stare back into her eyes. There's a steely look in them; she's beautiful but there's something about her that makes me shiver. I know it's not really her out there looking in at me, but she feels so close, like I could touch her. I open up the window as far as it can go and stretch out my hand, straining it towards the light radiating from her, but my fingers clasp at nothing.

It's when I see her, dancing across the sky, that I make the promise to myself. Whatever happens, whatever Mother and Father say, I'm going to the Cirque.

HOSHIKO

The children lining the fences all cheer and shout as we arrive. Most of them are actually jumping up and down with excitement, their hands clasping for the sweets that Silvio cascades into the crowd.

I beam my smile down at them as I tumble, waving and blowing kisses every time I land back on the wire.

I hate them.

I hate them all.

I think about spitting on them.

This is it, then: London. It's been ten years since the circus pitched up here – just before I was selected. It can't be later than five o'clock but it's dark already and the buildings stretching out all around me twinkle with a million lights.

Right up in the middle of the vast sprawl, towering over the labyrinth of skyscrapers and office blocks below, rises the famous Government PowerHouse. It's bathed in yellow light and is so huge that I can make out every detail, even from up here as I flip and dance. It's just like Amina described it. From the bottom, in gleaming black ebony, hundreds and hundreds of sculpted bodies rise up in a great column. Coiled around each other, on top of each other, entwined with each other, crushing each other: a massive pyramid of writhing Dregs.

On top, right there on the peak, gleaming and glistening above the world, a huge gold statue stands supreme, supported by the hundreds of clustered, crouching bodies beneath. A man – a superman – rippling muscles, face smiling tenderly down at the city below him.

I shiver, and feel my feet wobble as I lose concentration.

It stands for everything that's wrong with the world, that statue. It stands for dominance and pride and power. It stands for oppression: the many being crushed by the few. It stands for evil.

I can't tear my eyes away from it. I keep staring at it as the trailers wind their way through the great metal gates which then slam shut with a resounding clang.

At least that will be the last I see of it until we leave. That will be the last any of us see of the outside world for two weeks, until we dismantle and pack up and make our way to a new destination. It shouldn't really matter where we are, what town we pitch up in; the people who flock here night after night are the same wherever we go.

But it feels different, being here, right at the centre of it all: right where the laws are made, right where the PowerHouse squats.

I shiver again before I jump down from the wire.

As soon as the gates shut, Silvio disembarks his Palomino stallion. "Round them up and get them building!" he orders the guards. "Time is money!" The smiling, benevolent bestower of sweets has vanished and his lips are curled impatiently.

I try to reach Greta and Amina but I can't get to them quickly enough. They're herded off to one field and I'm left behind with another group.

Crack! A whip lashes across my back as we're herded over

to a big pile of building materials.

"What are you waiting for, you fools?" Silvio shrieks at us, his whip catching me again, catching all of us as we huddle together while it rains down relentlessly. "Get down there, crawl on your hands and knees and start building!"

BEN

All that evening I sit up in the library and watch as a vast walled town is erected before my eyes. Huge scaffolds, great metal walls, all nailed and hammered together painstakingly by dozens of Dregs. The billowing fabrics of golds, silvers and reds which are finally pinned on give the illusion of dozens and dozens of tents, all with domed roofs reaching up into the sky; but they aren't tents at all. They are real solid structures built like that to keep the animals in, I guess, and the Dregs too.

There are a few bigger buildings and lots of smaller ones, all linked from above with loads of enclosed aerial walkways. It means the Dreg performers never even have to set foot outside once it's built. It keeps them nice and separated from the Pures, like a giant ant colony in the sky. They're like worker ants, I suppose, scurrying busily here, there and everywhere for our entertainment.

I try to spot the girl again, but it's getting dark and everyone looks the same from this distance. I see her image though; it plays on repeat, one of the ten or so they keep beaming up into the sky.

I keep trying to figure out how I can persuade my parents to let me go and watch a show. They'll never agree – not with the way they feel about Dregs. I have to though. I have to see if it's true, what everyone else is saying about the shows. I have to see her, dancing on the tightrope.

HOSHIKO

It's pitch black by the time we've finished working. My hands are bleeding and I feel myself swaying as we're finally pushed into the dorms and the doors are locked shut.

Finally, six whole hours with no guards, no Silvio, no Pures. They don't bother to supervise at night – it saves money, I suppose, and it's not as if any of us can go anywhere.

I scan the room for Greta and Amina, taking in the appearance of everyone else as I do so. At first glance, you'd think we had nothing in common at all. All different colours and creeds make up this crazy circus; a more diverse group you'd be hard-pressed to find. When you look more closely though, we're more alike than you'd initially think.

It's rare for a member of the Dreg Cirque to make it to adulthood, so pretty much everyone's young, but most people look miles older than they actually are. Every face, even the tiniest of the children's, is lined with worry and exhaustion, and many people bear scars and injuries – physical confirmation of how dangerous what we do is.

In another world, we'd all walk different paths, but in here we're a unit. We share a common existence: the same worries, woes and hatreds. We shore each other up when we can, bear each other's burdens as much as we're able to. They're my family now – the only family I really remember.

There are about fifty of us all together, sometimes a few more, sometimes a few less as new faces arrive and old, and not so old, faces leave.

I spy Greta across the room and she rushes over to me,

flinging her arms around my waist and pressing her head into my stomach.

"I missed you!" she says. "I hate it when we're not working together."

"Me too," I say. "Where's Amina?"

"She's in the san already. One of the new boys got his arm crushed while he was erecting the scaffolding."

I wince. That's not good. If his arm's too injured he might not be able to perform, and if he can't serve his purpose, he'll be redundant to them, and we all know what that means.

"Amina thinks she can fix it. Well, that's what she said to me, anyway." She frowns. "It might not be true though; she never tells me what's really going on."

I give a dry laugh. Greta's right; if the poor guy gets taken away, Amina won't tell Greta that – she'll make up some story or other. She tries to spare her from as many of the gory details as she can. We both do. It's an impossible task in this place but neither of us want to see the light that's still there in her eyes extinguished any sooner than it has to be.

Amina used to do the same thing to me all the time: offer edited versions of the truth. She'd still do it now if I let her get away with it, even though there's no point any more – any delusions I had about life in here are long since over.

There's not much chatter in the dorm tonight and the communal area is already thinning out as everyone makes their way to bed. We're all equally exhausted; it's painful, physical work building the circus up from scratch and they always seem to forget to feed us on the first evening.

I think about waiting for Amina, but there's no point. She

might be gone all night anyway, and she'd be cross if she found me sitting up.

"You need your sleep," she's always saying. "Look what happened to me."

She's right. We have to take our chances of rest when they come.

"I'm so tired," I tell Greta. "I'm going straight to bed."

She looks up at me, her blue eyes beseeching, and I can't help but smile; the unspoken question in them is blazing.

"No," I protest, weakly. "No way. There's not enough room in one bunk. You're right next to me, anyway."

"Please!" she begs. "I won't be able to sleep at all if I'm on my own."

"Well, I won't be able to sleep at all with you fidgeting around next to me!"

"I won't fidget, I promise. I'll be really still. I'll scrunch right up. You won't even know I'm there."

I shake my head. Every night Greta makes the same promise and every morning there I am, half hanging out of the bed, while she lays star-fished across it.

She grins up at me. "Please?"

It's a pointless conversation. She knows I can't say no to her. She's got me completely wrapped around her little finger, has done since the day she arrived nearly a year ago now. Anyway, if I say no, she'll only keep me awake with her crying.

"OK," I concede, just as we both knew I would. "But only tonight. Tomorrow, you're on your own."

She nods, earnestly. "Whatever you say, Hoshi."

We make our way into the women's dorm, down the

thin central passage to our usual bunks, right at the far end.

It's so quiet in here tonight, an exhausted hush. It's always like this on the night we set up; everyone's even more tired than usual and sleep becomes the most important thing of all. It's not normally that way. Night-time is the only time we ever get to be together and even though we're always, always bone-tired, we all try to make the effort to stay up, just for half an hour or so. Sometimes we practise reading and writing, but not as often as we know we should. It's hard to concentrate when every part of your body is aching and your eyes are struggling to stay open. Mostly, we just gather together and one of the older kids tells a story. Sometimes the stories are made-up; fantasies to remove us for a brief, precious time from this place of pain and carry us away on flying carpets to magical worlds – to beautiful princesses and handsome princes and gleaming palaces, to fairy godmothers who make everything better with a swish of their wand. More often than not though, it's a true story. An account or recollection, or a history lesson about something from the past, about our heritage and how the world came to be the way it is. It's the only way we get to learn about who we are, about what we are. The sense of injustice I carry around with me like an iron ball resting in the pit of my stomach is strengthened by these sessions. They make it heavier to carry, but they make it more powerful too. Everyone else feels the same, I know that, but most of the others seem to be able to deal with it better than me. Amina has somehow managed to turn it into resilience; into hope, not hatred. She's certain that things won't always be this way.

"Look at history," she says. "There's always a change; there's always an end. Walls come down, regimes are toppled, the people rise up."

I love Amina, but she's wrong.

This Cirque has been around for over forty years now. Forty years of Pures paying their money to come here. Forty years of Dreg kids being wrenched away from their families and forced to perform here in the name of entertainment. Forty years of brutality, of pain, of death. The evil at the heart of society is ingrained. How can it ever end?

I lay straight down in my hard little bunk and Greta shuffles in next to me, wriggling her tiny body so she's snuggled right up.

Just when I think she's settling, she jumps up again to grab Lucy, her doll, from her own bed. The filthy bundle of mismatched cloth, sewn together so lovingly, is all she's got left of home and she never sleeps without it.

She turns to face me and I feel her warm breath on my face.

"Greta!" I whisper. "Stop breathing all over me!"

"Sorry," she whispers back, but doesn't move away. "Did you see the statue?"

"Yes."

"Wasn't it huge?"

"It wasn't that big. I didn't think it was that impressive actually."

"Didn't you? I liked the big gold man."

The big gold man – she hasn't got a clue what he represents. I'm glad of it.

"It's exciting, isn't it?" she says. "Being in the capital?"

"No! Why would it be? What difference does it make? It's not as if we're going to be doing any sightseeing!"

"No. I know, but … there'll be loads of important people coming to watch us; that's what Silvio said."

"Greta, there's nothing special about any of them. They're not any better than you or me; none of them are."

"Still. I like seeing all the people in their fine clothes."

I swallow the retort that springs to mind. Amina's right; we have to try our best to preserve her innocence, to keep her a child for as long as we can.

I suppose you could say that Greta's like my little sister, but it's more than that really. I might be only sixteen, but I feel like her mother.

The truth is I love her and Amina more than anyone in this whole messed-up world. More than my own family, even – after all, it's been eleven years since I saw them.

The main reason I fight to survive every night is so that I can keep training Greta. I don't want her to have to get out there and perform, God knows I don't, but I have to make damn sure she's ready for it when she does. I have to keep her safe, even though I know that the better she gets, the less vital I become.

I can still remember every detail of the day she arrived like it was yesterday. It wasn't long after Amina's accident and we were in the arena, rehearsing.

Silvio had given us three days to adapt the show to feature just me, instead of the two of us. I was really jumpy, we both were; scared he'd suddenly change his mind about keeping

Amina, about her being useful. That he'd sweep in and take her away and I'd never see her again.

I kept losing my balance and slipping on the wire. Amina was trying not to get irritated, but even she couldn't hide it. She didn't say anything, but I knew she was scared: for me as well as her. If I couldn't carry the show all on my own, it wouldn't just be her who'd be at risk. She was trying to keep it all inside but every time I made a mistake I could see her shoulders tighten, her jaw clench.

There was an unfamiliar tense silence between us and then the big doors swung open and Silvio came in, dragging this dirty little scrap of a girl by her white hair.

"Meet our newest recruit!" he sneered. "She's just passed selection. Hardly with flying colours, but beggars can't be choosers. The rest of them were bloody awful; this one at least has some potential, I suppose, some flexibility." He pulled her arm behind her back, hard, and she cried out.

He looked me up and down, appraisingly. "How are the rehearsals going?" he asked suspiciously.

"Fine," Amina and I both answered at once.

"I hope so. High wire is still one of our biggest pulls, God knows why. You'd better be able to draw the crowds in on your own, girl. I don't want to have to rip the whole thing up and start all over again."

The threat hung in the air.

The whole time Greta was just staring at me, her lip trembling, her big eyes wide, pleading with me to do something. He released his hold eventually though, and pushed her so that she landed in a crumpled heap at my feet.

"Anyway, this street rat is my insurance policy, for now. Train her up, fast," he ordered and swept out of the room.

She looked up at me and she said exactly the same words we all say. The same words she repeated night after night after night when I held her as she cried herself to sleep. The same words she's stopped saying now. The words I stopped saying too. When? I can't remember. When thoughts of home faded from memory to myth, when this place took its evil hold and became more real to me than the time before.

"*I want my mummy.*"

We didn't get any more rehearsing done that day.

Amina and I picked up the broken little creature from the floor and tried to fix her, to patch her up and mend her tiny wings. And we've kept her going so far, with Amina's bandages and plasters and cream, and with a lot of protection and love and support. She's stronger than she was, I suppose, but she still doesn't belong here. None of us do but Greta especially is too good for this world: too gentle and delicate. She won't survive in a place like this much longer. She's like a butterfly, and butterflies need sunshine and air, space and freedom, not spotlights and locked doors. Butterflies are vulnerable; their wings can be too easily crushed.

Any day now, Silvio will call for Greta to make her debut. I'm surprised he hasn't already. And, when he does, she'll be OK; I know she will. I keep telling her she's nearly ready, even though she doesn't believe me. She's so talented, such a natural up there; the crowd are going to love her. How could they not? Fierce pride swells up inside me every time I look at her, bringing with it such an intense sense of protection.

I'm not the only one who thinks she's like a butterfly. It's the name Silvio's already coined for her: *the Butterfly*. He sees her beauty and frailness as a commodity, something he can turn into a brand. The Butterfly and the Cat, that's Greta and me.

BEN

I can't sleep so I wait until it's quiet and then do what I always do when I need someone to talk to – creep down to the kitchens to find Priya.

She's baking bread. The warm smell fills the air as soon as I push open the heavy door.

She looks up and tuts when she sees me.

"What are you doing up at this time of the night?" she chides. She's only pretending to be cross though – I can tell by the twinkle in her eye that she's pleased I'm there.

I sit down on the stool and watch her working. It's cold down here, despite the ovens, and I hug my knees up to my stomach. Priya glances over at me and immediately stops what she's doing to go over to the cupboard. She carefully takes out her sari. I wrap myself in it gratefully, remembering the first time I saw it. How I was down here, chatting to her one cold morning, and I started to shiver. She was clicking her tongue and telling me to go back upstairs where the heating was on or at least to get myself a jumper, but I ignored her, and stayed sitting there, huddled up on the stool.

She kept looking at me doubtfully, like she was making her mind up about something, and then she went to the food cupboard and pulled it out from the back. It was hidden under a bag of rice and wrapped in brown paper. I'll never forget what it looked like when she shook it out. The weak winter sunshine filled the room that day, like it does sometimes when it's that low in the sky. The sari seemed to catch the light as it billowed, casting it back across the room. Turquoise satin, shimmering with gold and purple: like peacock feathers. Heavy and cool to the touch.

"Don't tell anyone," she whispered. "It's contraband."

I didn't know what that meant, but she told me all about it, eventually. It had been her grandmother's wedding dress, from the time before. Her mother had kept it and passed it on to her. When they outlawed traditional Indian costumes she'd hidden it away at home, but it was so damp there that she was worried about it spoiling. She'd smuggled it in here after that.

"One day I will give it to my daughter," she said. "Perhaps she can get married in it, when things improve for us."

That was the first time it dawned on me that she had her own family. The first time I realized that her life didn't revolve around me, around being a servant for us.

After that, I managed to persuade her to talk about them more and more. She was cautious at first, but she couldn't stop herself. Especially when I asked about her children, Nila and Nihal.

I've always been a bit envious of them, this boy and girl I've never met. I know that's absurd – I have everything and they have nothing – but the way her eyes shine when she talks about them always makes me feel a bit sad and empty inside. She loves them so much, it's obvious. She only sees them for a few hours a month, on her half day off, but she talks as if she lives for those times.

I wonder if my mother's eyes shine like that when she talks about me. I can't imagine that they do. I don't suppose she ever mentions me at all – she's far too busy discussing more important things.

Priya has already started making more bread and her fingers work quickly as she kneads the flour and water together until they merge into one.

"What's up then?" she asks. "What's stopping sir from sleeping this time?"

"It's the Cirque," I tell her. "I really, really want to go but I already know Mother and Father won't give me permission."

She stops what she's doing and looks sharply at me, her face uncharacteristically hard for a moment. "Why would you want to go there?"

"Why wouldn't I want to go?" I say. "Everyone says it's amazing."

"Yes." Her tone is dry, her voice brittle. "I bet they do."

She's working the dough now, pushing into it with her fist and pummelling it into submission. Again and again she slams it down heavily on the surface and pounds into it. It almost looks like she's punching someone, the way she's going at it. The atmosphere's really different all of a sudden. She's completely ignoring me and concentrating on the bread. Her lips are tight, her shoulders are hunched up.

It doesn't feel like it usually does when I slip down here. Normally, we chat away for hours, even though we both know it's forbidden.

I sit there awkwardly, watching her.

It's ages before she says anything.

"If that's really the kind of thing you think you'd enjoy," she says, finally.

"Why wouldn't I enjoy it?"

She looks at me again then, and there's a strange look on

her face I've never seen before.

"Do you really want me to tell you why?" she says.

"Yes, I do."

"Well..." she pauses for a moment and then she seems to collect herself. "Oh, ignore me. It doesn't matter what I think. I'm just a Dreg; it's not like I know what I'm talking about." She turns away and then with her back to me she says, "I think you should go to bed. It's not right, you being down here with me."

She's never said that before. She picks up a bag of carrots and starts dicing them really quickly, *chop chop chop,* with the knife.

Why is she so bothered about whether or not I go to the Cirque?

"Priya?" I don't know why I feel so awkward. "Are you OK?"

"Fine." Her voice is more restrained than normal. "Why wouldn't I be?"

"I don't know," I say. "I don't understand what I've done wrong."

She sighs and turns to me. "No," she says, more gently this time. "I don't suppose you do." She puts down the knife and leans on the work surface, her body slumping down like it's an effort to hold herself up. When she looks up at me, her eyes bore into me. "The Cirque isn't some magical wonderland, Ben. It's a prison camp."

She crosses the room and looks out of the window at the city. You can see the rooftops of the Cirque from here, all lit up and twinkling. "That place is full of kids, most of them younger than you." She laughs then, coldly and mirthlessly. "There don't seem to be many adults in there, from what I understand. Do you think they make a choice, Ben? To leave their families, to live as orphans?"

"I don't know," I say. "Maybe they like being free, away from their mums and dads. And anyway, they're only..." I stop myself before the words come out.

"Only Dregs? Is that what you were going to say?"

I hang my head. I didn't mean to upset her even more.

She walks back to the counter and starts chopping the carrots again. "You're right, of course. It's only Dreg kids in there; they don't really matter at all. Dregs don't have feelings anyway, isn't that right?"

I don't say anything.

"It must be right. That's what they tell you at school, isn't it? That's what your parents say, what your government says. Of course it's right."

I'm not sure whether she wants me to answer her. I don't know what to say, so I just sit there silently.

There's a strange feeling inside me as I sit, watching her back while she keeps furiously chopping the vegetables; it feels a bit like guilt, a bit like shame. It doesn't make sense. Why do I feel like I've done something wrong?

In the end, I fold the sari up, leaving it on the stool, before I skulk away out of the room and back to bed.

HOSHIKO

Amina's still not back and everyone else is asleep, except for me. In my arms, Greta's breathing is deep and calm. I bury my head into her soft hair and pull her in tightly.

How would I feel if she finally agreed to sleep on her own? I'd hate it, I know I would.

This night-time comfort I bring her, it's a two-way thing. Usually, cuddling up to her helps stop the pain a little. Not tonight though. Tonight, all the memories, all the pain, all the fear won't behave themselves. Not content to be held at bay, they seep in through the cracks of the walls I've built up inside to torment me.

I try to think about other things, but the images whirl in my brain like crazy black-and-white snapshots, revolving round and round.

For a second, I see Mum, Dad and Miko, how they were when I last saw them, a frozen tableau, arms stretched out to me. I try to reach back, to touch those trailing fingers, but they're gone, a blur, receding into the distance. Before I can fully focus on their eyes, their faces, before I fully remember what they were like, they slip from my grasp, like they always do.

Why can't I remember? Why has it all gone? All faded away to nothing, so that all I get are these torturous glimpses?

Greta still remembers. She takes herself back home sometimes, when things here are really bad. She gets this glazed look on her face and you know she's gone away to another place altogether. It makes it harder for her, I know, but sometimes I envy her, this little girl next to me. She hasn't lost them yet, her family, not like I have.

It frightens me how detached my thoughts have become. Pictures of the place that was home are all blurry and fuzzy, like wisps of smoke. I try to grab hold of them, but they vanish in my hands. It's as if I'm telling someone else's story when I try to remember anyone clearly, even my mum. I can't work out any more which is a real memory and which is my own detail, added to fill the gaps. That's exactly why they ban members of the Cirque from having any contact with their family: to cut the ties that bind, stop us pining for home.

I hate that it's worked.

I used to cry for them all the time. I used to be filled with a desperate, hungry longing for my mum and dad, and my baby brother. He was only one when I left. A chubby little thing, I remember, as impossible as that seems. How could he have been chubby, living in the slums like that? My mum was still feeding him, that's why. She was very pale and weak, like a tiny twig. He must have been sucking away all her nutrients, as I did before him.

She was sacrificing herself for him, for both of us, quietly wasting away with a gentle smile on her face. That's what she was like: very selfless, very soft, very patient. That's all I see when I look back: an increasingly faded outline. One day I'll find out, somehow, what happened to my family.

I turn away and face the wall, my fingers picking at the cracked and dirty plaster.

A trickle, a flow, a flood: the dam bursts.

Out of nowhere, a great sob rises up from deep inside me. I bury my head in the thin pillow, trying to suppress the sound. It won't work though; if anyone's still awake they'll be able to hear me. I've heard others sobbing in the night often enough before to know that.

I never cry any more. What's wrong with me tonight? The last thing I need is to wake Greta up. It would distress her: she's never seen me like this. No one has. Apart from Amina.

In the end, I ease my arms from underneath her and get out of bed, as softly as I can. I pad silently over to the window and cling on to the bars, leaning my head against them and looking out.

Nestled up high, almost touching the stars it seems, are the huge houses of the rich and famous, ring-fencing the city. There's one with a light on still, right at the very top, and there's a figure silhouetted at the window.

I hear a sound behind me and I turn around to see Amina, stretching and yawning her way over to where I stand.

"How's the patient?" I ask her.

She gives a rueful smile. "He's OK, I guess. I mean it was a clean break, it would heal fine if..." She doesn't need to say it; I know what she means. If he was allowed time for the bone to knit then it would be OK, but if he's out of action and not making money for the Cirque then Silvio won't be inclined to be patient.

Amina has the dubious honour of being the only Dreg ever who's been kept in the Cirque even though she can't perform any more. She's twenty now: that's old for someone in here. Until a year and a half ago, she was one of our best performers. She fell one night though, and that was that. She'd been up all night with a sick child – Aran, his name was – trying to coax him back to life after he'd been set upon by a group of Pures visiting the circus for their sick sport. It didn't work – he died in the end anyway – but she didn't get any sleep, hadn't had for days. That's why it happened.

There were archers in the arena that day, twelve of them. Timing is always imperative when you're on the trapeze, but when you're also dodging the deadly sharp arrows being fired at you from all directions, it makes it kind of tricky to concentrate.

I remember it so clearly, swinging across on the trapeze, holding my hands out, waiting for her to catch hold, like she'd done a million times before. I remember the arrow, soaring through the air, piercing her neck, quivering there while the audience exploded with glee. I remember her mouth, opening in shock, her eyes widening. She only lost her concentration for an instant, that was all, but an instant's too long in our business. She missed her moment. She didn't catch my hands and her foot flashed past the centre-point of the wire. Just a millimetre, just a fraction, that's all it took.

It was like slow motion, swinging up there, watching helplessly as she fell. Her arms, reaching up to me; her eyes, so big and frightened as she dropped down, down, down into the crowd below.

The Pures surged the arena that night, ignored the security warnings, pushed through the guards and the barriers. Hundreds of them, all desperate to get to her first. A seething, crazed mob.

One moment I saw her land, the next they were on her, tearing her to pieces.

And they say *we* aren't human.

It's almost laughable. These Pures, with all their airs and graces, that sense of superiority they wear like a crown. They're animals, beasts, every last one of them.

God knows how Amina didn't die that night. They left her for dead. They thought she was dead. They'd have torn her into pieces if the guards hadn't finally seized control. She's never been the same since. You can't perform on the wire when your arms and legs have been broken multiple times, when your ribs are crushed and fingers bent and useless.

The only reason Silvio let her stay was because of her healing skills. She's never been officially trained, obviously, but her mother taught her the basics when she was tiny, before they took Amina away, and she's been doing it ever since. No one tells her what to do; she just seems to know. It's in her blood. It's been in her family for generations, apparently: healing, medicine.

That's why Silvio tolerates her. She's still of use to him, unlike all the others. She cuts costs, keeps people alive for him who would otherwise have died, fixes and mends his best assets, gets them up and back out on the stage. He never bothers with the cost of an actual trained doctor, just calls on Amina to get him out of scrape after scrape.

The only time I've ever felt anything but hatred for him was when he spared her life. That night, I felt like hugging him.

I took her strength for granted, before then. She'd always seemed so strong, so tough. My hero. I'd never have made it through without Amina teaching me, supporting me, making me believe there's life after here; that there's an end in sight to this wretched existence. She's still my hero, of course, but I know she's not invincible now. I know I have to try and protect her, just as much as she tries to protect me.

I can feel her scrutinizing my face. "You've been crying," she says. "What's up?"

"I don't know really." I sigh. "Nothing. Everything. You must be exhausted. Go to bed, honestly, I'm fine."

She smiles, but she doesn't move. She wraps her arm around my waist and we stand there, side by side, gazing out on the moonlit night.

I lean my head on her shoulder, resting it on her mass of wild curls.

"I was thinking about my family," I tell her. "I can't remember what my mum looks like."

She doesn't say anything for a moment.

"It's hard," she says. "I forget things too."

"Do you?"

She nods sadly.

"Just don't let them take away who you are and where you've come from. That's the way you keep your family with you, that's what I tell myself. The details might get a bit fuzzy at times but we never lose our loved ones; they stay here, deep inside us. They make us who we are."

Amina always knows what to say to make me feel better.

"Do you think it can ever change?" I ask her. "The way things are?"

Her reply is immediate and resolute.

"Yes. If we keep on believing. If we don't give up hope. If

we stay united. Yes, it will change. Look over there," she says, pointing over the city to the distant horizon. There's a faint pink tinge to the sky. "There's a new day dawning."

She strokes my hair softly and I feel my shoulders relaxing.

She takes my hand and leads me back to my bunk. When I curl up next to Greta, she tucks the thin sheet around me and sits on the floor next to me, still stroking my hair like she used to, long ago, in the early days.

I feel myself drifting off.

BEN

By the time I make it down to the breakfast room, everyone else is already eating in silence. Francis has his phone out, as usual, playing some violent game or other – *Dreg Destruction*, it looks like, Father's reading the news on his tablet and Mother's checking through her emails.

I try to catch Priya's eye when she's putting the plates down but she doesn't look at me and give that secret little smile like she usually does.

Mother suddenly gives a derisive snort. She sounds so disgusted that we all look up, even Francis. She silently hands her tablet over to Father and he scans through the message on the screen. He chuckles and hands it back to her.

"I take it the answer's going to be no?"

"Yes! The answer will be no!"

Her cool blue eyes turn towards Francis and me. "They've offered us first-night tickets at the Cirque," she says. "VIP. Opening night. That's tonight."

I look at Priya, standing in the corner now, with her head bowed. I don't want to make her cross again but I can't miss this opportunity.

"I think I'd like to go," I say tentatively. I have this funny feeling Mother's not going to like me saying it.

She looks at me and tuts. "You actually want to go and see that load of rubbish? Watch a load of Dregs degrading themselves?" She raises one eyebrow in that sardonic way she has. "Why, exactly, Benedict?"

I feel myself squirming under her scrutiny.

"Everyone at school's going," I say, realizing as soon as the words come out of my mouth what a weak answer it is. "And it would be educational," I add, "seeing what happens out there for once. Know thy enemy, and all that."

"Hmm. Everyone at school, you say? Francis, what's your view on this?"

He shrugs. "Might be fun, I suppose. Especially if there's any action, if you know what I mean." His eyes light up. "I think I'd like watching that!"

My father slams his cup down, sploshing coffee out on to the table.

"Don't even think about it." His voice is uncharacteristically firm.

"I have to think about it, Peter," says Mother. "I have to keep my eye on the party leadership now. Raising my profile at a major event like this could be the difference between winning and losing."

"No! I will not have you putting the boys at risk in order to further your own reputation!"

"You speak as if I'm doing it for my own vanity. This is for you too, and them. I work hard for everyone in this family. I'm doing this for us all!"

"You're doing it for yourself. We agreed, after what happened before, that we'd protect them, no matter what."

What happened before. They always use those words to describe it. As if we don't know exactly what they mean.

It's still so vivid in my mind.

A hand in a crowd, grabbing me, pulling me away from them. A knife at my throat. Gunshots.

"It's been two years, things are different now. The Dregs are under much tighter control."

"That just makes them more resentful, can't you see? It makes another attempt *more* likely, not less."

"We'll take extra security guards, the police will be on hand. What can they do, really?"

"Plenty! They can do plenty. Why on earth would you want to expose the boys to any of that rubbish anyway?"

Her tone is diplomatic. "We can't keep them wrapped up in cotton wool for ever, Peter."

"We're not wrapping them in cotton wool, we're protecting them, as best we can. Parading them in front of a load of angry, embittered Dregs is foolish. Foolish and dangerous. And these aren't just any Dregs; these are circus Dregs. The lowest of the low!"

She acts as if she hasn't heard him. "There'll be cameras there, thousands of people, all posting about it online." A smile forms at the corners of her mouth as she pictures it.

"We are not going. I absolutely forbid it."

They both lean forward, glaring at each other. Her, dressed for power as always: crisp white shirt, expensive blue jacket, sleek red bob. Him, not quite pulling off the same effect; shirt a little too tight these days, tie slightly askew, hair thinning on top.

I hold my breath.

It's not long before my father looks away. "Do what you want. Do what you bloody well want." His voice is exasperated, resigned, defeated, all at once. "You were always going to anyway!"

My mother's smile returns; a little smirk of victory. "Well, that's settled then. Get your glad rags ready, boys." Her voice is dripping with sarcasm. "We're going to the circus!"

HOSHIKO

The morning alarms jolt me awake. I must have only fallen asleep about an hour ago and now my head feels even more heavy and fuzzy than it normally does. There's a warm indent next to me where Greta was lying. She's probably up already and running about in the communal area with all the other little ones. God knows how they find the energy to play. Amina's not around either – she'll be checking on her patient in the san.

I join the long line filing its way into the canteen, grab my rations and suddenly notice Amina's mass of dark, curly hair. She's already here, in the corner, at the end of one of the huge wooden tables which fill the room.

The big room is busy already but there are two places free opposite her, for Greta and me.

I slide in on the bench and stare down at my tray. Two vitamin tablets, which allegedly contain all the nutrients we need, a grey-looking oatcake and a glass of milk.

I can't remember the last time we had milk. Amina smiles at me wryly.

"Don't get too excited. Have a sniff before you think about drinking any."

I lower my head down to the plastic beaker. My stomach heaves – it's completely rancid.

Amina's chuckling to herself. "Looks like we'll be going thirsty today."

"It's not funny." I frown at her. She raises her eyebrows and glances around. A guard is pacing past the table, glaring menacingly at everyone as he makes his rounds. Once he's moved on, she leans forward.

"Better to laugh than cry. Remember, don't let them break you," she whispers.

Greta makes her way over to us, balancing her tray precariously. She's cutting it fine today; she's only just made it. The shutters slam down on their timer. Anyone who's not here yet will miss out on the tantalizing treat that is breakfast.

"Do you think we'll get it right today?" she asks me, straight away. I know exactly what she means. We've been working on her quadruple somersault and she's struggling with it. She can't quite keep her balance when she lands; she wavers just a little every time.

"Bound to," I tell her. "You've practically got it nailed already."

We bolt down our vitamin pills and make our way straight to the arena for rehearsals, while Amina heads back to the san.

We get to work on the somersault straight away. "It's all about keeping your core tight," I tell Greta, holding her steady around her tiny waist as we practise on the floor mats. "You take a fixed point, focus your eyes on it, focus everything on it, flip and land. Hold your stomach steady. Lock your eyes in position. Like this."

We practise again and again. Six times, she wobbles when she lands. On the seventh go, she gets it. A perfect tumbling quadruple somersault.

"That's it!" I tell her. "You've done it. Now try on the wire."

Her eyes widen. "No, Hoshi, I can't."

"You can. You can do it, Greta. I'll drag over the landing mats." Our eyes lock. "You're running out of time," I say, as gently as I can.

I've been trying not to let her see how desperate the situation is becoming but I can't protect her from it, not any more, not if I want to keep her safe. Any day now Silvio's going to make her perform; it's a miracle that he hasn't already and there'll be no crash mats then to break her fall, just a very high wire and a very steep drop down. Into nothing, and that's if she's lucky.

She looks up at me and nods, bravely. "OK. If you think I'm ready."

"Good. I'll show you one more time."

She waits down below as I mount the ladders.

"So you grip with your toes, like this, you focus on your fixed point, you bounce to get the momentum going: one, two, three, and that's it."

I leap upward and somersault.

"You did it five times!" she gasps. "You never said I had to do it five times!"

"You don't. Four is fine."

"I'll never be able to do five!"

"You will. When you've been doing it as long as I have, it'll all seem easy. You don't need to now: four is fine. That's what Silvio said you have to do."

I spring back across the wire and scoot down the ladders.

"Come on," I tell her. "You can do this!"

There's a sudden crash as the double doors are flung open. There he is, as if me speaking his name has summoned him, the devil himself comes sweeping in. Even though it's the middle of the day, he's still wearing his full ringmaster get-up. Those shiny boots, the crimson trousers and blazer, always crisp and impeccably pressed, the frothy frill of the shirt; they're as much a part of him as the gelled hair and curled moustache. Bojo, his tiny little monkey, all dressed up in the same costume, scurries along at his feet as always.

Greta's eyes widen in fear and she steps backwards, instinctively hiding behind me.

"Well, has she got it yet?" he barks.

"Yes," I say with certainty. "Yes. She's got it perfectly."

"You'd better be telling the truth!" He grabs Greta, pulling her out from behind me. She stands in front of him, her eyes downcast. She's shaking.

"Come on then, girl, let's see it!" Silvio gestures up at the wire. "Now!"

The panic on her face must mirror my own.

"But Silvio, the mats aren't out. She's not ready yet."

"You said she was! Is she, or isn't she?"

I stare at him. What do I say to that?

"She'll be ready soon. She's nearly ready. Not today though, not without mats."

The ringmaster leans forward, staring at Greta with disdain.

Putting his hand to his waist he takes his little jewelled dagger out of its sheath, holding it up to her throat.

"A year, she's been here. A whole year on my time *perfecting her craft*." Silvio sneers. "Time's up, little girl. Time is up."

I clench my fists together, my nails pressing into my palms.

"Get up there!" he yells sharply. At his feet, Bojo whimpers.

Silvio picks him up and strokes him as Greta makes her way up the ladder to the wire.

"Greta," I say, keeping my voice as steady and firm as I can. "You can do this. Remember, fixed point. Toes gripped."

She mounts the stairs, looks down at me, her eyes brimming, her bottom lip trembling. I give her a thumbs up.

My heart's in my mouth. If she falls now, she'll never be the same again. She might die straight away, or she might just break a few limbs. Either way, her life's over. She won't have a purpose to serve if her bones are broken.

She tiptoes lightly across the wire, her little toes daintily pointed and stands there, arms out while it steadies.

"Get on with it, girl!" Silvio calls. In his arms, Bojo has his eyes covered; even he can't stand to watch.

Greta stands there, motionless. Beside me, Silvio curses impatiently.

The seconds tick by.

Finally, she soars. Shooting upward like a rocket. High, tight, she tumbles. One, two, three, four... *five* perfect somersaults. She lands: her arms above her head, her body arched.

I can't hold the elation in.

"Yes!" I call. "Yes! Yes! Yes!" I turn to Silvio. "Told you!"

It's a mistake; talking to him like that.

"You *told* me?" he says, incredulously. "Who are *you*, to tell me anything?"

He grabs my hair, wrenches my head back and leans in close to me, so that my eyes are staring up at him.

"She looks as good as you now," he smiles. "Makes you less ... valuable."

I know what he's suggesting. It's not true though; ever since Amina's accident he's wanted a double act up there. Greta and I should both be safe. For a while.

Greta's back down the steps and she stands hesitantly next to me, whimpering quietly, a tiny, petrified sound, like a puppy. Her eyes are wide, her face deathly pale.

"Hmm," he says. "Fear suits you. I must remember that."

The burning embers of hatred I feel for this man are always there, glowing in the pit of my stomach, but now they've flared up again: a forest fire, a raging inferno…

"She's done what you asked!" I cry out, but he only throws back his head and laughs and then pulls back his arm and punches me, as hard as he can, right in the stomach. "I've warned you not to challenge me!" He punches me again, so I fall to the floor and then he kicks and kicks and kicks me while I cower helplessly at his feet. I can hear Bojo and Greta both whimpering. I don't cry though, and I don't beg. I don't make a sound; I'll never give him the satisfaction.

Maybe it's the monkey's distress that saves me, as Silvio stops suddenly. "It's OK," he croons. "It's OK, my little man." He scoops Bojo up in his arms and showers him with kisses before turning on his heels and heading for the door.

He turns as he reaches it. His eyes meet mine and he smiles again, a smug smile, before spinning out of the room. He's pleased with himself. I think of all the harm he's caused, all the people he's destroyed, murdered, tortured, and I make a silent vow to myself: one day, somehow, some way, I will make him pay.

BEN

At school, everyone's still talking about the Cirque. Most kids are going at some point or other over the next two weeks.

"I guess none of you will be there tonight?" Francis asks loudly. "Thought not. It's only VIPs like us on opening night."

I cringe. I should have known he wouldn't have been able to stop himself from broadcasting it, even though Mother and Father both warned us not to.

The more important Mother has become, the more gleeful Francis has been. God knows how he'll contain himself if she wins the party leadership battle.

By the time I get out to the football field at lunch, the word's already spread and the boys crowd around me.

"Oh my God! You're so lucky!"

"Can you get me some autographs? That African warrior guy who's on all the posters, and the tightrope walker: the Cat. I've seen her on TV; she's awesome!"

"Why didn't you say anything? I would have!"

"I don't need to say anything with Francis for a brother," I reply.

When I was younger, when Mother was Minister for Education, she'd be sent tickets for cup finals and film premieres and I used to love going to all those exciting places, being treated like royalty and then showing off about it at school afterwards, but it's not really my style these days. Anyway, we never go anywhere any more, not since the kidnapping happened and she took on her new role in government, the one which changed everything.

My eyes flick to Stanley, standing vigilantly on the sidelines. It's like having a permanent prison guard with me. He must be able to hear what's going on, although his face is a passive blank as usual. I wonder if he'll let Mother know that Francis has told everyone where we're going tonight.

She won't like it if she finds out.

We're not supposed to tell anyone where we're going to be spending our evenings any more, not even the kids at school. I've had enough security training by now to know I've got to keep my cards close to my chest. *You never know who's listening;* that's what we're always told. *If they don't know where we'll be, they can't go planning any surprise attacks.* I trust all the lads at school – they're my mates – but it's still prudent to be careful. *Prudent* – Mum's favourite word, since the day Francis and I were nearly kidnapped.

I think back to that day again. We were at a cup final; Arsenal v Spurs it was. I remember it being controversial because there was a Dreg on the Spurs team. They'd discovered him kicking a tin can about in the slums and had made a special petition because this guy was so good but there were loads of protests about it and the crowd were booing and throwing things on to the pitch.

Spurs won and it was when they were lining up to receive the cup that it happened. These two Dregs had somehow got into the ground and they came at us with knives and grabbed hold of Francis and me. I felt the knife at my throat and heard everyone start screaming. I could smell the guy's breath on my face, warm and rancid. It all happened so quickly that

I don't even remember being scared, just confused. It must have only been a few seconds before the snipers shot them down. I remember just standing there in the middle of the chaos breaking out all around us and looking down at this Dreg lying dead at my feet. They found out afterwards that they were members of one of the militant Dreg groups: the Brotherhood, they were called – terrorist lowlifes who make it their mission to go around killing innocent Pures.

Mother was so angry about it. She was affronted, she said, that such creatures would have the audacity to approach us like that. She was angry with the government too, and the security forces for allowing such a thing to happen. People lost their jobs over it – a lot of people, I think and everyone in the Brotherhood was hunted down and destroyed. They hanged them in front of the PowerHouse. Twenty bodies swinging there: a warning to anyone else who even thought about repeating such terrible actions.

It's never really left her since, that anger. She said the attempt wouldn't have happened if the Dregs were properly controlled and contained. She said if no one else was going to do the right thing, she would. She changed positions as quickly as she could, became the Dreg Control Minister and introduced a much tougher line.

It changed her for ever, that day. She's never around any more. She says what she's doing at work is more important, that she's determined to make the world a safer place for all of us. She says she's found her calling now and it takes priority over everything, even us. Especially us. Being the Dreg Control Minister isn't enough for her any more. She says she feels too restricted – that she can't do as much as she wants to because she always has to run it past someone higher up first. She wants to run for the leadership so she can get rid of all the red tape and make it easier to do what needs to be done to suppress the Dregs. They can't vote, of course, and the pledges she's making are so popular with most of the Pure public that she's bound to win. When she does, she's promised to make the Dreg problem a thing of the past.

Until that happens though, we're more at risk than ever. There are Dregs out there intent on targeting my mother and her family, causing trouble; Dregs who want to destroy the country, destroy us, so when we do venture out there are always armed guards and security forces following us around. Going to the circus tonight will be the first time I've been anywhere except school and back for such a long time.

Sometimes I sit in my room, reading or drawing or staring out of the window and I feel like I might explode. Everything in my life is so ordered and safe and controlled. My food is prepared for me; my clothes appear neatly ironed in my closet; I'm driven to school and back in an air-conditioned car by a driver who calls me sir, a driver whose name I don't even know.

I haven't even got any proper friends any more, not since all the security stuff started. I mean, everyone's nice enough to me at school, I don't get bullied or left out or anything but it's not the same as it used to be.

The party invitations stop coming when you politely

decline every single one of them for long enough. And when you aren't allowed to play any away matches, you soon get dropped from the footie team.

My father's always been quite removed from us. Present, but not there, if that makes sense. Quietly fond of us from a distance. It wasn't always like that with Mother though. When I was younger, she was around all the time, like any other normal mum. Every assembly, every sports day, every football match, I'd look up, and there she'd be, waving at me from the sidelines. She took us to school every day, picked us up, ate dinner with us. I took her for granted, I suppose; assumed she'd be around like that for ever.

It isn't like that any more. I can't remember the last time she showed an interest in anything Francis or I did. She just works all the time, and even when she is there there's always a distance in her eyes, like she's somewhere else entirely in her head. She gets so irritated by our "petty questions" that I've stopped asking her for much.

It doesn't really bother me; I'm not a child any more, I don't need her like I used to. And anyway, it's been a lot easier since she took Priya on.

It's crazy, really, that a Dreg servant, of all people, should seem more interested in my life than my own mother, but sneaking downstairs and talking to Priya always seems to reduce that empty feeling inside me.

Sometimes I wonder if everyone feels like this, but they just don't talk about it.

I did ask Priya once, if she ever felt sad, deep inside. She laughed and said of course she did, of course she felt sad deep inside, every second of every day.

"Show me a Dreg who doesn't," she said. "Know how often I see my family? Once a month. Know what we do together? Huddle up to keep warm usually, and try not think too much about food."

She's not supposed to tell me things like that, but I didn't say anything. It's not really her fault: Dregs are often fiery and unpredictable; it's part of their nature. They live on the fringes of society because they aren't capable of being civilized, kind, cultured. That's what Mother says.

Rather than feeling empty, like I suppose hers must do all the time, my stomach feels queasy – especially when I think about the girl on the tightrope. It must be excitement, because tonight will finally be a break in the monotony: I'm finally going somewhere, doing something. I haven't felt *excited* about anything for so long.

HOSHIKO

As soon as Silvio's gone, Greta sits down beside me on the floor and we hold each other tightly. We don't say anything – what is there to say? – we just stay like that for ages before we eventually pick ourselves up slowly and head over to the san. I'm stiff, which makes it hard to walk, and I have to stay all hunched over because it hurts when I stretch my stomach out, but thankfully nothing has been broken.

Amina casts a critical eye over me. The bruises have appeared and my whole midriff is an angry purple colour.

"He's been very clever; the marks won't show under your costume," she remarks wryly, "and he's kicked you just hard enough to avoid any breakages or internal damage." She looks at me. "He's protecting his assets; and that's a good thing. Once he stops seeing you as valuable, that's when you're in real trouble."

I look at Greta; there are dark rings under those big blue eyes and an anxious look on her face which don't belong on a six year old.

"Hurry up and get better," she pleads. "If he's going to make me go out there, I won't be able to do it without you."

"I'll be fine by show time, Greta, I promise. Won't I, Amina?" I try to reassure her.

"Right as rain," Amina agrees but adds gently, "You know you'll have to go up at some point, Greta." She sighs. "And Hoshi might not always be there with you."

Greta gives a brave little nod, but her bottom lip is trembling again. "Not yet, though," she says, firmly. "Not yet." As if repeating it will make it a fact.

I think about what Amina's suggesting. Does she mean that one day Greta might replace me? Or that one day I might just go and die and leave Greta alone? Both things, probably.

A feeling of intense frustration floods through me. It's the same old miserable realization that we're stuck here, enslaved, totally without hope. Being born a Dreg is to be the lowest of the low – to be crushed underfoot by the Pures and their domination and doctrine, the doctrine which defines us as the sludgy, worthless sediment floating at the bottom of society, while the Pure elite – the superior, the virtuous, the worthy – rise upwards to their rightful place at the top.

The Pures think that Dregs have always been scum, that it's in our nature but it's not true. They did this to us, used us a scapegoat for all the wrongs in the world. It's been over a hundred years now since the government started turning on the country's immigrants and ethnic minorities, blaming them for everything. Back then, opportunities were open to anyone in this country. People just like us were doctors, police officers, teachers, judges – until we took the fall so epically.

They segregated us first, moved anyone not *Pure* English to the slums on the edges of the cities. Then came the shutting down of access to schools and hospitals, to good jobs and any hope for the future.

It's a tough life, living in the slums – I'll never forget the feel of the cold and the damp, even if I do struggle to remember my family's faces. There's no electricity or heating and the roofs all leak, everywhere is filthy and there are rats, as big as dogs some of them, roaming around as if they owned the place. People work in return for rations and most just about manage not to starve to death, but the jobs are all menial, degrading ones that the Pures themselves don't want to do.

The Cirque didn't come along until a few years after the slums were set up. It was just an ordinary circus at first, full of trained Pure performers, until a couple of Dregs were drafted in for the more dangerous stunts. When one of them died, there was a huge fuss made about it on the news and in the social media. It wasn't all negative though – turned out a lot of the Pures were happy about it and the circus suddenly became more popular. More Dregs were drafted in, the acts becoming increasingly more dangerous, the death count higher and higher. The more deaths there were, the more popular the place became and so it grew and grew and grew: the wealthiest and most successful circus in the world.

Sometimes, when I'm putting the horses into their stables for the night and look into their soft, dark eyes, I envy them. They aren't weighed down by that same heavy burden of fear and pain that we are. They don't know regret, or fear, or anger, not like we do. No one tells them that their ancestors were once free, that the world wasn't always this way. That it's not right, the way they are kept caged up like this, the way they are forced to perform. They don't miss their families, or worry about how they are and they don't feel the grief either, every time there's another death. Whenever I try to think of the future I can't picture anything except a black hole. I just feel cold. A cold that's buried so deep under my skin I don't think it will ever go away.

BEN

Passing through the big metal turnstiles into the Cirque is like walking into an alternative reality. It punches you in the face the moment you enter, an assault on the senses which refuses to let up.

There's so much colour. The bright and beautiful performers all dressed up in their spangles and sparkles. Lights everywhere: neon signs shamelessly flashing and tiny twinkly fairy lights winking seductively, beckoning you in. The smells of popcorn and candy floss and sizzling burgers all vying for attention. Gaudy music spilling out of every tent. It makes me feel dizzy.

The ringmaster, Silvio Sabatini, is there to greet us at the entrance. I recognize him from the parade. He seems beside himself with excitement as he rushes forward to greet Mother, bowing down as if she's some kind of queen.

"Let me escort you straight to the action, Madam," he gushes. "We're so excited to have you here, watching our little show."

Francis, Father and I trot along behind them as he sweeps Mother along the queue of people waiting obediently in line. I feel their eyes all turn towards us as we are ushered past them into the empty arena.

"Please, come this way," he simpers at Mother, practically drooling at her as he shows us up to the royal box. His slicked-back hair and greased moustaches gleam and he's all dressed in his circus finery – frilly white shirt, red waistcoat buttoned over his barrel chest, tight little breeches and shiny heeled boots. There's a monkey, dressed up in exactly the same clothes as him, perched on his shoulder.

"It's a huge honour to have such an esteemed guest here, among us. And your wonderful family, of course." He gestures benevolently towards Francis, Father and me. I look at my family. They all have the same expression on their faces as they look down on this strange, costumed creature ingratiating himself at their feet. Their nostrils flared, haughtily, their lips curled upward in a sneering look of disdain. No, it's more than disdain; it's disgust. He disgusts them.

It's against protocol, him standing this near. I can sense the tension as the guards all ring-fence us, their hands resting on their guns. He's too close to us, can't he see that?

He scuttles up a sweeping staircase, and gestures towards our seats like he's performed a conjuring trick.

"We have had this addition to our usual arena erected in your honour. I trust you will be comfortable."

We are up on a platform, elevated above the rest of the seats which circle the central performance ring. At the front are four large chairs: red velvet and encrusted with gaudy jewels, like thrones from a fairy story. A dozen other chairs are grouped behind them; for the guards and the rest of Mother's entourage, I suppose.

I look at Mother again as she scans the area he has set up "in our honour", the area he is evidently so proud of. Her expression hasn't changed.

I don't know what this man, Silvio Sabatini, was expecting from her. Gratitude maybe? Awe and wonder? Instead, she is insulted. He has insulted her with his pathetic efforts. He should be careful. It is not a good idea to insult my mother.

From his pocket, he pulls out a little camera. "Madam, I wonder if you would be so kind as to have a photograph with me? It would take pride of place on my wall."

Mother's face is tight with outrage. She doesn't say anything, no one says anything; she just raises one eyebrow and stares down at him.

There's a terrible silence.

Finally, the ringmaster breaks it.

"Well," he laughs, trying for hearty and booming. I look at his face and there's panic in his dark little eyes. He's realized, finally, that the woman in front of him is not easily impressed. "I will leave you to enjoy our show. I hope you will find what you see to your liking." He makes a hasty, bowed retreat.

Mother's voice is ice-cold. "I suppose we ought to take our seats."

I feel a little ridiculous, perched there on the big ornate chair as the public file in below us, quickly filling up the vast arena. I try to push it down though; I don't want anything to spoil this evening.

The band strikes up, the lights dim.

It's show time.

HOSHIKO

The dressing rooms are busy as everyone prepares for their performances. There's one main hub where we all get ready before heading off to our different locations. My show is always in the arena, but there are loads of smaller sideshows happening at the same time for those who don't get in to the main events.

The crowd are lively tonight. Their cheering and chanting travels all the way down the tunnels. Lots of nervous glances are exchanged; the lion show is always one of the riskiest. It's a lottery, pure and simple: luck alone will determine the fate of Emmanuel and Kate.

That's why it's always quiet down here, despite the traffic constantly passing through. Everyone's at their most nervous pre-show: facing their own mortality, wondering if tonight will be the night they don't make it back. Plus it feels disrespectful to chatter away when you know that someone out there might be dying, that very second.

It's always surreal watching everyone transform. A group of thin and poorly dressed children enter, and fifteen minutes later they leave as a troop of jolly clowns: red noses, curly wigs, beaming smiles painted on. Three average-sized teenage boys walk in and leave ten feet high on stilts, ducking down under the door as they exit.

But it's the girls who all change the most dramatically. We're drab when we walk in and sit down at the make-up booths. Half-emaciated, pale, exhausted. It's amazing how they manage to change us. A bit of lipstick, some heavy-duty eyeshadow, a sweep of blusher, top it all off with a sparkly costume and – hey presto! – out walks a circus star.

Only a few of my costumes are kept down here; most of them are up in the space above the arena. There's a huge room hidden away up there, full of props and costumes, so that I can make a quick change during the act whenever I need to. Tonight, I'll be staying in my black cat leotard for the duration of the show. I'm trying out a new routine. It's a risky one, I suppose, but I'm not nervous. I feel confident enough with it and I need to make sure I keep things fresh to stay on the right side of Silvio. It's not as easy to vary things so much when you're performing solo, even though I still draw in a really good crowd every time.

I miss Amina out there, when I'm on the wire. We worked so well as a pair, before her accident, and I always felt safer knowing she had my back.

Silvio hasn't mentioned Greta performing again, thank God. I don't want her with me, not ever – it's far too dangerous – but it is lonely out there on my own. They put the acrobats down below now, to try and add more drama and colour, but it's not the same as the two of us soaring through the air towards each other, our hands grasping hold at just the right time, working together to get the symmetry and balance perfectly on point. That's why the dangers they've thrown at me have been getting more and more extreme lately. The crowd aren't satisfied with artistry alone, no matter how good we are – that's not why they flock to the Cirque.

They want risk. They want to see the fear on our faces.

They want to watch us die.

BEN

The lights all dim at once, and we're plunged into blackness. It's so dark that I can't even see my hand when I hold it out in front of me. Everyone's murmuring to each other: *What's going on? Is this part of the show?*

Loud music suddenly fills the arena, a dramatic fanfare. There's a full orchestra in here by the sounds of it.

The lights turn back on, brighter this time. I squint as my eyes adjust and then I see the lions. They prowl around the ring, their coats gleaming, eyeing the audience up hungrily: two huge lions and five lionesses. A thick glass partition protects us from them but I still feel vulnerable; I'm relieved that we're higher up than everyone else.

There's a feeling of communal anticipation in the air. It's the thrill of being so near such wild animals – they'd tear us to shreds if they could. And then, underneath that, the delicious knowledge that we're safe, protected by impenetrable glass. After all, what would happen to the Cirque if a Pure was injured, or worse, killed?

The lions pace around the ring for ages before anything happens. Seven of them, snarling at us and each other, their massive mouths open wide, their huge teeth bared and threatening. The two male lions begin fighting, ripping into each other's necks so violently that I start to wonder if they're actually going to kill each other.

The lights dim again and a single spotlight picks out the ringmaster. He stands on a podium right in the centre of the ring, monkey perched on his shoulder, lions leaping up below his feet, waiting imperiously for the applause to subside.

"Ladies and gentlemen, welcome to the greatest night of your lives! Sit back, relax. Prepare for amazement! Prepare for bewilderment! Maybe even prepare for … *death*!"

We all gasp, but it's a theatrical, excited gasp. We're playing our part too: we're lapping it up. Then, beneath his feet, bright, blazing light. A ring of fire. He's posed dramatically above it, arms raised high, chest thrust forward. He cracks his whip and, one by one, the lions leap through it, their golden coats just skimming under the dancing flames.

"These beauties, ladies and gentlemen, are wild beasts, straight from the plains of Africa. They are used to tearing on flesh, ripping it, devouring it! They have not had meat since yesterday! They are hungry! Shall we feed them, ladies and gentlemen? Shall we give them what they want?"

"Yes!" everyone cheers. "Yes! Yes!"

"As you wish!" He cracks his whip again and, seemingly at his command, two wire cages descend, apparently out of nowhere, hanging enticingly just above the lions.

I crane my neck and see that they're full of meat: red, raw meat, the blood slowly seeping from it, dripping out of the sides of the cages and on to the arena floor.

The lions really go crazy now, hurling themselves upward at the cages. They can see it and smell it, but they can't get to it.

The cages lift up higher, dangling mockingly. The lions are jumping up, roaring.

Eventually, the cages rise further again, disappearing back into the ceiling.

There's a pause for a moment and then Sabatini flicks his whip once more and another cage appears, wobbling precariously in the air. From our elevated position, I can see what's inside it before the rest of the audience and before the lions. Two Dregs: a man and a girl, back to back.

The guy is huge. There's only a loin cloth around his waist and he's all rippling muscles. He must be the African warrior guy they were talking about at school. His dark skin is greased and shiny and, when he looks up, I see a gash running from where his ear must once have been all the way across his cheek so that his mouth stretches out into a deranged-looking leer. It must have been recent; it's gaping open. You can see the flesh inside his cheeks. It's red raw. The girl is tall as well; lean and athletic.

After a few moments, the cage lowers further. On every side, the lions leap up on their hind legs, swiping their great savage paws through the bars. The only way the two people can avoid them is by curling up tight, right in the middle. They cling together in a ball, burying their heads.

I turn to look at Mother; there's a wide smile on her face. It's not often she smiles these days. For someone who didn't even want to come to the circus, it certainly looks like she's enjoying herself now.

She catches me looking at her and leans over.

"Their behaviour is very melodramatic," she whispers. "They aren't really afraid at all. They love it."

I look again at the man and the girl, huddled together, millimetres away from those gnashing jaws, those ferocious claws.

It doesn't look like they love it.

They're left there for what seems like an eternity. The lions get more and more agitated. My heartbeat, thundering now, matches the tempo of the clashing cymbals.

I start to feel a bit sick. I don't like it here as much as I thought I would. What's going to happen next?

Eventually, the cage begins to rise again, the lions still leaping up at it.

"Emmanuel, Kate, choose your positions!" Silvio Sabatini's voice booms out. I only notice now that there are three trapdoors in the floor of the cage. Video screens light up all around the arena, showing us what's happening inside. The man and girl, it seems, have to each pick one door to stand over, pushing a bucket full of meat over the remaining door. They raise their hands into manacles protruding from the roof, locking them into position; I suppose so they can't change their minds.

A big digital clock descends, the display showing one minute. It begins to count down, accompanied by the beat of a drum. A loud ticking sound every second – like a bomb is about to go off.

The time goes really slowly at first, every agonizing second creeping past, but then it seems to get quicker and quicker and quicker. My hands are clenched so tightly my nails are digging into my palms.

"What are we waiting for?" I ask Mother.

"One of the doors to open. Keep your fingers crossed for the guy's door."

"Why?"

"Your father got one of the guards to put a bet on when we arrived. We get three thousand pounds if it's the guy who falls – four thousand if he dies."

The expression on her face chills me to the bone. I've never seen her enjoying herself so much.

I look at Francis and Father; the same smile is on both their faces. Am I the only person in the whole place who isn't sure about this? I turn away from them.

Magnified on the TV screens are close ups of the Dregs' faces. They aren't screaming, or hysterical, like you might think; they look blank and emotionless, both of them staring into the distance.

The seconds keep ticking down. I notice that Mother and Father are holding hands now – a rare moment of affection – and Francis is filming everything on his mobile phone, like a lot of other people in the crowd.

Looking up at the doors, I close my eyes tightly and pray with all my might for the right-hand one, the one with the meat above it, to open; willing the other two to remain closed.

In the end, it all happens really quickly.

A door shoots open. Its contents drop. The lions finally get their feed.

It's the meat.

Thank God.

Fighting over every piece, they tear into it, ripping it to shreds. It's devoured in seconds.

The arena goes dark again then, except for a spotlight shining on Emmanuel and Kate, the ringmaster between them, raising their hands aloft. Released from the shackles, they bow to the crowd.

Around us, below us, everyone's on their feet, booing and shouting, their faces twisted in anger and frustration. Did they all want the Dregs to die? Mother doesn't join in; she's regained her composure now and is sitting there motionless, her usual aloof expression back on her face.

She turns to me.

"Talk about an anticlimax," she tuts, crossly. "The lions didn't even get near them."

My heart sinks. Surely she doesn't mean it?

"But they'd have killed them if they had," I say. "You saw what they did to the meat."

She snorts. "No such luck, probably. The statistics in this place are weighed too heavily on the side of the Dregs; I've been looking at the figures. Even when they're dropped into the arena, they get away half the time. Sometimes they actually manage to outrun them, sometimes the lions aren't hungry enough. They shouldn't bother feeding them beforehand. That black creature, Emmanuel? He got away from them a couple of weeks ago, hardly a scratch on him afterwards."

That explains the gash; not exactly what I'd call a scratch.

"Last year," she frowns crossly, "only eight Dregs died in the lion enclosure over the whole season. That's simply not good enough."

Francis and Father are listening to her now too, both nodding in agreement.

Father looks at me. "Don't tell me you're feeling sorry for

them, Benedict, you great big softie! They're vermin: the scum of the earth. Even the poor lions probably couldn't stomach them." He laughs and Francis joins in – Mother manages an icy smile.

I feel cold, suddenly, and more detached from them than ever, as if I'm watching them through glass. As if they're predators too, and not my family at all.

Once I'm dressed and made up, I stand at the foot of the passageway to the main arena until it's time to go on. I have to wait for Emmanuel and Kate to return from the lion show and then make my way up the ladder to the wire. I keep my fingers crossed tightly and whisper a prayer to a god I don't believe in that they'll both come back.

Kate's only just arrived; she was brought here after one of the slum raids. All Dreg kids are assessed at the age of five, but the Cirque often wants older performers too – teenagers usually – and so every few months, Silvio and some Pure policemen go into the slums of whatever town we happen to be in, and take as many Dreg kids as they want to perform in the Cirque. One minute these poor souls are going about their daily business of eking out a living and trying not to starve to death, the next they're bundled into the back of a van and bought here to paradise. That's what happened to Kate, just a few weeks ago, and she hasn't really figured out how it works in here yet. She's desperate to return to her family and she still seems to think she'll be reunited with them at some point. I don't think anyone's had the heart yet to tell her that she'll never see them again.

Everyone knows who Emmanuel is; he's been here since before I arrived and he's one of the longest-serving performers. Like mine, his face always features on the promotional posters and he's one of the holographic images that are beamed into the sky to advertise the show. Powerful frame, rippling muscles, ebony skin; the Pures fear him and love him, especially since he got his scars last year.

We lost eight souls to the lions last season. The first one was Emmanuel's partner, Sarah.

She was the opposite of him in every way, physically at least. Tiny, fair, delicate – she only came up to his chest. Seeing them together was a bit like seeing Greta with her doll. Sarah wasn't weak though, physically or mentally. She was strong, fiery, charismatic. I loved her. We all did. Emmanuel, especially.

I never saw two people as in love as they were; they made you believe that light and goodness still existed in the world. They were the glue that held the rest of us together, right up until she died in front of him.

I was standing right here the night it happened.

I knew someone was being killed because the crowd went crazy, like they always do when the lions get fed. You could hear them cheering, whistling, screaming in rapture.

I tried to tell myself I might be wrong, but I knew I wasn't; the only time the crowd are ever that loud is when there's a death.

There was a different sound, all of a sudden. A roar. Not a lion's roar, a human's roar, rising above the rest of the tumult. A roar of pain. A roar of rage. It went on and on, that roar.

I think they kept him out there as a bit of extra entertainment for the Pures; it must have been a real treat for them to witness such raw grief.

When he was eventually chucked into the corridor by the guards, all the anger had gone from him. He lay there, curled up in a ball on the floor.

I sat down next to him. I'll never forget the expression on his face when he looked up at me.

"They ripped her to pieces," he said. "I had to watch from the cage while they tore her to shreds."

He wept then.

I wept too. And then Silvio came with his whip and made me climb the ladder and I had to go out there and perform for the people who'd just watched my friend get mauled to death.

Please don't let it be happening again.

They're taking ages.

The sound of the band striking up and the crowd's jeering calls and thunderous feet stamping tells me the show's over. It's such a relief when I see Emmanuel and Kate push their way through the arena doors and walk wearily towards me.

There's not much time to chat, but we have a quick hug. A hug that says: *I'm glad you made it*; a hug that says: *I hope you make it too*; a hug that says: *You're not alone out there*.

There's a feeling of doom in the pit of my stomach, all mixed up with that betraying flicker of excitement. And a knowing, deep inside, that something's going to happen; things are going to change.

There's a loud cheering from the arena all of a sudden. What's going on out there?

"They're hyper tonight," Emmanuel says, "and there's some VIPs in, so be careful. Silvio's guaranteed them lots of action, apparently. He won't be happy that we made it out alive."

"Who's in?" I ask.

"Vivian Baines."

My heart plummets. Vivian Baines: the Dreg Control Minister.

We may not often get access to the papers or the PureWeb, but there's not a Dreg in the country who doesn't hate Vivian Baines; who doesn't wish her dead. Rumours about her fly around at night, frightened, fearful whispers: Vivian Baines has issued another decree; Vivian Baines has made another speech; Vivian Baines is on the rise.

She's the person who is paid mega bucks to find new ways to torture and humiliate us. The person who dishes out all the bullshit media propaganda the Pures get about us being dirty and evil. The person who "controls numbers". She's running for power in the next election, apparently – just when we thought things couldn't get any worse.

Why is she here? She usually issues her decrees from afar; I don't suppose she likes to get her hands too dirty by getting up close and personal with any real Dregs.

The hatred runs cold through my body. There's no way I'm dying tonight. Not in front of her.

BEN

Once the lions and the performers are removed from the arena, there's a few minutes' interval while they get ready for the next act and the crowd below us mills around, people queuing for refreshments or making their way out to the toilets. There's still a buzz in the air from what we've all just witnessed. This is so far removed from my usual life, by rights I should be excited too, but I feel sick, subdued, anxious about what's coming.

Silvio Sabatini crosses the arena again and rushes up the stairs to our box. The spotlight has him picked up and the people below us all look up to see what he's doing. The camera swivels to point at us and focuses on Mother, so that her face appears on the big screens at either end of the room. Francis points them out to her excitedly and leans in towards her, grinning and waving at himself. Mother smiles serenely, waving a hand elegantly at the crowd below. There's a hum as the arena buzzes with the realization that she's here. The guards around us move forward a little, glaring at Sabatini as he scurries his way to our seats.

He's carrying a cardboard tray, laden down with wrapped-up food. Burgers, French fries, fizzy drinks. Baby-pink candyfloss. Spun sugar as light and airy as a cloud. Popcorn, still warm and encrusted with thick golden caramel. Chunky slabs of different flavoured fudge. We never have food like this. It smells delicious.

"May I tempt you with some traditional circus fare?" he croons, smiling at Mother.

"My family do not eat junk," she informs him icily. His face drops.

"Madam, I'm so sorry for the imposition. I merely wished you to have an authentic circus experience. I thought your delightful children might enjoy it. I do apologize; I should have realized."

Francis and I look at each other. He grins at me. For once, we actually agree on something.

"Oh, Mother, go on!" he pleads. "Just this once."

She turns to my father. "You brought them to the circus," he says. "Don't look at me."

My mother coldly examines the ringmaster.

"Very well, little man, but how do I know they aren't poisoned? How do I know you don't mean us harm?" Her face is etched with false concern. She's making him squirm, playing with him like a cat does with a mouse.

"Oh, Madam, never, never would I wish any harm on you and your dear family! I am so honoured you are here."

"Eat one, then," she commands.

He looks at her, he doesn't know what to do.

"Eat one," she repeats. "Eat one of those greasy chips you're trying to force on us, so I can be sure."

The camera is still fixed on him, and the whole arena watches as he reaches into one of the little oil-spattered cones, extracts a fry with his two fingers and nibbles it delicately. Mother looks on disgustedly.

"And now, the drink," she says. He gives a funny little bow and then takes a cup and sucks on the straw, his cheeks drawn in as he looks up at Mother uncertainly.

"Very well," she says, after a moment. "You've convinced me they're safe. Boys, if you insist on wanting to eat that rubbish, you may, just this once. Not the cup he's drunk from, of course. Don't touch that one."

She reaches into her pocket, pulls out her black leather gloves, and puts them on, spending time working the creases from her fingers as the crowd looks on expectantly. She reaches for the cup and stands up, smiling down at him.

"This one has been contaminated," she says, and pulls the plastic lid off before holding the cup aloft and emptying the contents of the drink all over him. Coke drips down around his ears, and collects on his eyelashes and nose. His carefully gelled hair is a bedraggled mess.

He stands there, unmoving, as the crowd below whoops and cheers and stamps its feet.

My mother always knows exactly how to please a crowd.

This ringmaster, Silvio Sabatini, is small anyway, but he seems reduced now. There are two little purple spots on his cheeks. The Coke pools at his feet as he stands there, head bowed.

"You may leave," Mother instructs him. But as he turns to go, she calls him back. "Ringmaster?"

"Yes, Madam."

"My sons felt a little let down by the lion show. There was a distinct lack of action, if you know what I mean. Please make sure we aren't disappointed again. So far, this circus has been a trifle dull. I've promised them they'll have something to tell their friends about."

His eyes meet hers in an unspoken exchange and he nods.

"Let me assure you, there will be no disappointment next time, Madam. I'll make sure of it."

He retreats respectfully, bowing and nodding his way back down the stairs as the Coke continues to dribble and drip from his forehead.

The lights dim for a minute or two, and then red and orange flashes appear, focused high up into the roof. There's a wire up there, a thin one, reaching all the way across the arena, and a trapeze drops down from a hatch in the centre.

It must be the high wire act; it must be the girl.

For two days solid, her image has been imprinted on my mind. It's there when I gaze through the window at night, beamed into the sky above and below me and it's there too in the day, every time I close my eyes. I'm going to see her now in real life, dancing on the wire, just above my head.

What did Mother mean just now? She wasn't ordering Sabatini to kill her, was she? No, she can't have been; she wouldn't do that, would she? I hear his words again.

Let me assure you, there will be no disappointment next time.

I'm wrong. I must be, so why do I suddenly feel consumed with dread? As the act begins and she tumbles and soars through the air, I can't escape the feeling that something is about to go horribly wrong…

HOSHIKO

My act has gone perfectly – I am poised, triumphant upon the wire, the roar of the crowd's approval washing over me. My eyes meet Silvio's as he reaches one hand forward and clasps hold of the tightrope. Grinning wickedly, he jerks it back and forth, sending his message of execution down the wire.

I can't maintain my balance and I plunge, head first, the collected gasp of the audience audible as I plummet once more.

My bare feet are what save me, momentarily at least. They clasp the wire, so that I dangle precariously, upside down. Below me, the stool crashes loudly to the ground, shattering on impact.

I can't swing myself back up. If I loosen this grip, even a millimetre, I'm dead.

I hang there, right in front of the VIP box. They're higher here, in their privileged position, kept away from the crowd, closer to the action.

I can't see Vivian Baines; all I can see are guards, five of them, cordoning off the VIPs, shielding them from me.

They're frightened of me, a girl dangling from a tightrope in front of them. What on earth do they think I'm going to do, knock her out with a killer somersault?

A boy breaks through the circle and stands there, looking at me. He's not shouting, or laughing, just staring at me with this strange expression on his face. A still point in the panicked frenzy.

For the briefest of moments, the crowd fades away. It's just us, me and this Pure boy, eyes locked together. Only six feet of air and one hundred years of history dividing us.

I feel as if he's trying to tell me something. I wonder what it is.

I can't hold my grip any longer. One of my feet finally slips, then the other. I launch myself forward and land heavily in the box. There are cries of horror as the guards push everyone away from me.

This has never happened before. A Dreg, landing right there in the VIP box. Tonight, of all nights, when Vivian Baines herself is here. What's Silvio going to do now? I'm not dead, as he intended. I'm here, contaminating the Pures.

I look up at the wire. It dangles, enticingly, above my head. Maybe I can reach it, pull myself back up. No, it's too far away.

Suddenly the boy is there, right in front of me. He puts out his hand to me, gently, tentatively, smiling.

"It's OK," he whispers. "Let me help you."

He edges forward. "I'm going to lift you up. On the count of three. OK? When I do, grab the tightrope."

A piercing whistle sounds from behind me. They'll shoot me if I stay here any longer. I'm a dangerous animal, and I've escaped from my cage; let loose and savage.

Behind him, guards are rushing towards us, ready to remove him from this imminent threat. There's no time to lose. I don't have a choice. I look into his eyes. I'm going to have to trust him, going to have to let this Pure boy touch me.

I nod. He lifts me up and I reach the wire just as the guards pull him away. It slices into my hands hungrily as I swing.

Clasping it tightly, I swing again and spring, crouching like the cat they've christened me as.

I rise, holding my hands high, arching my body. Standing tall once more.

I look down at him, surrounded by guards now. Riot shields up, guns out, all aimed at me. Our eyes meet again.

Why did he help me?

It takes me a moment or two to pull myself together, to remember that he's chosen to be here – he queued up and bought a ticket with a smile on his face. Paid to witness the public torturing of Dregs, maybe even a death or two, if he's lucky.

I scowl at him and he looks away. His head hangs low, almost as if he feels ashamed. Not likely – whoever heard of a Pure with a conscience?

Beneath me, the rest of the fickle crowd are jubilant. Seconds ago, they were ready to tear me limb from limb but now I am, once again, their champion. A sea of white roses is tossed into the ring as they chant my name: *the Cat, the Cat, the Cat*.

BEN

She grasps the wire with her feet and hangs there, impossibly, holding on with just her toes. She's right in front of the box and there's chaos all around me as the guards try and jostle us to safety into the corner. I can't see what's going on, can't see if she's fallen. I wrench away from them. She's still there.

All of a sudden, I swear, she looks right at me. I tear myself free from the guards pushing me away from her. I can't break eye contact. I have to let her know that she can survive this, that she must survive it.

When she lands, I don't even think about what I'm doing; all I know is that I have to help her. I hear myself talking to her.

"It's OK," I tell her. "You can trust me."

My hands encircle her waist and I lift her up to the wire, which she reaches at the same time as the guards force me back. A part of me can hear Mother and Father screaming at me furiously, but it's white noise.

Nothing else matters except that she makes it.

I watch her as she springs lightly back up again, leaping on to the wire in one easy movement.

I become aware that the room has stopped crying out for her death. Everyone's calling out her name euphorically now, as if she's suddenly become their hero.

She's looking at me again, but her eyes are angry now. Hostile, like I've offended her, not saved her. She performs a backflip. Her whole body tumbles, but the eyes remain in exactly the same place. They burn a hole in me. She hates me. This time, I can't hold her gaze – I have to look away.

HOSHIKO

As soon as the show's over, Amina rushes me through the overhead tunnels and into the san. "They should be OK," she says, examining my hands, "if we treat them straight away."

She rubs cream into them and then roots around in her box for a bandage, pulling out a grey-looking rag.

"This is the only one I've got left." She peers at it, dubiously. "It doesn't exactly look sterile." She winds it around my hands anyway, frowning as she does so.

"I nearly lost you tonight," she says crossly, as if she's telling me off. "What on earth happened out there?"

She's right to be worried; if that Pure boy hadn't stepped in when he did and helped me back on the wire, I'd never have made it.

"It was Silvio," I tell her. "He was trying to make me fall. He shook the wire."

Her eyes widen.

"Hoshi," she says gravely. "If that's true then you need to be really careful."

She stops winding the bandage around and just sits there, biting her lip and staring into space. When she looks at me, her face is deathly pale.

"We need to think fast," she says. "You must do something quickly to persuade him you're worth hanging on to."

"I *am* worth hanging on to!" I tell her, a little hurt. "I've been the most popular act all season, even on my own."

"That doesn't guarantee anything – you should know that

by now! Look at all the acts he's had cut off in their prime before!"

She carries on bandaging my hands, pulling the thin material tight around them.

"Make sure you toe the line from now on, do you hear me? No heroics, no defiance. You do exactly what he tells you, understand?"

"Understood," I sigh.

BEN

All the way home, all the way through the horrified lectures from Mother and Father, all I can do is think about the expression on her face when she looked at me.

A poisoned arrow, right on target.

"Everyone saw you!" Mother is livid. "Everyone in that damn arena saw you. With your arms round the waist of a Dreg girl. Treating her like she was a princess! I can't even look at you. I'm horrified! Go and have a shower! Right now. Scrub yourself clean. And stay out of my sight! I can't bear to talk to you!"

I've never seen her lose her cool like this before.

I suppose I should feel guilty, should feel contaminated, but I don't. I feel oddly detached from her anger. I look at Francis, silent for once, smirking at me as Mother and Father rail and rant. He's loving this.

I let their words wash over me. I don't argue back, but I don't apologize either. As soon as I can, I get the hell out of the room and go upstairs, all the way up to the little attic room.

Far below me, the lights of the Cirque are still twinkling.

It's not like I thought it would be; it's not like any place I could ever have imagined. It's beautiful and beguiling and intoxicating. It's dark. It's evil. People are killed there, murdered for entertainment. Surely that's not right? It can't be, can it?

She's down there, somewhere, under those billowing roofs. I wonder if she's lonely; I wonder if she's scared. She must be.

I can't stop thinking about her. It's as if she's inside me, somersaulting around in my head.

HOSHIKO

By the time we leave the san, most of the other girls are already in bed asleep. Greta's sitting outside, biting her nails.

"Look," I tell her, "Amina's fixed them; they'll be fine."

She seems to accept what I'm saying for once, maybe because she's so tired.

The three of us creep in to the dorms as quietly as we can, past the long line of bunks to our own. The springs above me creak as Amina gets into bed. I don't even bother having the usual conversation with Greta; I just scoot over to make room for her in my bed.

She curls up next to me with her doll and closes her eyes.

I can't stop thinking about what just happened.

I've never fallen before. I've always felt kind of invincible, even when others have died. The horror I've felt has been grief for them, not fear for myself. I'm lucky up there on the wire – I always have been. And I'm good too, although I'd never say it to anyone else.

In another life, I'd have found the tightrope anyway. It's a part of me. That's why they call me the Cat: surefooted and nimble, I'm the best there is. I've made it through scrape after scrape, dancing through all of my nine lives and then some. It's what makes the Pures flock to the show night after night; what makes them call so loudly for my death, and then cheer so wildly when I survive, yet again.

But I don't feel invincible any more. I wonder how much time I've got left; how many performances before I fall again, and nobody's willing to save me.

Silvio shook the wire. He must have decided to kill me off. Imagine the publicity it would bring: the Cirque would be notorious again. I've got to stop this. I try to concentrate on other things but the face of that boy staring at me creeps into my mind.

The only people I hate more than Silvio are the Pures. I wish they would all die a painful death; wish they would all burn in Hell for eternity.

What kind of a fool am I? That boy's not some gallant hero. He's a *Pure*.

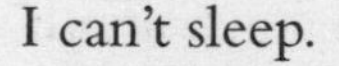

BEN

I can't sleep.

I get my tablet out and look up the Cirque on the PureWeb.

The Cat has been performing in the main shows since she was six – the longest surviving high-wire act in the Cirque's history. That explains why the crowd went so crazy when they thought she was going to fall.

There's loads of details online about the dangers of the act. She's had to deal with arrows being fired at her, electric shocks, cannons: loads of stuff. Other times there are lions – the ones we saw today, I suppose – waiting for her below, or a pit of crocodiles. There's always a fantastically high drop. There's never a safety net.

Her real name, I discover, is Hoshiko.

Hoshiko: it means "child of the star". I look out of the window at the stars twinkling above me, jewels illuminating the night sky. I wonder if she's looking at them, too. I think of her spinning up high, picture again those eyes when they fixed on mine. The name suits her.

I pore through pages of images of her. Standing proudly on that wire; hanging suspended from a trapeze. Every time, that same defiant look in her eye as she glares at the camera. I think about her having to dice with death night after night.

The more I read about her, the more I see, the more desperate the feeling I have inside becomes. It starts off as a gnawing ache, but grows and grows until it becomes unbearable.

I understand now why Priya didn't like it when I said I

wanted to go to the Cirque. It becomes really important all of a sudden to tell her that.

I creep downstairs. She's not in the kitchen, so I search the huge, silent house, making sure I avoid any of the guards' posts and alarm points.

I find her eventually in the drawing room, polishing the silverware. She jumps when I walk in and gives a little shriek, her face breaking into an indulgent smile when she sees it's me. She's forgiven me then.

"Ben," she says. "You ought to be in bed. You seem to be making a habit of these nocturnal visits lately."

"I wanted to see you," I say. "To talk to you about the Cirque."

She turns away from me and goes back to dusting the candlesticks, slamming each one roughly back into place.

"I don't want to hear it," she says, bluntly. "You shouldn't even be talking to me. It's not appropriate."

I move to sit down at Mother's piano. "I need to tell you that I understand now why you were cross with me yesterday, when I said I wanted to go."

She shrugs. "It's not my place to be cross about anything," she says, coldly. "I'm no one. I'm nothing."

She's not making this easy.

"No," I tell her. "You're not no one, not to me. And I didn't like it there. I didn't know it would be like that. I *hated* it."

That's not strictly true. I mean, I kind of hated it, but I'm sort of fascinated by it too. Fascinated by her, the girl, Hoshiko.

Priya turns to me at last. She walks softly over to the doorway and peers through it, making sure no one else is around.

"Ben," she says. "There's something you should hear. I could lose my job for saying it. I could lose my life, but it's important."

It's true: Mother and Father would be outraged if they knew she spoke to me like this.

"What is it?"

She comes over, and grips my arm. It's the first time she's ever touched me. Her hands look old and worn, but they feel soft.

"Think," she whispers. "Think for yourself. Judge for yourself. Make up your own mind."

What does she mean?

I don't want to tell her that I don't know what she's talking about, so I stay silent. I just look at her.

She taps her head. "Use what's in here," she says and then puts her hand to her chest, "and what's in here. Judge with your head and with your heart and you won't go far wrong." She looks at me, her dark eyes intent. "Promise me," she says. "Decide for yourself. Heart and head."

"I will," I tell her. "I promise."

"Good," she says. She looks over my shoulder, her eyes landing on the piano. Its keys glisten in the moonlight. "I don't like it in here," she says and, for some reason, her words make me shiver. "Let's go downstairs and I'll make you a hot chocolate."

As we cross the hallway, I see something out of the corner of my eye, a shadow darting away and up the stairs. I step away from Priya and look up, but there's nothing there. It must have been my imagination.

HOSHIKO

It feels like I've been lying here for hours and I still can't sleep. Next to me, Greta tuts crossly. "Hoshi," she admonishes. "Will you *please* settle down?"

It makes me smile; so many nights she's kept me awake with her fidgeting and now she's here, in *my* bed, telling me off for having the audacity to move.

"I'm sorry," I whisper back. "I can't sleep."

She sits up suddenly, and I can make out her little face grinning in the darkness.

"Did you hear about Silvio?" she says. "A really important Pure lady chucked a fizzy drink over his head!"

"No way!"

"Yes way! In the arena, in front of everyone. They caught it on camera!"

"Why didn't you tell me before? This is the funniest thing I've ever heard! Why would a Pure chuck a drink over Silvio?"

"Don't know." She giggles, infectiously. "I'm glad they did though!"

I can't help feeling shocked. "He must have been mortified!"

All of a sudden, his attempted sabotage of my act starts to make sense.

"When was this?"

"Just before you went on, during the interval."

That explains his rage earlier; a high-ranking Pure humiliated him and so he took it out on me.

"Hoshi," Greta asks, "why would he be so upset that a Pure did that to him?"

"You know why. You know he loves the Pures; you know he thinks he is one."

"But why does he?" she asks, her tone puzzled.

I look at her in the darkness.

She smiles at me, cocking her head to one side expertly. My heart sinks. She's playing me again; she always looks at me like that when she wants something. I know what it is too – she wants me to tell her the Silvio story again. It's her favourite one of all. She makes me repeat it all the time, like it's some kind of fairy story, not the all-too-real account of our psychopathic dictator boss at all.

"Greta, please, it's been a really long night. Can't we just go to sleep like everyone else?"

"I was trying to. You woke me up." She wraps her arms around me. "Please, Hoshi, please tell me why he does. You said you couldn't sleep anyway."

There's no point telling her no; she'll only keep going on. I learnt that a long time ago. It's much easier to give in and give her what she wants.

"OK..." I sigh and I pull her closer, so that her head is nestled on my chest and I can whisper the words into her ear without disturbing any of the others.

"Long ago, there lived a beautiful ballerina, famous across the world. She was not just beautiful and talented, she was wealthy too. Her family were very important Pures; her father was a millionaire financier and she had everything she could ever wish for, everything except love. She dreamed that one day she would find her true love."

Greta has stopped fidgeting now, her body is calm and still.

I wonder if she's asleep already. Maybe I can get away with not finishing the story. I stop talking and lie there quietly, holding my breath.

Her head lifts up suddenly. "Carry on," she yawns. "Tell me how she finds him, her one true love."

Damn; looks like I'll have to finish.

"One night, she found that she was missing her favourite ballet shoe and she went back to the empty theatre to find it. As she walked into the huge auditorium, she saw that a man was there, on the stage, singing. His voice was the purest sound she had ever heard. She watched as he sang, standing silently in the shadows, and was astonished to see that it wasn't any of the singers she knew on the stage but a Dreg, the poor worker who swept the theatre every night.

"When he saw the ballerina the singer was terribly afraid, for he knew the punishment would be death if she told anyone what she had seen. She didn't call the guards though, or sound the alarms. Instead, she asked him to keep singing and she sat and listened to him as the tears rolled down her cheeks. Afterwards they spoke into the night, until the sunbeams crept through the windows and she dashed away, back to her chambers.

"They met every night after that, in the empty theatre. Sometimes, he would sing for her, sometimes she would dance for him, sometimes they would just sit and talk. As the months passed, they fell more and more deeply in love.

"Their passion could not be contained and, eventually, she discovered that she was pregnant. The pair were desperate. What could they do? The Dreg would be killed if their love was discovered, and the authorities would destroy her unborn baby.

"The lovers had no choice but to run away together. For a while, they were safe, hiding in the Dreg slums where she gave birth to a baby boy.

"The ballerina was happier than she had ever been, but she was also weaker than ever before. She was not used to the hard, deprived life of a Dreg and she became very, very sick after childbirth. The singer knew it would mean their secret would be discovered, but he could not bear to see her in pain. Picking her up in his arms, he carried her to the hospital, pleading with them to save her. When they realized who she was, he was immediately arrested and executed. Word of his death came to her hospital bed and the ballerina was overcome with grief. She threw herself from the window and her body shattered to pieces on the pavement below.

"The ballerina's parents were horrified at the shame brought upon their family, and shunned their new grandson. The baby boy was placed in a grim orphanage in the Dreg slums where he somehow stayed alive and grew to adulthood. His parents' theatrical blood was in his veins and he joined the circus and grew up to become the world's most famous ringmaster.

"But that's where the similarities to his parents end, for he had none of their softness, none of their goodness, none of their love inside his heart. He vowed that he would one day become a true Pure and take back his rightful heritage, and he's been striving it for ever since."

I hate this story. I hate the way it makes out that Silvio is some kind of poor unfortunate lost soul. He's been luckier than the rest of us, if the story is true. His mother's family own the circus, and although they can never openly acknowledge him, they've protected him. It can't be just coincidence that he's the one who calls the shots in here, literally most of the time.

Greta is asleep in my arms, lulled off by the story. It's magical to her, but not to me.

This story of his past doesn't make Silvio any more human, nor does it does excuse what he's done. It makes it worse, not better. His parents risked everything to be together and look where it got them. Both of them are dead, and their love child is a monster. They must be turning in their graves.

BEN

I'm still awake when the cold fingers of the morning creep around the curtains and another boring day claws its way in. I think about staying right here, pulling the duvet over my head and pretending I'm ill. I crawl out of bed eventually though. Put on my school uniform, eat breakfast, smile politely at the driver, get in the car, just as I always do. But my mind is still there, in the Cirque, with Hoshiko.

Next to me Francis has his phone out, looking again at the footage he filmed last night. He thrusts it towards me.

"Ben," he says, laughing loudly, "have another look at the lion guy from last night. Look at his face! He's absolutely bricking it! I'm so gutted we didn't see him get mauled!"

I can't believe we're related. I floated alongside him in Mother's womb, shared oxygen, food, everything with him. How can that be?

"You wanted to see him die?"

"Err, yeah!" His face is puzzled. "Didn't you?"

"No! I thought it was terrible!"

"Terrible? It's just a bit of fun, Ben. They're only Dreg kids: parasites, sucking the state dry." He sniggers. "Be better for him too if he'd died, put him out of his misery, end his pointless little existence." He looks at me, curiously. "You've got a thing about them, you have. It's weird."

"What's weird?"

"Thinking about their feelings, wanting to talk to them. I know what you get up to." He smiles mysteriously. "And I know how to stop it."

"What do you mean?"

He shakes his head. "Never you mind; you'll find out soon enough."

I turn away from him and push my headphones into my ears. I stare out of the window but I still can't drown him out.

"Are you turning into some kind of girl? There's some great footage on here."

The churning feeling inside my stomach gets stronger and stronger. I don't think I can contain it much longer; something's going to snap – break into a thousand pieces. Perhaps it'll be me.

HOSHIKO

As soon as the alarms go off, Greta sits bolt upright. "How are your hands?" she asks.

I hold them up, wriggling them tentatively. They feel a lot better, actually. God knows what's in that cream Amina uses but it's started to work its magic already. The cuts are healing over neatly and the swelling has virtually gone.

"They're fine. I think."

"It's OK." Amina leans over from the bunk above, her wild hair hanging down. As usual, she somehow knows everything. "There's not going to be a full show tonight. They're closing the arena down for two nights so they can finish off the preparations for Saturday."

Wow. They *never* stop the show. Mind you, Saturday is November 4th – the weekend between Halloween and Bonfire Night – the night of the Cirque Spooktacular: always the biggest event of the year and this year Silvio's vowed to make it more dramatic and action-packed than ever.

"What, the whole place is going to be closed?"

"Not quite, Silvio's got some big new act he wants to try out; he's invited all the press along for an exclusive."

A big new act. I don't like the sound of that.

"What is it?"

She shrugs. "I don't know. No one does."

She indicates across the dorm to where Astrid and Luna are curled up in the same bunk. The twins are escapologists and contortionists and they've been in the Cirque nearly as long as Emmanuel. They're completely identical, and you never see one of them without the other.

Their act always involves them working together to escape from being chained and bound. Locked up in tiny boxes; buried underground in a coffin filled with snakes, rats or fire. You name it, they've survived it. As the years go by, escaping seems to get easier and easier for them. The more locks and chains Silvio has added, the more quickly they seem to defeat them.

They don't really talk much to the rest of us. They're friendly enough, but they keep themselves to themselves. It's as if their bond is so strong that they don't really need anyone else. When I was younger I used to think they must be magic: the way they look so alike, and they seem to have this weird sixth sense between them. They aren't like individuals at all, but two halves of one person.

"All I know is that the new act is something to do with the twins," Amina whispers.

"Don't they know what it is?"

"No. He's told them it will be better off as a surprise, apparently. He said he wants the shock on their faces to be real. He's promised it will be unforgettable."

Two guards enters then, tasers raised, and we all jump quickly out of bed and start getting dressed.

"Come on!" one of them shouts and they both begin randomly jabbing at people. The female one goes for Amina as she's climbing down from her bunk and I see her eyes widen as the jolt goes through her body. It only lasts a few seconds, but it's long enough. It's horrid, seeing that pained look in her eyes.

I look away from her, across to Astrid and Luna again, as they dress silently with eyes downcast: mirror images of each other. I shiver, because if there's one thing you can say about Silvio – he always delivers on his promises.

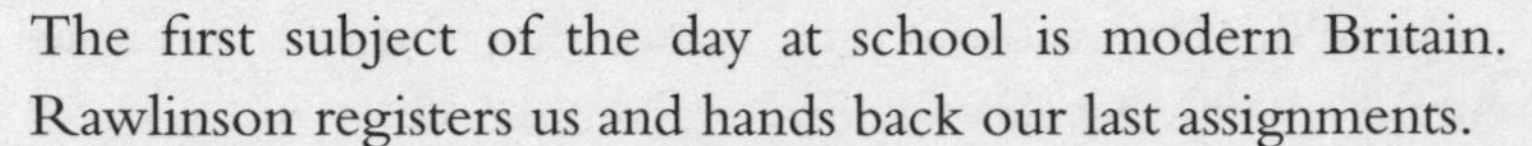

BEN

The first subject of the day at school is modern Britain. Rawlinson registers us and hands back our last assignments.

"What did you get?" Alex asks.

I glance down at my grade. I can't even remember what the homework was.

"B minus," I tell him.

He tuts. "You're so lucky," he says. "I bet you didn't even try. I only got a C and I spent hours on it."

At the front of the room, Francis is holding up his paper gleefully, waving it in the air.

"An A* again!" he shouts across to me. "What did you get, Ben?"

I shake my head. He's always so competitive. Doesn't he realize that I don't care? That no one cares, not even our parents?

"My mother said I can have a PS25 if I stay top of the class all year," Francis calls out to no one, to everyone.

The other kids roll their eyes; they're all used to him by now.

Rawlinson smiles indulgently at him. "Francis, that's enough. Remember, not everyone can be as brilliant as you are. Now, back to the syllabus."

I slump in the chair, staring at the same boring old teacher drone about the same boring old things and the tight feeling in my chest gets more and more unbearable.

What would everyone do if I stood up now and told them what I really thought? What if I punched Mr Rawlinson full in the face? What would happen? What would Stanley, standing discreetly at the back "protecting" me, do? What if I pushed this desk over? Threw my chair through the window? What would the other kids say? I stare around at them all. What's going on inside their heads? Does anyone else feel like this? Like they're unravelling?

The lesson is the same as always; I've heard all this a hundred times before. I let the words wash over me as Rawlinson drones on. "Dregs are vermin." His tone becomes slightly hysterical. "They have poor hygiene, carry germs and spread disease. They are intellectually, morally and emotionally inferior to the Pure English in every way. They nearly destroyed our Motherland, and would do it again, given half the chance."

He keeps rising up out of his chair, and banging down on the desk with his hands every few seconds to reiterate his words.

"They took our jobs, drained our healthcare system and claimed our benefits, bringing a huge wave of violence and crime with them."

He pauses dramatically and looks around. What are the effects of his words on his enraptured audience? Half the class are staring out of the window, the rest have their heads on the desk. Where I'm sitting, in the back row, the others are all whispering to each other about something or other. Maybe Rawlinson actually registers for once that no one's listening to him, because he stands up, moves to the middle of the room, and coughs.

"Ahem. As you know, your main assignments are due for submission next week. You should have spent the last few weeks researching your area of interest. Now is the time to finish writing up your findings and looking for interesting ways to present them."

My heart sinks. I haven't even started my assignment; I don't even know what I'm going to do it on.

A couple of desks down from me, Johnny Parker raises his hand.

"Erm, sir. Could you recap what we should be doing, please?" he asks, innocently. "I want to check I've included everything I need to."

The rest of us snigger and grin at each other. At least it looks like I'm not the only one who hasn't started yet.

Rawlinson nods. "It's good to see you taking it so seriously for once, Jonathan. OK, each of you should be preparing an individual presentation on your chosen aspect of modern history and its impact on society today. This is your time to shine; your time to explore something you find particularly fascinating. As you know, the grade you receive will go towards your final examination mark."

Jonny raises his hand again. "I don't really get it, sir."

We all know exactly what he's doing. We've all been doing it for the last two years – reeling Rawlinson in and letting him go. You just need to feed him a question every now and again to get him straight back on to his favourite topic. Our books are pretty much empty and we hardly ever have to do any essays. Listening to him waffling on about the Dregs for an hour seems a small price to pay. Usually.

Rawlinson sighs. "Well, you might like to look at the history of the Pures for example, at the laws and traditions of modern government, or Dreg management – and the methods we have developed to curb and control them. The best presentations will be the ones which do more than simply dredge the PureWeb for information; try to make them innovative, different, personal. Can you gain any first-hand accounts, access any primary sources, for example? What about speaking to your grandparents? Neighbours? Think outside of the box; access newspaper archives, go to museums, look at what's around you."

Look at what's around you.

Suddenly it dawns on me. I know exactly what my presentation is going to be on. Why didn't I think of it earlier?

I raise my hand. Everyone looks at me; I never say much in class usually – that's Francis's style, not mine. I keep my head down and try not to draw too much attention to myself.

"Benedict!" Rawlinson's delighted. He's always trying to get me on side.

"Could I do mine on the Cirque?" I say. "Seeing as it's in town at the moment?"

The teacher's eyes widen in horror. "You don't mean to tell me you haven't started yet?" he gasps, as if I've committed a serious crime.

"No, I have started," I answer. "My family went to the circus last night. And I've been researching its history," I add. It's not even a lie.

"My mother was given VIP tickets!" Francis blurts out. "We were on the news!"

Everyone groans again; he's already been talking about it at every opportunity, already shown everyone his footage, answered all their questions: *What was it like? Did you get to see any deaths?*

I hate the way he shows off all the time. But this time it's me who's about to use Mother's status to get what I want.

"If I asked my mother," I say to Rawlinson, "she might be able to get me in again. Maybe I could interview some of the performers."

"Hmm." He is suddenly cautious. "You don't want to waste your time talking to them; they'll only fill your head with rubbish. You need to access reliable sources."

"It might be interesting though?" I say. "To find out what their take on it all is? Look at how they're managed and stuff?"

He looks very unsure about this. "Speak to your parents," he says. "Tell them to contact me if they have any concerns. You've left it very late, Benedict. You'll need to act quickly if you're to have enough time to write everything up correctly."

The heaviness that's been sitting at the bottom of my stomach like a lead weight suddenly feels lighter. I don't know why I'm so desperate to go back. It's like the place is some kind of drug, taking hold of me, intoxicating me.

Maybe, if I play my cards right, I could get to speak to some of the performers. Maybe I could get to speak to Hoshiko.

HOSHIKO

For the first time I can remember, rehearsals are cancelled today and we're all ordered to help start preparing for the Spooktacular instead. Some people are painting signs, some are sewing costumes, others are working on lighting and holograms, and the remainder are making props.

To our mutual delight, Amina, Greta and I are put together, along with a load of other performers, in the main arena. Our job: to transform it, for one night only.

The red, gold and silver drapes which are usually pinned up over the building are being replaced with huge polystyrene segments, painstakingly painted orange by a team of workers in order to turn the arena into a giant pumpkin. We've been instructed to make the internal area look like the inside of a scooped-out pumpkin: all fleshy and orange. Huge crate-loads of frothy orange cloth are dumped in the middle of the arena and we work together to pass them around the room and pin them up securely.

Greta and I have to climb up into the rafters and swing down to attach the cloth to the ceiling. It's almost impossible for me; my hands are really painful and the thick wadding of the bandages makes it hard for me to hold on to anything. Greta covers for me as best she can, banging in all the nails while I unravel the cloth; gradually feeding it through to her.

Hanging upside down, watching everyone working busily, I'm struck again by how much they all mean to me. Even the newer members like Kate, the ones I've barely spoken to yet, are family already. Being in the Cirque together, sharing our worries and woes, supporting each other through death and desolation, it makes us much closer to each other more quickly.

There's almost a holiday atmosphere in the room. If you ignore the guards lining the walls, pointing their guns at us and glaring ferociously, it almost looks as if we're preparing for a huge party, not decorating a public torture chamber at all.

I think it's because we're doing something different to normal. Rehearsals take up most of the day usually, and the thought of the evening's show is always there: a dark shadow ominously approaching. We never, ever get a night off.

Saturday seems a long time away, suddenly. Two whole nights. For two whole nights, I won't have to perform. For two whole nights, death isn't coming for me; isn't coming for any of us. We're not free from guards and locks and semi-starvation but there's much less likelihood of a sudden and violent death; we're as free as we could ever be. No wonder everyone's happy.

Below me, a team of workers are pinning up the thick black segments of cloth to form the pumpkin's slanted carved eyes and jagged mouth. A soft light eerily shines through; it's unbelievably effective. Suddenly, it really does feel we're all inside a giant pumpkin.

I glimpse Astrid and Luna out of the corner of my eye, sewing little pinpricks of fairy lights into the orange drapes, and a feeling of shame instantly replaces the bubbly happiness I felt before.

I hadn't even thought about them. They haven't got a night off; while the rest of us are resting in the dorms, they'll be out there, performing to the press. I hope they'll be OK.

BEN

As soon as I get home, I cross to the other side of the house to Mother's office. It's never been officially declared out of bounds or forbidden for us to come here, but I can't remember the last time I did. I tap on the door and wait outside nervously.

She's talking on the phone, I think. I can't make out what she's saying, but I can hear her voice. She opens the door crossly while she's talking and her eyebrows raise in surprise to see me standing there. She gestures me inside and I perch nervously on the edge of one of the big leather chairs while she finishes her conversation.

"Look, I really do have better things to do with my time. I'm not a puppet. I showed my face last night; once is enough."

She hangs up the phone and glares at me.

"I hope this is important, Benedict; I'm incredibly busy."

She's still cross with me and she's finding it hard to deal with. My mother isn't a sulker – she prides herself on it. If she doesn't like something, she changes it. Take the world and mould it into the place you want it to be: that's Mother's motto. That's why she wants to be the next leader, so she can make the country a safer place, she says, by whatever means necessary. If she wins, we'll have to move into the official Leader's Residence in the PowerHouse. We'll live in the apartment, right on the top. The windows are built into the eyes of the huge gold Pure who stands tall, crushing down the Dregs below him. It will please Mother, living there.

I'm not sure what to say. It isn't important, what I have to ask, not in the great scheme of things, not to her. It's a school project. I'm asking about a school project when she has the weight of the whole country to deal with.

But I don't think I've ever wanted anything more than I want this.

"It's not about much, really," I say carefully. "But I do want to speak to you about something, if you can spare a minute. I can wait though, until you're not so busy."

"Not so busy?" She laughs dryly. "When will I be not so busy? Erm, let me see, in about ten years when we've finally rid the world of the plague of Dregs who create so much work for me?"

I stand there, looking at the floor, while she stares at me from behind her desk. It's never bothered me before, her saying stuff like that. I don't know why it makes me feel so uncomfortable now.

The plague of Dregs.

How on earth am I going to convince her to let me go back to the Cirque?

"I seem to be very in demand with my sons today, Francis has already sent a text message requesting a hearing later on," she says. "I can give you a minute or two before my next conference call. Will that be sufficient?"

A hearing... Will that be sufficient? It's like she's talking to one of her office clerks or something. Has she always been this formal and cold? I suppose she has. I've got used to it generally, but today it makes me feel twisted and sore inside.

What if I was being bullied at school? Or I was worried

about something? Who would I talk to? It wouldn't be her. It wouldn't be Francis or Father, either.

It wouldn't be any of them.

It would be Priya, probably. And what could Priya do? Nothing – she's just a Dreg.

I feel tears swimming in my eyes. What's wrong with me? I haven't cried for years. I blink them away hurriedly. She'll be displeased if she spots me behaving so weakly. I needn't have worried though; she's far too distracted to notice.

I need to play this right; tell her what she wants to hear.

"I wanted to apologize," I say. "For my inappropriate behaviour yesterday."

She raises her eyebrows. "Really? Seen the error of your ways, have you?"

"Yes. It was the whole Cirque experience; it made me feel confused for a while. I forgot they were all just Dregs; that they don't have the same feelings as we do."

"That girl," she frowns, "is an example of everything that's still wrong with this country. Parading her up there like she's something to be admired! It would have been a blessing for everyone if she'd fallen."

I try not to wince at her words.

"It has made me think," I say, carefully, "about the Cirque and how, like you said, Dregs need to be regulated in better, more efficient ways. I came up with an idea of something I could do to make more people realize."

"Go on."

I take a deep breath and then blurt it out. "We've been set an assignment for modern history. We have to do a presentation about contemporary society and I was thinking of doing mine on the Cirque, seeing as it's in town."

Her lips curl angrily and there's a sneer on her face. "Why would you want to do that? I thought you'd finally seen sense. You said yourself; it's a vile place. Creatures like that should not be put on display as if they are something exotic and wonderful. I'm more convinced than ever about that after our recent experience. The whole place would be shut down if I had my way. I'm sure we could think of a more economical way of dealing with problem elements of society."

"That's why I want to do it," I tell her. "I want to use it as a case study about what's wrong with society today. I want to show the other kids how cost-ineffective it is, and suggest other, more efficient methods of Dreg control."

She look at me, her eyes narrowed. "What are you after, Benedict?"

I take a deep breath. "Well, I was hoping that maybe you could arrange for me to spend a bit more time at the Cirque, just to study it a bit more. I would be looking at it from a critical stance and I'll show you anything I write before I hand it in. I could interview you about it too. My teacher would love to hear what you've got to say."

There's a daddy long legs buzzing around the room and she bats it away angrily, before peering at me dubiously. She likes what I'm saying, but she's not convinced I mean it. My mother is not easily fooled.

"This is not like you, Benedict. You've never shown any particular political motivation before." She grabs my face suddenly and stares at me intently.

"Why did you help that girl last night?" she says. "Why didn't you let her die?"

What do I say? Because I couldn't stop myself? Because it was the right thing to do? Because I couldn't bear to watch her, or anyone else for that matter, plunge to her death? Because I can't stop thinking about her?

"I don't know," I reply. "I just panicked."

"You haven't got any silly romantic notions in your head, have you?" she says, suspiciously. "About the tightrope walker? It was a very touching scene, watching you save her."

It's like she's examining me, peeling back the layers to see what's inside.

I feel my cheeks redden. I laugh. "No! As if I'd ever look at a Dreg like that!"

Her eyes narrow. "Good. You do know why she's able to leap around up there like that, don't you?"

I shake my head, nervously.

"Because she's closer to the apes than she is to the human race, that's why. All that balancing on a wire; she'd be better off jumping from branch to branch in the treetops!"

I don't like what she's saying, it doesn't feel right any more, but I just nod, contritely. I will be out of this room any minute.

She keeps looking at me like I'm a puzzle she's trying to solve.

"You do seem peculiarly keen on visiting the circus again. You never usually feel the need to come and discuss your homework with me and you've never really exhibited a tendency for bloodlust before, unlike your brother." She laughs, dryly. "Unlike your mother, either."

"I wanted to make up for my behaviour," I say, and then I play my trump card. "I thought it might even help you to get rid of the place once you get elected. Your son spending time there, and condemning it in a school assignment; it might be good PR."

"Hmm." There's a pause while she considers it. I hold my breath. "I'm not sure I want either of my sons near there again," she says. "Then again, it might dispel any misconceptions you and your classmates have about it, I suppose."

She looks at me, properly looks at me, for the first time in ages. "You're growing up," she says softly. "Where's my little boy gone?" She sounds almost surprised. "You're very handsome," she says. "You always were the pretty one."

She touches my cheek and her expression softens. I have this unlikely desire to suddenly throw myself into her arms, hold her tightly; cling to her. I don't do it, of course: she'd be horrified, and anyway, she swiftly moves her hand away and the moment's gone. She's back to being hard and detached again.

"I've been dealing with Cirque issues far too much this week already. I've got to go back again tomorrow during the day to supervise a selection, and my PR clerk's just told me he wants me there tonight too, on another ridiculous marketing mission. A-ha!" She smiles suddenly. "I've had a good idea, a very good idea."

The daddy long legs drifts around our heads again, then lands, foolishly, on the desk next to her. As quick as a flash she lifts up her paperweight and slams it down on top of the insect, crushing it underneath. "That's the last we hear of you, my little friend." She looks at me. "That's how to deal with irritating pests," she says. "Eradicate them. Crush them."

With two fingers, she pulls a tissue from the box on the desk and delicately picks the remains of the daddy long legs up, wiping away the bloody smear from the bottom of her paperweight and tossing the tissue in the bin.

"If you're so desperate to return, you can go in my place. Sending one family representative has got to be better than none."

My heart leaps. "Really? When?"

"As I just said: this evening. Go and get ready, I'll have a car sent to pick you and Stanley up."

She opens her tablet and clicks on the secure link.

"Vivian Baines," she says wearily. "Access code one-four-nine-eight-six." That's her personal code: the one she uses every time she's dealing with sensitive government business. It hasn't changed since the last time I heard it and it's years since I've sat in this office.

"It's me," she says to someone. "I'm sending one of my sons, instead. Surely that's better than nothing. Yes, he's looking forward to it. No, I'll send my own guard."

She ends the call.

"Thank you, Mother."

I'm not sure what else to say, but it looks like I've already been dismissed anyway. She's back on her computer, typing away. I think she's already forgotten I'm there. I stand up.

"Benedict," she says quietly, as I'm turning the door handle. "Don't tell your father; he'll only make a fuss."

"I won't."

"Good." She smirks at me. "Enjoy your evening."

HOSHIKO

At dinner time they send our food in to us – so that we eat more quickly, I suppose – and we all sit down in the middle of the arena. The party atmosphere intensifies; it's as if we're having a big picnic together. The food's better than normal too; there's even a slither of cheese in between the thin pieces of dry bread which are passed around, and there's a big bucket of lukewarm tea for us to dip the tin cups into.

I fetch some for Greta and Amina, handing the mugs over awkwardly with my bandaged hands.

"Your wine, my ladies. I've taken the liberty of pouring it for you."

"Thank you, waitress." Amina smiles. "And what is on the menu tonight?"

"Well, there's all sorts of wonders, madam." I rack my brain. What do the Pures eat in restaurants? I don't have a clue.

"There's fish," I say. "Cod in a herb crust. And there's steak. And creamed potatoes."

"Lovely, and for dessert?"

Greta chimes in, playing the game immediately. "Is there chocolate cake?" she asks, excitedly, as if she really believes I'm going to be able to produce these things.

"Why yes, of course. Chocolate cake *and* ice cream," I tell her.

Emmanuel makes his way over with one of the kids who arrived yesterday, and we shift around, making a space for them to join our little circle.

"Amina, Greta, Hoshi, meet Anatol," Emmanuel says, introducing the new boy.

He's not one of the tiny children, so he hasn't been drafted in through the selection process they put all Dregs through when they turn five. He must have committed some kind of crime, or maybe he was just pulled in from the slums in one of the raids. Either that, or he chose to come here. It's still unbelievable to me that anyone would appear here through choice, but it happens more often than you'd think. People in the slums are so starving and desperate that they don't know what else to do. They quickly regret it of course, when they realize just what kind of institution they've been brought into, but it's too late by then.

The boy has the look all new kids have: shock, disbelief and terror, mingled together in equal parts. His left arm is cradled in a sling.

"We've met already," says Amina, brightly. "I patched Anatol up yesterday, after his accident. How are you getting on?"

"Not very well," he answers. "I can't seem to grasp things as quickly as the others, and now this has happened," he gestures helplessly to his injured arm, "I can't even keep rehearsing."

"Don't worry; we all felt like that at first," she says, sympathetically. "You'll get there in the end. It was a nice, clean break; it should heal quickly."

"That's what I said," Emmanuel agrees.

There's an awkward silence.

"We were just discussing the menu," Amina says, and gestures towards me, "and our waiter here was pouring the wine."

"Ah-ha. I'll have a glass of your finest red, please," grins Emmanuel. "And whatever my friend here would like."

It's nice to see Emmanuel joining in; he doesn't often go in for humour these days. I don't think Anatol is in the mood for games, though. He looks down at the thin, dry sandwich in his hands, stares at the murky grey tea we're holding, and gives a huge sigh.

"I never thought I'd miss the food in the slums," he says.

There's a sudden hush in the room as Silvio sweeps in dramatically and stands, poised on the stage above us, cradling Bojo in his arms. Everyone looks down at the floor, trying not to draw attention to themselves.

He looks around, critically, surveying the decorations. "Not bad," he says, "if I do say so myself."

If I do say so myself. Like he's had anything to do with it.

His eyes continue to scan the room.

"You two!" He calls to Astrid and Luna. "What are you doing in here? You should be getting ready. Go! Now! Quickly!"

The twins get to their feet and rush out of the room.

He looks down at Amina, Greta and me, sitting almost directly below him with Emmanuel and Anatol and he laughs. "Ah, the African King, the three amigos and the incompetent acrobat. I've reallocated you to a different act, boy: you clearly aren't destined for any skilled activity. Don't worry, I'm sure you'll find your new role *explosively* exciting!"

I don't know what he means, but it definitely doesn't sound good. From the corner of my eye, I see Anatol nodding nervously. I'm looking at the floor, but I can still feel it when Silvio's eyes land on me; feel him coolly examining me.

"Did you enjoy the show last night, Hoshiko? Very frustrating, you defying the odds like that again. Still, I must admit, I do want you around for Saturday night. I've got big plans for you." He places Bojo gently down on the floor, takes out his whip, flicks it with his wrist so that it extends, and then reaches down with it, prodding Greta in the chest, right where her blood-stained bandage sits. "For *both* of you!" he laughs, then clicks his fingers in the air, suddenly. "Supper time's over!" he barks. "Get back to work!"

He sweeps out of the room, Bojo scampering after him. Everyone immediately starts getting to their feet. I turn to Greta, still sitting there, not moving. There's an expression of complete terror on her face.

"Did you hear that?" she whispers. "He's putting me in the show. On Saturday. The Spooktacular." She clutches hold of me. "I can't do it." She turns to Amina, on the other side of her. "What shall I do?"

"You *can* do it," Amina tells her. "You can and you will." She puts her arm around her. "It's OK. Hoshi will be there with you."

Greta's lips are trembling. The tears welling in her eyes flood over, trickling down her face.

"Look," I say, cupping my hands together, and holding them towards her. "I've brought you your chocolate cake."

She stares blankly down at the dirty bandages.

"No thanks," she says, sniffing. She looks up at me, her big eyes deep and grave. "I don't feel hungry any more."

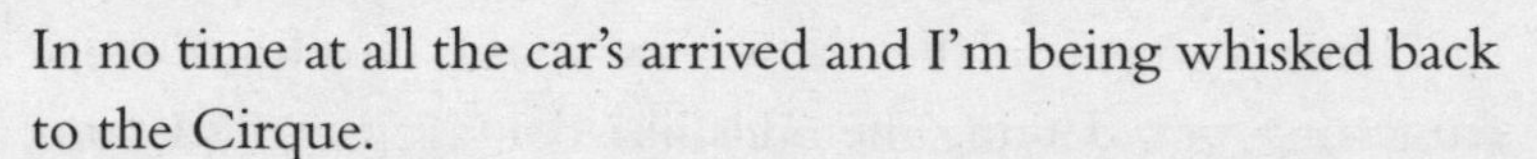

BEN

In no time at all the car's arrived and I'm being whisked back to the Cirque.

The gates are already open as we approach and there's a long line of traffic filing its way in. I see the ringmaster, Silvio Sabatini, waiting at the entrance. I feel really embarrassed after the way Mother treated him last night. He doesn't seem to mind though; as soon as the car glides to a halt, he opens my door, bowing deferentially as I climb out.

"Benedict. It's wonderful to see you again so soon," he smiles. "We're so pleased you could be here!" He leans towards me, his face beaming. "We've got some real treats in store; I think you're going to really enjoy it!"

"Thanks." I'm sure he didn't even know my name yesterday, but suddenly we're best buddies; he's obviously been doing his homework. Silvio Sabatini glares at Stanley, who's opened the other door and is standing silently behind me.

"The Cirque is very secure," he says, defensively. "You didn't need to bring your own bodyguard."

"Sorry," I say. "My mother insisted. We had a bit of trouble a while back."

"Yes, yes, I heard about it. But the guards here really are very efficient, and we're not even open to the public tonight anyway." He gestures to the dozens of people leaving their cars and making their way across the courtyard. "All of these men and women are members of the press. They've all been fully vetted."

The ringmaster scowls accusingly at Stanley, whose face

is passive and professional as always, but then the mask goes back on and he turns to me with his fixed smile.

"There's a new show debuting tonight, hence the media showing up en masse. I really think you're going to love it, and then there's a press conference with the performers afterwards. If they make it out alive, of course!"

My stomach lurches. "Who's in the show?"

"Oh, two of our finest artistes, Astrid and Luna. They'll put on a wonderful display, I'm sure."

"Are any of the other performers going to be at the press conference?"

"Well, possibly, time permitting. It's mostly to promote this new act tonight, though." Sabatini looks at me, his eyes searching my face. "Who were you hoping to see?" he asks lightly.

I move slightly away from Stanley and lower my voice; I don't want him feeding back to Mother.

"The tightrope walker," I say. "From last night. I'm not that bothered," I add hastily. "I just thought she was quite good."

He nods and smiles. "Oh yes, your rescue attempt was very endearing! Developed rather a soft spot, have we? Don't worry, she'll be there; I'll make sure of it, Master Benedict." He nudges me again, and winks knowingly. "I was young once you know; anything for a pretty face!" He laughs as if he's told an excellent joke. I feel my cheeks redden.

There's something really weird about this guy, something sinister. I wonder what his story is. He's obviously a Dreg but he struts around as if he owns the place. He takes my arm and starts to manoeuvre me over to one of the buildings, the same one all the press have been filing into. Within seconds Stanley is by my side, clamping his hand firmly on to Silvio's arm and removing his grip from me. Silvio glares at him and his cheeks flame. He must realize that he's broken protocol by getting so close to me.

"The performance is in here," he says. "In our new custom-built aquatic room. I've reserved you a seat. There isn't one for your guard; he'll have to stand." Anyway, please go on ahead and I'll join you shortly. Our seats are at the front. I just need to see to a few matters."

And then he scurries away across the square, his little monkey bounding after him.

HOSHIKO

By the time we've finished decorating the arena, it really does feel like being inside a huge magical pumpkin. The lighting is all flickery, like candles, and a ghostly orange glow fills the room.

Although we haven't been rehearsing, I'm exhausted and relieved when we finally start packing away. My whole body aches and my bones feel heavy as I make my way back to the dorms for the first night off in a year. I don't think I could have performed tonight even if I'd had to.

The press are all in for the new show, apparently, so we're ordered to leave discreetly through the aerial tunnels that spread all over the place. They've built them so that we're separated from the Pures – so we don't contaminate them too much, I suppose, and also so that the illusion is maintained. They don't want to see what we look like before we're all dressed up and sequinned and the tunnels mean that we appear, perform and disappear again, all in the blink of an eye. They're very useful after a fatality too. If a body has to be scraped off the floor and carted away, the Pures don't always want to be exposed to it. They prefer the drama of a violent death to the inconvenient aftermath.

It's always dusty up in the tunnels; they're made of great metal tubes that are pulled apart every time we leave town. They chuck them in a trailer and then when we arrive in a new town we have to click them all back together, holding them up with pre-made scaffold frames. There's not much room in them either; it's OK for someone small and agile, like me, but for the larger guys it's horrible, having to scramble through them every time the Pures are about.

The tunnels are so narrow that we have to go in single file and I'm queuing up to take my turn when Silvio steps out of the shadows suddenly and grabs hold of me roughly.

"You're coming with me," he hisses in my ear. In front of me, Amina and Greta have stopped too and I look towards them, helplessly.

Is this it? Is he going to kill me?

"Where are you taking me?" I ask, hating the shakiness in my voice.

"How dare you ask questions?" he barks, angrily. "Say goodbye to your friends," and he pulls me away from them, dragging me out of the arena and across the square.

He marches me into the costume rooms and slams me down in one of the chairs. Minnie, the make-up artist, jumps up guiltily from where she's been sitting at one of the booths. It looks like the performers weren't the only ones hoping to enjoy a bit of time off.

"Get her ready," Silvio demands. "Lots of grease paint and make sure she's wearing something revealing."

"What for?" I ask. I can't help myself, even though I know I'm not supposed to ask questions. "I thought there wasn't a show tonight."

He stands behind me, glaring at me in the mirror. "You're on press call," he says. "Make sure you stick to the script."

Press call. My heart sinks. I suppose it's better than having to perform, but only just. Press call is one of a million reasons why I hate the Pures. It's not enough for them to watch us getting maimed and tortured every night: they like to hear us telling them how it feels. Of course, we don't get to tell them the real truth; no one's interested in our actual opinions. The answers are heavily scripted, and we're monitored to make sure we don't say anything untoward or inappropriate. We're not allowed to show any animosity or anger towards the Pures – we have to appear grateful for the opportunity they've given us. It's not easy for anyone to fake that, but I'm particularly bad at it.

"Why?" I ask. "You've said it before: I'm not very good at press conferences."

"Well, you'll have to do better, won't you?" He pulls back my hair so that I'm staring up into his cold eyes. "We've had a special request for you. There's no accounting for taste, I suppose." He smirks. "Don't let me down," he snarls, and then turns and heads back out of the room, leaving me sitting there numbly while Minnie smothers my face with make-up.

BEN

Walking into the new show is like walking into the middle of a coral reef.

It's a round building, nearly as big as the main arena, and the walls aren't really walls at all, but thick reinforced glass. Behind them, an array of marine life meanders its way round a circular tank, encompassing the room. When the doors shut, they too form part of the transparent walls, so that we are entirely surrounded by sea life. It's as if we're in the hollowed-out centre; a magical bubble in the middle of the ocean.

The turquoise blue water is teeming with kaleidoscopic life: so many fish, a myriad of different colours and sizes, huge sting-rays, great ancient turtles. There's music playing: a calm, plaintive tune. It's very haunting; I think it must be whale song.

The ceiling above our heads forms part of the tank too, its water an inky black colour mingled with the brilliant blue glow of plankton, peculiar and alien. Hundreds of bio-luminous sea creatures meander along up there, their skeletons and organs bright white and visible. Strange, long-tentacled squid-like creatures; puffy pink and green jellyfish rippling their way by; illuminated sea horses bobbing along in shoals. It's hypnotic, mesmerizing, the spell it casts over me only broken by a sudden cry from a lady opposite me, pointing excitedly at a pod of six dolphins that comes weaving its way around the room.

The rows of chairs we sit in are circular too, facing inward to an empty stage. Everyone's craned round in their chairs, looking behind them at the closest walls. There's a sudden cry from opposite me and I see a lady pointing excitedly at a pod of six dolphins that comes weaving its way around the room.

Suddenly the lights in the tank dim and the middle of the room is illuminated instead. The tempo of the music speeds up, throbbing intensely as a new tank is lowered down into the ring. There's a collective gasp as we all realize at the same time what's in it.

Four huge sharks are gliding through the water. Nature's deadliest, sleekest of weapons, great whites, without a doubt. Their tails swish and their huge mouths gape open, seeming to leer at us, as they patrol the tank. You can see their teeth, jagged white zigzags, like something a child would draw.

A shiver runs down my spine just from being this close to them. No wonder Sabatini was excited about this latest show.

I wonder where they come from, how they are caught, transported, penned.

There's something in the middle of the tank. An extra spotlight shines on it, so it becomes clear what it is. It's a diving cage. Inside are two women, huddled together and bound up with chains.

Standing on a platform above the tank, cracking his whip and beaming at us, beaming at me, especially, Sabatini appears.

"Ladies and gentlemen!" he calls out. "Welcome to the inaugural performance of our newest Cirque act. We are proud to say you are the first audience to witness this show – the first people *ever* to witness this show, in fact, for it has not even been attempted in rehearsal before! Please refrain from photography, but do tell the world all about it afterwards! In the tank below me are the world famous escapologists, Astrid and Luna. You will, I am sure, have heard of them, maybe even seen them perform before, for they have been one of our most popular circus acts for over ten years!"

There's a roar of applause. He waits for it to die down before he continues. "I'm sure I don't need to remind you, ladies and gentlemen, that Astrid and Luna have survived every single situation they have faced so far. And they have faced many difficulties... except one..." He pauses and then in a horrible, piercing singsong voice wheedles, "That's right, except for nature's deadliest predator... Except for Great. White. Sharks!"

The audience erupt again and he basks in the noise as he waits for silence.

"Astrid and Luna, you will see, are currently breathing with the support of oxygen tanks. In a moment, these tanks will be removed and the safety cage around them will be lifted up. Astrid and Luna must find a way to escape the twelve chains which bind them both to the bottom of the tank. They must do it before the air runs out. They must do it before..." he pauses dramatically, "before the sharks get hungry!" The crowd cheers again, there's a frenzied stamping of feet, wolf whistles, dramatic screaming.

I thought the press would be a bit more subdued, but no; they seem just as crazed as last night's crowd.

I don't want to be here; it's not why I came. What would Priya say if she knew?

"Ladies and gentlemen, without further ado, I give you the Great White Gamble!"

With that, Sabatini leaps down off his platform and bounds across the room to sit in the chair reserved next to me. He turns to me, a self-satisfied smile on his face. "I told you it would be good," he says.

The oxygen canisters and cage are lifted out of the water. The tank is lit up so well that as soon as the cage is gone you can see the two women really clearly. They don't have protective masks on and their eyes are wide open as they begin to struggle with the chains. They look exactly the same as each other. They must be twins, like me and Francis, identical ones though.

The sharks immediately swim towards them. Some people say sharks are beautiful, but I don't think they are. To me, they just look menacing and cruel; soulless, heartless predators with blood on their brains.

In the centre, Astrid and Luna are frantically trying to work their way out of their chains. They make fast progress for a while; three great metal bindings and four locks are quickly released and drop to the bottom of the tank in heavy coils.

"What do you think?" Sabatini leans towards me so that I feel his horrid breath on my face. "I thought of this one myself. Am I not a genius?"

I've had enough. Enough of him, enough of the Cirque, enough of everything.

"I think it's disgusting," I tell him, watching as his face drops. "Disgusting and shameful. This isn't anything to be proud of. It's sick."

He laughs nervously. "Don't worry," he says. "It's all an

illusion. These people aren't really in any danger at all!"

I look at the tank, at the two women, struggling.

"It looks very real to me," I tell him, doubtfully.

"What I mean is, sharks don't feed on people. Shark attacks are much rarer than you think. They aren't at all interested in attacking anyone; they've just had a good feed."

I feel a bit better when he says that. It's true, I think. I remember reading something about it being a myth that sharks ate people, even great whites, like these ones.

The twins haven't got any oxygen though and they're chained to the bottom. How much longer can they last for, even if the sharks decide they don't want breakfast?

"Don't worry," Sabatini croons at me. "Luna and Astrid are the best in the business. They'll be free within minutes."

Sure enough, there's a sudden commotion in the water as one of the girls swims free from her chains. She pushes up through the water to the surface, her head thrown back as she sucks in great lungfuls of air.

"There, didn't I tell you she'd be fine?" Sabatini says. "She'll climb out now, right as rain."

He's wrong though. Instead of moving towards the steps and getting out of the water, she plunges back in again and dives down into the tank. The other girl is still struggling below the surface, her eyes bulging and panicked. There's only one chain left holding her down, but it's a huge one, wrenching her back every time she tries to rise up.

The first twin swims towards her and grabs her head between her two hands. She puts her mouth to hers. She's giving her sister air, breathing it into her mouth, trying to keep her alive. She swims away from her and down to the chain, working to try and untangle it. The chained girl's movements are noticeably slower than hers now.

The first girl swims back up to the surface, and then dives back down, repeating the same moves as before, breathing air into her twin's mouth and then trying to untangle the chain.

The audience are silent now.

The submerged twin's face looks pale and her eyes glazed. She's stopped moving. She looks like she's dead.

The sharks swim about the tank uninterestedly, ignoring the two figures struggling so desperately.

Something changes though. The unchained twin turns suddenly and swims quickly up to the surface, holding her arm out of the water in front of her.

"Her finger's bleeding!" someone shouts. I lean forward and I can actually see it. A tiny cut. She must have caught it on the chain, or scraped it on the bottom.

She swims quickly towards the steps and starts to pull herself out. It's too late though; the blood has already dripped into the water.

In horrifying symmetry, the sharks attack. They whip towards her and one of them launches up, out of the water, pulling her downwards with its great jaws.

It's hard to see what happens after that because the water turns red. It churns, seething. Like it's alive, when all it really means is death.

This doesn't feel real. Maybe it's all part of the act, maybe it's just pretend. I look at Sabatini, next to me; his face is stricken.

"Damn," he says angrily. "They weren't actually supposed to eat them; not until Saturday night at least."

He stands up and beckons over one the guards. "Get everyone out of here! Now!" he orders. I think he's actually forgotten I'm there. "Show's over."

Once I'm ready, I slump down in the chair, trying to summon up some energy and enthusiasm from somewhere, rehearsing in my head the script of acceptable answers.

When Silvio comes in, I can tell straight away that he's angry about something.

"Get out there," he orders. "You're on straight away."

"I thought I was on after Astrid and Luna?" I say.

He regards me coldly. "I'm getting sick of telling you not to question me. Things are not going well for me at the moment; I've got a whole new show to plan in time for the Spooktacular and I do not have time to stand here answering your questions. Do as you're told, girl."

He turns to leave, pausing at the door to face me again. "Astrid and Luna are dead. Is that clear enough for you?"

And then he walks out, slamming the door behind him.

BEN

The aquatic room is a sudden hive of conversation as fifty journalists simultaneously give live broadcasts about what's just happened. I force my way through the mass of people, and stumble over to the edge of one of the pathways, vomiting up my lunch.

I turn around and Stanley's there, as always, pretending not to see. What does he think of it all?

Those girls must both be dead. No one could have survived that.

In my head, all I can hear is Priya's voice. *Make up your own mind; judge with your heart and with your head.*

I know what she meant now. All I want to do is go home and tell her that.

That's not true; all I want to do is see Hoshiko again, and then go home and tell Priya that.

I stand there for a bit longer, waiting for the queasiness to subside, then I head over to the press conference room. There's no one here yet; they're all still broadcasting their gleeful reports live on the rolling news channels.

I sit in a chair a couple of rows back. I try to stop my hands from shaking, but I can't. Eventually, the room fills up around me. Any minute now, I'm going to see her again.

Once everyone's seated, the trademark Dreg Cirque fanfare crackles over the tannoy and Silvio Sabatini appears again, prancing on the stage like some kind of evil goblin. Maybe he's actually got demonic powers which enable him to be in more than one place at the same time.

"Ladies and gentlemen!" he cries in his wheedling voice. "What an eventful night! Here at the Cirque, when we promise a treat's in store, we never fail to deliver! And now, yet another gift for you: welcome to this evening's press conference!" Ever the showman, there's no sign now that anything's amiss. His smile is syrupy, his tone grandiose. "Well, I know you're not here to see me and so, without further ado, please welcome the Dreg Cirque's star performer: trapeze and tightrope artiste extraordinaire, the amazing, the phenomenal, the sublime – the Cat!"

The whole room around me is on its feet, everyone clapping furiously. I stay seated, looking around.

A door at the side of the stage opens and there she is, flanked by two security guards.

She's wearing an emerald green gown – the sheer silk ripples when she walks, fluttering at her thighs. The neckline plunges down to her waist, where it's tied together with a black, looped bow. I feel my cheeks burn.

I wonder if she remembers me.

I wait for her to look up and see me in the crowd, but she spends most of the time looking down at the ground; her eyelashes are really long and dark. Her hands are bandaged up; she must have damaged them last night.

Silvio Sabatini kicks things off.

"Ladies and gentlemen, this is not our show, it's *yours*. The Cirque only operates with your generosity and support. Young Hoshiko here would be delighted to answer any questions you may have."

Nothing happens for a few seconds and then a

journalist in the front row tentatively puts up her hand.

"Madam?" the ringmaster beams.

"Erm, yes." The woman seems nervous. She's about thirty, I guess, quite plain and dowdy looking. "I'd just like to say that I've watched your act loads of times now, and I'm totally in awe of you! What I would really like to know is, when did you first realize that you wanted to be a performer here in the Cirque?"

If the question makes me feel this angry it must make her feel furious, but her face is a mask of indifference.

"Every Dreg dreams of being in the Cirque," she answers. "To be able to enrich the lives of the Pures in some way is all I've ever longed for, ever since I was a child."

The first question has opened up a tidal wave, and there are dozens of hands up now.

"How many hours a day do you practise?"

"What's your favourite part of the act?"

"How many times have you been injured?"

Every time, she answers in the same measured, monotone way. It's as if it's all scripted: a carefully rehearsed performance.

I look at Sabatini. He's watching her every word, a steely glint in his eye. A chill runs down my spine. She can't say what she really thinks, she's not allowed to.

The questions keep coming, quickly getting more personal, more offensive, as the audience become more comfortable.

"How long do you think you've got left?" one guy asks. Her expression alters as her eyes narrow and flick up. It's just for an instant though, before she looks back down and her face resumes its neutral expression.

"Every day I risk my life, but it's a small price to pay if it entertains the audience."

I'm sitting on my hands, but I still can't stop them. I raise one in the air. I have to connect with her again, although I don't know what I'm going to say.

The ringmaster points to a few more people.

"How many deaths have you seen?"

"What's the goriest one?"

"How old were you when you started performing?"

I keep my hand aloft, straining it up high now, trying desperately to catch his eye. Eventually, his gaze lands on me. "Yes, young sir?" He smirks at me, knowingly.

I will her to look up, to see me, but her eyes remain downcast.

"Yes?" he prompts me. "Do you have a question for Hoshiko?"

"Erm. What I would like to know is … do you… I mean, have you…"

I stop. What do I want to ask her? What do I most want to know? It's suddenly simple.

"Do you ever wish things could be different?"

Finally, she looks up. She strains forward in her chair and she stares, really stares into the crowd for the first time. "Can you repeat that please?" she asks.

I stand up and repeat the question. Her eyes lock on to mine. She's seen me.

HOSHIKO

The questions are exactly the same as they always are. Pathetic Pure journalists, desperately wanting to know about every gory detail of my life. They lap them up; the more bloodthirsty and chilling they are, the better.

I've rehearsed the answers to all these questions time and time again; there's nothing new here, but I can still feel Silvio watching me carefully.

I really don't want to do anything to make him angry, not after everything that's happened recently. He nearly killed me while I was up on that wire last night. For some reason, he's no longer as keen to protect me as he's been before. In fact, it feels like the opposite. All of a sudden, it feels like he's desperate for me to die.

So I answer the questions exactly as I've been drilled to do. I manage to not scream at them, manage not to tell them how I really feel. It's agonizing sitting up there going through the motions after what he's just told me about the twins. All I want to do is get back to the dorms, find out if it's true. He might have been lying; he could have just wanted to upset me.

I need Amina, she'll make me feel better. Surely there can't be much longer left?

Then, a new question: one I haven't heard before.

"Do you ever wish things could be different?"

Something about the voice makes me look up. I can't see where it's coming from.

The spotlights shining on me from the back of the room are so dazzling that the audience, even though they're just a few feet away from me, are in darkness.

I strain my eyes, trying to see more clearly. It's the first time I've looked at the audience, so it takes a while for them to adjust.

That voice: gentle, apologetic in its tone. I've heard that voice before.

"Can you repeat that, please?" I ask.

A figure in the middle of the room stands up, and a spotlight moves obligingly, illuminating him.

It's him. The boy from last night. Why is he here again?

I look at him and his eyes stare back into mine. He asks the same question again, softly, quietly, his voice trembling a little.

"Do you ever wish things could be different?"

I keep looking into his eyes; they're pleading with me, somehow, to tell the truth.

The room is silent; they're all waiting for my answer.

My eyes turn to Silvio. He shakes his head at me. I daren't defy him. Then again, if he's already got my cards marked, how can things get any worse?

I look back at the boy, wonder again what he's doing here. I lean forward; it's as if there's an invisible chain linking us, pulling me towards him. I take a deep breath.

"Yes," I tell him. I whisper it at first, but then I think of Astrid and Luna. They must be dead. Silvio never lies about stuff like that. He never needs to. I know, somehow, that they are truly dead. Rage fills me up, it boils up inside, it cannot be contained.

I stand up, I speak loudly, clearly. My voice rings out across the room as I stare at him. "Yes, I do wish things could be different."

BEN

For a few seconds it's as if there's no one there but me and her; as if the room, the Cirque, everything, just melts away. It was the same in the arena last night. It's as if the rest is just background, just outlines and she's the only real thing there is; glorious, iridescent colour in a world of silhouettes.

The spell is broken abruptly as Sabatini comes to the centre of the stage, grinning maniacally.

"Right, thank you, everyone. That's all for tonight. I'm sure you'll agree it's been eventful. On your way out please take an exclusive press pass for Saturday night's Halloween Spooktacular! Thank you, thank you."

She's dragged out of the room by two security guards. Sabatini looks at me coldly, then turns on his heels and rushes out after them.

Everyone gathers their things together and begins to leave. Most of them aren't even talking about what Hoshiko said at all; they're all still going on about the shark tanks. Two deaths at once to report on; they must be more than happy with the night's events.

I suppose I should wait for Sabatini to come back and escort me out, but I can't bear the thought of seeing him again tonight. I wish I could see Hoshiko though, check she's OK.

The room's empty now except for me and Stanley, who is standing impassively at the back. I wish I could talk to him about it. There's no point though – he never engages in conversation with me, no matter how much I try. Ever the professional, he just maintains his detached façade.

I sink back down into my chair.

I definitely wasn't imagining it. She did look at me. She recognized me, I'm sure of it. The way she whispered the words – as if she was just talking to me. As if it was just us, as if she was really answering me.

There's a sound, a polite cough. It startles me; I was so deep in my thoughts. I look up and there's a cleaner there, waiting to tidy the room.

"Sorry," I tell him. "We were just leaving."

I look at him. Old, wizened, olive skin, frail emaciated frame. There's nobody here. Just me and him and Stanley.

"Do they treat you well here?" I ask him. What a stupid question. Look at the poor guy: of course they don't.

He glances around hurriedly. His voice, when he speaks, is weak and hoarse.

"Yes," he replies, in the same monotone voice Hoshiko used. "They treat me very well. I am very happy."

He's not looking at me; his eyes are on the ground, like hers were for most of the time.

I reach forward and place a hand gently on his arm. He flinches and takes a step backward, as if I've injured him.

"I'm sorry," I tell him.

He looks up, his moist eyes meet mine, just for a second. I can't read the expression in them; it's not hatred and it's not fear. It's sadness, I think.

There's a silence for a second or two. And then he turns suddenly. "I'll come back later," he croaks. For someone who doesn't look very well, he moves fairly quickly and I'm left there, with Priya's words running through my mind. *Judge with your heart and your head.*

What if my heart and my head don't agree?

My heart is crying out to me that this is wrong. Her, me, all of it. The Cirque, the world – wrong. My heart is telling to me go after her.

My head tells me not to be a fool. This isn't some silly fairy story; this is the world we live in. This is the way things are; what's the point in wishing things could be different? I'm just a boy, just one boy, that's all. Look at my family; look at my life; look at who I am. I'm one of the lucky ones. I'm on the right side of the gulf that splits our worlds in two: the deep, un-crossable chasm. I can't change that, even if I want to.

I look at Stanley, expressionless as always. What would it take to make him react? To tell me what he really thinks? I sigh heavily.

"Come on," I say. "Let's get out of this place. Let's go home."

HOSHIKO

I know I've taken it too far, even before Silvio drags me out of the room. As soon as we're out of sight of the audience, he pushes me into the wall and grabs me by my throat. "What do you think you're playing at, girl? You went completely off-script there – that answer was inflammatory!" His eyes, millimetres away from mine, are flaming with fury. "Do you know who you were talking to? Do you know what you may have done?"

What does he mean, who I was talking to? Does he mean that boy? He was in the VIP box last night. Who is he?

"I just told the truth," I answer. "You're a Dreg too, Silvio, you must feel the same!"

He lets go of my throat and thrusts me away from him, so that I fall to the ground.

"How dare you compare yourself to me? I'm not just a Dreg! Not like the rest of you! The Pures value me."

I stare up at him. My God. He actually believes it.

I start laughing, I can't help it. "You're just another performing animal to them, Silvio, don't you see? They'll kill you off like all the rest of us once they've had their use out of you."

"No." He kicks me hard again and again as he speaks. "You're wrong! I'm nothing like the rest of you!" My poor tender bruises protest helplessly at another beating. I ought to keep my mouth shut. Then again, I never could do the sensible thing.

"Silvio," I say, smirking up at him. "They'll never accept you."

He pulls me to my feet, and then hurls me against the wall. My head slams backwards, cracking painfully.

"How dare you! I've had about all I can take out of you, girl! You aren't such hot property that I won't have you taken out to the firing squad and blasted off the face of this planet right now!"

I look at him, my head still reeling, and I laugh. I laugh in his face.

"If that's the best you can do," I say, my eyes meeting his, unflinchingly, "bring it on."

We stay there, eyes locked for a long moment and then he turns away. "Fortunately for you, I've got a last minute show to plan or I'd do it right now, but I won't forget this, Hoshiko. I'll deal with you before too long, I promise you that."

He grabs me again, throws me back down to the floor and marches off.

My bravado vanishes as quickly as it came. What have I done? You can't speak to Silvio like that and get away with it. He's going to have me killed.

What am I going to tell Greta and Amina?

BEN

As we're leaving, I hear raised voices in the corridor: Sabatini's and another voice. I think it's her.

"I won't be a second," I tell Stanley, and move towards the sound. The door is open a crack and I peep through it.

It is her.

She's on the floor, looking up at Sabatini who's standing over her.

"I'll deal with you before long, Hoshiko, I promise you that!" he snarls, and then whirls around and leaves through the other door.

She stays there, curled up on the ground. Her face is pale, with spots of colour high on her cheeks. She looks really frightened. I don't blame her; I'd be frightened.

Stanley is standing behind me, impassively. God, I hate it. Hate having this silent witness there all the time, stuck to me like a limpet.

I move forward quickly through the door, shutting it behind me. She looks up, shocked.

"Are you OK? Your hands, I saw the bandages," I say. "I wanted to check. Let me help you up."

She scrambles to her feet, smoothing down the green dress and hugging it around her.

"I'm fine," she answers abruptly. She glares at me. "What are you doing here? Who are you?"

"I helped you yesterday, in the show, and I saw you again just now, in there. You answered my question. I wanted to check you're all right..."

"All right? No, I'm not all right. I nearly died during that show. I do hope you enjoyed the performance?"

She's really angry. It's as if she *hates* me. She does hate me.

"I didn't enjoy it," I protest quickly. "Not one bit. That's what I wanted to tell you."

"Poor baby, did the big lions frighten you?" Her tone cuts me deep. "Two performers died tonight, did you know that?"

I hang my head, but I can feel her staring at me. "My God! You did know. You were there, weren't you? You were there when they died! Enjoy it, did we? Entertaining enough for you, was it?"

"No. I hated it. I'd never have come to the Cirque if I'd known; I was here for a school project."

My words trail away too late. As soon as I say it I realize how it sounds. Everything I do seems to dig the hole I've made for myself deeper.

"A school project? Well, this keeps getting better! And talking to me now, that's going to help improve your grades, is it? I'm *so* pleased to be of service to you!"

"No. I wanted to see if things were really what they seemed. I'm sorry. It's horrific here, I know that now."

"And you're telling me that *because*?"

I stand there, silent and stupid. This was a really, really bad idea.

"Look," she says. "I don't know who you are and I don't know why you came, but you need to leave. Right. Now."

I turn to go, but something makes me spin back around. I have to know that it wasn't just me.

"You must remember me," I beg her. "Today, when I asked

you the question. You recognized me, I know you did."

"No!" She spits the words out. "I don't remember you! You Pures all look the same to me. You *are* all the same. Now get lost, before I scream."

I look at her, drinking her in for one last second.

"Sorry," I mutter, cursing myself for never knowing the right words to say.

I turn away. Stanley's waiting there in the doorway. I'm moving towards him when she speaks again. "Wait. There's something I want to tell you."

HOSHIKO

He's like some weird stalker, appearing everywhere I go. He was in the arena, he was in the press call and now he's here, in the corridor. Every time he looks at me with those deep brown eyes, as if he really cares about how I feel, it makes me so angry; at least with most Pures you know where you stand. You know they hate you; you know they'd rather you were dead. Even ones like that stupid woman in the press conference who develop these weird obsessions with you because you're in the Cirque, you know they don't see you as a real person, not really. They don't actually consider what might be going on under the surface.

This boy though, helping me back on to the wire yesterday, saving my life. *Trust me,* he said. And then today: *Do you ever wish things could be different*? What a ridiculous question. How dare he come in here and pretend to care like that?

"Wait," I say to him, and he turns back towards me, all hopeful. "You can't come here and ask questions like that. It's not fair."

"I'm sorry," he says again. "I know that now." He sighs, and his lip trembles. "I don't know what I'm doing here either."

He looks so lost, so dejected. I feel my heart give a tiny involuntary tug. I have this ridiculous urge to comfort him; as if it's him who's been pushed around, him whose life is in danger.

What the hell's wrong with me?

"Is there anything I can do," he says, "to help you?" His

tone is so concerned, so respectful. It makes me angry again.

"Yes," I tell him. "There is. Leave me alone! Leave this circus, go back to your safe little life in your safe little world and don't come near me again."

A guard has appeared now, standing in the doorway, so I turn and run the other way. I look back round when I get to the end of the corridor and he's still there, staring after me with that lost look on his face.

BEN

By the time we get home, Mother, Father and Francis are all in bed and the house is in darkness.

I don't even get changed; I wait in my room until I hear Stanley relieve the other guard and reset the alarms, then I go downstairs to find Priya. The only light is coming from the kitchen, so I guess she must be there.

When I walk in though, it's not her I see at all. There's someone else there, washing up. A man, in our house uniform. He looks up at me briefly, then back down.

"Hello," I say. "Who are you? Where's Priya?"

"I'm sorry, sir, I'm not permitted to discuss that with you."

"What do you mean? Who said you can't discuss it with me?"

He carries on washing up, scrubbing away vigorously at the pots and pans.

"I'm sorry, sir, I'm not permitted to discuss that with you."

I walk over to where he's standing and push myself between him and the sink but still he won't look at me. He stands there, eyes downcast.

"Where's Priya?" I ask him. Why won't he tell me? "Tell me where she's gone, please!"

"I'm sorry, sir, I'm not permitted to discuss that with you," he says again, his voice shaking.

I turn away. What can I do?

I walk slowly back upstairs. Where is she?

I pause outside Mother and Father's room, then turn the

handle and thrust open the door. It's dark, but I can make out their sleeping forms in the bed. I turn the light on, and they both sit up, blinking in the glare. Mother gasps, the covers clutched up to her neck, and Father grabs instinctively for the pistol on his bedside table, pointing it at me. As soon as he realizes it's just me and not some evil Dreg kidnapper, he drops it on to the bed.

"Benedict! What on earth are you doing?"

"Where's Priya?" I demand.

"How dare you?" Mother's voice is outraged. "How dare you come barging in here during the middle of the night asking such impertinent questions?"

"I said, where's Priya?"

She reaches for her glasses and puts them on, glaring at me through them. "Why should the whereabouts of a Dreg servant be of any concern to you, Benedict?"

"Where is she?"

"She's gone and she will not be returning," my father says firmly.

"Why? Why has she gone?"

Mother sighs heavily. "Do you really think we don't know what goes on under our own roof, Benedict? Do you think we are that naïve? We know all about your cosy midnight chats with that woman, that's why she's gone."

My mouth goes dry. I stare at her.

"What were you thinking of, fraternizing with her like that – as if she was an equal, as if she was of value?"

"She was of value," I say. "Is. She is of value."

She chuckles. "Was," she says. "Right first time."

I think I'm going to be sick again. What have they done to her?

"Benedict," she smiles. "We have eyes and ears everywhere. Speaking of which, what a peculiar question you asked the little Dreg tightrope walker tonight. You wish things could be different, do you?" She laughs, "You don't know you're born!"

"I warned you," my father says to her. "I warned you that allowing them to go the Cirque was bad news. It's turned his head, given him false notions."

"There's no point in recriminations now, Roger. Benedict, Priya has gone and that's all you need to know. And there will be no more visits to the circus; you'll have to find something else to do your little school project on. Now, I suggest we all go back to sleep."

She puts her glasses back on the table and lies down. "Turn off the light on your way out, will you?"

HOSHIKO

By the time I get back to the dorms it's obvious the news has already spread about what happened to the twins. There's a heavy silence and everyone's gathered in a circle. Amina stands up and comes over to hug me.

"We've been waiting for you," she says. "We've lost the twins."

"I know," I say, "Silvio told me. What happened?"

She looks towards Greta, cradling her doll, and the other youngsters all sitting there, forlornly. "Sharks," she says in a low voice. "They didn't stand a chance, apparently."

I join the circle, next to Greta. Emmanuel moves to the door and checks that the coast is clear. He nods gravely, and Amina goes into the san, coming back out with the candle and matches. We used to have five candles when I first started. I don't know how Amina got hold of them; she just seems to be able to acquire things like that. We light them every time there's a death so they've gradually melted away. There's only one little stub left now. Amina lights it and places it in the middle of the room. It casts an eerie glow on the circle of solemn faces. She sits down next to me and we all cross our arms together, joining hands with the people on either side of us forming one great circular chain.

There are quite a few unfamiliar faces here tonight: new Dregs, just drafted in. They're part of us now though, part of who we are and they sit among us, their eyes shadowed, their faces pale. If they were ever under any illusions about what sort of place they have pitched up in, they aren't any more. Talk about a baptism of fire.

We sit in silence for a long time, united together in grief.

The mourning ceremony is one that has evolved over time. It's not religious; the faiths in here are too diverse. Some people still cling fiercely on to their religious heritage, their Jewish, Islamic, Hindu, Christian roots. They use their belief to give them hope. I admire them for it, and envy them it sometimes. Others, far more of us, have no faith, unable and unwilling to believe in a God who maintains a steely silence at what the world has become. That's not to say that this process is any less important to us. Saying goodbye, remembering and celebrating a life that's been snuffed out too early, it's a part of what makes us human. Far more human than they'll ever be.

We feel every death. It never gets easier, and nor should it. We will never, ever become indifferent. We will never let them take away our humanity, even though theirs vanished long ago. They try to reduce us to animals, but they never will. Never. Astrid and Luna may have been nothing to them, but not to us, never to us. Their lives mattered as much as anyone else's in this cold and cruel world.

The silence is broken by the first note of song, and then we all join in, a sombre, lyricless dirge; an outpouring of emotion and grief.

When we finally cease, Emmanuel speaks, his deep rich voice filling the room.

"Brothers and sisters, today we remember Astrid and Luna. They lived together, they died together."

He pauses and when he speaks again his tone is no longer

gentle; it is sharp, angry. "They had a terrible death. A violent death." He raises his voice, "An unnecessary death. Astrid, Luna, we wish you peace. We mourn for you. We will give your life, and your death, meaning. We will never break. We shall be strong."

He looks around the room as he cries out the words which draw us together.

"We shall overcome."

We echo his words, a chorus, faltering at first but then stronger and stronger as we chant.

We shall overcome.

We shall overcome.

We shall overcome.

BEN

I don't sleep all night; I just sit at the window, looking down at the circus far below.

Every time I close my eyes, I see those twins again in the water: the way the first girl supported her sister, breathed life into her like that, the way the water turned a terrible red.

And I see Hoshiko, again and again I see her, looking up at me, looking into me, whispering: "*Yes. I do wish things could be different,*" and then, in the corridor, so cold, so angry: "*Leave me alone... Don't come near me again.*"

I try to put her out of my mind, try to put the Cirque out of my mind, but I can't. It's like the place has got hold of me, somehow.

How did my parents know about me and Priya speaking once the rest of the house was asleep? And where is she? What have they done to her?

I remember the shadowy figure the other day, in the hall. Was that one of them? Mother or Father? No, it's not their style to be sneaky. They'd have dealt with things there and then.

Suddenly it's obvious. I don't know why it took me so long to figure it out. I know exactly who betrayed Priya and me: Francis. Mother said he'd requested a meeting with her and it's just the kind of thing he would do.

I think about those poor twins in the shark tank, one of them dying to try and save the other one, and I think again of my own twin.

I hate him. He wouldn't risk his life to save me, and I wouldn't save him either, not now. I couldn't care less if he was dead – I wish he was. I wish they all were.

HOSHIKO

Amina removes the bandages from my hands before breakfast the next day.

"Hmm," she says, dubiously, rubbing cream into them. "They don't look great, if I'm honest. I told Silvio you shouldn't rehearse at all today if he wants you up there tomorrow."

"Don't tell me he agreed?" I look at her. She's biting her lip like she always does when she's not telling me everything. Something's up. "What does he want me to do instead?"

She winces, and gives me an apologetic smile. "He's put you on selection."

I stare at her. "No. Amina, I can't."

"I'm sorry, I did try to persuade him otherwise. He was insistent."

He's done this on purpose. He's punishing me for what I said yesterday.

All the years I've been in this place I've managed, somehow, to avoid being involved in the selection process. Until now.

"I'm not doing it. How do I get out of it, Amina?"

"You can't. You have to go along with it, Hoshi."

I look towards Greta, perched on the edge of the bed, and she stares back at me, her huge eyes wide and haunting. Her doll, Lucy, is clutched to her side, as always. *Where would she rather be?* I wonder. Here, in this living hell, or out there, starving to death in the slums?

She's not exactly spoilt for choice, whichever way you look at it, but at least out there she'd be with her mum, with her family, even if they only got a few years together. At least she wouldn't be on the brink of embarking on an exciting new career where the promise of death loomed large, night after night.

"I'll fail them all then," I tell Amina. "If I say they're inadequate, they'll have to send them all back to where they came from, won't they?"

Amina shakes her head. "It's not that simple. They're not stupid, Hoshiko, far from it."

Why is she always right about everything?

She looks at me closely. "Don't do anything foolish, not now. Please."

I stare right back at her. "So, I'm supposed to condemn a load of little kids to their deaths, am I? No. No way."

"Be sensible. You wouldn't be sparing them anyway. If you don't play ball, they'll just get someone else to do it, and God knows what they'll do to you. You can't afford to make any more waves, Hoshi."

I stare at the ground. What does she want me to say?

"Promise me," she says. "Promise me you'll be sensible."

Greta joins in with her pleas. "Please, Hoshi. I don't want you to get in trouble."

I love them both so much. "Fine," I say. "Fine. I'll behave myself, I promise."

I can't cross my fingers; my hands are too sore, plus they'd both notice. Instead, I swing my feet under the bed and cross my toes. Promises don't count if you cross your toes.

BEN

As soon as we're in the car on the way to school the next morning, I interrogate Francis angrily. "Why did you tell them?"

His eyes widen in mock surprise. "Tell them what?"

"About me and Priya."

His face breaks into a stupid, smug grin. He's enjoying this. "Ben, she's only some old Dreg servant; don't get so worked up about it."

"Why?" I ask again. "What could you possibly gain from it?"

He shrugs. "I didn't like her, that's why. I'm not blind; I used to see her giving you that special secret smile. She never bothered looking at me like that."

"That's because you treated her like dirt!"

"She *was* dirt. Muck, tramped all over our house. I'm glad she's gone."

I can't even look at him. He's vile. A vile little weasel.

The day carries on after that, time trundling ever onwards like it always does. I sit in the car, ignoring Francis, just like yesterday. I sit still and quiet during break-time, ignoring Francis, just like yesterday. I sit in modern history, hating the teacher and ignoring Francis, just like yesterday.

Rawlinson is droning on about the inferiority of Dregs as usual. I scowl at his big, bulbous nose and the beady little eyes which peer over his glasses. At the greasy, combed-over hair trying, and failing, to hide a shiny bald scalp.

Use your head, Priya said.

My head is telling me that it's not possible that he's biologically superior to her. To Hoshiko.

I can't stand it here any more. I feel a panic fluttering in my chest. I want to smash something.

I look behind me at Stanley – his eyes are fixed on me as ever. I stare at the walls, the cameras with their beady eyes swivelling around, logging everything. I feel like I'm suffocating.

I make a sudden movement with my arm, and sure enough, the lens on the one nearest me immediately expands as it focuses on this unprescribed action.

The end of lesson alarm sounds and everyone stands up behind their desks. It's lunchtime, usually my favourite part of the whole day. Time for a kick about on the field. For nearly a whole hour I'm almost free, as long as I block out the guards lining the fence and watching my every move, of course.

But I can't do it today, can't pretend that I'm not being followed everywhere I go. It doesn't feel like protection; it feels like I'm being smothered. I've got to get away.

I push my chair back and head straight out of the door, ignoring Alex and the others as they call after me. I head off quickly down the corridor. Not quickly enough though; I can hear Stanley hurrying along behind me. I turn around and confront him.

"I'm going to the toilet. Is that OK with you?"

Stanley nods. I feel guilty immediately. It's not his fault he has to watch me. I don't suppose it's very exciting for him either, trailing me about all the time.

I attempt a smile. "Sorry, Stanley. I feel a bit fed up with everything today. I know it's not your fault."

He nods again. "It's perfectly fine, sir."

I walk to the toilets. I don't even need to go, but I suppose I'll have to now I've told him that's where I'm going. The room's empty and I slip into a cubicle, locking the door behind me.

I can see Stanley's black shoes as he waits outside. This thin bit of wood, gaping at the top and the bottom, it's the only degree of privacy I've got. This is the only moment of the entire school day when someone's not actually watching me.

I look up. Directly above the toilet, there's a window, open. The weak autumn sunshine has momentarily overcome the grey of the morning and its rays filter through. The blue sky beckons to me.

It's a small window, but I could wriggle through it, if I wanted to. I could go to the slums and look for Priya.

No, that's a ridiculous idea. I've had it drummed into me often enough that the slums are dark, dangerous places – I'd have a knife at my throat within seconds. I could go to the Cirque, though. Maybe I could see Hoshiko, find out whether she's OK.

Outside the door, Stanley coughs politely.

I look at my watch; it's one o'clock. The lunch break lasts for an hour and I don't have any more lessons today, just a double study period in the science centre. The driver's coming for me at three. Just for me though; Francis has got chess club until late. If Stanley kept quiet then no one would notice I was even gone until then.

I pull open my bag, tear a page from my history book and scribble hastily.

Sorry. Don't want to get you in trouble. Don't report it. Back by three, I swear. I underline the word swear a few times and leave the note on the floor before climbing up on to the toilet seat. I throw my bag out of the window, hoist myself up and pull myself after it. I jump down. I'm on the move.

HOSHIKO

After morning head-count, I make my way outside with everyone else and stand in the courtyard, watching them all bustling busily away to their different activities and assignments. I feel a crushing sensation in my chest. I can't do it. Not selection. Not me.

I look all around at the high metal walls which separate us from the outside world. Maybe they would work for most people, but they'd never keep me in, not if I really wanted to get out of here. I could scale them in seconds, drop down the other side and be away from here before the alarms had even gone off.

For a few moments, I actually consider doing it; picture myself running into the city, vanishing into the slums. I could go on the run, keep going until I find my family. Why not?

Because I know I'd never make it. The walls are electric, for a start – I'd be fried as soon as I touched them. And even if they weren't, I'd be caught, mown down right outside, peppered with bullets. Silvio would probably display my body for a while, as an example to others – *this is what happens if you disobey*. Amina and Greta would see me. I'd rot away in front of them.

I take a few deep breaths. I need to calm down. Maybe it'll be OK; maybe none of the kids will be good enough to be called up.

Behind me, I hear the *thud*, *thud*, *thud* of authoritative feet. A guard is making his way over to me, his taser out and a scowl on his face. I've been standing in open view doing nothing for too long. I don't stop to make conversation.

BEN

As soon as my feet touch the ground I scoot away fast to the left, ducking down low against a line of hedges. I can see the school gates, tantalizingly close. They're locked, of course, but it's a safe bet that they'll be opening soon; lunch is the time the coaches leave for away fixtures, and there are loads of lower school teams due out today.

I stay where I am. I can see a whole bunch of first-year girls in the car park; they must be waiting for a coach. Out of the corner of my eye, I spot Stanley's worried face appearing at the little window I've just jumped out of. He's discovered I'm missing, then. He disappears. Will he report it? No. He'd lose his job over it. I feel a bit guilty. Not guilty enough to go back though. As long as he keeps quiet and I make sure I'm back in time for the driver it'll be fine.

The coach finally arrives, and the girls pile on to it. After a minute or two, the engine starts up and it rolls towards the gate. As it passes me, I duck out of the hedge, positioning myself directly behind it. It's only moving slowly and I can keep up with it by jogging. I stay central, pressing myself close to it, so that the driver can't see me in his mirrors and I won't be visible if anyone looks out of the back window.

It's easy. The big gates slide open when the driver holds his pass-key up to the security post. I move forward with the coach, out of the gates.

As the coach gathers speed, I duck out away from it, behind a fence post. I look back – no one's behind me, no one's seen. I'm free, and it's a feeling that's totally exhilarating.

I feel really exposed, being out of school in the middle of the day like this. It's the first time I've ever been out alone. I've always been safely in view of some figure of protection or other: a guard, a teacher, my parents. I don't exactly blend into the background dressed like this. Everyone knows our school uniform; the school's the most expensive in the country. I may as well be carrying a banner, declaring my status: "Elite schoolboy – bunking off," maybe, or worse: "Person of Protected Status, inadequately guarded." I pull off my tie and blazer and stuff them into my school bag.

I smile to myself at the autumn leaves which swirl around me in the wind, clustering together in rebellious gangs on the regimented, perfectly cropped lawns, brazenly defiant in their bright golds and reds. I bet it drives the people in charge mad having to make someone sweep them up every day: trying to tame the untameable.

It's easy to navigate my way back to the Cirque; it's visible for miles around, nestled amongst the city's cold grey skyscrapers. From up here in the hills, you can see just how vast it is.

Dozens of round buildings, joined by all those aerial tunnels and walkways, encircle the huge main arena, where I sat that first night here. Each roof is domed and ornate, painted in bright metallic swirls and patterns and encrusted with gems. With the red, gold and silver tents underneath, they look like giant sweets, tantalizing and delicious.

The roof of the arena is the most beautiful of all, bright turquoise and deep purple, overlaid with shiny gold plate. It reminds me of Priya's sari, and a chill comes over me. I hope she's OK, I couldn't bear it if anything had happened to her because of me. The sunlight catches on the shiny surfaces of the roof and winks at me.

I feel a tingle run down my spine, just standing here, looking down at the circus. It annoys me, the effect it has on me. It's a bad place, an evil place.

I cast an eye over the rest of the city. All the skyscrapers, all the towers, pale into insignificance now the Cirque's in town. There's only one thing that can dwarf its vastness: I see it every day, so I guess I've stopped noticing how imposing and dramatic it is, but today I see it again, through unblinkered eyes. There, right in the middle of the city, so high that its shadow ripples over the whole Cirque when the clouds move over the sun, is the huge monument of the Government PowerHouse; the place that will be my home if Mother becomes the new leader. The gold statue, raised up on the bodies of all the crawling and clamouring Dregs below it, beams its bounteous smile down upon us all.

I shiver again.

I jog down the hill steadily, keeping to the shadows. It's quiet out at this time of day. All the Pure children are in school, while their parents work in their offices, or take lunch in the city's wine bars and restaurants. The Dregs who aren't working are all locked in the slums.

I pause for breath for a moment or two when I reach the big quarry. Below me, hundreds of Dregs are mining stone, chained together at the ankles in groups of four. I can hear the clink of their shovels as they work. There are some Pures down there too: security guards with their tasers raised in case there's trouble.

I turn away and start running again, reaching the gates without incident. They're locked shut and two armed guards stand outside.

Damn, how am I going to get inside?

I look back up the road and see flashing blue lights as a police car comes round the corner. Another one follows immediately behind it, and then another, and then three motorbikes. Behind them I glimpse a familiar sight: a sleek black Mercedes bearing the government crest on a silver shield.

It must be Mother's. How could I have forgotten? Yesterday in her office she said she had to come back here today. The motorcade seems over the top enough for it to be her, or someone like her; it's as big as the one that escorted us in the other day. There are at least a dozen cars and bikes in it and, flanking the car with the crest, snipers stand in open-air trucks, their guns aimed in all directions. I duck back and watch as the procession glides past me, through the gates. I can't see through the blacked-out windows, but it is Mother's car; I know the number plate – PURE 1.

As soon as it's through, the gates slam shut with a resounding clamour.

I look down at what I'm wearing. Even without the tie and blazer, it's so obvious that I'm a schoolboy. I'm never going to be able to get inside, especially not today with all this extra security around.

Then I realize what I have to do – I have to *use* who I am, not hide from it.

Before I can change my mind, I march straight up to the two guards on the gate.

"Benedict Baines," I announce, confidently. "My mother has told me to meet her inside."

They look at each other, doubtfully.

"We haven't been told to expect you," one of them says.

"That's right," adds the other one. "We're under strict orders not to permit any unauthorized personnel."

How would Mother react if someone inconvenienced her like this? I try to channel her sense of superiority, her coldness.

"Are you actually questioning me?" I ask them. "My mother won't like that. She's told me to meet her inside. I don't suppose she was aware that she'd have to run it by you first."

They look at each other again.

One of them pulls a phone from his pocket.

"Stop," I tell him. "If you waste my mother's time, she'll make sure you regret it."

The other guard puts his hand on his colleague's arm.

"It is him. I saw him here yesterday," he tells him. "With Silvio, and he was here the night before. He was on the news – look."

He passes the guard his phone; he must be showing him footage from the arena.

Since the kidnapping attempt, I haven't made any public appearances; Mother and Father decided it was better if nobody knew what Francis and I looked like. The other night was different though: Mother was going for maximum exposure, and there's photos and video of me, as clear as day, sitting next to her on those stupid thrones.

The first guard's tone immediately becomes deferential and nervous.

"Sir, I'm so sorry. I had no idea. We were trying to protect your mother. You do understand, sir?"

I nod, coldly. "Just open the gates."

"Of course. Do you need escorting anywhere?"

"No. That will be all."

He presses a button and the gates swing open, obligingly.

I stride confidently through, right into the courtyard. I'm back in the Cirque.

HOSHIKO

Outside the selection room, a dozen little kids are lined up. They must all be five – the same age I was when I was selected – and they look as awestruck and anxious as I still remember feeling. Bedraggled and skinny, they cower together in that primitive, mistaken instinct that tells them they will be safer that way.

I hang back for a bit, watching them. The first boy in the line immediately stands out. His blue eyes and dark skin are incredibly striking and he's taller than the others, stronger looking. Most of them look as if they're about to collapse, but he carries himself differently.

The rest of them stand silently, eyes downcast. The child right at the back is tiny; surely she can't be five. Then again, most Dreg kids are a lot smaller than they should be. She's crying and one of the boys tells her crossly to "shh!" The girl in front of her turns around, sees her crying, and wraps her two little arms around her.

"Don't be horrid!" she scolds the boy. "She's scared."

She whispers in her ear. The tearful girl giggles and whispers back.

I wonder where I'd be now if I'd failed selection.

It feels like a hundred years since I stood there, leaning against that same wall. My mum warned me loads of times not to get carried away, not to show off, but I didn't listen. I was excited when all those important-looking Pures kept coming back to me, smiling at me, making me do more of the exercises than any of my friends. I wanted to please them. I tried as hard as I could, sealing my own fate.

After that, the men came to take me away.

I stand there in the square and it all comes back, all those memories. They sent three guards for me. They didn't even bother knocking on the thin wooden door of our little hut; they just kicked through it and grabbed hold of me.

They were all so big: heavy black boots, great black coats, cold faces. I screamed, I remember, begged them not to take me, clung on to my mum's legs. My baby brother was in my mother's arms and he started wailing too.

"Shut your bloody children up before I do it for you!" one of the guards barked and then he cracked Miko across the face with his gun, so that he screamed even more. There was a big welt on his cheek and his eyes were all wide, his little face bulging red with shock.

My mum tried to calm him down but he was too distraught. My dad knelt down to me then. He told me I had to brave now; I had to be a big girl and do what the men said, or they would hurt me.

"You'll be OK," he said. "We love you. Don't forget that. *Don't ever forget.*"

He kept saying that as they wrenched me away from him and threw me into the back of the truck with some other kids. It was the last thing I heard as they slammed the doors shut. The last thing I ever saw or heard of any of my family again.

Don't ever forget.

I wonder what he'd say now if he knew that I do forget, that I can't remember, exactly, what he looked like. Do I look like him or my mum? I don't know. I can't see their faces properly in the faded pictures that remain in my head.

He was right about them hurting me. They beat me again and again in those early days, every time they didn't think I was trying hard enough. I'd never been so much as slapped before.

I know why they did it: they were trying to break us. To curb our will, to turn us into automatons – human machines. It didn't work though; it made me hate them so much that I began to fantasize about getting my revenge.

After a while, I refused to do anything, wouldn't even get out of bed or eat. Then they told me they would hurt my family, put them into hard labour camps, or that they would just disappear, in the way that Dregs do. At the time, I thought they were probably lying, but I was unsure enough to go out there and try damn hard, just in case.

I know now that it was true. After Amina's injuries, Silvio tried to make her perform, even though she could barely walk. I remember walking into the changing rooms, seeing her trying to get changed into her costume. Her ribs were still broken and she was wincing as she pulled the fabric over her body.

"Amina!" I couldn't believe what she was doing. "You can't be serious."

"I don't have a choice. He's told me I have to go out there."

"You can't. It's not possible. You'll have to say no."

She stared at me. "Say no? Do you really think it's that simple, Hoshi?"

Silvio walked in then without knocking, ignoring her

desperate attempts to cover up. He gave that oily little smirk of his.

"I sent a little visitor to your parents, Amina. You'll be delighted to know they are both still alive, for now. Anyway, I have a picture for you; never let it be said I'm anything but generous!" He leaned forward and spoke into her ear; it was a whisper, but I could still hear what he said. "If you don't get back on that stage and put on a show tonight, they'll pay the price for your laziness." He held something between his fingers and dropped it at her feet, before pivoting around and leaving the room.

She picked it up and looked at it. A noise came from her then, like something was breaking inside her. She cradled the paper to her chest and for a long time I couldn't get her to move.

In the end she scrambled to her feet and carried on getting dressed. I picked up the paper – it was a photograph.

Her eyes met mine: "My mum and dad," she said quietly.

I looked at the photograph. A man and a woman stared back at me. They were handcuffed together; behind them two armed guards held a gun to each of their heads.

"Are you sure it's them?" I asked. "It's been a long time."

"Of course I'm sure! Do you think I'd forget my own parents?"

I still didn't understand what was going on. "Why are they tied up like that?"

"Hoshiko, he's threatening me. If I don't perform to his standards tonight, he'll kill them!"

"Why?" I was confused. "It's not their fault."

"To get at me!" she wept.

She tried her best to do what he wanted – went out there, got on the wire, started the show.

It was impossible though; she slipped again, and that was that. He didn't put her out there again – the Pures don't like to see inadequate performances; they like to see us die when we're at our best. They're sensitive like that.

Amina has never found out what happened to them. She asked Silvio once and he just laughed and said he'd been true to his word. She doesn't talk about them much any more. She says she knows they're dead, that it's better to think of them like that. She says she keeps going for them, to honour their memory.

She kept the photo. She thinks I don't know, but I've seen it. She takes it out at night when she thinks no one's watching. It can't be healthy for her to keep seeing them like that, with guns to their heads, but she seems stronger than ever now. She's somehow turned this terrible thing into a reason to keep going. She's strong, my Amina. Resilient. She's amazing.

The doors swing open, and a tall security guard appears, jolting me back to the present.

"Children." Her voice is cold and authoritative. "Pass through these doors in single file. You are about to enter a sanitization unit, and you will feel a light spray on your head. Please do not panic or make an unnecessary fuss."

They make their way obediently through the doors. The spray is to make sure they're disinfected and clean in the presence of Pures.

This is it then, the selection.

BEN

It feels so different, being in here in the daytime. It's disconcertingly quiet, like a ghost town, and then I hear a chatter and noise as a group of performers walk by.

I duck back behind one of the tents and watch as they pass. I recognize them; it's the acrobats, the ones who were performing in the arena on opening night. They looked magical then, in their sparkling costumes and glitzy make-up. In the harsh light of today though, dressed in their rags, they just look pale and ill.

I wander off, skirting the edges and ducking low behind the buildings. I don't want anyone to see me, and I especially don't want to bump into Mother.

In the centre of everything, the main arena looks different today. It's covered in what appears to be orange polystyrene – it looks just like a huge pumpkin – and I guess that what it's supposed to be, ready for the Spooktacular.

The smoky, sweet, magical aroma of night has vanished too; there's an earthy, pungent smell in the air which intensifies as I walk further in. I don't need any signs to tell me I'm approaching the animal enclosures.

I look around but can't see anyone. All the performers must be busy rehearsing and the guards will be wherever Mother is, I suppose.

There's a noise, a kind of humming murmur, coming from the cages which stretch up and down in long lines.

In the first one, the horses are lined up next to each other. There's no room for them to move or turn around, and just enough to be able to flick their heads in their futile attempts to get rid of the mass of flies gathering about them and crawling into their eyes. At the performance, they looked white and gleaming but today, close up, they just seem skinny and sad. The Palomino horse Sabatini arrived on is on its own. I reach a hand in and stroke its velvet nose. It whinnies, and nuzzles me softly.

The next cage is the same size, but there are elephants in there. Huge elephants, three of them squashed into a space no bigger than they are. I touch the skin of the nearest one; it's dry and cracked. He reaches towards me with his trunk and I let him snuffle my fingers.

I wish I had something to give him.

"I'm sorry, boy," I tell him. "I don't have anything for you."

It's almost as if he can understand me; he looks like he's nodding, sadly, as his eyes meet mine.

In the next cage, there's a paddling pool. It's tiny, like the one Francis and I used to play in when we were younger. It's half full and there are five sea lions in it, laying there listlessly in the murky water.

I move to the next cage. The lions are in here. I draw back again, instinctively, but they don't even move; they all lie there and stare at me, apathetically. They don't seem scary at all now. I can see their ribs through their coats, dirty in the cold light of day. The male lion's mane is all matted and tangled up. He yawns, and I see the sharp teeth and smell his rancid breath.

How do they reduce a wild beast to this? He was jumping through rings of fire yesterday. What do they do to it, to make it comply?

Same thing they do to all the animals, I suppose; same

thing they do to the Dregs. Use violence and fear. It doesn't seem right, once majestic beasts like this being locked up in these tiny cages and made to perform like that.

It must be even worse for the Dregs than the animals. It must be far, far worse. I think about Rawlinson, in class. *The Dregs aren't really people at all*, he always says.

I think about the sneer on Mother's face, when she discusses anything Dreg-related. She's always hated Dregs, but since the kidnapping attempt she's channelled all her anger into a white hot loathing; it's as if it's taken over who she is.

I think about Hoshiko's face, when she looked at me last night. I think about her eyes.

She looked like a real person to me.

I hear Priya's words again.

Heart and head. Judge with your heart and your head.

From the next cage comes the unmistakable chattering of apes. I don't want to see them. I can't bear any more sad eyes and the smell of all the dung is making me feel sick.

"Sorry," I tell the lions ridiculously, as they regard me impassively. "Sorry it's not much fun for you."

As I look around, I see the exit doors of the main arena are open a crack. Moving cautiously over to them I peep through. It looks really different in the day, without the twinkly lights and the crowds. The walls are orange now, like the outside, but it still feels vast and empty and cold.

It's not empty though; a group of boys are hunched up together in one of the far corners.

I wonder what they're doing.

I check behind. No one can see me, except the animals,

who all seem to have moved right to the front of their cages and are staring at me, accusingly.

Creeping forward, I slip through the doors and into the arena, ducking down into one of the rows of chairs and squinting through the gaps.

HOSHIKO

I follow the children into the room. The only way in is under the spray; it wafts around me, a mist of chemicals.

They cluster uncertainly at the back of the vast hall. Various pieces of gymnastics equipment are out – mats, climbing ropes, vaults, beams. At the far end, behind a desk raised up high on a platform, three people sit, pens in hand, waiting.

I recognize them straight away.

The two guys are the financial trustees of the Cirque, both city big-wigs. They look kind of the same as each other: grey hair, black suits, blank faces. I forget what their real names are, but all us Dregs refer to them as Tweedledum and Tweedledumber.

They flank the woman in the centre. She's wearing a navy-blue suit and her red hair frames her face in a sleek bob, accentuating her cool, icy-blue eyes.

Vivian Baines.

Wow, two visits in two days. We *are* honoured.

Guards line the back wall, their guns aimed at me and at the children, although I have no idea how they think we could pose any threat to them.

Mind you, there were kidnapping attempts a couple of years ago; I remember hearing about them. Vivian Baines and her kids were nearly abducted by one of the Dreg hate mobs. They caught them though, before they got very far, strung them up, hung them to rot at the front of PowerHouse.

Shame they didn't succeed; shame it wasn't her and her

kids who ended up dead: at least that would be three fewer Pures to worry about.

She notices me, loitering at the back, and she raises her hand and curls one long, manicured finger at me, beckoning me over.

"You, Dreg girl. Come here."

The look on her face isn't disgust, or contempt, like you would expect to find when someone like her looks at someone like me. It's more passionate than that, almost as if she's angry with me. Her eyes bore into me. I meet them with a steady gaze as I cross the room. If she wants to intimidate me, she'll have to do better than that.

"Let's get this over with as quickly as possible; I have places to be. Put the dirty little brats through their paces and then report back to us. Could they be useful in the circus, or not?"

I nod curtly at her before heading over to the little group of children. They're all sitting down now, huddled together, cross-legged. I hate the way they all look so scared of me – as if it's me who's the bad guy, not the child-snatcher behind me.

I turn back to look at her. She's not focused on us at all; she's got a laptop out and she's typing with determination. The two guys are both doing the same. I kneel down and whisper to the group of kids.

"It's OK. You'll all be able to go home at the end of today."

Their faces light up. They must live in cold, dingy squalors, they must be practically starving the whole time, and yet none of them want to be here. Maybe they know, already, what kind of place it is; maybe they can sense the evil, hanging in the air.

A place in the circus means certain death. Maybe you can

escape it this time, maybe you can survive another a week, maybe a month, maybe a few years, if you're lucky. But the one thing you can be sure of is that Death's waiting for you. He wears a fine suit and he carries a monkey on his shoulder and he's coming for you; one crack of his whip and you're done for.

I don't care what Amina says, I'm not passing anyone.

BEN

There's a sudden commotion at the back of the hall and a group of workers enter, pushing a giant contraption between them: thick black metal, vast, imposing. The last time I saw one of these was in the Imperial War Museum on a school trip, but this one is even bigger than those they used hundreds of years ago.

It's a cannon.

It takes twelve men to manoeuvre it through the door and across the arena. They edge slowly forward. Dregs are naturally weak, or so we're told, but it must be really heavy for them to be moving it that slowly. Finally, they get it in position at the back of the arena, on a wooden stage that has been erected since I was here on opening night.

Once it's in place, four Dregs with tape measures come in. They spend ages tilting it left and right, up a bit, down a bit, lining it up with a target point on the opposite wall. Finally, they seem satisfied. They step back and one of the guards begins hauling the boys roughly to their feet, pushing them over to the central stage.

They're all aged between fifteen and eighteen, I reckon: around my age. That's where the similarity ends, though. Their translucent skin seems to barely stretch over their bones, which jut through at sharp angles. I think guiltily of the hot school dinner I've just turned my back on, knowing there'll be plenty more food for me to eat when I next get hungry.

Most of the Dregs leave then: just one man remains, his critical eye fixed on the cannon. He must be some kind of technician, taken from his family as a child just as the performers were and trained up. The security guards push the boys roughly into a line in front of some metal steps which lead up to the muzzle of the cannon.

Oh God. Surely they aren't going to?

HOSHIKO

The test has three components: agility, core strength and balance. For the agility part, the children take it in turns to lay on a mat while I inspect their flexibility. I call each one over and try to get through my fake assessment as quickly as possible. I'm supposed to put them in lots of uncomfortable positions: make them arch backwards and push their little legs forward and back, right and left, to see how much pressure and resistance they can take. Instead, I try to make it fun for them, telling them curl up into tight little "bouncy balls", and stretch up tall "like trees".

For a while, it works. Even the tiniest girl stops crying as she concentrates on jumping up into the air like a great big star.

It's when Silvio comes in that it all starts to go wrong.

The metal doors swing open and smash heavily against the walls, announcing his presence with a loud clang. All the children stop their little jumping exercises to stare at him, open mouthed.

He's all dressed up, as he always is, with Bojo perched on his shoulder in his little matching suit. He must look like something from a story to them.

Silvio dashes across the room, ignoring us, and approaches Vivian Baines, who stares at him over her laptop.

"Madam." His voice is all sickly sweet and syrupy, it turns my stomach. "We're honoured to have you with us again."

"Really." She glares at him coldly. "And you are here because?"

He falters. "Erm. Well, I always try to be present at selection, when my schedule permits. I like to keep a close eye on all aspects of the Cirque, check the Dregs are working as they ought to be. Show them who's boss."

"The Dregs?" she glares at him. "Are you not one yourself? A Dreg, I mean?"

"I suppose, strictly speaking, you might say that, but my position is somewhat ambiguous."

"Ambiguous?" Her smile is icy. "Well, *boss*, you are either a Pure, or you are not. Which is it?"

Silvio glances over at me. I look quickly down at the ground, but I can't stop the little smirk on my face. He mumbles something so quietly that I can't hear him.

"I beg your pardon, little man," she says. "You will have to speak more clearly. What was it you said?"

He coughs, nervously. "I said I am not a Pure, Madam."

"I am not a what? I repeat, you need to speak more clearly."

"I am not a Pure, Madam."

"Yes. I can see that. Now, if you've finished taking up my time?" She looks over at us, all watching. "Show's over. Continue," she demands.

Silvio crosses the room, and stands uncertainly in front of us. I've never seen him lose his cool before. My eyes meet his and I turn away. I know it's a really, really foolish thing to do but I can't help the laughter that bubbles up inside me.

She reduced him to nothing, right there, in front of all the Dreg kids, in front of Tweedledumb and Tweedldumber, in front of me. I can't wait to tell Amina. This ludicrous notion he has that he's somehow different from the rest of us, better than the rest of us. His crazy little fantasy that one day his Pure family will welcome him back with open arms: she crushed it.

I know I mustn't let him see me laughing, so I keep my back to him, but I can't stop the convulsions that start in my stomach and rise up, making my shoulders shake. But then a sharp jolt runs through my body, making it convulse for a different reason, as he digs a cattle prod into my ribs.

"Get on with it." His words are clipped, angry; I think he's clenching his teeth.

He marches towards the children and grabs hold of the nearest one. It's the little girl, the smallest one of all. She reminds me of Greta when she first arrived.

"Get on with it!" he repeats, jamming the cattle prod repeatedly into her ribs. She cries out, her eyes widening in pain and fear as the electric shock shudders through her body.

For a while he patrols around, randomly prodding the children as they try their best to perform.

They're petrified now, cowering away from him instinctively.

"Ringmaster?" Vivian Baines calls.

"Yes, Madam."

"Haven't you got anywhere else you need to be?"

Silvio splutters something unintelligible. I never thought I'd see him floundering. Then again, I never thought I'd see anyone who sent more chills down my spine than he does but the woman across the room makes him seem like a pussycat.

"I hear your big new show met with a dramatic end last

night?" she says. "I hope you'll have something to replace it with in time for the notorious Spooktacular?"

"Oh yes, Madam!" he crows, nodding profusely.

"That's good," she says. "Care to share the details?"

"I'd rather not say yet, Madam." He laughs, nervously. "But if you'd like to come to the event, you won't be disappointed!"

"Once is enough," she snorts, derisively. "Just make sure it's explosive enough, will you? Two deaths in one night almost makes it worthwhile keeping you open. Presumably the great Spooktacular will be even more eventful?"

"Oh yes, Madam. Of course!"

There's a silence as she, Tweedledumb, Tweedledumber, me, the children – all of us – stare at him.

"OK." The fixed smile on his face is more like a grimace. "Off I go, onwards and upward."

He turns and dashes quickly out of the doors.

Her eyes settle on me.

She claps her hands sharply together. "Well, come on, Tightrope Walker, proceed as you were. I don't have all day!"

BEN

The front doors swing open and Sabatini appears. He strides across the arena, his little monkey hopping along behind him. I look at his dark, greased moustaches, his olive skin, and I'm left wondering how someone who is so obviously a Dreg manages to wield so much power. The usual rules of society don't seem to apply here, under the colourful roofs and the sparkling lights. Here, he seems to reign supreme. How does he do it?

The syrupy smile of last night has gone. He's rude and abrupt with the man in charge of the cannon.

"I want this ready by Saturday!" he shouts out to everyone in the room.

A Dreg in overalls steps forward. "But, Mr Sabatini, that's impossible. We haven't even started rehearsing."

"Rehearsing? How hard can it be to blast a few kids out of a cannon?"

"Well," the man answers nervously. "It's more complicated than you might think. We have to make sure we allocate exactly the right amount of ammunition each time, adjusting it accordingly depending on the weight of each person. And then we have to instruct the men on how to position themselves, and—"

"Oh, for goodness' sake!" Sabatini interrupts him. "This is not up for discussion. Show time is tomorrow night, do you hear? If this act fails, I fail. And I do not like to fail." He dashes up the stairs on to the stage and looks down at the group of Dregs below him.

"If it fails, we will have no use for any of you. You do not have skills, you have not been selected because you show any talent." He laughs. "Oh no! You are the lowest of the low. You have been picked because you are, how can I put this? Disposable." He says the word slowly, enunciating every syllable. "Yes, that's it. Disposable. To put it quite simply, you are irrelevant. It matters not to me, or anyone else here, if one, or two, or all of you die. However, the Pures will want to see at least some of you emerge intact once you've been fired out. There's not much point to the act otherwise. And this, people, may be enough to save your life. We don't really want you to die yet. We'd rather you were catapulted across the room a few times before that, so we can really recuperate the time and effort we've spent on you. Well, I can see you're all *dying* to begin!" He laughs and claps his hands together, "Let's go: Load. Aim. Fire!"

Selection is as horrific as I thought it would be, even after Silvio has left, and most of the children are sobbing as I ask them to complete the activities. Each child has a number pinned to them and I am given a clipboard and a red pen. Beside the corresponding number on the paper, I have to pass or fail them, a tick or a cross for each section. Next to each number, I put a large red cross. I don't even have to lie about it; Silvio has caused such terror amongst them that none of them manage to do anything even half successfully. They try their best, but they're trembling and weeping so much that it's impossible.

The boy who stood out in the line is last, and he's the only one who doesn't seem petrified.

"What's your name?" I ask him.

"Ezekiel." He grins, his teeth still white and shining.

I put him through the motions, like the other kids. He's miles better than they were, much more flexible, with an easy grace to each fluid movement.

It's the same with every section. He's stronger, quicker, more supple than the others. When they walk along the beam a couple of them totter right off and even those who manage to stay on waver and sway as they shuffle from end to end. Not Ezekiel; he dances across, eyes fixed in front, not at the floor like all the others. There's something poetic about his movements and I can't help picturing him on the tightrope. He'd be a natural, I know it.

I look across the hall at the directors. All three of them are paying attention now, watching the boy too, eyeing him up like a tasty dish they're about to devour. You can almost see the pound signs gleaming in their eyes.

He's too good.

I lean into the beam, shift it with my shoulders so that it jolts. His eyes widen and he wobbles slightly, but he still doesn't fall. At the end, he springs up into the air, landing perfectly, hands raised.

I pick up the clipboard. There are red crosses in every box for every child. This is the last one.

I think about it for a moment or two, weighing up the possibilities. The truth is, he's had it either way – they all have. If he goes back to the slums, he'll grow up in some squalid pit, sharing a bed with the rats and the lice. If he's lucky enough to make it through his childhood at all, he'll have to do some menial, soul-destroying job in order to earn a few measly tokens for food and clothes. He'll spend the rest of his life feeling hungry and cold and dirty.

Maybe he'd be better off here? At least he wouldn't starve. He'd have clean clothes, get a wash every night. And we'd try to look after him; we'd do our best for him.

I see it suddenly, clear in my mind, my own little hut, the one I struggle to picture at all sometimes.

It was cold, always cold, or that's how I remember it anyway: so cold that your fingers and toes always felt numb and your breath came out in cold little puffs, so cold that your bones ached with it and there were never enough blankets to go around. We'd all huddle together on the tiny bed, seeking warmth and comfort.

As well as the bed, we had a little table, made out of an upturned wooden crate, but there were no stools or chairs; we just sat or crouched on the floor. There was a bucket in the corner, for going to the toilet, or you could walk across the slum to the communal ones: stinky, muddy little sheds they were, with big cavernous holes in the ground for us to use. I was scared of the thick cloying cobwebs in them and the smell always made me feel nauseous. My mum said the communal ones bred germs and disease anyway, so she always let me use the bucket.

I remember her telling me stories, while I sat there, dress hitched up, perched on it. She used to sing me songs sometimes too. I used to love hearing her sing, she had a beautiful voice.

I'm filled up, suddenly, with a wave of longing for her. I'd take the cold, I'd take the bucket, I'd take all of it just to hear her sing again; just to snuggle up with her in the cold.

I can't do it. I can't be the one responsible for taking Ezekiel away from his family. I can't condemn him to a life here, no matter how good he is; can't train him up and then see him perform up there on the wire, risking his life every single night; can't watch as he turns into someone broken and bitter.

Someone like me.

I look back over the directors; they're all still watching him. I take the pen, mark a large red cross next to the number twelve and march over to them, waving the list in the air.

They peer over the large desk at me as if I'm a cockroach, scuttling towards them.

"They've all failed," I announce. "None of them are good

enough." I slam the paper down on the desk and turn away.

"Stop," Baines commands. "Come back here. Right now."

I spin around, my eyes meeting hers again. We glare at each other.

"That last boy. Don't try telling me he was inadequate; we all saw him cross the beam."

"He was too wobbly, he's not flexible enough. He's untrainable," I tell her.

Tweedledumb finally speaks. "That's not right. He definitely had potential."

"Yes, we all remarked on it," agrees Tweedledumber.

"Well, I'm telling you. He's not good enough."

They all stare down at me. Vivian Baines leans forward.

"How many selection processes have you assessed at?"

"Loads," I tell her, confidently. "And he's no good."

"Come here." Her curved red fingernail is a claw, beckoning me closer to the table. "Closer than that."

I'm right up next to the desk now. I'm barely tall enough to see over the edge of it and I have to tilt my head back to peer up at her on her big chair. She's done it on purpose, to make me feel as small as she possibly can.

She rises up from her chair. Her eyes burn; hatred seems to seep out of her every pore.

"I've got your number," she hisses. "You're an insolent little madam, too big for your boots by far." She turns to the others. "The boy passes. Agreed?" They both nod their assent, smirking at me. She leans towards me again, so close I can feel her breath on my face. "I don't like your attitude, Dreg girl. I don't like it all. You'll be hearing from me."

She turns back to the two men. "All of this fuss over a bunch of bloody Dregs. I don't know why we don't just terminate the lot of them; save everyone a great deal of time and expense."

They laugh, nervously; I think even they are afraid of her. She waves her hand towards me, dismissively. "Well, go on, get out of here."

All the children are watching in wide-eyed wonder. It takes all my nerves, but I walk steadily, slowly. When I reach the exit, I turn around and face her again. She's still looking at me. I smile as sweetly as I can at her and leave, slamming the door behind me so hard that the sound resounds across the empty courtyard.

BEN

I can't watch this. I glance over at the doors I came through; they're still open. Maybe I can get out of here before it's too late.

Suddenly, the arena is flooded with light. I'll never make it now, not without all of them seeing me.

I don't want to watch, but I can't help it. My eyes are drawn to the front and I stare in fascinated horror as the first boy slowly ascends the steps. Years ago, in the wars of the olden days, they'd have stuffed great round balls of metal in here, wedging them in and blasting the enemy to smithereens. Now, a boy of about my age is taking the place of a solid sphere of iron.

He hasn't got a costume on, just the thin rags all the performers seem to wear if they aren't on stage, and his feet are bare. It's so quiet that you can still hear his steps as he mounts the ladder.

The atmosphere is so different to during the performance. There's no glitzy costumes, no pounding drum beat, no vigorous crescendos. This is the Cirque, stripped to its bare bones, like the poor boys on the stage.

I put my hands up to my face, watching through the cracks in my fingers.

Once he reaches the top of the steps, he bends down, taking something out of a large sack on the platform. He clips a belt into place. There's a bag bulging on the back of it. He looks down at the boys below him, an expression of terror on his face. I feel sick.

He crawls into the gaping muzzle, curling into a ball, so all you can see is the bag, poking out of the rim. It's a tight squeeze, even for someone as skinny as he is. That's why all the boys are in such a state – the Pures must have seized the scrawniest ones they could find.

Another boy steps forward. I see him look upward and mutter a prayer, before he pulls swiftly on a black lever at the bottom of the cannon.

Sparks fly and there's a sizzling noise before it explodes with a loud boom. The boy shoots out of the other end, still curled up tightly like a ball. He tumbles in the air above, round and round before landing, perfectly, on the thin mats opposite. He quickly throws off the belt, plunging the smoking bag into a huge water vat at the side of the arena. Then he gets up and scurries away, seemingly completely unharmed, as Silvio claps slowly. I feel pure, sweet relief that he's still standing: maybe this won't be so bad, after all.

The next four go in exactly the same way, a different boy catapulted across the arena each time. It's only on the sixth that things stop running so smoothly.

He looks even more nervous than the others did, and it's harder for him to manoeuvre himself into the dark mouth of the cannon because his left arm is already bound in a sling.

"Get on with it, boy!" Silvio barks impatiently at him. "If you can't get your arm in, we can always hack it off!"

The boy pulls himself in then, concertinaing himself inside, the pain visible on his face.

For the first time though, the cannon doesn't fire when the lever is pushed down. There's no spark, no boom, no flinging human ball across the arena.

The technician comes forward, frowning. He mounts the ladder, peering in at the petrified boy still nestled in the gaping O of the cannon. He says something to him and the boy scrambles out, standing nervously on the platform. He turns, suddenly, to the part of the arena where I'm hiding, staring with his big, hollow eyes. Can he see me? It feels like he can.

"What's going on?" Sabatini demands.

"I'm not sure," the technician answers. "Maybe there's not enough powder."

"Well, what are you waiting for? Pour some more in, man."

The technician starts to slowly spoon more powder from the keg.

"Come on," snarls the ringmaster. "Get on with it."

The technician is hesitant. "We aren't really supposed to mess around with the quantity," he says. "Fire safety and all that."

"Oh for goodness' sake!"

Silvio lifts the large keg up off the floor, heaving it up on to his shoulder and tipping it into the bag on the boy's back, pouring until it cascades out of the sides.

Slowly, the boy climbs back into the cannon and the other boy pulls the lever again. Still nothing.

Silvio Sabatini steps forward once more. He looks carefully at everything and then picks up a bottle. "What's this?" he asks.

"Lighter fluid," the technician answers, nervously. "You don't need it. It would be very dangerous with all that gunpowder; these wall coverings are flammable."

Ignoring him, Sabatini unscrews the bottle and pours it over the bag strapped to the boy's back. Everyone's so quiet that you can hear the glugging liquid as it drenches the bag.

The boy doesn't say a word, but I can see him trembling as he climbs back in for the third time.

This time, the spark ignites straight away, flaring up dramatically. The boy is flung out of the cannon, a roaring ball of fire. The force is much harder now and he blasts over the mats, crashing with a thump into the wall opposite and landing in a crumpled heap on the floor.

The orange drapes catch alight, the flames quickly licking their way higher, before the Pure blasts at them with the white foam of a fire extinguisher.

He doesn't spray it on the boy though. He's still on fire. He rises up and runs around the arena, manically. He must finally see the vat of water because he heads for it and plunges into it, headfirst. There's a hissing sound and clouds of smoke buffet out, and then the other boys all surge forward to help him.

"Stop!" the ringmaster commands from the stage. "Stop where you are, all of you!"

They look up at him and then towards the boy, torn.

"If any of you so much as move forward one further inch, you will all lose your lives!" he cries. "Rehearsal is over. Leave this arena immediately." They still remain, looking at him, looking at the boy who is screaming helplessly from the tank.

"Get out!" Silvio Sabatini bellows. "Get out of my arena!"

They turn and head away.

He blows his whistle and two security guards appear. He gestures towards the screaming boy. "Take him away."

"To where, sir?"

"To where? I don't bloody care. Do what you like with him, just get rid of him!"

The poor Dreg is dragged out and now there's no one left in the arena, apart from the ringmaster. Him, and me, hidden away, silently watching.

Sabatini stands up on the stage, bowing and blowing kisses dramatically to an imaginary crowd before turning and leaving too.

I let out a long breath I wasn't aware I'd been holding. I'm horrified: I just crouched down over here, watching, doing nothing. Maybe I could have stopped it, if I'd stood up, told them not to do it. They'd have to have listened to me – I mean, look at who my mother is.

But I didn't even try. Even when that boy was running around on fire, I just watched him burning.

HOSHIKO

Once I'm outside, my bravado quickly subsides. I keep looking behind me, expecting the doors to open and the security guards to rush out after me. I run across the courtyard, ducking quickly down one of the little pathways before sinking to my knees behind one of the hot-dog stands.

What was I thinking of, behaving like that? Showing disrespect towards any Pure would be asking for trouble, but I've just gone and offended Vivian Baines, of all people.

I was deliberately rude to her. I answered her back. I slammed the door on her.

She's never going to let that go.

I've just signed my own death warrant.

BEN

Outside, the courtyard's deserted.

I can't leave yet, not without seeing Hoshiko again, one more time. She doesn't want me here, she made that perfectly clear yesterday, but I have to try and explain that I'm not like all the other Pures. Not any more.

It's when I'm looking around that I see him lying there, down one of the narrow walkways which lead into the main courtyard. The boy – the one from the cannonball. I can't just leave him there. I walk quickly down the path.

He looks dead.

I touch him, tentatively. His eyes flicker open. When I take my hand away, there's something stuck to it. Something flaky: it's his skin. One leg and both arms are red and raw. He's lost his shirt and his charred chest is shiny. His face is bruised, one eye swollen shut. The arm in the sling is twisted away from his body, jutting out at a peculiar angle.

"Let me help you," I tell him. Trying to put as little pressure on him as possible, I gently ease him up, so he's leaning against the tree trunk behind him. He looks dazed; I think he's about to pass out. Or worse.

I take my water bottle from my bag and kneel down, letting a few drops trickle between his cracked, dry lips. He reaches up his hand and seizes the bottle from me, draining it in long, desperate gulps.

It's only when the whole bottle's gone, that he opens his one undamaged eye. It widens in fear when he sees I'm a Pure.

"Sorry," he wheezes. "Sorry."

"It's OK. I don't mind," I tell him. "I promise I won't hurt you."

There's blood trickling down from a cut on his head. I dab at it gently with my shirt sleeve, wiping it away so it doesn't trickle into his eyes.

He glances around weakly. "I need to get inside," he whispers.

"Let me help you up."

"No!" He looks so panicked. "If they see..."

"It's OK. There's no one else here. Let me help you up and I'll leave." He looks helplessly at his legs, and then back at me, warily. Our eyes meet. "You can trust me."

"Fine," he agrees. "Thank you. But quickly."

"I'm Ben," I tell him, ridiculously, as if he cares about that. "What's your name?"

"Anatol," he breathes, so faintly that I have to lean my head right down to his mouth to hear what he's saying.

"OK, Anatol. Let's get you up. Lean on me; I'll help you stand."

I put my hands around his waist and slowly ease him on to his feet. As soon as I let go, he collapses to the ground again.

He looks at me for a second, his eyelids flickering and then he slumps forward. He's lost consciousness.

If he doesn't get some help quickly, he's going to die. What can I do though? If anyone sees me with him, they'll go straight to Mother. And that doesn't bear thinking about. I'll have to leave him and hope someone else finds him in time.

HOSHIKO

After a while, I stop shaking. I rise up from my knees and turn to walk back to the living quarters, trying to work out how I'm going to prepare Greta.

The courtyard's deserted as I approach it but then, out of nowhere, he appears.

The boy, again, running away from me, down one of the pathways.

I look about. Nobody else is around and I move quietly after him; I stand behind one of little merchandise kiosks and peep out.

He's crouched down on the floor, helping someone by the looks of it. It's Anatol, the boy with the sling.

The Pure boy is talking to him, but he's too far away for me to hear what he's saying. Anatol looks up at him, and says something back, then the boy helps him to his feet. As soon as he lets go, Anatol falls back down to the ground.

My heart sinks; not another death.

The boy stares down at him and then turns away.

He's going to leave him there to die. I should have known all along: he's not different at all. He's just like all the rest.

BEN

I turn to go. There's nothing I can do for this Dreg, I need to get back to school, this was all a stupid mistake…

Priya's words, *Head and heart, Ben, head and heart,* crowd my thoughts suddenly. Then Hoshiko's accusing, angry *You Pures are all the same.*

Was she right? Am I just the ignorant, over-indulged Pure boy she thinks I am? Am I just like all those people, paying their money night after night, to come and watch the destruction of the Dregs? Am I even worse than that, a cruel coward? Am I like Francis? Am I like *Mother*?

It's time to decide who I want to be.

I take a deep breath and turn back to Anatol.

HOSHIKO

I watch as he begins to walk away, then stops. He looks behind him at Anatol, lying horribly still on the ground. The Pure boy glances at the gates, then he bends down and lifts Anatol gently, carrying him, like a baby, back towards the courtyard.

I duck out of sight behind the kiosk.

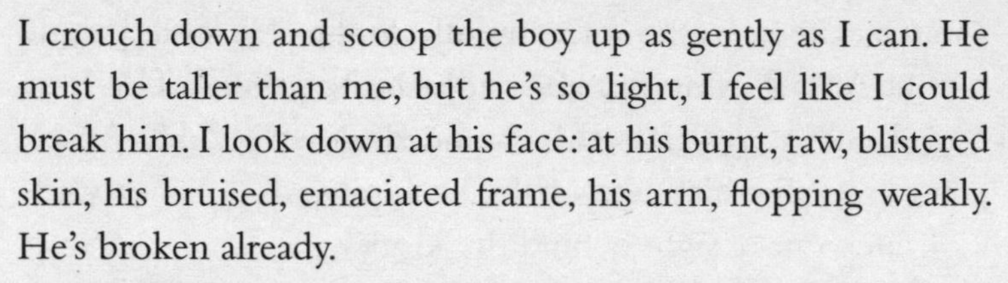

BEN

I crouch down and scoop the boy up as gently as I can. He must be taller than me, but he's so light, I feel like I could break him. I look down at his face: at his burnt, raw, blistered skin, his bruised, emaciated frame, his arm, flopping weakly. He's broken already.

I carry him into the main courtyard and look about, desperately.

How can I help him?

HOSHIKO

He stands there, right in the middle, looking around.

"Help!" he calls out. "Help, somebody. Please!"

I step out from the shadows and run towards him.

BEN

It's a waste of time; there's no one there.

Then, suddenly, she is. Out of nowhere Hoshiko appears, running towards me. She looks down at the unconscious figure in my arms, her face etched with concern.

"We need to get him to Amina," she says. "This way."

She turns and starts hurrying down another one of the pathways. I follow her, though I have no idea what, or who, Amina is. She turns back towards me as she runs and our eyes meet for an instant.

Suddenly, there's a whistle. From behind us come the sounds of guards in pursuit.

"Quickly," she says. "If we don't get him to Amina, he'll die."

I speed up.

There's another whistle – a louder, shriller one – and an authoritative, commanding voice: a voice I'm more than familiar with.

"Benedict Baines. What on earth do you think you're doing?"

Mother.

HOSHIKO

I lead him down the pathway so we can cut across the fields, but as soon as the whistles start blowing I know we're not going to makc it. We keep running anyway and that's when another whistle blows and I hear her voice, hard and clear, calling down the path.

"Benedict Baines, what on earth are you doing?"

I stop in my tracks.

I look at him, his mouth open in a little round O, his eyes wide and shocked; I look back up the path towards her.

Vivian Baines.

It's not a sudden realization; it dawns on me slowly.

She called him Benedict Baines: same surname. No, surely not.

I look at him. There's no family resemblance, even now, when I'm searching for it. Vivian Baines has red hair and those icy cold eyes. He looks so different. But looks can be deceiving.

He was in the VIP box, the other night.

Why didn't I realize before?

He can't be; it's not possible. Vivian Baines is evil – really, really evil. He seems so different. He helped me in the arena, and now he's trying to save Anatol's life.

His eyes meet mine again. His face isn't pale any more; his cheeks are flushed, like he's embarrassed.

"Keep going," he says. "You said it yourself, there's no time to spare."

We both glance back up the path. At the woman standing

there in the centre, at the guards, running towards us, and we flee.

"Quick!" I tell him. "This way!"

We sprint down the path, but it's no good; they're gaining on us.

Just when it seems things can't get any worse, *He* appears; running towards us from the other path in front of us, flanked by guards.

Silvio.

BEN

I look at her, helplessly, as they advance on us from two sides. We're totally surrounded.

Mother doesn't run, of course; she strides calmly towards us while Sabatini dashes up, arms flailing dramatically.

He doesn't know what to do, what to say. He looks at me in confusion, an uncertain smile on his face, and then turns to Hoshiko, fury burning in his eyes.

Mother reaches us and I see the same fierce anger in her eyes as she stares at me, stares at who I'm with, stares at who I'm holding.

"What are you doing?" she barks, again. "Why are you carrying that filth-ridden creature? Benedict? Don't look at the ground, look at me."

My eyes meet hers. It's hard, but I hold her stare.

"Drop him," she says. "Drop him immediately and come with me. You are in a lot of trouble, my boy."

I look at Hoshiko. Then I look down at the boy, slumped in my arms. I don't even know if he's still alive.

"No," I say. I turn back towards Mother. "He's hurt, Mother, really badly. He'll die if we don't get him help; he might already be dead. Please," I'm begging her. "Please. Let me get him some help. I'll come with you straight away after that, I promise."

"And why is it a concern of yours whether he lives or dies?"

We don't have time for this.

"Excuse me," I say to the ringmaster. "I need to get past."

He looks at my mother.

"I don't think so," he says. He's still not sure how to treat me. I think that's why he turns on Hoshiko. "What on earth is going on here?"

She looks straight back at him, her eyes fiery and unflinching, a scowl on her face. She's not even afraid of him. She's so brave; I want to be brave too.

"We're taking him to Amina," she says.

He laughs. "I'd really like to see you try." He turns to Mother. "Madam." He bows his head. "I can only apologize. If you would like to take your son home, I'll deal with everything from here."

Mother looks at him in that same repulsed way she always does.

"This Dreg girl has been openly rude. To *me*." She laughs, incredulously. "It beggars belief. And now, here she is, with my son. *How*, exactly, will you deal with her?"

"Oh, I'll teach her a lesson she'll never forget," he answers. "Don't you worry about that; I'll make her pay."

"That's all very well, Ringmaster, but I would rather see her … obliterated. No time like the present?" She turns towards the guards.

"No!" I cry out. "No! Please!"

Sabatini steps forward again.

"Madam, if I might be so bold? She has a leading role in tomorrow night's Spooktacular. Perhaps you would permit me to keep her alive until then?" He grins. "The performance should be more than enough punishment."

Mother nods. "Very well. You have twenty-four hours. If

she's not dead by then, I'll shoot her myself. Guards, escort my son to our car." She turns on her heel and walks back up the path.

The guards immediately close in. They take Anatol from Benedict Baines and then begin dragging the Pure boy away. He's struggling with them, but it's no good; there are five of them and one of him.

"No!" he shouts out. "No! Leave her alone! It's not her fault; it's my fault!"

I look into his eyes as they take him. Ever since I saw him, I've tried so hard to hate him, but I can't do it, not even now I know who he is.

I hate his mother but I don't hate him.

He stood up to her; that must have taken some guts.

It's then that I notice the stillness that has fallen over Anatol. His eyes are open, staring sightlessly. He isn't making any sound at all. Horror floods through me and I lift my head to see Silvio standing there, smirking.

"Oh, how sad," he croons at me, making my skin crawl. "It's too late. No point taking him to the san now! What a tragedy."

My tears – of sadness, of anger, of loathing – begin as I'm hauled away from Anatol's dead body.

BEN

I wrench away from the guards, shake their arms off and run back down the path. They chase after me but not before I see her being dragged away. Then I see the boy lying there dead on the pathway.

The guards quickly catch up with me and drag me away, back up the path.

"I'll save you!" I call to her. "I won't let them hurt you!"

I'm pushed into the back seat of the car, where my mother is already sitting, staring straight ahead.

"I hate you," I tell her. "I *hate you*."

She laughs. "Benedict, you think you hate me now but you'll realize, one day, when you've grown up a bit, that all I've ever done has been for you. You're a teenage boy; I suppose it's natural that you should want to rebel. But you've had your little piece of action, your little piece of fun. You must have known what a futile activity your attempt at running away was. Stanley works for me, Benedict, not you. He called me the moment he found your note. He'll escape punishment on this occasion. We need to go home, forget this ever happened and get on with things in the real world."

I turn away. What's the point in responding? She'll never listen. She'll never allow herself to let compassion back in; it would mean becoming human again, and she's done with all that. She's turned to stone now, that's all she is; stone and ice and steel.

I've changed though.

I close my eyes and I talk to Hoshiko instead, inside my head, as if I'm praying to her.

"*I meant it,*" I tell her. "*I'll save you. I don't know how yet, but I will.*"

HOSHIKO

The guards drag me back to the dorms, tossing me in like a bag of rubbish. Next to me, they hurl Anatol's body; I have to scoot to one side to stop him landing on me.

Emmanuel comes forward, picking Anatol up effortlessly and carrying him into the san, placing him gently on the bed. Amina rushes in after him, gasps when she sees that he's dead.

We'd all been looking forward to tonight; it's so rare to get a night off together. It's quiet now though; the atmosphere in the dorms is strained as everyone realizes what has happened.

Anatol is brand-new, he hasn't even been with us a week. I feel responsible for him, somehow.

The boys who were in the arena with him describe what happened and the story spreads around the dorms in whispers.

Things have always been horrific in this place – it's always been a dance with death for everyone but, lately, it feels like Silvio's lost the plot altogether. At least he used to try and preserve our lives for as long as he could. Before, when the Dregs met their deaths, he wanted it to be on stage, in front of a packed house of Pures. He's reckless now, in a way he's never been before. It's like he doesn't care how or when we die, as long as we do die, like every death is a notch in his belt that will somehow elevate him up the slippery ladder to Puredom.

My own death has always been inevitable, I know, but it's different now: it's imminent. He promised her he'd have me killed tomorrow. This is my last night on earth.

I should want to be with Greta and Amina, or my family.

That's what you're supposed to want in the last few hours of your life, isn't it? Your family, friends, your loved ones, the people who mean the most to you.

I don't though. I find myself avoiding conversation with Greta when she comes over and sits beside me, turning away from her coldly. I see the hurt in her eyes, but I can't seem to stop myself. I mustn't let myself feel too much, that's why. I mustn't let the emotions out.

I keep seeing him as they dragged him away, Benedict Baines.

Benedict bloody *Baines*.

It's like someone's playing some kind of sick joke on me. The only Pure I've ever felt anything but hatred for and he turns out to be the son of the most evil woman on the planet. What on earth was he doing wandering around the Cirque on his own? And why did he help Anatol like that? Why didn't he just turn away and run?

I think again of when he asked that question during the Press call and then, after, when he apologized. How can someone like him have anything but evil inside him? Still, there's something in his eyes I've never seen in any Pure's before. Something soft, something deep, something good. He stood there just now, side by side with me, a Dreg girl, and refused to obey his mother's command. Why?

Stop being soft, I tell myself: he's back home now, probably sitting around the dinner table and discussing his eventful day with Mummy.

But even as I think this, I know it isn't true, that it's my grief and anger twisting things. I'm drawn to this Pure boy – his story is starting to become mine.

BEN

When I get home I run upstairs. The pictures play round and round in my head, as if I'm watching a slow-motion film on repeat. I see the boy, Anatol, being catapulted across the arena. And then, later, dead on the path.

And I see her. Again and again I see her. Looking up at me, looking into me, whispering: "*Yes. I do wish things could be different.*"

I hear my mother, coolly ordering her death, arranging it with Silvio Sabatini.

I can't let them kill her.

I take out my tablet and get on the PureWeb again. The home screen of the Cirque has changed and the whole site has been revamped to promote the Halloween/Firework Spooktacular.

The screen swirls hypnotically in an orange-and-black kaleidoscope and then Hoshiko's face appears. I touch the cold screen with my fingers and the camera zooms in on her eyes. I stare into them. They're like the eyes of an animal: untamed, somehow, savage but beautiful. The screen freezes like that and then the picture colour slowly changes, turning redder and redder, until her eyes fade away completely. It's just red. Blood red.

It stays like that for a few moments and then Silvio Sabatini appears on the screen, flicking his whip and grinning at the viewers. He winks and then whispers something: it's so quiet that I can't make out what it is. He says it again though, louder, and then again, faster and louder. In the end, he's shouting it, frantically, joined by hundreds of other voices, faster and faster, louder and louder. The same chant, again and again:

See the flames go higher, higher.
Who will survive the funeral pyre?
See the flames go higher, higher.
Who will survive the funeral pyre?

There's a tap at my door: I slam the tablet shut.

"Come in."

My father pokes his head tentatively into the room.

"I'm not angry, Benedict," he says. "I heard it's been an eventful day; just wanted to check you're OK."

"Do you know what she did?" I blurt out. "Do you know what she is? She has people killed! She doesn't even care!"

I search his face. I need so desperately for him to be different, for him to be shocked. For him to feel the same pain I do, clawing at me inside.

His eyes meet mine and he smiles, softly. "I know it's hard to understand, but it's her job, Ben. It's important."

"Important! How can having people killed be important?"

He comes into the room and closes the door, sitting down on the edge of my bed.

"We've all felt like you do at one time or other, but it's not people she has killed, Ben – it's Dregs. She does a good thing, an important thing. What would the world be like if we let them run free? They'd breed and spread and before you know it, they'd have taken over."

"They aren't rats!"

"No. They're much more dangerous than rats. Rats would

be easier to control. You should know better than anyone what Dregs are like."

He's talking about the kidnapping attempt.

"Why do you think they tried to take you?" he says. "What do you think they wanted?"

"Maybe they wanted to be heard," I say. "Maybe they wanted someone to pay attention."

He laughs, patronizingly. "It's time you stopped being so naïve." For the first time the gentle edge is gone from his voice. "They wanted to kill you, make no mistake about that. They wanted to punish you for being Pure, for being superior to them. They're all the same, Ben. They're angry and dangerous and evil. Do you hear me?" He raises his voice a notch further. "One day, you'll understand what your mother is doing. She's making the world a better place. She's not a bad person, Ben, none of us are. If she gets into power, she'll stop places like that circus. She doesn't want Dregs paraded in people's faces any more than you do. That's what she's campaigning for – to get things done in a more professional way. She'd do it all much more quietly, make much less song and dance about it."

I stare at him. "Where's Priya?" I ask.

His face clouds over. "She's the reason your head's been turned. We should have regulated things with her far more closely from the start. Your brother did the right thing, reporting her."

"Where is she?" I repeat again.

"Ben, she's gone – that's all you need to know. Look, the sooner you stop romanticizing and start accepting the world for what it is, the better it'll be for all of us. You mother can't afford any more scenes like the one today. She needs to avoid any scandal if she's ever going to stand a chance of becoming leader."

"Please." I'm begging him now, pleading with him to understand. "Please, speak to her for me. Please tell her to speak to the Cirque, tell them not to hurt anyone."

He sighs and shakes his head, then he stands up; he's not pretending to listen any more.

"Stop being so melodramatic. Your mother doesn't have the time to deal with this now."

I stare at him.

Why am I wasting my breath? This is another one of those pointless conversations. I don't have time for it, either. I need to get Hoshiko out of there.

I look back at him; force myself to nod meekly.

"Sorry, Father," I say. "I understand how it is now. Sorry I've let you both down. I won't behave like that again."

He stands up, leans forward and ruffles my hair awkwardly. "That's a good lad. I knew you'd see reason."

He leaves the room.

There's no way I'm going to let her die. Accept the world for what it is? No, never again.

HOSHIKO

After they come and take his body away, everyone congregates together, sitting mutely.

The silence is broken by the door crashing open and a security guard enters, ushering in a child. It's Ezekiel, the boy from selection.

The guard shoves him in and leaves without a word, slamming and bolting the door behind him.

He looks so tiny, standing there. The bravado of earlier has gone and his lips are trembling as he looks around, wide-eyed. He sees me, and rushes over, throwing his arms around me as if I'm a long-lost relative. He clings to me, sobbing.

What can I do? I crouch down on the floor, and return his desperate hug, holding him as tightly as I can.

"It's OK," I whisper to him. "It'll be OK."

Over his shoulder, I see Greta looking at us, her eyes narrowed. I hold my left arm out and gesture her over. She runs into the hug and I hold her tightly too, so the two of them are enveloped in my arms.

"Greta and I will look after you. Don't worry. Everything will be fine," I lie.

Amina catches my eye and winks at me. I wonder if she's remembering my first day and how she took me under her wing, right from the start.

Around us, the preparations for another memorial service begin. This can't be the first thing Ezekiel experiences in here, surely. I take him into the women's dorms and sit down on one of the bunks with him. Greta doesn't leave us for a second, so I'm sandwiched in between them the whole time.

His confidence increases quite quickly and he asks us hundreds of questions about the Cirque. I don't lie, but I don't exactly tell the truth either. I try to leave out all the really nasty bits, which is pretty much everything, so there's not much to say; I just go on about the lights and the music and costumes, the buzz of performing, and how he'll be a natural.

Amina comes in. She smiles at Ezekiel.

"It's about to start," she says gently to me.

What do I say to this little boy? How the hell do I explain to him what's going on?

I can't.

The two children either side of me need me to be strong, but I don't think I can be. I can't go and sit out there, between him and Greta. I can't. I can't be strong any more.

Suddenly, I can't breathe. My chest rises up and down rapidly and I'm gasping for air, choking, rasping for breath.

I look up, panicked, and see Amina, gazing at me, her brow furrowed with concern.

"Greta," she says, "I'm going to check on Hoshi's bruises. You two stay here, I'll be back in a minute."

"But I can come too."

"We won't be long, I promise," she tells her.

Amina puts her arm around me and manoeuvres me out of the door and into the san.

"Take deep breaths," she keeps saying. "That's it. In. Out. In out. Concentrate on your breathing. Be calm. Nice and calm, nice and deep."

Gradually, I feel my breath slowing.

"I don't know what happened," I pant. "I couldn't get any air."

"It was a panic attack," she says. "This day has been too tough on you. Sit quietly now, you'll feel better soon."

I can't tell her what's happened with Vivian Baines, not after what she's been through tonight.

"It's fine. I'll be OK. I'm sorry," I say. "This is the last thing you need."

"It's not your fault, Hoshi."

Behind the door, the melancholy song of grief begins. The mourning ceremony has started.

"It's time," she says.

Suddenly, I can't stand the thought of it. I can't do it – can't sit out there with everyone else; can't sit amongst them, knowing that this time tomorrow they'll be singing for me.

My breath starts getting faster again. I clutch at my throat, sucking desperately for air.

"Shh, shh." Amina is rubbing my back. "It's OK, Hoshi," she says. "You don't have to go out there; you can stay in here." As soon as her words sink in, I begin to breathe more slowly. Eventually I can speak.

"What about the service?"

"You aren't well."

"What about Greta? What about Ezekiel? They need me out there."

"I'll tell them you're sick. You can stay in here. I'll look after them; they'll be fine. Greta can sleep next to me and Emmanuel will look after Ezekiel."

"Anatol is dead," I say. "It's disrespectful to miss his memorial."

"It's not. He'd understand. You did your best. You need to rest. Look," she points down at the bed. "I even managed to find some clean sheets."

"I can't," I say. "It's selfish. There's nothing wrong with me."

She takes me firmly by the shoulders.

"Nurse's orders," she says. "Stay in here tonight. Rest. I won't take no for an answer."

She pushes me down gently but firmly on to the bed, stretches my legs out and puts a pillow behind my head.

It's nice, letting her take control. I nod, obediently. "OK," I say. "OK."

The song of grief outside the room is getting louder now. She stands up. "Try and get some sleep," she says and tucks a sheet snugly around me before leaving the room, shutting the door softly behind her.

I look at her face again, on the screen.

I made a promise to her. I said I'd save her and I will. I've got to get her out of there. How, I have no idea, but I push that inconvenient reality to the back of my mind and concentrate on the first necessity: escaping from this house.

No time like the present, I suppose. It's nearly midnight, pretty much everyone except the guards will be asleep. I slip into dark clothes – black jeans and T-shirt – and grab what little cash I have lying around.

Our security system was only installed a couple of years ago – after the kidnappings – and it's pretty much invincible: iris recognition, fingerprint recognition, voice recognition.

The latter part is the smartest because it means that, whatever the circumstances, no one can force us out under duress. The code words change every week and there's a standard word and a panic word. If anything happens to us – if anyone tries to hurt us or take us – we just have to say the panic word and the whole place will be flooded with police in seconds.

All that technology, all that brain work, put into making the place impenetrable. There's one flaw though, one thing they never even considered: the system is designed to stop Dregs from getting in, not one of us from getting out.

I'm completely trusted not to ever try anything like this, even now. Partly because I've always been pretty well behaved until the circus came to town, and partly because it's complete madness. A death wish. Why would anyone want to leave the safety of this fortress at night, venture out into the unknown where, we're frequently warned, lawless Dregs lurk on every corner, waiting for a chance to kill? No one. No one sane anyway, especially if they happened to be the son of one of the most important people in the country.

I head downstairs and look into the facial recognition screen, touch the fingerprint monitor and utter the safe word. This week, it's *challenge*.

Everything's silent. So far, so good. The cameras on every wall flash intermittently. Any second now, someone in security is going to see me, if they haven't already. I've got to move quickly.

As well as all the monitors, there are five guards on duty here at night: one on each exterior exit. The only way they'd ever abandon their posts is if they thought they were needed elsewhere. I'm going to have to create a diversion by deliberately triggering the alarm.

It should be easy: all I have to do is say the panic word, that's all. One little word, two tiny syllables. If I do this, there's no going back. Pandemonium will break out. No one's ever said the panic word before; no one's ever needed to. A shiver of excitement runs down my spine.

They'll check the video footage. They'll know I've done this on purpose. Mother will be livid, both my parents will be. What am I thinking?

I take another breath. I think of Priya. Is she still alive? One day I'll find out where she is. I think of Hoshiko. I think of her eyes, of her hair, alive with light. Suddenly, it's easy. I look at the camera above my head. Stare into the screen, say the word loudly, clearly. It resonates in the silence: "*Shatter*."

Instantly, the house is flooded with light and a high droning noise fills the air, more than enough to wake up the whole neighbourhood.

As quickly as I can I run into the hallway, hiding myself in the big cupboard under the stairwell. I hear fast footsteps straight away. Peering through the crack in the door I see Stanley rushing past me into the kitchen. Before he turns around, before anyone else appears, I slip out of my hiding place and head over to the door.

The iron shutters are already descending. There's about a foot left before they reach the floor. The lasers are darting hungrily across the room, frantically criss-crossing, waiting to take down anyone who ventures into their path. I take a deep breath and run straight through them, praying that the body recognition system kicks in.

It must do: I make it through unscathed, reach the shutters, inches from the floor. Pull myself under, just in time. I'm out.

I hear sirens straight away: hundreds of them, it sounds like, competing with the wailing alarm.

I dart sideways as quickly as I can, slipping through the trees in the garden. I stick to the shadows and run to the left. There's a back access gate down here, hardly used except by the gardeners. It's alarmed, but the face and fingerprint recognition works again. I just have to utter the password and I'm out on to the city streets.

I keep running for at least ten minutes before I even allow myself to stop and breathe.

I can't believe I'm acting like this. If I'm caught, Mother might actually have me killed too. Imagine how embarrassing it would be: her own son, breaking curfew to run off and see a Dreg girl, of all things. They'd keep it out of the press, of course, and she might get me let off a formal punishment. Anyone who breaks the rules is automatically thrown into the slums, but somehow I don't think they'd do that to Vivian Baines's son. She'd be absolutely horrified though; disgusted – they all would. I don't think they'd ever get over the shock. Their precious Benedict, out on the streets, prey to any Dreg who happens to come along.

It's too late now to change my mind. I can't go home. After the alarm, they'll all have got up. They'll be assembled in the main meeting hall for a roll call. Mother, Father, Francis, all the servants and guards. What are they going to think when I'm not there?

It would never occur to them that I'd be brave or stupid enough to do anything like this, even after I bunked off school today. They'll imagine the worst at first, think that the latest great Dreg kidnapping attempt has been successful.

They'll soon know though, when they watch the footage back; know that I've gone on purpose, that I've taken leave of my senses.

Good. Serves them right. They think they know me. They think they know everything. It's not true. They know nothing.

I push the thoughts of home out of my mind and focus on the next step – getting to her. The Cirque is calling me, a thousand tiny fairy lights twinkling down there in the valley, beckoning me back again.

It's an icy cold, clear night and there's an almost full moon lighting my path. The further I run, the fainter the sirens behind me become, until they're distant sounds. The air feels pure and crisp when I breathe it in, sharper than in the daytime.

I feel liberated, being out of that big old house with its guards and alarms and locked doors. It's the second time I've been anywhere on my own; the first time I've ever been out this late.

I'm jogging towards the Cirque at a steady pace when the noise of the sirens gets louder again. They must be out looking for me. A police car approaches, cruising its way down the road. I can't reach cover in time and it stops. I don't know what else to do, so I turn and run, as fast as I possibly can.

Behind me, I hear the car door slam. Then, footsteps, echoing along with mine, torch light shining on me and a deep voice shouting.

"Stop. Immediately. This is the police. Stop, or I'll shoot!"

What can I do? I keep running. The distance between us expands, but a shot rings through the night. The policeman obviously doesn't know who I am; he'd never risk hurting me, no matter how desperate he might be to catch me. He must think I'm some kind of Dreg criminal.

Another bullet whistles past my right ear. I turn a corner, and then another corner, trying to throw him off my scent. As I weave through the suburbs, the footsteps behind me quickly quieten.

I know I'm not safe though. They'll be looking for me

already. I stick to the side streets, always expecting to hear more sirens but, before I know it, there I am, outside the Cirque.

My eyes scan the vast iron fence. It stretches up, up, up, into the clouds. Impenetrable. I break a branch from a nearby tree and tentatively touch the fence with it. The wood crackles immediately, smoke snaking ominously from the end. Dropping it, I sink to my knees behind a load of rubbish bins. Frustrated. Helpless. Pathetic. My suicide mission is over before it's even begun.

BEN

I don't know how long I'm behind the bins for. I'm completely at a loss as to what I should do next; all I know is that I can't go back.

After what seems like for ever, I hear voices approaching. There's the screeching metal sound of the lock being pulled back, the gates swing open and two Dregs emerge, pushing huge bins. I wait, holding my breath, as they walk past but, just when I think I'm safe, one of them stops.

"Hold up," he calls in a low voice. "We might as well bring these bins in too; fill 'em up as we go."

There's nothing I can do but stay there, crouched down into as tight a ball as possible, as if that makes any difference, while they pull the bins away and both stare down at me. They're definitely Dregs; they've got that unmistakably grey look that a lifetime of semi-starvation and hard work brings. It's hard to determine the woman's age; she could be twenty or sixty, for all I know. Her face is lined with dirt and fatigue, and there are sores around her mouth. The man next to her looks in a better state, quite young and surprisingly strong.

They both jump with shock when they see me, but they pull themselves into action pretty quickly. The man grabs hold of me, twisting my arm behind my back.

"Stop!" I beg. "Please don't. I don't want any trouble. I've got cash!"

What an idiotic thing to tell them. The one thing Dregs don't have, the one thing they're desperate for, is money. He drops my arm.

"Let's give him a minute to explain before we call Silvio."

"I don't want to cause any trouble, I swear," I say. "I only came for a look around." They stare at me as if I'm mad, and the man starts laughing, cynically. "It's true!" I protest. "I've been here before. I just got curious, please don't report me."

He's still laughing at me: hardly surprising, my story sounds ludicrous, but she looks really angry and steps forward, glaring into my eyes.

"Enjoyed it, did you? What bit did you like best? The public humiliation or the fact that at any minute someone might die? You Pures," she tuts. "All the same."

I pull out all the money I have. It's hardly a fortune, but it's enough to take her mind off my apparent enjoyment of the Cirque, and she looks over at the man.

Their eyes meet in silent communication before she nods, tacitly.

"OK," he whispers. "We haven't seen you, right? We could take that money from you anyway, you know – you could hardly report us, considering. You've got a nice little Pure life, I'm sure. I don't know what the hell you think you're playing at."

He shakes his head at me. "Our shift is for two hours, that's all the time you've got if we let you in. We'll lock the gate when we've finished. If you're still inside, you're as good as dead. Be careful: if Silvio finds you, we're all for it."

I hand the cash over and slip in through the unlocked gate. I've made it. I'm back, and this time I'm not leaving without her. Now that I'm inside again, I have no idea what comes next. I haven't got a clue where in this vast prison she is; I don't even know if the Dregs are kept here at night. I circle slowly around in the shadows of the incongruous orange pumpkin of an arena rising up forebodingly in the centre of the courtyard. Everything is silent. There are signs to the animal enclosures, which I definitely want to avoid, and signs to the different shows and refreshment stands. They point every way, except one. I head in that direction and see a big, ugly metal building, tucked away out of sight, cleverly concealed by dozens of brightly coloured tents and a hot-dog stall.

The tents weren't here yesterday; there seems to be twice as much crammed in this space as there was before. It must be for all the extra exhibitions and shows they're putting on for the Spooktacular.

I creep up to the building. Skirting round the edges, I finally find a door. It's bolted, but from the outside. I guess they've only thought about keeping the Dregs in, not anyone else out. After all, who'd be mad enough to break into the Dreg Cirque?

I pull at the big iron bolt. It's old and rusty and I know it'll make a huge grating noise unless I ease it across really, really slowly. It takes ages before it finally shoots back and, despite my caution, the clang resonates through the silence.

A light goes on in a building opposite. I hold my breath, shrinking back into the shadows. A figure appears at the window, silhouetted in the light. After a couple of anxious moments it vanishes and the light goes back out. I make myself wait five minutes more, actually counting out the seconds before I let myself move even an inch.

Slipping my fingers around the door, I peep through the

tiny slit, making out a long, thin corridor. There's no one there, so I creep in.

I daren't use my torch, I just listen for a while, trying to figure out if there's anyone nearby. At first all I can hear is my own breathing, but then I start to notice other sounds. I can make out snuffling, sighing, snoring, the noises of people at rest.

The door nearest to me is ajar. I peer around it and can make out rows and rows of bunks, a sleeping form on each one. Damn it. I should have realized that the Dregs would all be cooped up together.

What am I even doing here? I'll never find her and, if I do, she's unlikely to be alone and able to speak to me. Even if by some miracle she is, what am I going to say to her? And how can I possibly get her out of here without us being caught?

But I can't leave – I can't abandon her here to die.

I notice a large green cross on the door at the end of the corridor, directly in front of me. It's the only one that looks a little bit different, that doesn't have a number on, just the word "SAN".

It's got to be worth one last look before I go. Edging slowly forward, I open the door as quietly as I can. It's not quietly enough though, because the one solitary figure in the one solitary bed gasps, jerks bolt upright and pulls the light cord, staring at me open-mouthed.

It's her.

HOSHIKO

I jump upright, scared out of my mind. All of my fears materialize and take on a life of their own. Silvio's sent for me. It's my turn to die. I turn on the light, my eyes take a second to adjust and I think I must be asleep and dreaming after all, because it's him standing right in front of me.

The boy.

Benedict Baines.

BEN

"What are you doing here?" she demands, as any fantasies I had about her throwing her arms around my neck in spontaneous joy instantly wither away and die. She is most definitely not pleased to see me. "How did you get in?"

I don't know what to say; I've never felt so awkward in my whole life. I've barged my way in here, invaded the space of some girl I don't even know, without even so much as considering what comes next. I take a deep breath.

"I wanted to check you're OK..."

"OK? No, I'm not OK. Your mother has just ordered my death!" She glares at me fiercely. "What are you doing here?" she repeats again. "What do you want from me?"

Her hair is a big, scraggly bed-head mess. She's wearing an old baggy T-shirt in a faded shade of grey and there's make-up smeared on her face and under her eyes – like she's been crying.

The glamorous circus star has gone, but she's still more beautiful, more *alive*, than anyone I've ever met.

At least I tried – at least I didn't just sit at home daydreaming about her. Now I know that there wasn't some crazy connection, that it was all in my stupid head, maybe I can get on with my life like before.

I stand there, looking at her. She glares back at me, but then her expression softens and, for a moment, I think her anger's gone, until she scowls again.

"Don't just stand there gawping! Last chance. Get out. Now!"

"I wanted to ask about the boy, Anatol," I say. "He's dead, isn't he?"

"Yes! Yes, he's dead and tomorrow they're going to kill me too and, you know what? I'm glad. Glad to finally get this rotten, pointless life over and done with."

She turns away from me. I think she's crying.

"Don't say that." My voice is trembling. "Please don't say that."

"Get out," she says. "How dare you come in here?"

What else can I do now except leave?

I can't. Not now. Not after Priya, not after her. I can't go back to my closeted little Pure life. My nice life, where I have all the food and possessions I need, where I live with good, respectable people, who like to spend their time watching those less fortunate than themselves being tortured and killed on a nightly basis.

I can't leave her here to die.

"No," I say. "I'm not leaving. I want to help you."

She laughs – it's brittle and cold – then stands up and faces me.

"You can't help me," she says. The anger's gone now and she's sad and quiet. "No one can."

She's right. I know she is. I stare desperately into her eyes and there's that pull between us again, like we're talking to each other without words.

We both move forward, slowly.

Suddenly, there's a piercing alarm. Everywhere is instantly bathed in a bright, searching light and there's the sound of pounding feet.

Hoshiko's eyes widen in horror.

"It's the emergency alarm. Quick, under the bed!"

"What?" I gape at her.

"For God's sake. Do it. Quick!"

The footsteps are getting closer and I stop hesitating, pick up on her panic and do what she says, sliding myself under the flimsy metal frame. There's just enough room for me to squeeze under there, but I'm totally squashed in, my nose pushed against the springs and the dirty old mattress.

Within seconds the door opens and a pair of the shiniest ankle boots I've ever seen appears in the doorway – the unmistakable Silvio Sabatini himself. I can actually make out my own face reflected on the sheen, so I hope he doesn't look down. A sharp voice demands:

"You see anything? Hear anything?"

"Huh? No... What's going on?" Hoshiko's voice is groggy, as if she's just woken up.

"Break in. Or break out, we're not sure which yet. The doors have been tampered with. Looks like it's from the outside." The syrupy silkiness of his voice whenever he speaks to me or Mother has vanished.

"No way!" The shocked tone she adopts sounds way too over the top to me, but hopefully I'm being paranoid. "Who would break in here?" she asks incredulously.

"Someone with a death wish. Get into the assembly hall right now for headcount."

"Why?" she asks. "You've already seen me, Silvio."

"Enough questions," he barks. "How dare you answer me back? Get up and get in there. Now."

The feet turn abruptly and the door slams.

A second later, her head appears, hanging upside down over the bed. Her hair brushes the floor and her eyes appear kind of googly and strange. The blood has rushed to her head too, so it looks all strained.

I'm hiding under the bed of this crazy, angry Dreg girl in the living quarters of the most dangerous circus in the history of the world. She could turn me in at any minute. She hasn't though. Why not?

She feels it too, that's why; I know she does.

I smile at her, hopefully. She scowls in return, cutting me to the quick when she speaks.

"Just when I thought things couldn't get any worse, you rock up and cause even more trouble. Thanks for that. Nice one."

She disappears from view and before I can work out how to respond, I see her bare feet on the dirty floor, the door opens, and she's gone.

HOSHIKO

We assemble in the hall. No one makes a sound; we all sit with our heads down, trying not to draw attention to ourselves.

There's a really charged atmosphere. The guards are pacing up and down, staring at us as if they'll aim those guns and fire if we so much as move which, let's face it, they probably will. Why not? It's been done before. No one would complain, well, no one who actually matters anyway. In fact, the guards would probably be given a promotion.

Greta files in with the rest of our dorm. Her nervous eyes flicker across the room, and I know she's seeking me out. She smiles when she sees me, trotting straight over to squeeze in next to me – no wonder people call her my shadow. She rubs her eyes, sleepily, and I can't help putting my arm around her, even though I know it's forbidden.

She's carrying her dirty old rag doll, hugging on to her possessively. She should be snuggled up in bed with her now, at home, safe with her family, instead of trapped here, in hell. If I die, she'll be totally alone. If she dies – the thought petrifies me, I can't even go there.

I clench my fists together as white hot fury floods me: I want to punch someone.

I try to focus on the faces in the room. Everyone's looking furtively around. They're all trying to work out what's going on; it's been years since we had an emergency night-time roll call like this. Everyone's anxious, no one knowing why we've suddenly been plucked from our beds, what we're supposed to have done wrong. No one except me.

Ezekiel, tiny and wide-eyed, is standing next to Emmanuel, whose hand is clasped protectively on his shoulder. It looks like they've bonded already; I'm glad about that. Emmanuel's been a shell since he lost Sarah; maybe Ezekiel will give him another reason for living – for however long they have together, at least.

Ezekiel sees me and his face lights up with a huge smile. I give him a quick thumbs up across the hall, but then turn my eyes quickly to the front when I catch a security guard frowning at me.

It's not until the atmosphere feels as if something will crack that Silvio enters. He's only a little man but, you have to hand it to him, he certainly knows how to make an impact – just as you'd expect from the world's most famous ringmaster. He was born for a life in the circus, and he plays his part flawlessly, on stage and off.

He's dressed in his finery even now, in the middle of the night. Surely he doesn't sleep in that costume? It's funny to think of Silvio at rest, or wearing anything other than that smart little red suit. I picture him in a pair of striped pyjamas, and for a second I almost laugh. I need to keep a tight grip on myself.

Amina's expression is stony but that familiar twinkle's there in her eye; I bet she's thinking exactly the same as me.

As always, Bojo sits on Silvio's shoulder, dressed in a tiny version of his red suit. That monkey must be the only thing he's ever given a damn about.

The steely glint in Silvio's eyes is more fervent than ever

tonight as he paces up and down on the platform in front of us. It must be a full minute before he speaks, and in that time, the tension keeps right on mounting.

Finally, he talks. Really quietly and calmly, his tone almost sing-song.

"Ladies and gentlemen."

He always calls us that – it's the same thing he says to the Pures – a compliment, you'd think, but the gentle and respectful tone somehow makes it even more menacing. We're scum to him. We know it, and he knows we know it. And we loathe him for it, every single one us: the only thing worse than a Dreg-hating Pure is a Dreg-hating Dreg.

"Ladies and gentlemen," he repeats. "There has been a breach of security. Someone has tampered with, and opened, the door. Since the head count shows no one is missing, we can only assume that one of you has tried, unsuccessfully, to leave the safe confines of our family home and, given that the lock is on the outside, has had help doing so.

"There is no need to remind you all, I hope, of the foolish nature of such an act. Even if the guilty party had made it from the building, we would have quickly found them – found them and destroyed them, and everyone else they care about."

His tone is still calm, gentle almost, but he's like a purring lion, and we know better than anyone never to trust a lion.

"You, my friends, are the property of this circus. And we will not tolerate the removal, the theft, of our property."

The silence seems to last for ever.

"Someone in this room must know something," he says at

last, diplomatically. "You have five more minutes in which to confess or there will be a withdrawal of all rations until the mystery has been solved."

There's an audible intake of breath across the room. We were put on food deprivation once before, when some money went missing. I must have only been about six, but I still remember it really clearly.

"As I said," Silvio reiterates, "the perpetrator has five minutes."

There is complete silence again. Even the guards stop pacing, no one moves, no one even appears to actually breathe.

Last time food quotas were cut back it wasn't that bad for me; Amina gave me pretty much all of hers, and I remember others too, who are no longer here with us, feeding me little tit bits. I think the idea was that we had just enough to survive, that we were almost starving, but that no one actually died. It didn't work though. Esmerelda, the old fortune teller, didn't make it.

I think she was the first person I saw die off the stage. She keeled over in front of us all, during group rehearsals. They made us carry on while they picked her body up and carted it away.

She was one of the few lifers. She'd been here from the age of four, as some sort of psychic phenomenon, and made it to middle age, old age almost. She was like a grandmother to everyone.

I remember asking Amina what they'd done with the body, and the way she wouldn't look me in the eyes when she said she didn't know.

One of the older boys told me though, a couple of days later.

"She'll be lion food by now," he said. "Much cheaper than buying in meat." When I said I didn't believe him, he laughed. "That's not the worst of it," he told me. "Not by a long shot. Ever notice that the only time we get meat is after someone's died or vanished? Think it's just a coincidence do you?"

I ran straight to Amina in floods of tears. She wiped my eyes and said he was just scaremongering.

"The truth is that none of us know what they've done with Esmerelda, or what they do with anyone who dies," she said. "We just have to hope they deal with them decently."

"They never treat us with decency when we're alive," I said. "Why would they bother once we're dead?"

She shrugged. "What's the point in thinking the worst? What good does it do?"

A guy called Dimitrios confessed to taking the cash in the end. He wasn't a performer, he was one of the circus riggers. No one ever knew if it was actually him. Maybe he couldn't stand it any more, or wanted to save the rest of us – who knows? They killed him for it anyway, I assume, because they hauled him away and none of us ever saw him again.

Do I think about giving him up? Standing up and declaring: *The intruder is here in this building. I don't know what he's doing here, but he's under my bed in the san.* I'd like to say that I do, but it'd be a lie, I'd rather subject all these people to starvation.

Why do I feel like I need to protect him? What would they do to him anyway if they found him? He's Vivian Baines's son, so they'd have to be careful but still, he's pushing his luck, surely. He's disobeyed protocol three times now.

The only reason I'm keeping quiet is curiosity. I need to find out what he's actually doing here, what he wants. If he's caught now, how will I ever know? Plus, I'm in too deep anyway. I didn't raise the alarm immediately, didn't scream. I'm complicit already and, while they might be lenient with him, they'd shoot me right now without even thinking about it. Big show or not, no one's irreplaceable; Silvio's made that crystal clear often enough lately.

"May I remind you, just in case you'd forgotten, what day it is tomorrow?" He knows we don't need reminding; we've been gearing up to it for months now. "If anything happens to jeopardize my show, I will be very, very upset."

He leans forward, scanning our faces, looking for any signs of weakness, and then speaks softly. "More upset than you've ever seen me."

I shudder.

BEN

It feels like I'm lying under that dirty bed, trying desperately not to cough from all the dust, for ever.

Finally, the door opens and I see her tiny feet again – don't Dregs have shoes? In that circus ring they looked completely pointed and perfect. Close up though, I see that they're covered in red raw blisters and hard skin from a lifetime of dancing on the wire.

"Don't move," she mutters quietly. "Don't speak. Don't do anything. They're checking the dorms."

I do what she says, mostly because I don't want to risk her anger again. There's a creaking of springs as she gets on the bed, and the mattress moves even closer to my face.

The door opens abruptly and a big pair of heavy boots appears.

"Anything unusual?" a gruff voice asks.

"No," she answers. "Nothing at all."

The door slams shut. I don't know what to do; I can't just stay here. She's centimetres away from me.

I pull myself out from under the bed. She's scrunched up into a little ball, curled right into the corner.

"Are you OK?" I whisper.

She whips around like a firecracker. "No! I'm not OK! Do you realize how much danger you've just put me in?"

"Danger? Why?"

"Why? Because you've broken into the circus and I'm hiding you under the bed! What do you think they'll do if they find out?"

I don't know what to say.

"They'll kill me, that's what! They'll take me outside and shoot me!"

"But it's not your fault. I'm the one who'd be in trouble … wouldn't I?" Even as I'm saying it, I realize she's right. Why would they punish a Pure, the son of Vivian Baines no less, when there's a conveniently placed Dreg girl they can blame instead?

"I'm sorry," I say. "I didn't think. I'll go and hand myself in, right now."

"You can't! It's too late now. They'll know I've protected you."

"I'll tell them I just hid here, that you didn't know."

"They won't believe you!" She shakes her head. "They won't care, don't you understand?"

"But what else can I do? I should never have come here."

"No! No, you shouldn't! What on earth did you think would happen?"

"I don't know. I wanted to see you; that was all."

She looks at me. There's anger there still and grief, but there's something else there too, the same thing that was there before. It's like electricity crackling, like fire.

She looks away. "I don't know what to do. If you tell them you're here, they'll punish me. If you don't, and they find out later…"

Footsteps echo outside. We both freeze, listening to them getting louder and then fading away again. She sinks down next to me.

"I'm sorry," I tell her. "I'm so sorry. I never wanted to put you in danger."

She shrugs, looks at me again, and gives a funny little smile. "It's OK. I haven't got much to live for anyway."

I want to reach out for her. I want to hold her, just once. She's so close to me that we're almost touching. She moves away, stands with her back to me on the opposite side of the room, arms crossed.

"My mother," I say. "What she said to Silvio Sabatini yesterday..."

"You mean about having me killed tomorrow night?"

I wince.

"It's no big deal," she says over her shoulder. "People die all the time in here, haven't you worked that out yet?"

"I'm sorry. I wish I could do something. Tell me what to do and I'll do it. I'll do anything."

She turns to face me, but she won't meet my gaze. Her eyes flick up for an instant, but then she looks back down at the floor. "How come you turned out like this?" she says.

"Like what?"

"Half decent, as if you actually cared."

"I do care. I care more than I've ever cared about anything."

There's a long silence. We stand there, inches apart, her looking at the floor, me looking at her.

"There was a Dreg working at our house," I tell her. "Her name was Priya. I used to talk to her about stuff. I ... I loved her, but she's gone now. My parents found out I'd been speaking to her." My voice cracks. "I don't know where she is. I think she's dead."

"So you put her in danger then? Like you're doing now, to me? It's your fault if she's dead."

Her words cut like a knife; she's right, I know she is. I hang my head.

Silence again.

"I shouldn't have said that," she says a moment later. "It wasn't fair."

"It's OK. It's true."

"What else are you supposed to do? Treat us like the rest of them do? I think my family must be dead, too," she says. "But I'm not sure either. I know how hard it is, being uncertain."

We stand there, looking at each other.

I know what this feeling is. I've known ever since I first saw her; first saw her perform, first saw her face, projected up into the sky. And every time I've seen her since, it's got bigger and stronger; it's overwhelmed me. It's turned me into a different person, a better person. There's no other feeling that could be this strong, that could take me over like this. I have to tell her, before it's too late.

She's still looking at me. I feel my cheeks flush; why can't I get the words out?

She breaks my gaze and turns away again.

"You'd better get back under the bed, they could come back at any minute," she says.

I just stand there, like an idiot.

"Go on then!" she hisses. "What are you waiting for?"

I slide back under the bed. Above me, the mattress sinks as she lays back down.

The tips of her fingers appear over the edge of the bed. Dangling there, just hanging over. Her body is centimetres away from mine, one thin layer of foam separating us. I can hear her breathing. We lie there in silence.

Her hand has an angry cut on it; it must be from when she grabbed the wire. I have this almost overwhelming urge to kiss it. If I moved my head up, and to the right, I could do it. Instead, I reach my hand up, brushing my fingers against hers, lightly as a whisper. Her hand jolts for a split second, and I hear a tiny intake of breath above me, but she doesn't pull it away.

It makes me brave enough to move my hand up. To wrap it right around hers. Ever so gently, so as not to hurt her. She still doesn't wrench away and, right at that moment, all the lights go off.

I'm scared to move in case she pulls her hand away, scared even to breathe. The two of us, connected. Joined. I wonder if she has this funny tickling feeling inside too.

Eventually she whispers, "I did feel it."

"Feel what?"

"In the arena. And earlier, when we were trying to help Anatol. I felt it too."

I squeeze her hand, not too hard, just softly. After a second, she squeezes back. So, there we are, lying together in the darkness, waiting for morning and the trouble that's bound to be coming.

HOSHIKO

I can't explain why I don't pull my hand away; I don't know what makes me say what I do. He's a Pure. He might seem a bit kinder, a bit more human than the rest of them, but it's just an illusion. I'm too tired, that's why; too tired to deal with anything else today, so I drift off to sleep, his hand encircling mine through the night.

BEN

The room starts to get lighter, and I can hear birds chorusing as dawn breaks. Who would have thought they'd sing even here, in the Dreg Cirque?

In the end, I can't resist having one little look, so I carefully ease my hand from hers and pull myself out from under the bed.

She's asleep. She looks younger than before, and softer.

I've never seen anyone more lovely in my whole life.

HOSHIKO

When the morning alarms go off – wailing sirens penetrating into the skull – I actually forget for a couple of seconds: about Anatol, about Ben. It all floods quickly back but, even then, I wonder if it was a dream. There he is, though under my bed, fast asleep.

He looks really peaceful. He must be in a really deep sleep not to be disturbed by that alarm.

What's wrong with me? Why don't I hate him? He's just some stupid Pure boy who's put me in danger. Worse than that, he's the son of *her*, the son of evil personified. If he was to get up and leave now, maybe people would believe that I wasn't aware he was hiding there. After all, everyone knows how much I hate Pures. Why would I let one seek refuge in my room?

The safest thing is probably to tell him to go now, before things get any worse. I don't know why I don't. It's all his fault. His fault for coming here; his fault for making my brain all muddled. I think about waking him up, shouting in his ear. I think about calling out too. About screaming and giving him away. "Help! He's in here. I've found him under the bed!"

But instead I watch him for a minute or two. His chest is moving up and down as he breathes, softly, peacefully, as if he hasn't a care in the world. He looks much younger when he's asleep. I guess he's got kind of a baby face anyway, with his floppy blond hair and long, dark eyelashes. His skin looks really soft, like only a Pure's can. It's the face of someone who's never known starvation or any kind of physical labour.

There's a tiny bit of blond stubble showing through on his chin. I wonder, if you touched it, whether it would feel soft or spiky.

I scowl at him, sleeping there obliviously, and leave quickly, hoping he'll have the sense to stay put when he wakes.

I need to tell Amina. Firstly, because she always knows what to do, and secondly, because she's going to be back in this room treating people before the day's out. I don't think it will take her long to discover there's a Pure hiding under the bed.

There's no breakfast today, so we're all ushered to work straight away, before I get a chance to track her down, and it's a busy morning, even busier than usual. There's always so much hype surrounding the Spooktacular, and it sells out as soon as the tickets go on sale, even though the price is quadrupled. It's obvious why it's so popular, obvious why they're all so desperate to come: tonight's the night, more than any other, that the Pures long to witness Dreg death. They don't just want façade and trickery; they want proper bloodshed, genuine screams, real-deal chills down the spine.

In the morning, we're all put on different work groups. Amina's on a team repainting all the signs; keeping them gleaming and fresh for the Pures, Greta's with Ezekiel, feeding the animals and I'm sewing costumes, which is really hard because my hand hurts and I had even less sleep than usual last night; my eyelids keep sagging while I'm supposed to be sewing. If I get caught dozing, or my output isn't good enough, I know what they'll do to me, so I try really hard, but end up just making stupid mistakes.

Thank God Emmanuel is next to me. He slides over half of his work while the guards aren't looking. He's always the best, the quickest, the most skilled at everything, so he can afford to lose a bit of work without it looking suspicious. I smile at him gratefully – I know he's putting himself at risk – but he just looks away.

I keep waiting to be grabbed and hauled away for interrogation, but it never happens. Benedict Baines's family must have realized he's gone by now and, after what happened yesterday, you think I'd be the first person they'd question about his disappearance. There's no sign that anything's wrong at all though, maybe a few extra guards and police officers around than normal, but that's about it.

It's not until much later that I have the chance to get anywhere near Amina. She's in the changing rooms during afternoon rehearsals, patching up bandages and giving on the spot first aid to people.

Sidling up to her, I whisper as quietly as I can, "I need to speak to you: I'm in a bit of trouble."

She looks at me sharply. "What kind of trouble? What have you done?"

"It's a bit complicated. I can't tell you here. Can you give me another appointment with you, please?"

"Hoshiko, you spent last night in the san. Only you could get in trouble in a room on your own."

I swallow the retort that springs to mind, but my face must give me away, because she gasps. "You weren't alone. Oh my God! What have you been doing?" I feel my cheeks reddening.

"Nothing like that, I swear. Look, please, I really need your help."

"OK. Play on your hand hurting today. Not too much, in case he writes you off before the show; just enough so that I can tell him you need another medical."

I don't see Silvio all morning. It's not until rehearsals that he appears, but he doesn't haul me out, or yell at me, like I expected. He stands in the corner, watching me quietly, his face thoughtful.

During rehearsals, I'm careful not to overreact, but I make sure I wince a couple of times when I know he's watching, and I occasionally glance down at my hand. It does still hurt quite a lot, so it's not even as if I have to fake it.

Along with his ruthlessness, one of the qualities that's got Silvio where he is today is that he doesn't usually miss a trick, and it's not too long before he makes his way over to me, Bojo hopping along at his feet.

Silvio doesn't walk like a normal person – he dashes in a neat little dance, kind of fox-trotting across the arena. That probably sounds quite innocent and charming, but it's not. He's so light and quick on his feet that he's able to suddenly appear, right next to you, completely without warning. There's something really scary about that: it's as if you can never escape him. One minute you're alone, the next minute he's there, breathing down your neck.

He reminds me of a squirrel. Quick, sharp-eyed and shrewd. A really evil squirrel though, dressed in his little red coat. A squirrel who's bound to find out sooner than later that I'm up to something.

"There's been an incident," he says. "The boy, Benedict Baines, he's gone missing, run away from home. Would you believe it? Run away from his bloody great mansion on the hill. You wouldn't know anything about that, would you?"

"Me? No! Why would I know anything?"

"Because the poor, deluded young man has obviously fallen under your spell, that's why."

"Silvio, I hate Pures. If I saw him, I promise you, I'd tell you straight away."

"Hmm. That's what I told the police – that they were wasting their time. He couldn't get in here, the place is too secure and, even if he could, none of my people would conceal him. They might tear him to pieces, but they wouldn't help him." He leans forward and looks at me. "I said that nothing happens in this place without my say-so. I hope I was correct?"

"Yes. Definitely, definitely correct."

He stares at me for a bit longer, his sharp little eyes like the tips of knives.

"His family want his disappearance kept quiet for now. They think he'll be at more risk if word gets out and they seem to believe he'll come crawling back with his tail between his legs anyway: he isn't known for his rebellious nature. I've been told to report anything suspicious though." His voice lowers. "Hoshiko, you wouldn't dare to try and deceive me, would you?"

"No," I say, narrowing my eyes. "There's absolutely no way I would ever willingly help a Pure do anything."

"Yes, that's what I told them. That's why I didn't even mention last night's false security alarm; I don't want them closing my circus down over a silly coincidence like that." He looks at me again. "Anyway, back to business. Your hand, girl; it's not going to cause me any problems tonight, is it?"

"It just hurts a bit. Just a tiny bit, that's all. I can still perform."

I watch his face carefully, judging his mood. It's still foul; I need to be really careful not to make him even angrier.

"It's just..." I begin tentatively.

"Just what?"

"Well, if it gets any worse, I might not be able to grip on properly at all. Then I'd probably slip straight away, before the act really gets going. It wouldn't be a very theatrical end. I'd hate to underperform. Especially tonight."

"Since when does the nature of your demise and whether it's dramatic enough concern you?"

"I'm only thinking of the Cirque, Silvio, honestly. It might be better if Amina has one more look at it."

He looks at me, in that calculating way of his. He's assessing my worth.

"OK," he agrees. "One more. After the rehearsal." He scowls. "It's been a difficult day, what with one thing and another. No deaths – at least they'd be cheap to deal with – but five injuries. Five people incapable of performing, wasting the Cirque's money without giving anything back. I'm warning you, Hoshiko, if Amina declares you unfit, you're finished."

He looks me straight in the eyes.

"I hope you'll be OK for tonight, my dear: I've got big plans for you."

BEN

When I wake up, she's gone, and there's just me there, for hours and hours, stuck under this dirty, smelly bed, wondering what on earth I've done. I've broken out of my own home, stayed out all night and bribed my way into the Dreg Cirque. Now, I'm trapped here, hiding under a bed. What's going to happen next?

I'll never get out of here without being spotted and, even if I could, how could I go home now, after everything that's happened?

Eventually, I can't stand it any more and I creep out from under the bed. The room is tiny, and there's no window, just the door I came in by. It smells like a hospital in here, that heady mixture of disinfectant and vomit, and there are boxes of bandages and medical supplies piled up in all the corners. I'm clearly in some kind of treatment room; Hoshiko must have been put in here last night because of her hand.

I think again of the disgust on Mother's face after I helped Hoshiko during her act, and the anger on it yesterday, when we were out there in the courtyard. They must be going frantic, looking for me. It wouldn't take a genius to work out where I am. I don't know how they haven't found me already.

I realize with a sudden jolt of panic that Hoshiko was right. I have put her in even more danger, coming here. Whatever punishment they give me, you can guarantee hers will be worse. *But they're going to kill her anyway*, a voice in my head says, *And that's your fault too.*

Even so. The only real option I have is to show myself. I'll tell them that Hoshiko didn't even know I was there, that I hid when she was asleep. I'll say I must have been sleepwalking, that I don't know how I got there, or why. No, they'll never believe that. I slide back under the bed.

I'm racking my brains trying to come up with a plan, when the door opens. My heart races. The feet which appear aren't hers.

This is it. I lay there, waiting to be found.

It doesn't take long to work out that this must be the doctor, and she's got patients to see.

The first one is a boy who's part of the knife-throwing act and has been caught in the chest by one of the blades. He explains what happened to the doctor.

"It was some Pure kid's tenth birthday. They'd bought one of those horrific party packages where they get to come to rehearsal. They were all allowed a throw – ten nasty little bastards, all throwing knives at me, their parents proudly filming it on their phones and cheering when anyone got close."

"They did this *before* a show?" The doctor sounds shocked. "Things are getting worse around here. After what went on last night, it wouldn't surprise me if they cull us all. You're lucky though; it's only superficial. I don't think I'll be able to get you out of performing tonight."

"I don't want to get out of it, Amina. The more I'm there, in front of those Pures, the more likely it is that someone gets lucky and finishes me off for good."

She hushes him softly. I get the impression he's crying.

"Hold on a minute," she tells him quietly. "I've got some

stronger painkillers somewhere. They'll numb the ache a bit, and I don't just mean the pain from the chest wounds."

I hear her rummaging around in drawers and cupboards, then my heart leaps out of my chest when she says, "I think they're under the bed."

Within seconds, a face appears, inches from mine. We stare at each other. She's a bit older than me, about twenty, I suppose, with wild, curly hair. This is Amina then. I expect her to scream, or shriek, or raise some kind of alarm, but instead she grabs a box from behind me and stands back up.

"Here they are," she says to the guy and carries on treating him, and the next five people, as if she hasn't even seen me at all.

HOSHIKO

After rehearsals, we're given "recreation time", although the very term is a complete joke. In reality, it means we have one hour to eat our measly rations, wash in the crammed communal showers – one block for girls, one for boys – and rest before we have to get dressed for the evening's show.

There's no dinner provided at all tonight though – Silvio's sticking to his decree – and the only thing left out in the canteen are buckets of murky tepid water. We have to go in there and plunge our faces into them, slurping like the animals they say we are.

This is the one hour of the day where there's usually time for an attempt at camaraderie – it's the only thing that keeps us going. Not tonight though. Tonight, grief and shock still hang around like unwelcome visitors; etching their lines on everyone's face, wrapping us up in their heavy shroud.

Three deaths in two days: that's pretty unusual even by Cirque standards.

I can't stand listening to the whispered analysis about everything that's happened so, instead of staying in the dorm like I normally do, I sit outside the san, waiting to be called to Amina.

Surely Ben will be discovered any second now and all hell will break loose. I scan the faces of everyone who comes out of the san but none of them look as if they've just stumbled across a Pure boy hiding under the bed.

Finally, it's my turn. I knock, but enter before there's a reply. There's no sign of him. He must still be hiding. Amina's standing in the corner of the room, her arms folded and her eyebrows raised.

"So," she says calmly. "You want to tell me what's going on?"

I don't know where to start. I'm floundering around trying to find the right words to begin, when she says, "Let me help you out. I reckon it's a pretty good bet that it's got something to do with the boy hiding under the bed."

There's a few seconds silence, and then a pair of trainers, some legs, a torso and finally a head emerge.

He looks really dirty; there's dust smudged all over him: in his hair, on his clothes, on his skin, even tiny little bobbles on his eyelashes.

In spite of all that though, you can still tell where he comes from a mile off. His cheeks are pink and healthy, his body doesn't have that malnourished look that Dreg boys have. His floppy blond hair looks shiny and soft and I can't help noticing that he's definitely got some muscle definition going on under that T-shirt. He might as well be carrying a placard declaring his status.

"Oh God, Hoshiko, a Pure?"

We all stand there in a little circle. I feel like we're wayward children, caught out up to mischief by their mother.

After a moment, he speaks. "I'm sorry. It's all my fault. She did absolutely nothing wrong. I crept in here. I don't know what I was thinking, and now I'm stuck and I've caused all this trouble. I never would have come here if I'd known, I swear. It's not her fault, any of it, please believe me. Whatever I've got to do, I'll do it, but leave her out of it, please. Just say you both found me."

Amina doesn't scream, or look panicky, or do any of the other things I thought she would. She just sighs.

"Let's start at the beginning, shall we? Who are you? And how did you get in? Don't spare any details; it might be important later on."

So he tells us his story. How his name's Ben, how he's never done anything like this before, how he saw me that first night here, and how he acted on impulse. He says he's ashamed, ashamed of being a Pure, ashamed of watching the show, ashamed of his family.

"So you should be," I spit the words out. "You think we're scum, but it's you who's repulsive, the whole lot of you!"

"Shhh, Hoshi." Amina is so improbably calm. "It's OK. He's done a stupid thing, but he's done it for the right reasons. What was the alternative? That he just sat at home and carried on? I've got news, for both of you. You're not the first Pure boy who's crossed the lines and you won't be the last. We've just got to figure out what the hell to do now."

"There's more." He's looking at the floor now and his skin has taken on a funny greenish pallor. "My mother … she's sort of famous."

"Who is she?"

He doesn't say anything at all for a few seconds. Then, still staring at the floor, he whispers.

"Vivian Baines."

My eyes meet Amina's. For the first time, even she looks shocked.

It hits me again now – what he is, who he is – like a smack

in the face. Last night, I actually let him hold my hand. What was I thinking?

I turn on him angrily. "Wanted another look at the freak show, did you? Looking for inside information? Don't suppose you cared if it meant people like us would die!"

I can't control the rage I feel. I punch him as hard as I can in his chest again and again; I can't stop myself. He doesn't stop me either, or try to fight me. He just stands there, while I pummel him with my fists. It makes me even angrier.

"Hoshiko! That's enough!" It takes Amina to physically pull me off him. "Give him a chance!"

"I'm sorry," he says. "I'm sorry for everything, for all of it. I know this sounds stupid, but I never really thought much about my mother's job before."

I want him to hurt; I want him to feel the pain we've all felt for over a hundred years.

"The show wasn't enough for you, is that it? Wanted to see it all a bit more close-up? You make me sick! I hate your mother and I hate you, and everything you stand for!"

For the first time, he's defensive.

"I didn't ask to be born a Pure, any more than you asked to be born a Dreg! I know it's all wrong. I hate it as much as you do. I'd give anything to change it."

His words incense me even more. "Your mum tortures Dregs, did you know that? Orders hundreds of Dreg deaths a week. She's just ordered mine, as it happens. Still, it doesn't matter, it's not like we're even human!"

Amina interrupts.

"What do you mean, she's ordered yours?"

"Yesterday," I say. "I didn't want to tell you, but Silvio's promised to finish me off." I don't tell her he said it'd be tonight.

"Oh my God!" She stands there, the colour draining from her face. "Why?"

"It doesn't matter why, does it? Because she hates me, that's all that matters."

She looks at me, still astounded. "You weren't even going to tell me, were you?"

"What would have been the point?" I say. "There's nothing you can do anyway."

She's angry. "Yes, there is. There's more than you know. Don't say anything, either of you. I need to think." She paces up and down the room.

I glance at him out of the corner of my eye. He looks so sad.

He looks at me; catches me watching him.

"I wish things could be different, too," he says, softly.

He's reminding me of yesterday, during the Q and A. I close my eyes and see his face again when he asked me that question; see him helping to carry Anatol across the square; hear him calling out, *I'll save you*; hear him last night, whispering, *I'm sorry*; remember him rescuing me in the arena, lifting me up so gently; feel him holding my hand through the night.

I open my eyes. He's still watching me, talking to me without words.

The rage has vanished as quickly as it came. I try to make it come back, to summon up that intense hatred of him, but it's gone.

"OK," Amina says at last. "There's people I need to speak to, things I need to do, but it's going to have to wait. It's show time in about twenty minutes; you'll have to stay here," she tells him.

Right on cue, the sound of the pre-performance alarm floods the room. "That's us," she says. "It's a big night tonight – biggest of the year. Come on, Hoshi."

This is it then: the beginning of the end.

Amina takes my hand in hers. "You'll get through this."

She tilts my chin up with her hand and gives me that knowing smile of hers.

"Your hands will hurt but you're the Cat; you'll be OK. Right. I'm giving you one minute, then you'll have to come, Hoshiko. They'll miss you in the changing rooms otherwise." She turns and leaves, closing the door softly behind her.

"Goodbye, Amina," I whisper.

We both stand there and then I hear my voice saying words I didn't even know I felt.

"I'm sorry," I tell him. "For being so horrible and rude."

He smiles at me, and my stomach swoops. Whoever his mum is, whatever happens to me, or him, right at this moment, I'm glad he's here.

If I die out there tonight, I'll never see him again; I'll never know what happens next in this crazy chain of events.

I don't say any of this to him, of course, but it's like before: it's as if he knows what I'm thinking and he's thinking the same thing, he just steps forward and I step forward and I'm there, his arms wrapped around me. Despite all the dust, he smells of washing powder. He's really warm, and his T-shirt is really soft.

He's the physical embodiment of everything I loathe and fear. He's put me in even more danger than I was before but, for the first time ever, I feel safe. It's like nothing can get me here, encircled in his arms; like I'm protected, wrapped in a cocoon. I feel like I'm home.

Eventually he breaks the silence.

"You can't go out there tonight. Please don't."

"I have to." I look at him. "Do you think I'm here through choice?"

He shakes his head, sadly. "No. But … I've only just found you…"

I lay my head on his chest again, hold him really tight. Neither of us moves.

I stay there for a bit longer, trying to capture this warm feeling, so I can take it with me. And then, finally, I wrench myself out of his arms and turn and run straight out of the door.

I stare after her. She's going to die, tonight; Sabatini promised my mother. I'll never see her again. I should have stopped her leaving, I should have done *something*.

The feeling of panic grows. I've been holding it all in but I can feel it getting stronger and stronger. What can I do? How can I help her? I've run away. I've – what was it Amina said – crossed the line. I have to concentrate on breathing, in, out, as slowly as I can. It works, slightly. My hands stop shaking as much and I try to calm my mind down too, but it keeps jumping back to the fact that she's up on that wire again and she's probably going to die. I can't stand the thought of it.

I can't stay here, hiding away, while she goes out and risks her life. That's not what I came here for. I'm pacing backwards and forward uselessly when a noise breaks the silence. I hear a door open and then footsteps, right outside, in the corridor. Two people, talking.

"Start at this end, John, and work your way through, and be thorough. Every drawer, every cupboard. In their shoes, in their beds, under their beds."

"Got it. What if there's nothing there?"

"Just find something. Anything. These orders are right from the very top; some rich kid's gone missing and they want answers. Anything dodgy, anything contraband, bring it to me."

The door slams again, and I hear just one set of footsteps walking towards me, then quietening again. My heart pounds in my chest. I'm about to be discovered. At least now I know there's no point getting back under this damn bed.

Pulling the door ajar as quietly as I can, I peep out into the corridor. It's empty but I can hear noises from the room near the entrance. It must be a guard, rifling through the performers' stuff.

I creep slowly out, edging my way down the corridor. It's pointless: I'm dressed in black, these walls are white, the corridors bare. If whoever's in that room comes out, I'm done for.

It's easy to identify the sounds of beds being pulled along the floor, tables thrown around. He's obviously being thorough and – what a surprise – doesn't have much regard for Dreg property.

Reaching the last doorway, the one to the room he's in, I pause. I have to somehow get myself past that open door without him seeing me. I wait, and listen, picking my moment.

Just when it sounds as if he's moved to the furthest end of the room, I make my move, running past the open doorway to the exit.

It's locked. I'm stuck.

Within seconds, I hear the words I've been dreading. "Hey! Stop where you are!"

There's nothing else to do but turn round. Face-to-face with a burly security guard. The same one, presumably, who's been moving beds and upturning wardrobes single-handedly. He's got a stubbly face and mean little piggy eyes and, for an instant, we stand there, staring at each other, before I see his hand reach down to his waist.

He must be going for a gun. Everything starts to move in slow motion as I watch him, helplessly. Instead, thank God, he takes out a walkie-talkie.

"This is SG9. I've got him. Send some back-up, just in case."

He stands there, leering at me. "End of the line for you, rich boy. I don't know who you are and I don't care, but you've caused me a lot of extra work. I'm going to enjoy watching them punish you."

I look around. There's nothing in the corridor except me and him. The door behind me is definitely locked, and he has the key. He's colossal, about three times the size of me, he's probably armed and he's just called for back-up. The walls and floors are completely bare, except for a fire extinguisher secured to the wall.

I don't know where what happens next comes from. I swear, I've never hurt anyone before. I've never been in a fight at school, never been into violent computer games, like *Dreg Destruction*. My brain rises to the occasion in a way I never would have thought possible.

I gasp, loudly, fixing my eyes over his shoulder, as if I've seen something, or someone, approaching from behind him. He swivels quickly to see what's shocked me so much and I immediately grab the extinguisher from the wall, wrenching it from the plastic clips that hold it. It's heavy, but I lift it up high, pull back as hard as I can, and swing it round towards his head. There's a clunking sound as the metal hits his skull and then he crumples to the floor.

I grab the keys from his hand lightning fast and fumble

with the lock, trying to find the right key. I'm never going to make it before the other guards arrive. There's no sign of them yet though and, finally, I manage to get the door open.

Before I leave, I turn and look at him. He's not moving. I don't know if he's breathing. Have I killed him?

In the distance, I hear dogs barking and footsteps running. I hesitate for a second more, then run, leaving him for dead.

HOSHIKO

The minute I walk into the arena, it's obvious something different's going on. Silvio's here already, directing the men setting up the ropes and trapeze. Today they're also erecting a tall wooden pole in the middle of the ring and carrying in huge piles of logs.

"What's happening?" I don't like this. Any change to the acts, especially at the last minute, especially tonight, throws me.

"Things are hotting up, literally!" He's grinning at me, wickedly, looking extraordinarily pleased with himself. The bad mood from earlier has obviously disappeared. "It's the perfect evening for another death. You're the talk of the town, after the last show. Everyone knows you're injured, and they all want to be the ones to watch you fall. You know me – I hate to disappoint the crowd. Besides, you heard what Vivian Baines said yesterday!"

"But Silvio, she won't remember that; she's got far more important things to worry about. And I'm the most popular act; it's me everyone is paying to see. You don't want to lose me." I hate the pleading tone in my voice. The begging, whining insistence.

"You're a liability, Hoshiko; you've pushed your luck too many times. Baines's order to destroy you has only reinforced an idea I've been toying with for ages. Astrid and Luna have inconveniently been chomped up too soon; the cannonball act is, I have to concede, not yet safe enough to perform to an arena full of Pures, and yet the Spooktacular needs something *spec*tacular, and you, my dear, are it. Doesn't matter how good you are alive; you're worth much more to me dead. Autumn's here, nights are drawing in, everyone wants to stay in their cosy houses and ticket sales are down. Tonight's the first sell-out show for weeks; it's time for another high-profile death."

It's true, what he says; every time one of our big acts gets killed it creates a really big buzz. The public and the press all suddenly go mad and we get mobbed at the doors for weeks. They increase the ticket prices to over double sometimes and they still sell them all.

I shiver as I look at his face, at the pound symbols gleaming in his eyes. He laughs at my expression. "Don't worry, I won't make you go through it alone; you'll have company up there with you." Smirking, he turns and looks across the arena.

I follow his gaze: Greta, fulfilling her unofficial role of monkey-sitting. She's the only one Bojo will ever go to, except Silvio. He sits on her shoulder, nibbling a banana. His adoring gaze follows his master everywhere, and her eyes keep surreptitiously flicking over to where we are too as she panics about what he's saying, about what's going on.

"You can't risk Greta getting injured, Silvio. You've said yourself; she's the future of the trapeze act."

He shakes his head, indulgently. "You will keep making the same mistake: assuming that any one of you is irreplaceable. You're not. None of the Dregs are, not like me. There are hundreds of kids out there who can do a few somersaults if they have to. We've already got a replacement lined up, in case something *terrible* should happen to both of you. A little boy – showed remarkable talent yesterday apparently, but then, you'd know all about that, wouldn't you? I hear you were trying to jeopardize his performance during the selection; realize what a personal threat he was, did you?"

I ignore what he's implying and turn the subject back to Greta. "Look how much Bojo loves her, Silvio! She's the only one apart from you who can look after him!"

He muses, thoughtfully.

"Hmm, maybe you're right. No, he'd forget about her at the first whiff of a peanut. Do you know, I think the best outcome would be if you both die? I mean, you're by far the biggest draw for now, but Greta's definitely got the cutesy factor going on. There's something about a little child dying that the Pures love. They'd have a field day if we could pull off another double death, especially after all the hype the press have created about the shark incident yesterday. Oh well, we'll leave it to fate. Sorry, Hoshiko," he grins. "Minister's orders."

He's still laughing to himself as he saunters off, clicking his fingers for Bojo who scampers off after him.

I will not let Greta die.

Greta's not broken, like I am – not twisted and ruined inside. There's an innocence there that they've not managed to take away yet. I don't think they ever will. She's just *better* than the rest of us. That's what will make her so compelling on stage, the light around her.

There's nothing I can do now to survive; I knew that as soon as Baines issued her decree. I'm dead whatever happens, but I can't let Greta die out there with me. Whatever it takes, I have to save her.

BEN

I hit a crowd of people as soon as I reach the top of the path.

The place has been transformed since last night. Carved jack-o'-lanterns hang from every tree, each one lit with flickering candle flame, casting an orange glow everywhere. There are huge models, towering over the buildings and trees: werewolves and devils, ghosts and zombies. All mechanized, so their mouths, eyes, hands, move up and down. Scores of bats flap above my head, swooping down and away again, their jewelled eyes flashing. There's a soundtrack playing too, screams and cackles, thunder and lightning.

Everyone I see has on a costume of some kind, and most of them are really convincing. Ticket prices for tonight are famously high, so it's not surprising that people are getting so into the spirit of things. There are witches, wizards, skeletons, the odd pirate.

It's hard to tell the ages of people, or their relationships to each other. The ghost and the vampire in front of me, arms wrapped around each other, they must be a couple. And the two little pumpkins who scurry past me giggling are being chased by a witch and a wizard who, I presume, must be their parents. An Egyptian mummy trundles past, pushing a buggy decorated with cobwebs. Inside, grinning at all the lights, a baby in the cutest fluffy monster costume I ever saw.

All these people here to watch people suffering, to watch people dying – bringing their children here, for God's sake. The thought makes me feel like screaming but, instead, I keep my head down and stay as hidden as I can.

The safest place is in the middle of the crowd, so I attach myself to the end of a large group of people, following them along the path.

The way the Dreg Cirque works is that there are loads of smaller buildings and sideshows all connected by the covered aerial tunnels splaying out like spider's legs above the main building which, amongst other things, holds the huge central arena where the big shows – the ones like Hoshiko's – all happen. It takes them a while to set up after each performance, and that's when the crowd spills out and visits the smaller shows and exhibitions.

They never get to see all the acts before the Cirque moves on to a new town but the idea, I suppose, is that they never see the same show twice, and they keep coming back to see their favourite parts again and check out the ones they've missed.

The first "act" I see tonight is on an open stretch of lawn, adjacent to the path. People are paying to throw things at a boy and girl in old-fashioned stocks.

They both have angry wounds on their heads, especially the boy. Blood is pouring down his face but no one seems to care: the group of Pures just keep on throwing things. I notice that they're aiming for him more, not less, as if they sense his weakness and they want him to suffer for it.

I read the sign next to the stocks.

Roll up for the Real Deal! Violent Dreg Criminals!

Acid Sponges, £2 for three.

Iron balls, £6 for three.

Loads of people are queuing up to throw the weapons. I

don't see any acid sponges being thrown – it's all iron balls.

I look at them, hurling the vicious-looking chunks of metal, and wonder if their costumes make it easier for them to do this, to inflict such pain. If they feel more anonymous, more detached from who they really are.

If I was a better person, I'd do something heroic now. I'd call out to them to stop, or I'd go and stand in front of the poor victims, block the missiles. I don't though. I just stand and stare. Everything I've ever been told about us Pures being superior, about us being more human, more humane, than Dregs: it's not true.

My whole existence has been a lie.

HOSHIKO

As soon as Silvio goes, Greta rushes over, throwing herself into my arms as if she hasn't seen me for weeks.

"What did he say? What's the big pole thing for?"

"Not much." It's hard to meet her big, trusting eyes. "He just said the act is changing, I don't know how."

"He said I've got to get ready for first curtain." She looks terrified, as well she might. "He's putting me out there with you. He said I should make the most of it; that it would be the only time we ever get to perform together. What does he mean?"

"I don't know what's going on, Greta, but you can bet whatever he's got planned it'll be dramatic."

I turn my head away from her. I can't tell her what he really said.

I've got to keep going, for her. It's hard though; there's a chill running right through to my bones. What would they do if I crumbled into a heap and refused to move?

I think about Ben and the thought makes me feel so sad. We're meant to have a story together, I just know it. It's not meant to end here, like this.

I've never been that bothered about my own life before; I've been more worried about the impact me dying would have on Greta or Amina than I have about anything else. That makes me sound like I'm a martyr or something, but it's not like that at all; it's just that it's easy to throw your life away when it has no value. What have I had to live for, really?

It's different now. Now, when I close my eyes, all I see is his face, all I feel is him holding me tight. He's changed me. He's already making me selfish, and weak.

I crouch down, so my face is level with Greta's. "Whatever happens, you'll be OK. I swear it."

"You can't promise that, Hoshiko. You don't know!" She's more forceful than normal, less willing to simply believe me. Maybe she is growing up, after all.

"I do know. Have I ever told you a lie before?"

She smiles at last, and holds out her hand, extending her little finger. "Pinkie promise?"

I curl my own sore, swollen finger around it, commanding myself not to cry.

"Pinkie promise."

BEN

I immerse myself into the crowd milling up and down the main stretches of promenade. Everything's going smoothly until I see a large group of police officers gathered up ahead, checking everyone's ID.

I don't know if they're looking for the intruder who broke into the Cirque and assaulted a security guard, or for Benedict Baines, son of Vivian, who's been missing since last night. Either way, identify me and they've hit the jackpot.

The tents holding the extra Spooktacular shows which are dotted about everywhere make it much easier to hide than it would be normally and I duck straight into a smallish sized exhibition named *The Evolutionary Tour*, another one I haven't seen before. If they're looking for me out there, I'm going to have to hide out in here.

The first section of the tent is filled with images. Some of them are recent; I recognize them from TV and from the newspapers. Others are from the past, but the sentiment behind each one is more or less similar: Dregs are dirty. Dregs are thieves. Dregs are evolutionarily inferior. Dregs are not really human at all.

The same face I've seen a million times stares back at me from about fifty per cent of the images. It's the dirty, leering, ugly face always associated with Dregs. It's the face of Vlad, the cartoon Dreg we all laugh at on telly. The one who is always desperately trying to steal from Honest John – the handsome, kind, mistreated Pure.

None of the Dregs I've seen have the shifty-eyed, evil look about them I've always been led to think.

The crowd I'm following files forward, through a narrow passage into the next part of the tent. The foot traffic moves much more slowly now as people stop to really soak up the sights: the live exhibitions.

The first one is a monkey, chattering away in a cage, apparently quite happy. Nothing too sensational or interesting about that.

Next, there's an ape, far too big to be confined in here. I gaze into his mournful eyes and wonder if he's thinking of home, or if he's always been here, under this artificial light, far away from sunlight and green trees.

The third cage is the same size but this one doesn't contain animals at all. Instead, sitting there, heads bowed as the Pures file past calling out abuse to them, are a whole family, brought here straight from the slums, by the looks of it. The two children look to be about eight and twelve, but you can't really tell how old their parents are. Their ribs poke out from under the dirty, ragged clothes they wear, and their faces are filthy.

The final exhibit isn't in a cage. There's a Pure standing there, bathed in golden light, high up on a pedestal. His muscles are flexed and his white teeth gleam as he grins at everyone. He must be a body builder; he's got bronzed, muscular limbs and is wearing only the tiniest of briefs. The sign above him flashes jubilantly: "Evolution is complete. Behold the Perfect Pure."

I'm ashamed to admit it, but I never even thought before

about what the word *Pure* implied. The way that it suggests that we alone are untainted. It's obvious, I know, but when you grow up with a word, you don't always dissect it in the way that you should.

Under each exhibit is the model of a brain. The Dreg brain is like a pickled walnut; tiny and shrivelled. The Pure brain is about six times bigger: pink, healthy, and swollen. It apparently confirms our superiority, our place at the forefront of God's world. I wonder where the biological *facts* ascertained here come from. There's no source cited, no evidence offered. Once, I'd have taken all this as gospel without so much as raising an eyebrow. Not now though – not now and never again.

There's music playing, the *Pure at Heart* anthem. The song I've sung every morning since I started pre-school. The one I've proudly joined in with at rallies, at sporting events, at weddings, christenings, parties. I know all the words, everyone does, but I've just been singing them unthinkingly – a dumb sheep, blindly following the rest of the flock. Now, I listen properly to the rousing chorus, probably for the first time ever.

Pure of Soul and Pure of Body,
Stand we proud with noble heart.
God's love shining on the righteous
His most perfect work of Art.

The words crawl under my skin.

I think about Priya. Where is she? What have they done to her?

I think about the Dregs in the lion tent, about the ones blown across the arena from a cannon. About Anatol, practically dying in my arms. About the girl in the shark tank, desperately trying to save her sister while the Pure audience looked on, enraptured. They were screaming with joy the other night when they thought Hoshiko might fall from the wire.

Who are really the evil ones here?

I think about Hoshiko; there'll never be another moment in my life where I don't. Those reproachful eyes, that haunted yearning in them, they're a part of me now, there, in my head the whole time.

Dregs aren't dirty, or wicked, or savage. Dregs are people; people who can be so achingly beautiful that they take your breath away; so magical that you leave your home and your family for them in a moment of madness that you know you'd repeat again and again and again.

I can't do it any more, can't just file through here, like everyone else, without saying something, without doing something. The time for standing by and watching is past; now, it's time to act.

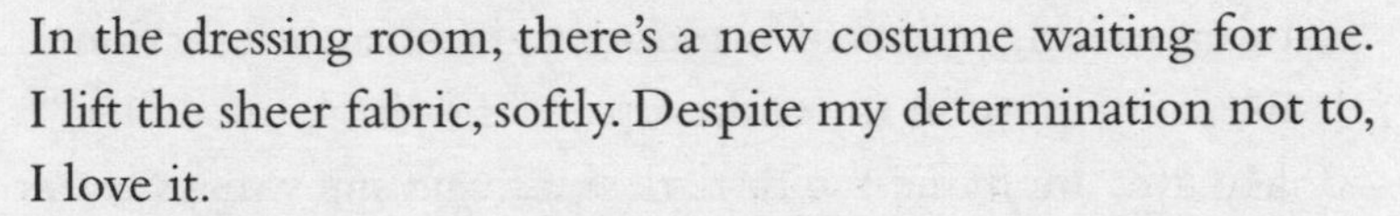

HOSHIKO

In the dressing room, there's a new costume waiting for me. I lift the sheer fabric, softly. Despite my determination not to, I love it.

It's a deep midnight blue, almost black, with thousands of tiny crystals sewn all over it. It's like the night sky. Someone must have sweated blood making this.

Minnie comes in to style my hair and put my make-up on, and her brief has changed too.

Normally, Silvio likes my hair down in loose waves, so that it sort of cascades around my shoulders, fanning around me when I somersault and drop backwards. It's always really annoyed me like that, falling in my face all the time and blocking my view. It's highly impractical, not to mention dangerous but, funnily enough, I haven't bothered to complain.

Tonight though, Minnie says it has to be pinned up.

"Dramatic and sexy, is what I've been told." She raises her eyebrows. "Think you can do dramatic and sexy?"

I look away, embarrassed. Ever since Benedict Baines arrived, ever since he looked at me like that, ever since he held my hand, I have felt more … not sexy, that's not the right word. I don't think there is a word to describe it; I've just felt more conscious of my body, if that makes sense. It's as if I can feel my blood pumping right from the tips of my fingers to the end of my toes; my nerve ends are all sort of tingly.

"Maybe," I tell her. "Maybe I can."

She sweeps my hair up right on to the top of my head,

rolling it up in sections so that it's piled up tightly in loops. She takes out hair grips, each one with a tiny bulb on the end, and weaves little points of sparkling light into each section.

Then she puts on my make-up.

My eyes are framed with dark liner, and she sweeps layers of black mascara over my lashes. She smudges shadow on my eyelids, blending it with glittery silver sparkles. There's a touch of shiny gloss dabbed on my lips and cheeks but, otherwise, she leaves them bare. Everything is understated, except the eyes.

When I look at myself in the mirror, the person staring back doesn't look like me at all. The costume clings to my breasts and hips. It fits perfectly, making me feel more curvaceous, more feminine.

My whole body fills with a sudden desire to see him again. It's so strong it makes giddy. If he was here, now, I wouldn't hold back. I wouldn't be cross. Or awkward. I wouldn't give a damn where he comes from, or who his mother is. Life's too short. *My* life will be way too short.

I'll never get to tell him how I feel now.

I'll never get to love him.

Minnie shakes me out of my daydream.

"Hoshi? You ready? It's show time."

BEN

I push forward through the line of people and stop in front of the grinning body-builder. Our eyes meet. I wonder how much he's being paid to come and do this. Does he feel proud of himself? Feel that he fulfils an important role? I take a breath; I have to say something, to him and the crowd of people who've paid to come and see this.

His expression changes from one of smug, self-delight to shock: he must see the animosity on my face. As I glare at him, the screens behind him flicker. They darken and then light up again as the images change. His eyes widen further as he looks from me to the screen opposite, then back at me again.

My face beams out from every corner of the tent. "Missing. Benedict, son of Vivian Baines. £1,000,000 reward."

I have to get out of here.

HOSHIKO

I stand at the top of the ladder, eyes screwed tightly shut, and count to ten slowly, like I always do. I daren't hesitate any longer, especially not after what Silvio did last time. God, has it only been two days since then? Forty-eight hours ago, I hadn't even met Ben yet.

When I open them, my eyes are immediately drawn to what is, unmistakably, a huge cauldron suspended from the ceiling, rocking slowly backwards and forward above the crowd. It's filled with a great, unlit bonfire. My mouth goes dry.

Thunderous music fills the arena all of a sudden and the crowd roar as the lights dim and a red spotlight shines on Silvio, far below in the centre of the ring.

For once he's in a different costume, dressed as a little red devil. An all-in-one leotard, little black horns, even a forked tail, swinging around as he moves. His usual whip has been replaced by a pitchfork and he's brandishing it up and down as he cavorts about. On his shoulder, Bojo is a miniature replica of his impish master. It's so absurd, it's comical, and the audience are laughing as Silvio leaps nimbly about the ring. He's captivating though. I hate him, but I can't take my eyes off him. Never was a costume more appropriate.

"Ladies and gentlemen!" he cries. "Welcome to the Spooktacular! I hope you like our little log pile!" He gestures above him, to the unlit bonfire. "Of course," he laughs. "Of course, there is one thing missing. For what November bonfire would be complete without a guy?"

The crowd are cheering and shouting.

"Bring on the guy! Bring on the guy!" Do they know something I don't? What are they expecting?

Another spotlight lights up the central ceiling hatch, directly above the bonfire. A little wicker basket lowers, swinging backwards and forward. Something's moving inside it.

After a couple of seconds, the lid raises and something rises, out of the basket. Concealed under a hessian sack, a figure fights her way out, and looks around, petrified, at the frenzied audience. Why didn't I realize before?

There, so small and far away that I have to strain my eyes to make out what I'm actually looking at, is Greta.

BEN

Head down, I push through the crowd to the back of the tent. I fight my way quickly under the heavy tarpaulin, just as he calls out: "Stop. Stop, he's here in the tent!"

It's darkening everywhere, but it's not dark enough, not yet. My face lights up every screen. Everyone's stopped in their tracks and crowds of people are staring up at it.

All around me, people are looking at my picture, reading the information. All they have to do is find me to get their hands on all that lovely money.

Behind me there are shouts, police whistles, running feet. I duck behind a tree just in time. It's the Pure from the tent, accompanied by loads of guards.

"He was here!" he's shouting. "I just saw him a second ago!"

Their sounds are drowned out as a marching band loudly makes its way along the circus promenade, seemingly oblivious to the latest drama. The music is booming, a deep monotonous chant, drowning out everything else. The same ominous words I heard last night.

See the flames go higher, higher.
Who will survive the funeral pyre?
See the flames go higher, higher.
Who will survive the funeral pyre?

Again and again, the same words, as they get closer, closer, louder, louder. On placards and banners they hold photos of Hoshiko on the tightrope, along with pictures of another, much younger girl.

She might be dying in there. Right now. She might already be dead.

I feel dizzy.

I turn and run through the trees, bursting through a fire exit into the nearest tent.

HOSHIKO

Around the arena, the big projection screens light up. The image is split, so that my incredulous face looks back at me from one half. The other side shows Greta, so I can see her really clearly now.

She's bound in chains, ankles and wrists, and is looking around desperately. They've dressed her as a butterfly. She's got a little pink flared tutu on and matching wings flutter at her back; they've mechanized them somehow, so that they actually move. The lights on them, and in her hair and on her costume, project tiny pastel butterflies all over the darkened arena in shades of lemon, lilac, baby blue and pink. Her hair's in pigtails and they've accentuated her make-up to give her two little rosy cheeks and big exaggerated lashes.

The desired effect is obvious; they want her to look as young and innocent as possible. And, my God, she does. She's crying up there, looking so frightened that I call out, desperately.

"Greta, stay there! I'm coming!"

Like she has a choice. Like she can go anywhere else.

Far, far below her, a deadly fall away, the orchestra strike up. They're playing the music Silvio always planned to introduce as Greta's signature tune: the Butterfly Lover's Concerto. The soaring notes of a single violin dominate, resonating through the arena. I know what the music's for. It lends a poetic grace and beauty to the deadly dance we're about to perform; makes the crowd feel like the spectacle they're watching is something artistic.

There's one slack wire between Greta and me. As soon as I step on to it, someone lights the log pile and the dead wood immediately roars into ferocious life. Before I've even taken one step, the flames begin licking their angry tongues around the base of Greta's platform.

I sprint across that wire like I'm on a running track. There are no props to steady me and all the careful balance techniques I've mastered go straight out of the window. If I don't think about falling, I won't fall. I run faster than I've ever run in my life, there, on a tiny wire seventy feet off the ground.

The crowd are beside themselves.

I reach her in seconds, scrambling over the sides of the platform. She's completely hysterical, screaming incoherently as the fire laps hungrily about my feet.

Below us, Silvio runs around, directing things like some crazed conductor. At his bidding, the flames produce their own little dance; higher and higher they climb, every time his whip decrees.

The pyrotechnic team have excelled themselves tonight. Somehow, they've managed to alter the colours of the actual flames and they curl from the cauldron in lurid green and a vivid, angry red. Thousands of tiny bubbles float up in the air, a myriad of twinkling colours, catching in our hair, spiralling softly, lightly on to my costume.

I grapple with the chains, but the metal is scorching hot, and it's becoming hard to see through the smoke.

My superhuman ability seems to be continuing though because, within seconds, she's free and clinging on to me.

A line of flames dances all around us now, even above our heads. We're totally surrounded by fire.

The drop below is a deadly one – there's only one way out of here, and there's no way we're both going to make it.

A slack wire works by careful observation of a vital system of balance. What that basically means is that it's impossible for two people to cross it together. You can travel from either side simultaneously if you're weighted exactly the same but, when you cross it from the same side, you have to wait until it's clear before you even so much as put a foot on to the line. Otherwise, it wobbles way too much, twanging the pair of you off. You must respect the laws of weight and balance. Always.

There's no way Greta and I can get on that wire together; we'll both fall and die. Maybe, with a bit of luck and a lot of skill, there might be enough time for one of us to cross it before the flames reach us, but there'll never be enough time for the two of us to make it.

This is what Silvio meant then. It's her or me. The Butterfly or the Cat.

BEN

It's pretty dark in here, and fairly quiet. That band were announcing the start of show time, so that's where everyone must be – in the arena watching Hoshiko. What's going to happen to her?

Lights flash suddenly about my head. Evil-sounding laughter cackles out of nowhere and creepy faces suddenly pop up in the dark.

I must be in the Haunted House. I've heard about it at school: a pop-up exhibition, here for October and November. I know what happens in here. This is the torture tent. It's where they showcase all the old-fashioned interrogation and punishment methods of days gone by. Dreg criminals in live exhibitions.

I run down winding, labyrinth-like corridors, each one leading to a door. There are a cluster of people queuing up patiently outside each one, the carved wooden signs above tempting them in. The Rack, the Iron Maiden, the Thumbscrew, the Tongue Tearer, the Rat Cage, the Spanish Donkey.

Everywhere I turn, there's another door, the sound of screaming coming from each one.

There's nowhere else for me to go. I'm going to be stuck in here for ever.

There's a sudden crack of light coming from the end of one of the corridors and I turn and see Silvio, dressed as a devil. His eyes gleam when he sees me and then the door closes and we plunge into darkness.

I rush forward and throw myself out of a door at the other end of the room.

Behind me, I hear his light footsteps.

At first, I think I've run down a dead end but then I see a handle and realize I'm standing in front of another door. I open it and slip inside.

There are real candles in old fashioned sconces lining the walls and casting an eerie glow over the room. A sign above my head creaks. *Welcome to the Mirror Maze*, it reads in big, jagged letters.

There's black panelling everywhere with just one small gap leading into the maze.

Behind me, I hear the footsteps again.

I squeeze myself through the gap.

Suddenly, I don't know where I am, don't know who I am. My face, petrified, desperate, haunted, stares back at me, once, twice, a hundred times. Mirror after mirror after mirror, everywhere I turn, I see myself.

I sprint down alleyway after alleyway. It can't be that big in here; I must be treading the same path again and again. I can't tell what direction I'm going any more; I can't tell what's left, what's right.

Then, I see him, not just in one of the mirrors, but in every single one – the same face, grinning at me.

Everywhere I look, I see him.

And he sees me.

His face is hungry.

"Got you!" he croons and laughs, a hard, victorious laugh.

It's as if his voice too is reflected from every mirror; the sound echoes all around me.

I don't know where he is. I don't know which of these is real and which are reflections.

"You might as well give yourself up," he says.

He moves then, his hand outstretched, clasping for me. The figure in the mirror nearest to me doesn't get bigger though, or closer: it recedes. He's taken a step away from me, not towards me. And then I realize: he doesn't know which of the images is me either.

"Never!" I tell him, with a lot more confidence than I feel. "You'll never catch me."

I turn and run back the way I came. At least, I think it's the way I came, I don't know.

He's running too: further away and then nearer again. I can hear his footsteps behind me, very close now. I suppose that means he can hear mine.

I stop. Stand still. Press myself against one of the mirrors.

He stops too.

He turns around, looking at every mirror – at the line of versions of me, of versions of him.

He still doesn't know where I am.

He pulls out a gun, aims it at my reflection, swivels around, aims again, pointing it at every version of me he sees. There's a deafening crack and an almighty smash and a mirror to the left of me smashes into a thousand pieces; the image of both of us, obliterated. There's another bang, another crack, and another one, and another.

He's going to shoot every single reflection until he gets to the real me.

I run again, gunshots echoing all around me as I trample over the shards of glass.

The mirror to the left of me explodes.

His face is huge, as if he's next to me. Maybe he is next to me.

Through the bullet hole in the mirror I see into the tent beyond.

I step through the shattered mirror, the cruel jagged spikes cutting into my skin.

I'm out.

I dash out of the tent, across the courtyard. Looking around, I plunge desperately down another path.

He must be seconds behind me; I'm too exposed here. I need to find somewhere to hide out before he sees me.

There's a group queuing outside another attraction and I make my way up to it and push myself amongst them. It's not a big queue; most people are in the arena. What's happening in there? I need to get to Hoshiko, but first, I need to escape from Silvio. We file quickly through the turnstile and in.

He's still not appeared. I should be safe in here for a while.

The exhibition looked quite small from the outside, but inside it's vast, expansive. It's an entire town, one of those you see in old Western films. There are cobbled streets and saloon bars and grocery stores. There's a gun store too, and people are lining up to get their hands on shotguns being handed out by a boy, dressed up as a cowboy.

I hear a gunshot then and see a Pure, crouching behind a powder keg and shooting at someone.

It's a zombie, a real life zombie. No, it's a Dreg; a man, dressed up as a zombie. His ripped clothes reveal black gangrenous flesh underneath. The make-up is so good that it looks real; it looks like his flesh really is rotting.

I wonder how they get him to play the part so well. His mouth hangs open, vacantly and his eyes are wide and empty. His arms are thrust out in front of him and his legs propel him forward in a slow, steady movement. The man shoots at him again and the bullet hits this time. He doesn't react. He wobbles backwards and forward and then crumples down to the floor and the Pure man walks over to him and starts kicking him.

Everywhere I turn I see the same thing. Zombie-like figures being attacked by Pures. Some of them have lost limbs with fleshy stumps where their arms or legs should be. Some of them have eyeballs missing, nothing there but black holes.

I don't think it's make-up. I don't know what to do; I don't know where to go. I turn and look down the movie-set style street for the quickest escape route.

Across the street, making her way into the "hotel", there's a female zombie. She's not dressed in dark rags like the others; the garment she's wearing is ripped and torn now but the vibrant colours still stand out.

Turquoise satin, shimmering with gold and purples.

I know that material.

Her back's to me, but her hair's hanging down in the long braid she always wears.

"Priya!" I call. "Priya! Wait!"

But she doesn't hear me. She keeps walking forward, vanishing into the hotel.

I run after her.

We're in an old-fashioned hotel lounge room, with shabby red velvet sofas and chintz wallpaper. There's no one else in here.

"Priya!"

There she is, turning the corner, moving slowly and steadily. I catch up with her easily and whirl her around.

"Priya. It's me! It's Ben!"

I reach for her. I grab her hands.

"Priya," I beg. "Priya, it's me."

There's no reaction. Her hands feel cold and her arms don't move from their static position. She stares blankly ahead. She can't see me, or feel me. She doesn't know I'm here. I see the contraption she's tied to, keeping her upright. The horror hits me. She's dead; all these "zombies" are dead. They've done something to their arms and legs – mechanized them somehow to make them move – but they're dead.

I sink to the floor and howl.

Not Priya. Not my Priya.

Her children, Nila and Nihal, they'll be waiting for her. Waiting and waiting and she'll never come home.

Suddenly, the whole place lights up. The music stops and an alarm sounds, accompanied by a voice over the loudspeaker.

"Emergency. Major security breach. Please head calmly towards the nearest exit point and assemble in the main courtyard."

I look up. A hooded dummy hinges out of the wall next

to me, a leering grin on its wrinkled face. I rip the hood and mask off the mannequin and put them on, heading out after the crowds. Looking like the Grim Reaper should buy me a few minutes to find Hoshiko.

HOSHIKO

The flames reach my feet first and I smell the disgusting, acrid stench of my own flesh burning.

Despite the pain, I feel calm, as if I've stepped out of my body. There's no fight left in me. I think about Ben, about how different things might have been in another time, another place, another world. I'll think about him now, only him…

I've retreated into myself so much that it takes a while to register that something's changed. The roaring flames are subdued and there's much more smoke now. Alongside the agonizing burning of my feet, there's a different sensation, cooling my upper body.

I'm getting wet.

Looking up, I see water gushing out of pipes in the ceiling, dousing the flames: the emergency sprinkler system.

What's going on? Is this part of the act?

I'm soaking wet by now, but I'm not on fire any more.

The smoke begins to clear. I'm able to see that the crowd are leaving the arena and I hear a voice repeatedly, over the loudspeaker.

"Emergency. Major security breach. Emergency. Major security breach."

My feet are angry and red, my lungs are bursting, and I'm overcome with coughing. I feel half dead, but I'm not.

Whatever's happened, it's saved me. For now.

BEN

I look behind me, there's no sign of Sabatini yet and I join on to the crowd filing obediently into the main arena.

Everyone's looking over their shoulders at the tents I've just come from.

"Did you hear all those shots earlier?" people are saying. "What's going on?"

"It's from the zombie town," someone says. "Haven't you been there yet? You really should, it's so cool. Loads of dead Dregs!"

I don't know what to do. The major security breach is obviously me. At least I don't stand out; everyone else is dressed up too. Still, I can't keep this bloody mask on for ever.

We're all shepherded into the main arena of the Cirque. Everyone's here, including all the performers, surrounded by police. I scan their faces, but there's no sign of Hoshiko.

Where is she? She could be dead too. The thought makes me feel as if someone's punched me in the stomach.

I should give myself up, right now. Who cares if they shoot me? I've already blown my chances of having a nice, sensible, ordinary Pure life by coming into this place, and I wouldn't want one now, anyway. The fact is, I can't go back to my old world, even if they let me. I've changed too much in the last two days to ever return.

I may as well go down fighting, may as well tell the crowds exactly what I think of them. At least I won't be conforming any more, going along with what *they* say. And if there is any sort of afterlife for this crazy, godforsaken human race I'm a part of, at least I can look Hoshiko and Priya in the eyes when I meet them there.

I push forward so that I'm towards the front of the crowd. The more people who see me and hear what I've got to say, the better. I need to get on the stage. If I even make one person think about what they're doing, it won't all have been in vain.

I'm almost at the front when there's a commotion behind me, amongst the performers. The door from the top of a stairway behind them has opened.

She's there, alive, framed in the doorway. Thank God.

She looks so different that I almost don't recognize her at first. The deep midnight blue of her costume is alive with a thousand points of light. Her hair is away from her face and there are sparkles dancing there, too.

She's dazzling.

Ho-shi-ko: an Eastern poem.

The child of the stars.

Burning bright in the darkness,

Lighting up the night.

HOSHIKO

I feel myself sway from side to side, even though I'm propped up between Amina and Alex, one of the fire eaters.

All I want is a bit of peace and quiet, but there's a whole crowd of Pures staring at me – at least, I assume they're Pures. They've all got costumes on, all dressed up as ghosts and monsters and ghouls, as if the costumes represent who they really are.

I don't know how I got here. I don't remember getting down from that platform, just the sound of Greta screaming hysterically afterwards and Amina trying to calm her down.

The pain isn't actually that bad any more. Apart from a dull throbbing and a numbness where I know my feet are, I don't feel much. Amina has some powerful medicines and creams which she just had time to hastily apply, along with bandages, before they ushered us out into the arena.

I didn't ask her about my prospects. There's no point, I know the answer; even if Vivian Baines hadn't given Silvio twenty-four hours, it'd be the end for me now.

I can't balance on that wire with burnt, swollen feet, and Silvio would never allow a Dreg to take up lodgings, food and medical resources without returning any revenue for so long, especially not me.

Still, neither Greta nor I died in the arena tonight – I guess neither of us have given Silvio quite the public acclaim he was after. I suppose I should draw consolation from that: he's failed, in a way. That's what I'll tell him, just before he puts a bullet through my brain.

Seeing her again, knowing she's alive, is such a relief that it takes me a moment or two to register that she's injured. Her feet and ankles are bandaged up, and she's propped up on either side by Amina and a performer I don't recognize.

The eyes of the whole room have turned to watch them; I'm not the only one she's casting a spell over. The crowd start murmuring and I strain my ears to hear what those around me are saying.

"She nearly died," one man reveals. "It was only the emergency alarm that saved her, apparently."

"I was there!" a woman exclaims. "There was a massive fire. She sacrificed herself for the girl."

"Who would've thought?" someone else near me declares, a smug-looking guy with glasses and a pot belly, dressed as a goblin. "A Dreg with feelings!" Everyone laughs, indulgently.

I want to smash his glasses on to his ugly little face. And I want to look him in the eyes when I do it. I'm about to rip my mask off and pull my fist back but, just then, I see Amina looking down at the crowd. She clocks me straight away and her head jerks back in surprise. As our eyes meet, she shakes her head, just a fraction. Not so that anyone else would notice, just enough so that I do. I get it straight away; get that she's telling me not to move, not to do anything, just to wait.

There's something about the Cirque medic that makes you do whatever she says. You just know, somehow, that she's the wisest person you've ever met, and the kindest. It was obvious yesterday that Hoshiko trusted her more than anyone else in the world, and that's exactly how I feel too. I just wait, calmer now, for her to save the day. I don't know how she's going to do it, but I do believe that if there's a way out here, she'll find it.

I lower the mask back down and wait.

Silvio has taken to the stage and all eyes immediately fall on him, the crowd instantly hushing.

He's another one with a commanding presence, but it's not a calming one, like Amina's, or an achingly lovely one, like Hoshiko's; it's a *look at me now and don't take your eyes off me* kind of presence.

How does someone with Dreg status gain such prestige? It's as if the rules don't apply to him; even the police seem to do whatever he says.

His voice when he speaks is so polite and formal that it sounds distinctly sarcastic when he addresses the audience.

"Ladies and gentlemen, we sincerely apologize for the disruption to your evening. Rest assured that you will each be given the opportunity to join us again here at the Dreg Cirque as our esteemed guests on a date of your choosing, absolutely free of charge."

There are mumbles of "too right" and "I should bloody think so" amongst the crowd but, simply by holding up a hand, he hushes them instantly.

"Unfortunately, the inconvenience you have suffered is not quite at an end. You may have heard gunshots tonight, ladies and gentlemen; I regret to inform you that some of them were not a scheduled part of the evening's celebrations. We are seeking a missing person, a white teenage boy, a Pure.

The situation is complicated and very delicate. His name is Benedict Baines – the son of Vivian Baines."

There's a collective gasp of shock.

"We have reason to believe he may be among us, even now."

Everyone immediately starts to look around at each other. Why do I get this feeling that they're all secretly enjoying the drama?

I feel my skin redden; thank goodness for the mask. The desire to be known, to speak out, has gone, replaced with a contrary urge. I need to survive, to get through this, to somehow, impossibly, find a happy ending.

"Ladies and gentlemen, I'm afraid we have no choice but to ask each and every one of you to file through the south exit of the Cirque in a calm and orderly fashion. Anyone wearing a mask, including women and children, we do ask that you briefly remove it for identification purposes. Please, ladies and gentlemen, do not be alarmed."

Sabatini gestures to the wings and two medics come forward with the guard from earlier. There's a bandage around his head but, apart from that, he's very much alive and kicking.

I know I should feel relief that he isn't dead, and I'd like to say I do, but I don't. I just feel that cold knot of fear in my stomach that's already becoming familiar.

He stands there, with Silvio, both of them scanning every person who files past them.

Behind them, the Cirque screens all light up with images of me, and the same message: *Benedict Baines, £1,000,000 reward*.

As soon as I take this mask off, I'm finished.

People begin ushering past the guard in an obedient line, starting from the left hand side of the arena, a few people away from me. I shuffle forward with the rest of the crowd, looking up at Amina helplessly as I get closer and closer to the front.

I count the number in front of me. There are eleven, ten, nine. Any second now they'll tell me to take the mask off. My heart pounds as I get closer and closer.

Suddenly, there's a loud cry from the performers' enclosure.

"Over there! I saw a man over there! He had a gun!" It's Amina, pointing off into the distance, "Behind that curtain!"

The guards and police take off en masse whilst, amongst the crowd, chaos and hysteria set in.

Everyone's screaming, trampling on each other to get out of here, away from the gunman. It's every man for himself as they push and fight their way through, scrambling madly for the doors.

One of the exits is straight through where the performers are being held and the barriers dividing us and them are pushed down as the Pures attempt to reach freedom.

I don't know what to do myself, except turn and head that way too. I work my way against the flow of the hysterical crowd, joining the people pushing their way into the enclosure.

Once I'm in, I fight my way through the crowd, trying to find Amina and Hoshiko, although I have no idea what I'm going to do if I reach them, or what I'm going to do if I don't. Without warning, I am hurled down to the ground and someone covers my head with a cloth of some kind so that I can hardly breathe. I struggle to resist, but I feel myself pushed by strong arms into some kind of box. It all goes dark and then there's nothing.

HOSHIKO

The pain makes me feel woozy and I find it impossible to stay alert. After a while, I become vaguely aware that I'm being supported out of the Cirque. It takes ages; we seem to all be trying to get out at the same time. In the end I think I must zone out completely because the next thing I know I'm back in the san and Amina's gently shaking me.

"Hoshiko? Hoshi?" She's repeating my name over and over again. "You need to concentrate on what I'm about to say."

I hear the urgency in her tone, and try to pull my mind back to consciousness. It's hard though, having to wrench myself back from the warm and cosy place I've been. I open my eyes, trying to focus on what she's saying.

"Listen to me. Listen," she repeats. "Don't move from this room. Stay here, the pair of you. I may be gone a while but, I promise, I'll come back."

I nod, and she must be satisfied, because she leaves and I'm left there alone, puzzling over her words.

She definitely said "the pair of you", but there's only me in here. Me and a big black equipment box. I look at it. When did it suddenly appear in here?

Things keep getting crazier. It begins to move and there's a banging sound coming from inside it. There's a latch, and without really thinking about what I'm doing, I bend down and open it. The show must still be going on, and I must be part of some crazy magic illusion because the box flings open and Death himself leaps out.

BEN

I feel myself being carried along and then, eventually, dropped down. Have the police got me, or someone even more sinister? I wonder if I'm going to be buried alive. Is this how it's all going to end? Is this my coffin?

I bang frantically on the wooden lid, just inches from my head. Whatever horrific things are waiting for me outside, I'd rather face them, rather face anything, than stay here like this, slowly suffocating. On my own.

Thankfully, I'm not banging for long before the lid starts to open. As soon as I see a crack of light, I push up and scramble out as quickly as I can. I can't believe what I see – not a group of police, not some kind of firing squad, but her: Hoshiko.

She looks even more confused than me for a minute but as soon as I pull off the mask her face lights up, and she smiles, this huge wide smile, and throws herself into my arms.

I've never really seen her happy.

The prickliness and awkwardness which radiated off her before in waves before has gone. She's soft and warm and clinging.

For ages, we stay like that and then I pull back.

"Are your feet OK?"

"Shh, I don't want to waste time. I don't know how long we've got. They're going to kill me tonight." She says it so matter of factly, like it hardly matters at all.

"Please – just tell me, how are your feet?"

"They're fine." She pulls back and grins at me. "Who

cares about my feet? I don't think I need them where I'm going!"

She's definitely changed from how she was before. She puts a finger on my lips and then she kisses me.

I thought I felt lightheaded before, in that box, but now my head reels. The fierce hunger in her lips seizes hold of me too. I don't think we could stop now if we tried. But we don't try, either of us.

HOSHIKO

When I kiss him, it's like I'm free-falling.

I should stop, but I don't. I couldn't, even if I wanted to.

They can torture me, burn me, kill me, but they'll never be able to take this away. I'll keep it safe inside me, always, no matter what.

BEN

After our kiss, we talk. About everything. About her life, and mine, about our families and our friends. About silly things and serious things.

I don't tell her about the zombies, about what happened to Priya. Perhaps I will do, one day, but I can't go there yet. If I speak about it, it will make it real, and it's too awful to be real, too horrible to acknowledge. I take the images, churning inside me like molten lava, and I push them back, deep down inside my gut. I bury them away, magma bubbling under the earth's crust; far too powerful, far too strong to be contained for ever, but, for now, obediently seething away inside.

I concentrate on her instead: the only good thing left in this world.

No one comes in for hours and hours, and it feels like we're suspended in this bubble where nothing can ever hurt us again. I know we should be panicking, should be afraid, but we're not. We're just relaxed and comfortable. Languid is the word I would use. The world has gone mad – it went mad long ago – and I don't know if either of us will get out of this alive, but right now, I feel calm. All that matters right now is here, in this room.

I know most people might think I've been lucky. I've always had everything I've ever wanted, materially at least: big house, expensive clothes, good school. Despite this though, I've never really felt whole before. It was always as if there was always something missing, something lacking.

It's not lacking any more. Here, in this crazy place, poised on the brink of death, I know with an absolute certainty that I've found myself.

HOSHIKO

Later, much later, Amina comes in. We're only sitting on the bed talking, but we both leap apart at the same time. We giggle, embarrassed laughs, as if she's caught us doing something we shouldn't be, which she hasn't, thankfully.

She's not laughing though, far from it, and the look on her face kills our humour dead too.

"Listen," she says. "We haven't much time. Hoshi, any minute now they're going to come for you. As for you, Ben, now your family have finally agreed to go public with your disappearance, they're running with the implication that you're here through coercion. They've drafted in pretty much the whole police force to find you; it's not going to take them long."

There's a few seconds' silence and then Amina speaks very slowly and carefully.

"Ben, if you've had enough, it probably isn't too late. I'm sure Mummy will be only too happy to cover it up. She has the power to make it all go away: a misunderstanding, a moment of teenage madness. You can go back to your old life and forget all about your circus adventure."

"No!" He puts his arm around me, squeezes me tight. "I'm staying with Hoshiko."

"This is the last chance you're going to get. If you make this decision now, that'll be it for you. There'll be no going back. Not ever."

Ben hugs me even more tightly. "I know."

"Good. Here's what's going to happen."

She looks specifically at Ben now.

"This is not something we would ever normally tell a Pure unless he'd been through months of proving himself, months of resistance work."

He nods gravely; he must understand this more than I do.

"It was the circus folk who saved you earlier. They surrounded us, concealed us while we got you into the box. They risked their lives for you."

"Why?"

"Because pretty much every single adult Dreg has made a pledge to do anything they can to end this madness. They're going to help us get you both out of here, for good."

I don't understand what she means.

"What do you mean, a pledge? Why didn't I know about it before?"

She looks a bit sheepish. "I kept meaning to tell you, but the time's never been right. I was going to do it the other night, when we were standing at the window, but you seemed so tired..."

"Tired? There's some secret pledge and you didn't tell me about it because I was tired! I'm not a child, Amina! I'm not Greta!"

"I know. I'm sorry. But you *were* a child, when I first found out. I had to keep it from you until you were old enough to understand."

"You should have told me years ago! Don't you trust me?"

"Yes." She looks directly into my eyes. "I trust you more than anyone. I'm sorry. I'm really sorry, but there isn't time for this now. Right now, I need to save your life."

"But why us? Why would anyone help Ben and me over everyone else? Dregs die every day."

"Because I managed to persuade the people who matter that you'll be useful, that's why. More than useful, maybe. The son of Vivian Baines, of all people, runs away from home, breaks into the Cirque and assaults a member of its security staff, all because he's fallen for a Dreg girl. And not just any Dreg girl: the Cat, the most famous Cirque artiste ever. It's massive. Can you imagine what this will do to the government's credibility when it gets out?"

She looks at me and her eyes soften.

"Hoshiko, you're the only thing that's kept me going in this place. I will not stand back and watch you die. You've been given a chance, both of you: make it count. Get the hell out of here and don't look back."

Why does it feel like she's saying goodbye?

"Aren't you coming?"

"No." She sighs. "It's too late for me."

"But you can't give up!"

She's smiling at me, but there are tears running down her face. "I'm not giving up. I'm helping you. Knowing you've made it. Knowing you're out there somewhere, free from this place, that's what will keep me going now. That's what will make everything worth it. You two, you're the future. Don't ever let anyone tell you that you can't change things – you can. I've known there's something special about you since you were five years old."

I know Amina well enough by now to know that she

won't change her mind, but I can't leave her behind; can't just forget about the people I love.

"What about Greta?" I ask her. "She has to come too."

"No." Her tone is firm. "It's too risky. We'll never be able to smuggle all three of you out. I'll look after her, I promise."

She's lying to me, just like I lie to Greta. She can't protect her, not really.

"I can't leave Greta! I need her! I need you!" Somewhere, a part of me knows that I'm making too much noise.

"Hoshiko, be quiet now. You don't have a choice. I have to go; I've got to get things in place."

I try to stop sobbing, to calm down, I really do, but I can't get control of myself.

Ben tries to hug me, but I push him away.

"How can I leave Greta here? How can I leave you? How can I?"

"You must." She takes hold of me. "Shhh," she whispers. "Shhh now."

She wraps me in her arms, rocking me back and forth until, eventually, I calm down. Then she makes her promise again.

"I'll watch Greta's back. I'll make sure she's next out, I give you my word."

I manage a nod.

"OK," I finally agree, reluctantly. "If you really think it's the only way."

"Good girl. Someone will come for you when the show starts. I'm not sure how yet. Until then, lie low."

She hands me a plastic bag. "There are some oatcakes in

here, and some water. It's all I could get my hands on, not much, but more than most of the performers are getting tonight. Make sure you eat; God knows when you'll get the chance for food again."

She wraps her arms around me and kisses the top of my head, and then she turns and leaves and it's just the two of us again.

We've barely known each other three days. He's giving up his family, his status, his world, for me. I'm leaving behind Amina, Greta and the only life I've ever known. It's madness, but it's the only thing there is to do.

BEN

When Amina's gone, we sit there, munching on dry oatcakes, both trying to take in the enormity of what's going on.

These four walls, this girl sitting next to me, they've already become more real than my family, than the place I've always called home.

It hurts my head, thinking about who my mother is, what she's done. In a way though, it makes it easier to face what I'm doing – walking away from everything over a girl I've only just met.

Her eyes meet mine, and my breath catches in my throat.

There's so much pain in her expression: the thought of leaving Greta and Amina behind is breaking her heart. There's a glimmer of something else there too though, and it's the same look I know is in my eyes.

This is real. What we've found is real and, alongside all the pain, it's exhilarating.

She stands up, and we move together, like a dance that we've rehearsed. Somehow, we're synchronized. Her skin is so soft, her dark hair feels like silk in my fingers, her breath on mine is sweet.

We're under that spell again. It feels like nothing will ever break it, like nothing will ever tear us apart, but it does. Suddenly and abruptly, the enchantment ends. There's movement outside, urgent footsteps marching up the corridor.

We spring apart and she whispers, "In the box!"

I jump into the equipment box and she closes the lid with a bang, just in time. I'm lying scrunched up in the dark, again.

A door opens and I hear muffled voices. I strain to make out what they're saying, but all that's distinguishable are the words, "Silvio… Benedict Baines… and interrogation," before I hear her yelling out in pain, the door slamming shut and then … silence.

HOSHIKO

The two guards who enter so politely obviously aren't ones for conversation. They hardly say anything, just pull me, kicking and screaming, down the corridors and outside. They keep dragging me, past all the buildings, past all the animals, past the sideshows. It's not until we're almost at the steps that I realize where they're taking me. We're at Silvio's trailer. Wow, hallowed turf. I don't remember anyone, ever, being allowed in here. I can't suppress the feeling of curiosity; I'm about to see into his secret lair.

They push me up the stairs, shove me through the door and leave me there, locking it behind them.

I look around, trying to see if there's anything here that might reveal the man behind the monster.

It's luxurious, I guess, but then compared to what we're used to, that's not hard. There's a couple of dark velvet sofas, a big TV screen, a table, chairs, a fairly modest kitchen area and two doors which lead off, presumably, to his bedroom and the toilet.

A huge display cabinet takes up most of one wall. Inside, dozens of gold trophies and awards – all the ones the Cirque has won over the years. *Best Entertainment Venue*, *People's Choice Award*, that kind of thing. I wonder how he manages to keep hold of them all given that, underneath his superior facade, he's a Dreg just like the rest of us. Not just any Dreg though, not if the whispered stories are true.

One of the walls is filled with photos. In each one, he proudly poses with some Pure celebrity or other. Pop stars, film stars, politicians – anyone who's anyone, basically. I don't recognize most of them – it's not like we get much access to news or media or music here – but I can spot a few who I remember watching the show from the VIP area.

Every time someone important comes to the Cirque, Silvio makes a massive fuss, creeping around them, throwing himself at their feet – *we're so honoured to have you here. I've always admired your work*. It always makes me want to throw up.

In every single photo, he's in full ringmaster get-up. This is his home, but there's no evidence of a real person existing underneath at all: no personal touches, no little trinkets or ornaments. What did I expect, pictures of his family? Hardly likely, given what they say.

There's the sound of footsteps on the stairs outside, the door lock turns; it's him.

He looks at me for a few seconds with that penetrating stare. "How about we cut out all the crap and you tell me where he is?"

"I'm not sure what you mean, Silvio, sorry. Where who is?"

He holds up Ben's poster. "Young Benedict Baines here. Quite the handsome young man, isn't he?"

"He's a Pure. I hate Pures. Why would I conceal one?"

"Oh, so he's concealed, is he?"

"I don't know, I thought that's what you were suggesting."

"I will ask you one more time... *Where is he*?"

There's a pause. I look at him and repeat, slowly.

"I don't know."

He stares at me again for a few seconds. His eyes are steely and then, he loses his cool; that slick façade seems to be slipping more and more often lately. He slams his hand down on the table.

"Where is he?"

"I don't know."

"My neck's on the line for this. They're asking me all sorts of questions. Why don't I know what's happening in my own Cirque? Why can't I keep a tighter track of security? Why are my Dregs out of control? And Baines, the boy's mother, breathing down my neck – *Where the hell is my son? Why haven't you found him yet? And why, why, why, why is that bloody tightrope walker still alive?*"

He's shaking. His voice drops and he snarls at me. "I will not lose my standing here because of you. *Where is he*?"

I look at him. Doesn't he realize what he means to Vivian Baines? What he means to all of them?

"Silvio, you're the same as me, don't you see that? You mean nothing to her, to any of them. You're just another dirty Dreg to them, just the same as the rest of us."

"No! I'm nothing like you! Nothing! I'm a Pure! I've always been a Pure, I just need them to see that!"

He's actually insane.

I try a different tack, a gentler one. Maybe I can reason with him, make him see what he's become.

"Your mother gave up everything to be with your father. Do you think she'd want to see you like this?"

I've made a mistake; his eyes bulge with fury, his face whitens with shock. He puts his hands round my neck, squeezes my throat so that I can't breathe. He's going to choke me to death, right here, right now.

"How dare you? How dare you mention my mother? How dare you presume to tell me how to feel? I'll tell you something, shall I? My mother was weak. A weak, careless fool. She sacrificed my destiny, sacrificed everything I should have been, everything I could have been, because she couldn't control her urges! My mother was nothing more than a whore!"

There's no breath left in my body. I can feel my head swimming, see everything fading away around me.

He lets go suddenly, and I gasp for air.

He stands back, watching me with his arms crossed. "Is that enough to change your mind, or shall I keep going?"

My throat is burning, and when I speak, the words come out in a hoarse croak.

"OK, Silvio, you're right. I do know where he is."

He nods, eagerly.

"That's my girl. Come on now, tell Silvio and the whole thing can go away. You won't hear another word about it."

He's practically purring.

"Do you promise? You promise you won't be angry any more?"

"Of course not." He strokes my hair, benevolently. "I'll be so proud of you. I'll protect you. I won't let anyone hurt you."

"I didn't know what to do it about it; I was afraid. It's a relief to finally confess everything," I tell him. "I know you only ever want what's best for the Cirque."

"That's right," he smiles. "I'm glad someone finally

appreciates how hard my job is. I have to think of the bigger picture sometimes."

"He's..." I keep looking right into those evil little eyes and I smile at him serenely. "Actually, I've changed my mind. I don't think I will tell you, after all."

I know it's reckless but he's going to torture me whatever I do and I can't help myself; seeing him so desperate makes me feel powerful. For the first time ever, I hold the trump card.

With an exasperated cry, he leaps up, twists my arm behind my back and pushes his ugly, ratty face into mine. I keep smiling.

"The thing is, I don't mean to disappoint you and all that, but it doesn't really matter what you do to me; I'll never tell you where he is. We're going to destroy your silly little circus. We're going to bring you down."

It feels like we stay there like that for ages, freeze-framed. Finally, he breaks my gaze, releases his hold – a minor victory.

"Do you know, I rather feel you're telling the truth? Looks like I'll have to rethink my strategy a bit, up the game. You've made your choice, Hoshiko. What happens now is all down to you. I'd like you to remind yourself of that later; all down to you." He leaves the room, slamming the door and locking it behind him.

I'm pretty sure I know where he's gone. Doing the dirty work isn't really his style, not often, anyway. He'll get his heavies in for that.

They'll probably start with my feet; they're so badly wounded already that the job's half done for them. Maybe not – when they catch Dreg thieves, they chop off their fingers.

Concealing a fugitive has to be a worse crime than that.

I think of Ben again and run my throbbing hand over my nose, eyes, mouth. I touch my arms, my skin. I've never really thought about it before, but now it feels alive, responsive, in a way it never has before. It's tingly, still, everywhere he touched it. He said it was soft, said it was perfect. Maybe it won't be for much longer. Maybe it will be burnt, all over. Or cut into. Mutilated.

What if he doesn't feel the same about me after that? What if he never looks at me like that again? Never touches me again like I'm something precious, something beautiful.

I don't know what they'll do to me. I don't know how intact I'll be at the end, but I do know that what I said is true.

I'll never give him up. I'd rather die.

Three days ago, I hadn't even met him, but I'd already die a hundred deaths for him.

BEN

It feels as if this is the millionth time now that I've lain helplessly in this room, wondering what the hell to do next. This time, it feels even worse than the others. This time, I know it's because of me that they've dragged her out of here. They're not going to ask her politely where I am; not going to just take her word for it when she denies knowing anything. The stakes are too high. They're going to torture her, because of me.

If they so much as harm a hair on her head, I swear I'll kill them all. I'll find a gun and I'll shoot them dead. There's no point in hiding out here now; the only thing left to do is hand myself in. There'll be no point in interrogating Hoshi if they've found me.

I get out of the box, running as quickly as I can down the corridor. I'll turn myself in to the first person I see.

In front of me, the door at the end of the building opens, and a policeman frames the doorway. I walk slowly towards him with my hands up, so that he can get a good look at my face.

"I'm Ben Baines. I'm the one you're looking for."

HOSHIKO

I pace the floor, waiting.

It's an awful feeling, knowing Silvio's going to come back for me. Or someone is. Come back to do what?

I turn the tap in the kitchen and water gushes out. Gratefully, I gulp some down.

I look in the fridge. There's nothing in there but a piece of dry cheese. I sniff it and then picture Silvio gnawing on it; holding it in his little paws, scraping it with his pointy little teeth. I put it back. I'm hungry, but I can't bring myself to eat that.

I try the handles on the other doors. They're all locked. I feel an inexplicable sense of disappointment. Why am I so curious? What does it matter to me where the great Silvio Sabatini sleeps? I'd love to peer inside his wardrobe though, rifle through his personal effects.

I search through all the cupboards and find a black marker pen in a drawer in the kitchen. With the pepper pot, I smash the frame on every picture and draw devil horns and a tail on to all the grinning Silvios.

I wish they would come and get it over with; do whatever it is they're going to do.

This waiting, it's torture too; it's torture waiting for the torture to begin.

Gradually the sky outside lightens and a pink smudge starts to blear the far horizon.

What's Ben going to do now? He doesn't know anyone else here, just me and Amina. I hope he makes it out, that they look after him when I'm gone.

Will his mother forgive him? Will they let him back into the family home? He poses a threat now, surely, to all the values she holds dear. She's not a normal mother; there's no softness in her – what if she has him killed? She'd do that, wouldn't she, rather than accept what he's done? Maybe she'll just disown him instead – but that would be even worse for someone like him.

How would he cope if he was thrown into the Dreg world? He's not been born to it; he's not like me.

People like me, we don't get happy endings. We live terrible lives for a few years, if we're lucky, and then we die terrible deaths, alone. I've known this all my life, so why am I so frightened now?

Because he came into this circus and brought me hope, that's why. I dared to dream, for the first time ever. He's made me feel things I have no right to feel. I should never have allowed myself to think, even for a minute, that we might have a future together – as if we live in some kind of fairy story, instead of right here in Hell.

I've existed for a while, and now I'm going to die. What's the point of it all been?

The worst thing of all is that sometimes, when I've been up there, under the lights, my body responding to the vibrating twang beneath me, the crowd calling my name, I've felt almost happy. I've liked their attention, liked the feeling of knowing how good I am. More fool me, then. I'm just their plaything. Just a cheap, replaceable puppet on a wire.

BEN

The police officer stares at me, open mouthed, for a few seconds and then whispers, "Be quiet. For God's sake, keep your voice down!"

"Why? I'm handing myself to you on a plate. You can call off the search. None of the performers know I'm here, I swear. I've been hiding out on my own."

He turns back round to the open door he's just entered through, shutting and locking it, before turning back to me. I don't like the way he does it: as if he's up to no good.

"Ben, Benedict, whatever you call yourself, you certainly know how to cause a stir. I hope you appreciate what everyone's gone through for you and your little tightrope walker."

He lowers his voice right down, so that I have to strain to hear him. "Listen carefully; I don't know how long we've got. It's OK; I'm not going to hurt you. My name is Jack: I'm a friend."

I look at him, what does he mean? Does he think I'm some poor innocent boy who's been kidnapped by the Dregs?

"Amina contacted me. We're getting you and the girl out."

I don't believe it. Everyone knows the police hate Dregs. It's a prerequisite for joining up – pretty much the only prerequisite. That, and a love of violence, of course.

"They're swarming over this Cirque looking for you," he carries on. "We have to get you out, now. Amina said something about an equipment box?"

I nod, dumbly; this wasn't what I was expecting.

"You need to get back in it."

"I can't," I tell him. "I'm giving myself up."

Now it's his turn to look confused.

"They've got Hoshiko!" I cry.

"Look, you playing the martyr isn't going to help her. They know you've been with her – you didn't do a very good job of hiding your trail."

He's far too calm about all this. Why can't he see how urgent the situation is?

"They're probably torturing her right now! Why are you wasting time on me? She's the one in danger!"

"I know that, but I'm not one of the bloody Cirque magicians, am I? Let's get you out and to safety, and then we can work out if there's anything we can do about your girlfriend."

"You mean there might not be?"

He looks at me, and shakes his head slowly. "Honestly, mate, you need to prepare yourself for the fact that we probably won't get her out of here. She's locked up; if I just walk up and try to move her, they'll smell a rat."

"But we can't leave her!"

"OK, you're worried about her, I get that. But you won't help anyone in this state. Calm down, get in that box, let me get you out of here to somewhere safer and then we'll see what we can come up with."

He looks towards the door, nervously. "Any minute now we're going to be joined by my less sympathetic colleagues, and you certainly won't see her again if you're both under lock and key."

Is he genuine? He has a friendly face; his mouth turns naturally upward, so it looks like he's smiling all the time and his twinkly green eyes look kind. If he wanted to harm me, he could have done that already. There must be a reason why he hasn't called anyone else.

The sense of what he's saying registers. If I'm going to get her out, I need to trust him. What choice do I have?

"I've got to be calm, I've got to be calm, I've got to be calm." Reciting it under my breath like that helps to keep the panic fluttering in my chest contained.

"I've got to be calm, I've got to be calm, I've got to be calm." I keep repeating it in my head as we hurry back to the san and I climb back into the box, as he lowers the lid and darkness descends, and as I feel the box move, wheeled down the corridor to God knows where.

HOSHIKO

It's ages before Silvio returns and, straight away, it's obvious something's changed. He's not tense any more; he's back in control.

He smiles at me, leaning in really close so that it's hard not to flinch. Then he treads, very carefully and deliberately, on my burnt feet. The pressure of his weight sears through to the bone, but I'll never let him see my pain. I stare back into his face, unblinking.

"Hoshiko." He's shaking his head at me, fondly. "I know you. I know how you work, know how stubborn you are. We'd be here all day if I let this go on." He grinds his feet down. "Never mind, I think I have a quicker way. Come with me."

He grabs me by the arm, pulling me out of the trailer and across the courtyard. The fact that I'm injured is hardly relevant, given the circumstances. He drags me across the Cirque, into the arena. A hushed silence fills the vast room. What's he got planned?

He sits down in one of the seats, leaning back, arms crossed.

"I know you, Hoshiko. I told you. Doesn't matter what I do to *you*, you won't talk. Now, have a good look around. See anything to make you change your mind?"

The gleeful, excited look in his eyes makes my blood run cold.

I look around the arena, look in the stalls and on the stage. I look at him again, and his eyes flick upwards. I raise my lids, slowly, and look up at the wire, at *my* wire.

There, high above our heads, the silhouette of a body hangs. Suspended, swaying gently like a huge pendulum – a grotesque parody of how it once swung on the trapeze during the shows.

Silvio clicks a button on a remote he pulls from his pocket. The screens light up, confirming what I already know.

It's Amina.

I don't really know what happens next. Everything around me disappears and it's just me, looking through a dark tunnel. At the end of that tunnel is Amina, dangling there, swinging backwards and forward.

Dead. Dead because of me.

I think I might be crying, might be screaming, but I'm not sure. I've split into a thousand pieces: there are fragments of me everywhere.

Silvio must realize that there's no point trying to get anything coherent out of me right now because he hauls me back down the corridor, towards the cells.

He stops, suddenly, and pivots back round in the other direction.

"On second thoughts, let's put you in here instead. There's some real food for thought here, literally in some cases. Once you've stopped being so weak and hysterical, you can have a good look round and see where you're going to end up." He laughs, and pushes his face close to mine, so that all I can see are his dark eyes, glinting. His breath is rancid.

"We don't like to waste anything here at the Cirque: have a good look round the Recycling Room, Hoshiko. I shall enjoy thinking of you in here!"

He pushes me into the room and I hear the sound of the door being locked from other outside.

I don't register anything about where I am, or take in anything about my surroundings, not for ages. It's a long, long time until I calm down. Until the strange wailing sound, which I guess must be coming from me, stops.

Exhaustion finally wins and there's just the shell of me, rocking backwards and forwards, backwards and forwards, like the swinging body on the wire.

BEN

I've never felt so useless in all my life.

All those times I watched my mother going off to work in her big car. I used to feel proud of how important she was. *Dreg Control Minister*. I never even though about what it meant that much. When I was younger, it was enough that all my friends' parents thought she was so great, that we got to go to all the top football games, got the best tables in all the most expensive restaurants. As I got older though, I didn't want to know. That's the truth.

It was easier not to know.

I keep hearing the words Hoshi said yesterday: *Your mum tortures Dregs, did you know that? She's the person responsible for hundreds of Dreg deaths a week.*

She was right; it's true.

Only last week, I heard her on the phone, issuing orders: *Their numbers are growing too rapidly. We need to cut costs, manage the situation.* What did she actually mean by that?

I don't need to think about it too hard. How many times has she told me that Dregs aren't really human, that they don't deserve any rights? She says we don't go *far enough* at the moment. She thinks Dregs should be, somehow, *eliminated*. That's the phrase I've heard her use, again and again – at conferences, at dinner parties, at family barbecues.

The public admire her because of her tough stance on Dregs. That's why she's the front runner for the leadership.

I love my mother.

I *loved* my mother.

I don't love her any more.

How can I love her now, after everything I've seen? After everything I know? How can anyone love someone who has been responsible for the repression and victimization of all these people?

I can't.

My childhood, my past, my whole life… when I look back, it all feels tainted, sour.

I remember all the times she'd be on the television, or the news feed on the PureWeb. How excited I'd get, seeing her face.

Sometimes, I used to hide outside and spy on her when she was working in her office. I'm sure she knew I was there really, peeping through a crack in the door, as she made her phone calls. *Minister Baines: access code one-four-nine-eight-six.*

Access code *one-four-nine-eight-six*.

No one's supposed to know that code. She should have been more careful, I guess, but she trusted me. Why would she need to be cautious around her own son?

A possibility starts to form in my mind. It's not a way to save Hoshiko, but it is a way to be heard. To do what I should I have done long ago: to speak out, to stand up.

There's not much in the little room I'm hidden in. A kettle, a desk, a computer.

"Jack? That computer. Is it connected to the PureWeb?"

"It is. Why? Fancy a little look at yourself? Don't turn it on unless you do, you're a celebrity now."

"So we could get a live feed up?"

He flips open the laptop. "Yeah. Why?"

"Because I've got an idea…"

HOSHIKO

I can't really remember much about my real mother, no matter how much I keep trying. She's this soft feeling I get inside when I try to look back: soft and sweet and insubstantial, like the candyfloss they sell here.

When they took me from her, Amina filled the big hole inside me. Amina's been a kind mother, a wise older sister, a best friend. Amina's been everything.

All I want to do is curl up and die, howl myself into oblivion.

I can't though. One thought manages to penetrate the grief. It starts off as a whisper, but then it gets louder and louder, so that it's a shout, a scream, a siren going off in my head. Greta.

Greta will be next.

Silvio knows how much I love her – everyone knows.

I have to concentrate on Greta now, have to take that wracking pain, so raw that I feel like my insides are being ripped out, and bury it away to take out and deal with at a later date.

I look up for the first time.

Where am I?

The room is large and poorly lit. I can make out rows of shelves stretching away from me and strange shapes lining the walls.

There's a switch by the door and, when I press it, the room is bathed in a clinical light from the old-fashioned fluorescent tube lights which reach down each row. What did Silvio call the place?

The Recycling Room.

At the very front, bound by a chain to a table, there's a large book. It looks expensive. I peer at its title. "Deposit Ledger. Only authorised personnel to enter details." I touch its front cover. It's bound in a very soft, very light material. It's not like leather and it's not like fur, but it's not like cotton either. It's warm, almost, to the touch.

It feels a bit like skin.

My hand shoots back.

I'm being ridiculous.

I walk slowly down the first row. It's lined with big chest freezers, quietly humming to themselves. I pause at the first one. It's got a big label above it: *Research Matter*. I'm scared to open it.

There was something about the excitement in Silvio's eyes when he locked me in here that, even amidst all the pain, managed to penetrate.

I open it slowly. It's crammed full of transparent bags, each one bulging with its tightly packed contents. I reach slowly in and lift one out. It's heavy, and inside is a frozen mass of purple. It's labelled, and I lift it up further towards the lights to read what it says.

Liver, lungs, heart: Slavic. 20/3/2045. I drop it, quickly, and it lands with a clunk on top of all the other bags, rocking gently.

I take a deep breath and force myself to pick up a bag from a different section of the freezer. *Kidneys: South Asian. 16/2/2045*, it reads. I shiver, and place it gently back down. I stare at the rest of the bags. I can't bring myself to pick any more up. There must be at least fifty in this one chest alone.

I slam the chest shut.

I don't want to see any more. Don't want to go on, but I have to. I have to know what else is in here, the dark underbelly of the Cirque.

The next chest has a different label above it. *Animal/Dreg Food: Flesh.*

I don't spend long looking into that one. I don't need to and I certainly don't want to. One glance in is enough to confirm what it holds. More transparent bags, bulging with diced meat.

The whole row is filled with chests like this. I count them. Ten.

Ten chests full of meat for the animals, full of meat for us, to eat. Where does it come from? My brain is screaming the answer at me. I shut it down. Breathe. Somehow. Keep walking down the long stretching corridors.

At the top, I turn around and head down the second aisle. There are no freezers in this row, just shelves, lined with jars. Jars with things floating in them.

I don't want to look.

I have to look.

I carefully lift down the first heavy jar. The labels on it are completely unnecessary. Dozens of eyeballs stare back at me, suspended in a vinegary liquid.

I drop the jar. It falls to the hard ground with a smash, the vinegary contents sploshing out, up on to my legs. Some of the eyeballs roll down the aisle, under the counters, but most of them stay there, looking at me in a mushy, accusing cluster.

I step over them, whispering an apology.

There are loads of jars on the shelves, at least twenty. More eyeballs. Fingers, disjointed and lost, for ever separated from the hands they once belonged to. Dismembered tongues, long and obscene looking.

What do they do with them all?

There are boxes too. I take one down. "Ivory." It rattles as I lift it. I prise open the lid. It's full of teeth. Big brown rotten ones. Tiny white milky ones. I slam it shut.

Further down there's a new section. Huge horizontal lockers line the sides. It takes all my strength to pull one open. Eventually, it springs out, nearly knocking me over.

Dozens of human skulls leer at me.

Who were they? Did I know them?

I must have known them.

I think about all the friends I've lost, over the years. Petra. Michaela. Andrez. Paul. Raj. Dozens of faces flood my memory. Is this what became of them all?

There are sacks hanging up in the next aisle. One is labelled Brown, another Black, another Blonde. I take down the first one, pulling it open by the drawstrings which seal it. I reach my hand in tentatively, jolting back when it touches something. It's like a big soft nest. It's hair; the sack is full of hair. Why? What's it for?

The final aisle has a large plastic sign attached to the shelf fronts, the same one on both sides. The writing is in thick black capital letters, underscored in red.

CIRQUE CADAVERS. FOR AUCTION. DO NOT TAMPER WITH.

There's something up on the top shelf but it's too high

up to see what it is. I grab a stepladder from the corner and mount the steps. There's a huge jar, but it's facing away from me. I prise it back round.

A decapitated head, floating in liquid.

I read the label. "Violent Death. Not in performance. Estimated value: 45-50K.

The next jar is bigger. There's a whole body crammed into it. I know who it is as soon as I see jagged tears on the flesh. It's Sarah: Emmanuel's partner. "Under auction," the label reads. "Performance death. Current bid: 300K."

There's another jar, next to it. It's got two corpses floating in it; they fit in there easily because there's not much left of either one. Astrid and Luna, or all that remains of them.

Their bodies are mangled red stumps but, for some reason, the sharks have left their faces alone and they remain intact from the shoulders upward. They float besides one another, mirror images even in death. This is how they started life, side by side, suspended in fluid. It's how they ended life, immersed in water while the sharks tore them apart.

Next to them is an empty jar. I rotate it around so that I can read the label. The ink is still wet; it must have just been written. "Death by hanging. Cirque veteran. Not in performance."

This jar is for Amina.

I push it away, get down from the ladder somehow and fall to my hands and knees, retching, and that's when I see it. Someone's been in here while I've been looking around. Right in front of me, in the doorway, gazing at me with its one quizzical eye, the head of Greta's doll. Just the head, the stuffing hanging from the bottom. Alongside, the pieces of her body. Arms, legs, a torso, all separated, in a neat little pile.

The message could not be clearer.

I start screaming. Once I start, I can't stop. I run down the aisles, pulling everything of the shelves, out of the freezers, out of the boxes. I hurl it at the walls, throw it to the ground, all of it. I trample on it and crush it and grind it beneath my feet.

I will destroy everything in this room. I will not let them make a penny's worth of profit out of these people they've butchered.

The door opens and three guards rush in.

I'm by the ladder and I climb up it again as quickly as I can. They run towards me.

I pick up the biggest jar I can manage, the decapitated head, unscrew the lid and rain the contents down on them. They're covered in a flood of vinegar and the head hits one of the guard's upturned faces before falling to the ground with a wet thunk.

They grab me and drag me away. It takes three of them. I scratch and bite and claw; the Cat has turned wild.

BEN

We go over things one more time. What I need to say, what I mustn't say, how I should look at the camera the whole time, how I should speak. Jack wants to write out a script, but I refuse. Better not to be too over-rehearsed, Mother always says – it never sounds as heartfelt if you are.

Funny, that I'm following her advice – the very woman I'm about to expose.

I take a deep breath. "OK. I'm ready. Let's get this over with."

"You really think this'll work?"

"Unless her code has changed in the last two days."

Jack clicks on the PureWeb explorer button. The news stream is all about our story, like he said it would be. There's a split screen: my face is on half of it, Hoshiko's the other. Except it doesn't look like the Hoshi I know at all, and it doesn't look like me either.

She stares menacingly at the camera, a huge scowl on her face. She's got the look on it she had when she told me about how much she hates the Pures, about what they did to her. She looks kind of intimidating.

The photo of me is about four years old. I'm all cute and baby faced. Grinning at the camera innocently, wearing my school uniform.

We listen to the report for a few minutes. *The search for Benedict Baines continues. Benedict, son of Vivian Baines, has been missing, believed abducted, since Saturday evening. Police are following several leads, and are now questioning the infamous*

Dreg Cirque tightrope walker, the Cat, in association with the abduction.

There's nothing there about me running away, or what I did to the security guy. It's a cover up, like Amina said it would be.

My parents come on the screen. My mother's crying. I've never seen her cry before. She speaks, her voice wavering.

"We just want our son back." She looks at the camera. "Benedict, if you're watching this, we will never give up. We know you love us. We know you would never do anything to hurt or shame us. It will be OK. We just want you home."

Her eyes bore into me. She's telling me that she knows I've run away with the circus, that this is getting embarrassing for her and I need to stop being so silly and come on home. As soon as I do, it can all go back to normal. To how it was before.

She forgives me, but I can't forgive her. Not ever.

HOSHIKO

I calm down, eventually. They've locked me back in a cell. At least I'm not in that room any more.

I need to think rationally.

Greta or Ben: who do I save?

I've got to protect Greta, she's done nothing wrong. She's just a child; she hasn't even started to live yet, not that there's a life worth living here. But there is always hope, even in the bleakest of days, that's what Amina told me, time and time again. While Greta's alive, there's a chance, somehow, that things might change for her, might get better.

I've got to give Ben up. Got to talk. But how can I actually say the words that might kill him?

I can't.

I can't sacrifice Greta. I can't give up Ben. There's only one option. I've got to get out of here. I've got to get out of this locked room, find Greta, find Ben and run.

BEN

Last year, Mother was given a special award for services to the country. There was a big ceremony and a commemorative service. The rest of the ministers all clubbed together and sent a gift over to our house: a huge grand piano, the one that sits in the drawing room: the one that gave Priya the creeps.

I'm not allowed to touch it; it's too valuable, Mother says. It's an ornamental piano, not one to be played.

She plays it sometimes though, when we're in bed. I've heard the tinkling keys, crept down and watched her, her fingers caressing the gleaming ivory.

I heard Mother one night, discussing it with my father.

"It must have cost a fortune," he said. "Collecting together all those thousands of teeth. Treating them and polishing them, getting rid of all the decay and discolouration."

"I love it," she said. "It's a permanent reminder of all the good work we're doing."

I crept back up the stairs. I pretended to myself that I didn't know what she meant. I never even thought about it again. I woke up in the night a lot, sweating and feeling sick, but I pushed it all away.

I ignored it, just got on with my life.

I can't sit on the fence any more, saying nothing about what they're doing. Even if it wasn't for Priya, wasn't for Hoshiko, I've seen too much now. I know too much. I can't be that boy any more. That privileged little rich boy, staring back at me, pleading ignorance.

It's all so easy. I click on a couple of links, type in her name, punch in the access code and that's it. There I am, online. Free to speak: to my mother, to the world. Live. Uncensored. *You should have been more careful, Mother.*

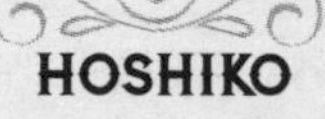

HOSHIKO

The pain in my burnt feet is intensifying, but it annoys me that I even notice. How can I let a foot injury bother me after what I've just seen? After Amina is dead? When Ben's in danger and, even now, they might have Greta?

I'm trapped and it's only a matter of time before Silvio returns.

Why's he taking so long?

Suddenly, I hear a shuffling noise from above. It's coming from the ceiling, and it's getting closer. I look up.

Someone's up there. Who?

I crouch down in the corner, holding my breath as the noise gets progressively louder.

There's a hatch, right in the middle of the ceiling – one of the dozens of ventilation hatches letting air into the tunnels above which spread their way all across the Cirque. As I watch, it's prised away, lifted out.

Who's up there?

I stay still. Watch. Wait.

A head appears. It peeps over the edge, then pulls back. Very cautiously, very warily.

Some legs appear, followed by a torso. A body springs down into the room, light as a butterfly.

It can't be. It is. It's Greta.

BEN

"Hi, my name's Ben Baines, I guess you know that by now. I don't have much time. Pretty soon they'll wipe this from the PureWeb. They won't report it, it'll be like I never spoke. But, if you're watching this, right now… Remember. Remember what I'm about to say. Think about it. Pass it on. Whisper it to others. Don't forget. Don't let them convince you it doesn't matter, that it isn't important. It is.

"I wasn't abducted. I wasn't kidnapped. I ran away. I left home. I made a choice.

"Everything you've been told is a lie. The Dregs who live all round you, in the shadows of your lives: they're not evil. They're not villains, they're not dirty. They are people. Just like you. Just like me.

"Here in the Cirque, they don't just kill people; they beat them, they maim them, they torture them – again and again and again – and we pay to watch.

"Is that right? Is it?

"Maybe this makes you feel uncomfortable? Maybe you avoid the Cirque; it's not your fault, you don't do anything wrong. What can you do to change things anyway? Why is it your problem? You're not the one who does anything evil, are you? No. Of course not. You just sit by and let it happen. What else can you do?"

I stare unflinchingly at the camera. I have to get this right.

"It's time. We have to fight for what is right. We have to resist. This is your problem; it's all of our problem, and it's all of our faults."

I hope Priya's looking down on me. I hope I make her proud.

"Use your head," I put my hand to my temples, "and use your heart. Listen to them, head and heart, hear what they say.

"It's not just the Cirque I'm talking about. It's everything. Our society is rotten; rotten to the core. Our government, our country, has forced thousands of people into poverty and slavery. Denied them an education, denied them food, denied them lives. We've let them convince us that they deserve it. But they don't. They have hearts and souls and brains, just like us. Now, the responsibility is ours.

"Each and every one of you who is watching; who gets that niggling feeling of doubt when you hear of another Dreg hanging, or another Dreg death in the Cirque; who sometimes wonders if this is really the right way of going about things; who's too scared to think too much – I'm talking to you. The time has come to speak out. To defy. To question.

"Yes, it's dangerous. Yes, it's frightening. But if we don't, if we allow this oppression, this torture, to continue, then we are guilty too.

"My mother..." My voice shakes a bit now, I can't help it, although I try to stop it. "My mother, the Prime Minister, the police, all of them, they are *wrong*. What they do, it's evil. They must be stopped. We must stop them. We must stand up for what is right. We cannot—"

The screen goes fuzzy. My face disappears.

"They've cut you off." Jack's grinning. "Doesn't matter though, it's out there. Well done, lad! You said what needed to be said, and more."

He claps me on the back. "You've done it, Benny-Boy! I

reckon you've done more for the cause in five minutes than we've achieved in fifty years!"

I shiver. I guess I should feel proud, but I don't. I just feel frightened. Frightened and alone.

HOSHIKO

She throws herself into my arms. A moment ago, I thought she might already have ended up like Amina and now she's here, in this room, with me.

"Greta? What are you doing here?"

"I'm rescuing you!" She beams at me. "You saved my life, yesterday, in the arena, now it's my turn. I'm saving yours!" Her expression changes suddenly, and she gently strokes my throat with her delicate little fingers.

"What's happened to your neck? Why is all purple?"

"Oh, nothing. It doesn't hurt much, honestly."

"Who did that to you? Was it Silvio?"

"Yes, it was Silvio. It's OK though, it could have been worse."

She crosses her arms together and narrows her eyes. "I'm not letting him hurt you again. Not ever."

I love that she wants to save me and I love having her here with me, where I can actually see her little face; somehow it feels like she's safer where I can protect her. The grim reality though, is that she's not – she's more likely to get hurt by coming in here, not less, and that, whatever she thinks, she can't rescue me. No one can.

"How did you get here? How did you do it?"

"They locked me up. They told me that you'd been bad, that you'd got together with a Pure boy and turned your back on the Dregs. They said they were using me as bait, to make you talk."

We sit down, and she slips her little hand in mine. "I knew

it wasn't true; everyone knows you hate Pures." She's looking at me a little doubtfully. She wants me to tell her it's all lies. Just one big mistake; that we can sort it out, and no one's going to come to any harm.

"Some of it's true."

Her eyes widen.

"I have got together with a Pure boy. It's a long story but, Greta, I promise, you'd love him. He's not like you'd think; he's really nice." She stares at me, open mouthed, for a second or two and then she giggles, infectiously.

"Is he rich and handsome?"

She thinks this is another fairy story, like she does the Silvio one. It's nice to see someone being happy for a change; it makes me feels happy too and, for a moment or two, I'm just a girl, giddy with love.

"He's gorgeous, Greta!"

"So are you!" she declares, proudly. "You're the prettiest person I've ever seen! Have you kissed him?" Her cheeks have turned rosy with excitement. I take a deep breath and whisper in her ear.

"Yes!"

She claps her hands, squealing in delight.

"What's his name?"

"Ben."

"Ben what?"

"Ben Baines."

"Ooh, Hoshiko Baines! That sounds nice! Do you love him? Does he love you?"

Suddenly I feel as high as a kite. I know I've got to get

back to reality in a minute, but it feels so good to tell her about him.

"Yes! I love him, and I think he loves me too!"

I let myself indulge in this warm, cosy pretence that's nothing's wrong for a few seconds more before I pull myself back down to earth. This really isn't the time and the place for childish fantasies and, somehow, I don't think we're heading towards a happy ending.

"Greta. I need you to tell me exactly what happened. Quickly. Any minute now, someone's coming for me, and they won't like finding you here."

"OK." She takes a deep breath, and all her words come out in a jumbled tumble. "These policemen came, they were really horrid. They took me and Amina out of the dorms. They took Amina away and I haven't seen her since. They put me in this tiny room, said they needed to get you to talk and I could help them. They took my doll away and then they left me there for hours and hours and hours.

"Then, Silvio came in – he was really, really mad. He said the time for being nice was over and that you'd run out of chances. He said Amina and I were '*necessary sacrifices*'. I didn't know what he meant, but it sounded really scary. I asked where you were and if he was going to hurt you and then he said that you were locked away, for now, and the one thing he could promise was that I definitely, definitely wouldn't see you again, ever. He was so horrible, Hoshi."

"Carry on," I tell her. "I know it's hard."

"Then, this big, creepy guy came in. He said, '*it's done, she's swinging,*' and Silvio left. Once he'd gone, I knew I had to get out of there and save you. The doors were locked though, and the windows, so the only thing was to crawl up into the tunnels. It was easy enough to get up there, and I knew you must be here somewhere so I kept moving along and pulling up the hatches until I found you."

Oh my God. She may be only six but she's far smarter and braver than me. I never even thought of looking at the ceiling, or escaping through the tunnels, but she says it so matter of factly, as if it's obvious.

"Greta." I try to let her down gently. "You're amazing. What you've done is amazing, but you haven't rescued me."

"Why not?" She looks confused.

"Because I'm injured, and even if I could get back up there with you, I can't stay up there for ever. As soon as I appear anywhere in this building, they're going to see me. See me and lock me back up. Silvio's probably noticed you've gone by now too; he's soon going to work out where."

She grins again, bouncing back quickly from her tears, as only little kids can.

"Don't worry! I promise it will all be OK." It's as if she's the grown-up and I'm the frightened child, and it makes me love her even more. "Wait there," she says. "I've got something to show you."

She drags a chair over to the space in the ceiling, grabs on to the gap, and pulls herself up so that she's sitting in the opening. I can just see her little legs with their scuffed, dusty knees swinging down.

I hear her rooting around and then she wriggles back

down. She keeps her back to me, turning to look at me, slyly. There's something in her hands.

"Close your eyes," she instructs me, as if it's my birthday and she's about to give me a present.

"Greta, stop messing around. I'm trying to work out what to do!"

"Just close your eyes. Please!"

She's so desperate for me to join in her little game that I decide it will probably be easier to indulge her.

"OK," I close my eyes and hold out my hands.

Gently, she rests something in them. It takes up both hands. It's heavy and cold: metal. I know what it is straight away, even though I've never held one before. I open my eyes. It's a gun.

BEN

I stare at the ground. I can't believe what I've just done. What will they do to me now when they find me? What will my mother say?

Thankfully, I guess, there's no time to dwell on these things, as Jack's voice shakes me back to the present.

"Ben, they're going to be able to trace you now, I'm sure of it; they must have ways of tracking the computer you used. We need to get of here."

He looks me up and down.

"Wait there. I'll be back in five. I swear." And then he's gone, locking the door behind him.

The silence in the room when he leaves is unbearable. How many times over the last three days have I sat in a room, waiting for someone to come?

The clock *ticks, ticks, ticks*. It reminds me of waiting for those lions, in the show the other day. It's driving me insane. I pull it off the wall and tear the battery out. That's better.

Where's Hoshiko? What are they doing to her?

The questions echo in my head, replacing the ticking of the clock. I think I'm going crazy.

Thankfully, I hear the key in the lock. Then, I panic. What if it's not him? I drop down, under the desk. The door opens and shuts.

"Ben?"

I stand up. He looks very pleased with himself. He's a really nice guy and he's saved my life, but I'm sure he's a bit mad. He definitely finds this all quite amusing.

"Here," he grins. "Try these on for size." He throws over two folded and sealed packages. Under the clear cellophane, a uniform, a police uniform.

HOSHIKO

I stare down at the gun in my hands.

"Greta, where did you get this?"

"It's Silvio's." She grins, cheekily. "He left the room in such a hurry he forgot to lock the desk."

I look at her, this young child I've always tried to protect. She's stolen a gun and escaped from a locked office to rescue me. Silvio underestimated her, I underestimated her. She's so brave, braver than me. It makes me proud, but also kind of sad: that we live in a world where she has to deal with cruelty and weapons, imprisonment and torture, and death. Always, waiting round every corner, death.

Greta doesn't seem to know it, thankfully, but I'm sure she was less than a day away from being killed. She probably still is, especially now; we probably both are.

If they'd have got here before her and started interrogating me, maybe I could have saved her, if I'd betrayed Ben. Would I have? I shudder.

"What next?" I ask her, helplessly; there's definitely a role reversal going on here. "Silvio wants me dead, Greta, whether I talk about Ben or not."

"I don't know. But you can't sit here and wait for him to kill you. At least if we get out of here, we might be able to find Amina, she'll know what to do."

Amina. I can't face telling her. I know I'm a coward, but I just can't, not now. The wound's too raw for me to say the words. If I try, I'll lose control again. I won't be able to comfort her: I'll be a mess.

I know what Amina would want me to do, though. It's like I can still hear her voice, in my ear, so clearly, telling me what to do. Perhaps I can; that's what she believed; that's what she told me, just two days ago, as she stood next to me and wrapped her arm around me. *We never lose our loved ones; they stay here, deep inside us. They make us who we are.*

When I asked her if things would ever change, she was so certain, so determined, so resolute. *If we keep on believing. If we don't give up hope. If we stay united. Yes, it will change.*

She'd say I have to keep fighting. She'd say I can't give up.

If I let Silvio destroy me, then what's it all been for? Nothing. Amina will have died for nothing.

I have to make her life count. I have to make all of our lives count.

Amina hasn't gone. She's here, even now, guiding me through everything like she always did. I cling on to that thought.

I don't have any clear plan, but the first step is to get out of this room, get past all the guards, all the police. Maybe, if we can make it out of here, we can find Ben, get him out.

It's more than a long shot, I know, but it's the best I can do.

I look again at Greta. She's covered in dust where she's been creeping along the tunnels.

"Right, let's get back up there then, shall we?"

She looks at me, her brow furrowed. "Hoshi, your feet, they hurt bad, don't they?"

Now she says it, I register again that they really do hurt, a lot. They're throbbing so much that each beat of my pulse seems to reverberate through my body. It's not a passive pain;

it's destructive, angry, biting. It feels as if I'm still being burnt, like the hungry flames are still feasting on my toes.

I look at the bandages, and look away quickly. Not quickly enough not to have seen the red blood seeping, and something else too: something green and sticky, something rotten.

I can be strong, though, I can. If I forgot about the pain once, I can do it again.

"They aren't so bad. I'll be fine. Did you pass other rooms, other hatches?"

She nods. "At least four."

"OK, this is what we're going to do. We get back up there. We find a room. We drop down. We pray to God it's not locked and that there's no one in there. We escape." Sounds almost easy.

She looks at me doubtfully. "What if there *is* someone there? A guard or a Pure? What do we do then?"

I consider the gun in my hands, caress the trigger with my finger, hold it up, aim it at the wall. Could I do it, if I had to?

I think of Ben, hiding somewhere. I think of Amina's body, swinging up high; think of all the other Dregs, all the deaths I've seen; think of that room, of all the horrors inside it; think of Amina again.

"I don't want to use this thing. It's dangerous, Greta. But if we have to – we shoot them."

BEN

I feel like a child wearing fancy dress.

I used to have a pirate costume when I was younger. As soon as I put it on, I remember, I'd feel braver, more swashbuckling. In my head, I wasn't me any more; I was Captain Hook, ready to sail the seven seas in search of treasure, ready to take on the Tick-Tock Croc.

I wore it all the time, to the shops, to the park, to bed. Father was always saying I should be wearing normal clothes, but Mother just used to laugh.

"Let him wear what he likes!" she'd say. "There'll be plenty of time for conforming!" She bought me a big wooden treasure chest to go with the outfit, and a telescope and a parrot. I was so happy. They were the best presents I'd ever been given. It's still there now, at home, stuffed at the top of my wardrobe. I could never quite bring myself to get rid of it alongside all the other toys I'd outgrown.

It was because of the memories it carried, I think. Not just of how much I used to play with it, but of the feeling I had when she gave it to me: my mother. She'd gone shopping, bought a gift, chosen it especially for me, because she knew I'd love it, and because she loved me and she wanted to make me happy.

She's not all bad. She used to be thoughtful, and kind; she used to be soft, and gentle.

She's the Dreg Control Minister, I remind myself. She's a mass murderer.

HOSHIKO

After a bit of trial and error, we establish that the easiest way to do this is for Greta to get up into the tunnels first, and then me.

I need to ease my poor feet through the ventilation hatch, but the only way it's possible is if she steadies me from above.

If we weren't tightrope walkers, weren't acrobats, we'd never be able to do this. Greta has more strength than someone twice her age, and we're both used to contorting into tight balls, to stretching in ways other people can't.

It's really hard work and we're both sweating by the end of it, but we do it; we make it up there.

The space opens out briefly above us but then narrows right back down as it forms a crawl space, connecting the rooms up. It stretches across the whole building, and it's tiny.

It's a really tight squeeze for me to even fit in the gap, and I have to crouch right down with my weight on my feet, so it hurts like you wouldn't believe. I can do it though; I've got to.

It's pretty hard to see up here already, even with the light from the room below, and it's about to get much darker. As soon as they see the opening, anyone who comes into the room will work out where I've disappeared to straight away. Sliding the ventilation hatch back into place might buy us a few precious seconds.

It's really fiddly and tricky, especially as we have to do it as quietly as possible. We're nearly there, we've nearly done it, just the final edge to seal, when we hear keys jangling in the lock from the other side.

We both shoot back, instinctively. Damn, there's still a few centimetres gap left. We were so close. I crane forward, peeping through the gap.

The door opens and a policeman enters, staring incredulously round him at the empty room.

BEN

I feel so daft, standing there in that uniform, but Jack looks me up and down approvingly.

"That's good. It fits a treat." He hands me something else. "Put these glasses on. I couldn't get hold of a wig, so they'll have to do."

I put them on. I feel like I'm getting ready for a school play.

He shakes his head. "It's no good. I'm going to have to cut your hair off. Those blond locks are too obvious, even under the helmet."

I run my fingers through my hair. After everything that's happened, a dodgy haircut really doesn't worry me. I reach for the scissors from the stationery tray. "Go for it."

He hacks away at my hair and then gathers it up off the floor, cramming it into a large brown envelope which he stuffs down into the bin.

"Got to cover our tracks."

He looks me up and down again. "That's better. That's much better. Right. Have you ever used a gun? Stupid question, of course you haven't. Hopefully, you won't need to, but I'm going to give you one anyway, OK?"

He hands me a revolver. I stare down at it.

"It's easy to use," he tells me, "like a water pistol – just aim and pull the trigger. Don't do it unless you need to, only if there's no other way. Once you fire that gun, there's no putting the genie back in the bottle."

He doesn't need to tell me that. Less than a week ago, I

was worrying about the football results. Now, I'm trying to prepare myself for the possibility of killing real-life policemen.

"Follow my lead," Jack instructs. "Don't speak unless it's necessary. I'm going to try to get you out of here and into the back of my van. OK?"

I remember my pirate costume again, how it made me feel and act differently. I need to be like that now, let the costume I'm wearing work its magic. If I skulk about, they're going to notice me more. I have to march out of this room, not creep.

I look at myself in the mirror. I don't look like me at all any more. I look stupid. They're going to notice straight away.

It's as if Jack can read my mind because he turns me round to face him and claps his hand firmly on my shoulder.

"You don't have a choice. There's no other way. Come on, let's do this thing."

I nod. Pull the cap down low. Put one hand on my gun. Turn, follow after him, out of the room. Right into the firing line.

HOSHIKO

The police officer reminds me of one of the Cirque clowns. Scratching his head in confusion, he looks like he's playing a slapstick role. He's really fat, in the way that only over-indulged Pures ever get to be, and his big wobbly jaw actually drops as he stands there looking around the room.

He peers under the desk, even trying to open the drawers, as if I'm going to have miraculously shrunk and be hiding in one of them. He rests his hands on his large belly and stands there, brow furrowed, shaking his head from side to side. After a moment, he turns and walks back towards the door.

I look up and give Greta a thumbs up; he's clearly so stupid that it looks like we might actually get away with this one.

No such luck.

He pauses with his hand on the door, turns back to the room and then reaches into his jacket, pulling out his police radio. He pushes a button.

There's no time to think now. No time to wait and hope. I mouth to Greta to stay where she is, then I grab my gun, pull myself over the hatch and drop down into the room, right in front of him.

His jaw drops even further. I don't think he's registered what's going on at all and is, instead, under the impression that I've momentarily vanished and then magically reappeared from nowhere.

Despite the searing pain which shoots through my feet, I manage to speak, inwardly giving myself a little pat on the back for how remarkably steady my voice is.

"Give me the walkie-talkie."

I aim the gun right at him.

He looks at me. I think he's trying to decide if I actually have the courage to do anything with it. He must come to the conclusion that I don't, because his hand reaches down to his waist again – this time it must be for his own gun.

"I said, give me the walkie-talkie. Now!"

He stares at me. I can almost see his little brain cells trying to work out what to do.

"Look," I whisper: I don't want Greta to hear what I'm saying. "If you're in any doubt about whether I'll shoot, let me put your mind at rest. One of the people I love most in the whole world has been murdered today by your lot, and all the other people I care about have been threatened with death and torture. If I'm caught, I die. I've got nothing to lose, and…" I move closer to him and enunciate each word as clearly and distinctly as I can. "I *hate* Pures."

Meek as a lamb, he passes over the walkie-talkie.

"And the gun."

He hands it over. What do I do now? If I let him go, he'll run straight to Silvio. I'm going to have to kill him anyway, but I can't do it when he's looking at me like that.

"Turn around," I order him, "and drop down to your knees."

"Please! I've got children," he begs. "And a wife. Please don't do anything. I was just doing my job. I swear, I won't tell anyone."

My eyes flick away from him, up to the ceiling hatch.

Greta stares down at me, wide eyed. She shakes her head; she doesn't want me to do it. I scowl at him, but I can feel my resolve weakening. That Pure boy has made me soft; I can't put a bullet in this man.

There's a tense silence, broken by his radio, crackling into life. "You OK, Joe? You've gone all quiet on me."

I hold the gun to his head. "Speak into it. Tell them it's fine. And if I think you're saying anything to give the game away, any secret code, or message, I will shoot you."

He nods, and I hold the radio to his face with one hand, keeping the gun pointing at him with the other.

"All fine here, Ma'am. Sorry, false alarm."

"Have you got the girl with you?"

"I'm escorting her to the interrogation suite right now."

"Good work, Joe."

I notice then that he's got a set of handcuffs hanging from his belt. "Give me those handcuffs."

He hands them to me.

"Listen, I don't want to shoot you unless I have to, but I'm going to lock you up."

He nods, vigorously: he's petrified of me. I feel a little thrill of power. All these years, I've lived in the shadow of the police and now there's a member of the establishment here, shaking in fear. It's really tempting just to hold the gun to his head. Bang, this one's for Amina.

I can't though, not with Greta following my every move.

"Sit down on that chair."

He sits.

"How do these work? Don't give me any bullshit."

His voice shakes. "The best thing is to restrain me to the chair." He must think I'm a complete idiot.

"The chair? That you can lift up? I don't think so. I'm only going to ask you one more time, how do these things work?"

He nods. "OK. Move me over to the radiator. You need something rigid: that pipe's the best bet."

"Right. Walk." He moves over to the side of the room. "Sit down."

"Now you need to click that half on my wrist and the other half on to the pipe."

I can't cuff him and hold the gun to his head at the same time. I was hoping to keep Greta out of this, but I don't have a choice.

"Greta. I need your help."

Immediately, she springs down. She stares straight at him and nods to me. "What do you need?"

"OK, I'm going to give you the gun in a minute. I need you to hold it, OK, I'm going to give you the gun in a minute. I need you to hold it, that's all – be careful with it. He's not going to do anything silly." I glare at him. "Are you?"

She nods. "You bet."

Without taking my eyes off him, I hand her the gun. I cuff him to the radiator. Now, all that's left to do is gag him, to stop him from crying out as soon as we leave the room. "Keep aiming the gun at him, Greta."

I pull off his tie as quickly as I can. My fingers fumble though and it feels like it takes ages. His neck is all clammy; it's disgusting.

I loop it round and round his head, over his mouth and tie it tightly.

I look at him once more. His flabby chest is heaving up and down really quickly, and his eyes are bulging. Maybe he's about to have a heart attack. The aggressive thrill of power I felt leaves me as suddenly as it came. If there's one thing Ben's shown me, it's that not all Pures are evil.

"I'm sorry," I tell him. "It's either this or we kill you."

I pick up his gun and walkie-talkie; they're bound to come in useful.

Greta hands me the other gun. She climbs easily back up into the loft and is about to pull me up, when she stops.

"Get his keys, Hoshiko!"

Genius. How could I have forgotten those? "Well done."

I cross the room again. They're poking out of one of his front pockets. "Stand up."

I reach my hand in there. It feels horrible and I'm scared of what I might end up touching. I hook one finger through the key ring and pull them out. I throw them up to Greta, and then she pulls me up after her.

Before we seal up the gap, I look down into the room once more. Nothing untoward there, just a member of the police, bound and gagged with his own handcuffs.

I check to see if Greta's OK. She grins at me. "Good work, partner!" It breaks the tension somehow, it makes me laugh. We slide the hatch back over.

"One down," I tell her. "About a million to go."

BEN

We head quickly down the corridor. I can see a load of police cars outside, through the windows of the building.

"My van's out there," Jack whispers. "We're seconds away now."

We hasten our pace, practically running down the corridor.

Suddenly, the exit door we're heading for opens from outside and three police officers run through it, towards us. Two of them rush past us without a second glance, but one of them stops.

"All right, Jack?" he says, and then looks at me. I fight the urge to run away. I make myself look up; make myself smile at him. He seems friendly enough; he nods at me, then claps Jack on the back and laughs. "You're going the wrong way, mate; they've called an emergency meeting."

"Really?" Jack sounds confused. "I was told to check down here."

"No. It was crystal clear – ignore previous instructions and check in at base."

He looks at me again for a second.

"I don't think we've met?"

"This is John – he's a cadet," Jack answers quickly. "First day out on the beat and all this kicks off."

"At least it's not boring," the other guy laughs again. "Jack here will look after you and, you never know, you might even get to shoot some Dregs!"

We join in his laughter, chuckling heartily. "Come on, we'd better get there quick." He turns away from us.

I look at Jack. His hand goes to his gun and he takes it out of his holster. He raises it up and points. He's going to shoot the guy. Because of me, he's going to shoot someone.

I want to tell him to stop.

I want to tell him to do it.

The door slams open again. Jack lowers his hands, quickly. Four more police officers come running through. The other guy turns round.

"Come on," he calls. "What you waiting for?"

"Nothing." Jack turns to me. "Let's go."

The decision's made for us. We're heading away from the vans, away from safety but maybe, just maybe, towards Hoshiko. Me, Jack and every other police officer in the city.

HOSHIKO

We head left, away from the direction of Silvio's office.

It's really slow going, dragging my poor, aching feet along this narrow space. The dust catches in my throat and makes my nose itch. I keep having to stop myself sneezing – not easy.

I've been suspended from the wire in boxes loads of time, bound up in chains from which I've had to escape – it's all been there in the act – and I've crawled through these tunnels hundreds of times, so why I suddenly feel claustrophobic now, of all times, I don't know, but there's a fluttering of panic in my chest and I feel like screaming, as if I'm going to lose control completely.

It's so dark and restricted up here and the pain in my feet gets more and more agonizing every time I haul them along the floor.

We reach the next ventilation hatch. At least there'll finally be some light and air, whatever else awaits us. I'm about to start pulling the cover away when I feel Greta's hand on my arm.

"Don't you think we should keep going?" she whispers. "We're hidden up here; we won't meet anyone."

Of course, she's right. If we go as far as we can up here, there's less distance to cover to actually make it out of the building, and much less likelihood anyone will see us. I suppress the fact that I still have no idea what we're going to do anyway when we do get out of the building, *if* we do get out of the building.

I know it's the best thing to do, but the idea of being up here any longer is almost unbearable. I take a few deep breaths and feel her eyes on me through the darkness.

"You OK?" For the first time, I can hear the fear in her voice.

"I'm fine. Let's go."

I resume the painful drag and crawl forward, making slow but steady progress, past one, two, three, four more rooms.

There's no noise from below. I guess it's early evening by now; everyone must have finished rehearsals. It seems funny, to think of them all carrying on as normal. I wonder how the others are all doing, whether they know about Amina yet.

I can't remember the last time I ate anything, the last time I slept. I must be running on adrenaline alone, we both must be.

The walkie-talkie breaks the silence.

"The young girl, Greta, she's escaped. Someone must have got her out of Silvio's office. Anyone seen her?"

We hold our breaths. There's a few seconds pause.

"Joe. Shouldn't you be here by now with the girl? Joe, are you there?"

The tone of the voice becomes increasingly more panicked.

"Something's not right. Immediate response required. Someone tell me we've still got her, or all our necks are on the line."

That's it then: there must be only seconds until they find out where I've gone. I grip Greta's hand in the darkness.

"Whatever happens now, thank you," I tell her. "For trying." She places her other hand over mine.

"Let's go down fighting," she says.

We keep moving forward, more quickly this time, and it's not long before the silence below is replaced by the heavy thud of more than one set of running footsteps. I should have killed that guard; he's going to tell them straight away that we're up here.

More and more footsteps rush down the corridors below. We turn off the walkie-talkie. It's a good source of information, but if anyone hears it from below, we're finished. We're going to be finished any minute now anyway, but we edge slowly forward, inch by inch.

BEN

So, in order to escape from the police, here I am right in the middle of what feels like hundreds of them, forming part of the man-hunt that's searching for me. There must be real criminals on the loose out there but, apparently, they've just drafted in even more officers.

What will they do to me when they find me? I'm not sure. Maybe they'll try to get me to conform; try to force me into retracting my statement. Maybe they'll just kill me.

We arrive in a building at the back of the Cirque, and an important-looking woman calls us to attention. She's wearing a black trouser suit and her hair is pulled back in a tight, functional bun.

"I'm going to keep this brief. There have been some major game changes in the last ten minutes. The girl, Hoshiko – you probably know her as the Cat – has escaped from right under our noses. We believe she's been helped by a young female Dreg accomplice: Greta Bukoski. They've gagged and bound one of our men, and stolen his radio and his gun and are therefore believed armed and dangerous."

An overwhelming sense of relief floods through me. She's alive! And she's not just alive, she's on the run. She's made them look totally incompetent. I want to whoop with joy.

She continues, grimly. "These are the worse kinds of Dreg: they are lawless and desperate. Our brief is simple: we must stop them. Anyone spotting them should shoot on sight. The boy, Benedict Baines, has well and truly nailed his colours to the mast; even his own mother has conceded that he cannot be relied on. He has assaulted a security guard, leaving him for dead, and his online incitements have already led to riots and unrest across the country. If you find him, keep him alive if you can, but if it's a choice between taking him down or letting him go, shoot the bastard."

There's my answer, then.

"The two Dregs escaped into the tunnels above our heads; they're up there now, inches above us. These tunnels are rat runs: they stretch all the way across the Cirque." She clicks a button and the projector screen behind her head lights up, displaying a blueprint of the overhead passageways.

"They could be anywhere up there, or indeed already back down below; there are ventilation points in most rooms. I need men on either side of the building and on every door and window, and I need someone to get up there and flush them out, to force them here," she points to the far left point of the map. "That's the direction we believe they'll be headed in, and where we will focus most of our manpower. Volunteers please?"

There's a silence. As I take in what she's said, I realize that the best *officer* of all to go after Hoshiko and Greta, is me. I'm certainly not about to fire a gun at them, and if I can reach them maybe, somehow, I can get them out.

It's too risky though; it would only take one person to recognize me and the whole game would be up. Not just for me, for Jack too.

I look sideways at him. He meets my eyes and gives a barely distinguishable nod. I hear a voice, my voice but a bit deeper, a bit manlier, calling out.

"I'll do it, Ma'am."

A hundred pairs of eyes turn on me – surely one of them will realize who I am.

"I'm only a cadet, I know, but I'm lighter than most of the rest of you, and shorter. I reckon I'm the best bet."

Jack claps a hand on my back and speaks up.

"I'll vouch for him, Ma'am. He's a good kid."

The woman nods.

"OK, Jack, if you think he can handle it. Get up there and get them out. There'll be career progression in it for you, young man, if you do. Right, people, let's go!"

Jack grips my arm tightly for a second.

"Good luck, cadet," he says. "Stay careful." Then he walks away without a backwards glance.

The officers file busily out of the doors. The woman takes me to an office room, and indicates upward, to an entrance leading up into the tunnels.

"The young girl escaped up there. Silvio Sabatini's gun's missing; we're assuming she took it up there with her, so that's two weapons at least they've managed to get hold of. Four doors along to the right is where the Cat escaped from."

She looks at me again, and again it's like she can see right through me. It's so hard to meet her eyes. I fight the urge not to turn tail and run.

"You got a gun?"

I nod. "Yes, ma'am."

"OK. Take this too." She hands me an oval object. It looks a bit like a sports drink bottle, but it's really heavy. I've got no idea what it is. "I don't need to tell you how dangerous these grenades are. You wouldn't normally get your hands on one of these unless you'd been in the riot police for a minimum of five years, but we've got to use all the tools we have at our disposal. You know what to do, right?"

I nod, but then ask: "Sorry, ma'am, can you go through it once, just to remind me?"

She tuts crossly.

"This isn't a training seminar. Every second we don't catch them, they're a step closer to escape. This is embarrassing for us, all these officers to catch three flaming kids." I nod again.

She sighs.

"If you need to detonate, pull the pin, aim and throw. You'll have about two seconds to get as far in the other direction as you can. It's powerful enough to kill on impact, but there's a risk to any of our guys in the vicinity, especially if they're stationed just below, so give us some notice, if you can. OK. You ready?"

"I'm ready."

"Right. Get up there and, for God's sake, finish the job." She shakes my hand, her grip strong. "Good luck."

She holds the ladder while I climb up. It's really dark up there and the dust clogs itch my throat. I shine my torch down the dim passageway. I can't see anyone. I pull myself up, and I'm off.

For a while we make slow but steady progress but, all too soon, there's a different sound: a clunking noise far back from the right, and a slither of light illuminates Greta's face.

"They're up here," she gasps. "They're coming. What shall we do?"

"I don't know."

"Hoshiko…"

She points upward. There are scaffold poles running horizontally just above our heads and there's about a foot's gap between them and the ceiling. "Can you make it up there?"

I see what she's thinking. Maybe we can hide above while whoever it is moves along obliviously below us.

My feet are beyond painful now. I'm glad I can't see them; they must be bleeding like crazy. As for all that dust getting into the open wounds – I don't need Amina to tell me that's not a good thing.

"'Course I can." The confident tone I adopt is for her benefit entirely. "I'm the Cat, aren't I?"

We only have a few seconds; the beam of light has nearly reached us. Simultaneously and silently, we pull ourselves up by the poles, coiling ourselves around them like snakes.

Greta's small enough to get her whole body up there, and she concertinas herself into the gap between the pole and the ceiling, but I just won't fit.

All I can do is stay here, wrapped around the pole as tightly as I can, holding myself up off the ground. My arms ache and

I can already feel the strain in my stomach muscles, but it's nothing more exerting than I do every day in the show, I tell myself.

Holding my breath as the light gets closer, I lift my legs up high, squeezing them round the pole, although I can see already that this isn't going to work.

My legs are too long. I'm too big.

The space below is less than a couple of metres. Unless the guy's tiny, he's bound to knock into me on his way past. What do I do?

I'll have to shoot him.

He's nearly reached us now.

I can see the top of his helmet as he moves along just below and to the left: police.

I cling on to the thought; if I do have to hurt him, that'll help. Since when have the police ever done anything for the Dregs, except destroy and torture us? It's about time one of them got what he deserves.

After that, everything happens really quickly. He passes Greta first, she's invisible as he passes. Then, it's me.

I push my legs up hard into the pipe, gritting my teeth with the effort it takes not to let them lower by even a millimetre. At first, I think I might just do it, but then the top of his helmet catches on one of my thighs and he stops.

I can't shoot him without letting go of the pole. There's nothing for it but to drop, right on top of him.

There's no time to think, no time to register his face. As I fall, I crack my gun down on to his upturned face and he tumbles to the ground beneath me.

We lay there, sprawled, just for an instant, before my stupid, idiotic brain finally begins to register what my eyes saw seconds ago. This isn't some bad guy police officer I've assaulted: it's Ben.

BEN

Ever heard the saying *you won't know what's hit you*? Well, that's quite literally how it is. One minute, I'm making my way along the crawl space. The next, something drops down on me, knocking me to the floor and taking a swing at my face on the way for good measure.

I lay there, dazed, for a moment, trying to puzzle out what's going on. My jaw is throbbing like mad, and there's something wet in my mouth. I think it's blood.

It's only when I hear her voice, a voice I'd recognize anywhere, that I realize that this thing on top of me, pinning me down: it's Hoshiko.

"Ben? Ben? Oh my God, oh my God, I'm so sorry." She's shining a torch right into my face.

I'm blinded by the light, lying injured in the dust, battered and bleeding. I'm on the run from the police and I've just been assaulted but I think I'd like to stay here like this for ever.

Half an hour ago I didn't even know if she was alive or dead and now she's here, and she's got her arms around me, covering me in kisses.

"Your mouth, it's bleeding. Oh my God. I was going to shoot you!"

"It's OK." My voice sounds funny through my split lip, which is already starting to swell. "I'm fine."

She pulls away from me for a second and shines the torch upward.

"Greta." There's a big grin on her face. "It's Ben!"

A tiny figure drops down next to us and looks at me, her head cocked to one side as she appraises me, curiously.

"Good to meet you, Greta." I hold out a hand, and she steps forward, shaking it formally before turning to Hoshiko. "You never said he was a policeman!"

Hoshiko snorts. "D'you think I'd have gone anywhere near him if he was? He's not, he's just dressed up as one."

She prises herself off me then laughs, burying her head in my arms again. "I've got no idea why though. Man, we've got some catching up to do!"

Of course, there isn't time to find out how and why he's suddenly appeared up here with hardly any hair, wearing a policeman's uniform, only a couple of panicked seconds in which we establish that there are over fifty officers waiting for us to come out, and that he's supposed to be finding us and doing one of two things – either shooting us on sight, or hurling a grenade at us at point-blank range.

"OK, here's what I think we should do." Ben talks quietly; there must be people inches below us. "They're expecting you to be heading away from the front of the building." I nod: that's pretty much what we were doing, getting as far away from Silvio's office as possible. "So, there are already a lot more police officers stationed to our left than our right. I reckon we need to head back that way, as quietly as we can. I've got a radio; maybe I can throw them off our scent for a bit."

We've come all this way for nothing.

"What do we do when we get as far as we can?" Greta waits for him to tell her, but he just looks at me helplessly.

"Let's stick to this part of the plan for now," I try to sound buoyant. "We don't want to overcomplicate things. The main thing is that we're all together."

"But..." Our eyes meet and she stops and nods bravely. "OK, let's go."

Ben takes his radio from his belt.

"I need you both to be really, really quiet now." He holds it up to his mouth and whispers into it.

"This is unit twelve. I can see them up ahead. Right to the far end of the building, heading away from the front."

The reply is immediate.

"What exactly can you see?"

"There's a light up ahead, and footprints in the dust. They're definitely heading that way."

"OK. Keep going. We'll reposition all the men up there. *Don't* let them escape."

"I won't." Lowering the radio, he turns to me. "Hope he believed me. Let's go."

He turns off his torch; the blackness around us is instant and entire. I reach for his hand.

"Ben? I'm glad you're here."

"Me too."

His breath is warm on my cheek as he moves forward. I feel his lip, tentatively, with my fingertips. It's puffy and swollen. I kiss his cheek softly. He moves his neck and his lips brush my ear, making all the little hairs on my neck and arms stand on end.

"Guys!" Greta's voice is already moving away. "Are we going, or what?"

I pull away from him, reluctantly.

"We're going," he answers, his voice cracking.

We move off, together, a team.

BEN

We edge slowly back down the corridor.

Greta flits along like a tiny ghost and has to keep waiting for Hoshi and me to catch up. I'm miles too big for this restricted space; my legs are stiff and my neck's aching like mad where I can't raise my head.

Hoshi's moving even more slowly than I am and I keep bumping into her. At first, I think she's waiting for me but, when I touch her face, there's sweat pouring off of it. She's struggling. Really struggling.

"Are you OK?"

She's breathing in short, laboured bursts. "I'm fine. Just – need – to – keep – going."

And so we do.

My radio crackles again. "Unit twelve. Any sign?"

I try to buy us a bit more time.

"They're up ahead. I think they've stopped. Another few feet and I'll able to reach them. I'm turning off this unit now. Too noisy."

I switch it off, and we keep on moving.

I look at her again; she can't go on much longer. At least if we're down there she can lean on me, maybe I can even carry her.

"We've gone far enough," I say. "Next time we come to an opening I think we should try and get down."

Greta looks past me, back at Hoshi.

"I think so too. Hoshi?"

She doesn't say anything, just nods, her brow furrowed, as

if every tiny movement takes concentration.

It's not long before we reach the next hatch. As quietly as I can, I prise it away while the two girls crouch back in the shadows. I ease it back a fraction and peer through the crack into the room below.

My empty stomach heaves. I slam the hatch back down, quickly.

HOSHIKO

I don't know what he sees in that room, but he jumps back from the hatch as if he's on a spring.

His face, when he turns to me is deathly pale, and his eyes are hollow and wide.

"Not that room," he mutters. "Let's keep going a bit longer."

He's different after that, as if whatever he's seen has reduced him somehow. He moves less decisively and he keeps looking back at us both and then looking away.

I don't ask him any questions about it. He's obviously trying to come to terms with whatever he saw, and by the look on his face, it's definitely not something I want him talking about in front of Greta.

We reach a sort of crossroads – the tunnel stops up ahead, but branches off to the left and the right.

Ben flicks the torch on; the light illuminates two more narrow passageways. Greta and I try to work out where we are.

"We must still be in the middle tunnel, but right at the end," Greta begins. "Which means there's a training room below us … and the main entrance to the building. That's no good. It's too open. If we go that way," she points left, "we reach the kitchens. If we go right, we'll hit…"

She turns to me and we both speak at the same time.

"The arena!"

BEN

"So what do we do?" I ask them. I can't work out if reaching the arena is a good thing or not.

Greta's tone when she answers is slow and clear, as if I'm daft. "We've got to head to the arena."

"Why?"

Hoshiko answers for her; they're both working this out a lot quicker than I am.

"You said they've shut the Cirque tonight, right?" I nod. "OK. So, one: it's going to be dark in there. Two: no one's using it – got to be good news for us. Three: that's *our* arena! We know every inch of it: every fire exit, every backstage corridor. The police don't. If nothing else, we might be able to hide out for a bit."

It seems obvious now she's spelt it out. I put out the torch, and we move down the narrow passage.

I try not to think about what was in that room, but the image won't go away.

Directly underneath me, an open bin of bodies, with limbs missing. A head, tossed in on the top of a huge pile of bone and sinew and visceral matter. A head with a bullet through it, the head of a boy about my age – the head I cradled in my arms just yesterday.

Anatol: the poor, injured boy they set alight and fired out of a cannon.

What's going to happen to him? I close my eyes, a wave of nausea hitting.

Grateful for something else to focus on, I move on down

the corridor. We quickly reach an opening. It widens above us, and I rotate my stiff neck around gratefully. There's a metal ladder, rising up and disappearing into what looks like another tunnel.

Wordlessly, we climb up, and then I turn the torch back on. We're in a huge, expansive attic-type room. There are rails full of clothes up here and boxes everywhere.

"This is it," Hoshiko whispers. She looks at me and her eyes glow. "The arena!"

HOSHIKO

It's spooky up here, amongst the racks and racks of costumes, waiting silently to be brought to life. The ghost of every part I've ever played is here, watching, waiting.

So many memories. Looking at each costume, I'm instantly transported back to when I wore it. My performance... The roars of the crowd... I'm betrayed again by that same sense of belonging I get on the wire. There's something about the lights, the crowds, the action that's made me feel most alive there, teetering on the brink of death every night.

Until now, I reprimand myself. This circus is my prison. It's torn me away from my family. It's taken my beautiful Amina away from me. I feel Ben next to me, and Greta the other side. I reach for their hands and we stand there in a little circle.

These two people with me here, they're all that matters now. The only things I care about.

It must put us at an advantage, knowing this place so well. We've spent loads of time up here, Amina and I, and Greta too, during rehearsals. Sometimes, I have to wait up here and then drop down on the trapeze, to shock and thrill the crowds below. Other times, I'm pulled up here to make it look as if I've vanished mid-act, or to make costume or prop changes during the show.

Ben has turned his radio back on and it crackles into life again. "Unit twelve? Are you there? We're all waiting."

He flicks his torch on and turns to me without responding to the urgent voice.

"We haven't got much time."

The radio starts again.

"Unit twelve? Unit twelve? Right, that's it. Something's up. Send another man up. Send another ten men up. Let's flush those rats out, once and for all: this has gone on long enough."

Ben puts the torch on the floor. It sends a low beam through the attic and his face looks haunted in the dim light. He looks broken, afraid; he looks like I feel.

He sighs, heavily. "I think we're about to be rumbled. Any bright ideas?"

BEN

There's a few seconds' pause, while we all rack our brains desperately. There's nothing for it though; we're going to have to drop down into that arena and hope for the best.

"I have an idea!" Greta squeals, excitedly. "They know what we're wearing. Let's get changed, Hoshiko!"

It's not a miraculous solution by any means, but it certainly won't do us any harm if we aren't all so instantly recognizable. It might throw someone off our scent, even if it's only for a moment or two.

"Well done, Greta," I praise her. "That's a great idea, but you're going to have to do it really, really quickly. Is there anything I can put on?"

They both stare at me, look at each other and burst into laughter.

"Don't worry; I'm not into women's clothes. But they're going to work out I'm lying any minute now. Then they'll be after me too – they'll be looking for the uniform."

The pair of them collapse against each other, shaking with silent laughter. Hoshiko actually has real tears running down her face. I really don't see what's so funny. They're wasting vital seconds we don't have.

"Come on girls. We don't have time for this."

"I'm sorry," she splutters, wiping her eyes. She takes a deep breath, obviously trying desperately to compose herself. "I just pictured you in one of my leotards!" She bursts out laughing again and Greta joins in.

"Did you straight away think of that orange sequinned

one? The really skimpy one? Me too!" They're giggling again. This is infuriating. Why are girls so annoying?

"I just meant was there a guy's costume? That's all. Come on, any minute now they're going to work out what's going on, if they haven't already."

Finally, the urgency of the situation seems to hit home and they calm down a bit.

Both girls carry on rifling through the boxes, searching out the most sensible costumes. They even find one for me.

We all turn our backs to each other discreetly and get changed. Mine's a tight fit, but I manage to squeeze into it.

"Can I turn around?" I ask when it's on.

"Hold on." Hoshiko is the slowest; I'm sure she's not in a good way. "OK. I'm ready. On the count of three." We all turn around and, just as I knew they would, they explode into fits of laughter again.

HOSHIKO

I know it's warped to find anything even remotely funny right now. Amina is dead, and we're being hunted by the police; tonnes of them, ready to shoot us down.

But if I didn't laugh, didn't let Greta's infectious giggles work their magic, I'd collapse in a heap of despair right now. Better to laugh than give up and, my God, he does look bloody hilarious.

The costume we've given him is a suit, but it's a suit made for me; a suit that has been especially designed for a girl to look sexy in. It's based on some guy called Charlie Chaplin, who lived hundreds of years ago. The trousers are black, but they're made of Lycra and they're really, really tight – they don't leave much to the imagination, if you know what I mean. They're too short for him as well and the shirt won't fasten properly. He's managed to do the middle button up, but the others won't close and it strains across his chest, gaping open at the top and bottom. I can't help staring at his body.

That's another thing about all this life and death stuff; you'd think I'd be far too frantic and panicked to notice anything like that but, oddly, I feel more aware of it all than I ever have before.

I've only just met him and now we're going to die.

I'll probably never get to be on my own with him again, never get to feel him close to me, never get to touch him.

OK, deep breath, back to the costume. He's wearing a really old-fashioned hat. It's called a bowler hat and it's this little round, black thing. He's tried to pull it as low as he can but his head is too big for it and it perches there, precariously.

I know he's embarrassed and that it's not fair of me to keep laughing like this, so I try really hard to stop. Avoiding any eye contact with Greta, which would definitely set me off again, I somehow manage to speak.

"It's no good. You look too silly. You'll have to put the police costume back on again." He stares down at his clothes, forlornly.

"But any second now, they'll click. Then they'll be looking for a police officer."

"Ben, if you get shot down and there's a picture of your body on the news, trust me, you don't want to look like that!" Greta and I both burst into peals of laughter again.

"Fine." He lets out an exasperated sigh. "Turn around, ladies."

Greta turns away, but I grin at him, one eyebrow raised. His cheeks have gone all red and he's looking coyly down at the floor; it's so sweet.

"You too, please," he instructs me. "Come on, turn around."

I snort derisively, but do as he says and slowly turn away. I can't resist one more look back over my shoulder though. "Hoshiko! I mean it. Turn around!"

So I stand there, waiting for him to change. I can't stop smiling to myself. But it's not really because he looked so daft, and it's not the thought of him in a leotard either. It's because he's here, with me. Because he came to get me, and because whatever happens now, whether we live or die, at least for a few days, we found each other.

BEN

I prise off the tight trousers, putting my first outfit back on again as quickly as I can.

"OK, you can look now." They both turn around and I give them a grin. "I guess women's clothes aren't my thing?"

It's only now that I really notice what they're wearing. They've both changed into tight black leotards and leggings.

Hoshiko is sitting on the floor, her legs elevated on a box. Her stage name seems to suit her more than ever; those huge dark eyes have a feline slant to them and the gloss of her hair catches the torchlight as it shines on her.

I keep shining the light on her, and she stares back at me. Then I notice her feet. The bandages have turned black and they're shredded and frayed so that they don't cover all of her flesh. It gapes through in an angry red colour, moist and sticky.

"My God. Your feet." She moves them away quickly.

"They're fine. It's not as bad as it looks."

"I thought Amina said they'd be OK?"

"I know." She looks up at me. "That was if I rested them. I don't think she thought I'd be running from the police and crawling along miles of dirty tunnels." She attempts a smile. "Honestly, they don't hurt that much."

I know she's lying. I look at Greta and her eyes meet mine in an exchange of mutual concern. Hoshiko's not having any of it though.

"Come on, guys. You said we had to hurry, Ben. What now?"

It's as if my radio wants to know too, because it suddenly resumes again.

"Unit twelve? Unit twelve? Unit twelve? Something's not right here. We have to assume they've taken him down. Officer down. Again! For Christ's sake, get up there!"

That's it then. There's only one thing for it, I guess. If they're all coming up, we've got to go down. Right now. Back where it all began, back into the Cirque.

HOSHIKO

The plan, if you can call it a plan, is to turn off the torch, open the hatch, drop down from the ropes into the Cirque and head out of a fire exit, all without being detected. Once we're outside we make a run for it, I guess, although I don't think any of us have a clue where to.

I've been trying so hard not to pay attention to the pain in my feet, but when I think about the drop, about having to land on them once more with the full force of my body, it's enough to make my eyes water.

Ben catches me looking at them. They don't look like feet any more, just grey and red lumps attached to my legs. They're disgusting. I don't want him to see them and I hide them away again as quickly as I can, but he eyes me doubtfully.

"You can't land on them. I'll catch you."

He must have read my mind. I fight my natural instinct to resist his help: the time for stubborn pride is gone.

"OK. I'll drop into your arms."

"Perfect. Greta, you go first, then me and then Hoshi." He pauses. "What about the radio, and the guns and the grenade? We might need them."

"I'll drop them down to you."

"You can't drop the grenade. When it hits the floor, it might go off. I can probably hold it while I jump."

An image of the grenade going off in his hands flashes in my mind. A slow motion shot: one massive explosion in his face and then … obliteration … no more Ben.

"No!" my cry is involuntary. "It's too risky. We'll have to leave it behind."

He nods. "OK. You're right. I'd rather not blow my own head off."

"What if they come?" Greta's voice is small and frightened. "What do we do?"

"We do whatever we have to." Ben's reply is loaded with intent. It fires me up. Every time I close my eyes, I see Amina swinging there. Whatever happens now, I have to make sure she hasn't died for nothing.

"Ben's right. Greta, these guys have done really, really bad things and they want us destroyed. Listen to me, none of this is your fault: it's our mess. If they come and we tell you to run, just run, OK. Don't stop. Don't look back. Don't try to save us; you've already done that."

She looks down at the floor. I've come to realize that she's as stubborn as I am, and as determined.

"Greta? Do you hear me?" Her eyes flick up to meet mine.

"I'm not leaving you behind."

"You might not have to. I just want you to promise that you'll run if we tell you. Please."

She looks back at me, holding my gaze.

"No. Not unless you're running too."

"Guys, I don't think there's any point worrying about this now. We've got no idea what's going to be waiting for us." Ben's tone is focused. "Hoshiko and I will take the guns. Greta, you're in charge of the keys: they might come in really useful. We've got to go. Every second we're up here, they're one step closer."

Right on cue, a beam of light appears from just down the corridor. He grips my hand, I grab hold of Greta's too and she reaches out for his. For a second, we stand again in our little circle.

Ben nods, looks at me and gives a funny little grin.

"Let's go."

BEN

We ease back the hatch from the nearest opening and I peer down into the arena. There's enough light creeping in from outside to be able to see that it's completely deserted.

It's so quiet, without the noise of the crowds and the sound of the music. There's the same smell from before of beer and popcorn, sweat and smoke, but it's different too, like everything is waiting in the hushed silence. Waiting for something to happen, waiting for a show.

The beam of light wending its way down the low attic corridors is getting closer. There's no time to lose now.

We feed the rope out and Greta scrambles down it, landing lightly. She looks up at us, gives a thumbs up and creeps away, ducking down behind the nearest row of seats.

I'm next. I'm bigger and much clumsier, but I lower myself through and, eventually, down. I'm standing there, waiting for Hoshiko, who seems to be taking much longer to appear than necessary, when the ring is suddenly flooded with light.

HOSHIKO

At first, I can't even bring myself to peer down, into the ring. I'm so scared that Amina's still going to be there, hanging.

I should have told Greta before, softened it somehow for her. She doesn't deserve to find out this way; doesn't deserve to have that swinging corpse imprinted on her mind too.

Finally, because of Greta, I find the courage from somewhere. I push my head tentatively through the opening and make myself look, upward and leftward.

She's gone. Thank God. Maybe she's already floating around in that jar. I shiver. Wherever she is now, I couldn't face seeing her again. The noose still hangs there, ominously, where she was.

I've wasted precious seconds.

I'm about to lower the first gun down to Ben when the light glare hits. I jerk back quickly, pulling my head back.

Edging forward a little, I can still see Ben, but not much further. He's looking to his left. Frozen there. A rabbit, caught in the headlights.

There's no alarm or sirens. Not hundreds of footsteps approaching, just one pair. A tap-tapping of feet, echoing in the empty ring and then the voice of the devil himself breaking the silence.

"Well, well, well. What have we here? Benedict Baines, as I live and breathe. This is a pleasant surprise! I've been so looking forward to meeting you again. Playing dress-up, are we? How delightful."

I lean forward a little more, just enough to see what's going on, although I'd know those sarcastic tones anywhere.

Silvio stands in the centre of the ring, Bojo at his feet. The spotlights shine down on him. He has a gun and it's pointed at Ben.

He looks up at the hatch. I draw back, but it's too late: he's seen me.

"And Hoshiko's here too. What a fortunate reunion."

I don't know what to do. I stay there, silently, crouching in the attic, the light to my left coming increasingly closer as whoever's on the end of the torch clambers along the crawl space towards me.

"Darling, if you think this all going to end happily for you and your little Romeo here, you really should know me better than that by now." He holds the gun up, aiming it at Ben's head. "Get down here, my dear, right now, or I'll blow his brains out."

"No!" Ben's eyes don't move from Silvio's. "He's lying, Hoshiko! They need me alive. Stay there. Don't come down."

Silvio laughs, indulgently.

"You really do have an elevated sense of your own importance, don't you, young man? Think you're something special because of Mummy, do you? Well, Mummy's washed her hands of you. They all have. You're just another criminal, and you've threatened my Cirque. You've made me look weak. Look around you. Why are we shut tonight? Because of you and Juliet, that's why. Let me assure you, nothing would give me greater pleasure than putting a bullet through your skull."

"Don't come down, Hoshi; he's going to shoot me anyway," Ben cries out.

"My dear little feline, if you come down right now, I give you my word, I won't shoot either of you. I'll hand you over to the police." He laughs again. "They'll probably shoot you anyway, but presumably you don't want to sit up there and watch while I pump lead into him here and now."

"Stop!" There's a cry from across the arena. Greta must have crept away while we were all distracted, and now she stands defiantly on one of the podiums. An easy target. What's she doing? There's something in her arms: Bojo.

"Let them go or I'll break his neck!"

Silvio laughs.

"No you won't: you're besotted with my little friend. Give him back to me." He takes a step towards her, the gun still pointing at Ben. "Bojo. Come on, little fella. Come to Daddy."

"Bojo, stay here with me, there's a good boy." She croons, stroking him softly. The little monkey looks back and forth from Greta to Silvio, leans forward and chatters into Greta's ear.

"You're wrong. I might care about him, but I love Hoshiko more. Come on, Bojo, come with Auntie Greta."

Holding Bojo tightly in one arm, she starts to climb up the bars of podium. She's getting higher and higher. Eight feet, ten feet, twelve feet up.

"Maybe I can't break his neck, but I will drop him, if you don't let us go."

Silvio laughs again, not quite as confidently this time. "You won't. You haven't got it in you, girl."

He waves the gun at Ben, then up at me, and back to Greta.

He fires.

The sound is deafening. I reel backwards. He's fired up here. The metal ceiling above me is ruptured and bent. He's missed me by millimetres.

"He's next. Now, let Bojo go, and come down." Bojo is clinging tightly to Greta now, whimpering and looking down fearfully.

Silvio takes another step towards her, still aiming at Ben.

I quickly throw a gun down. It clatters and spins across the floor, resting at Ben's feet.

Silvio swivels his arm to the hatch.

"So, she's survived!" he calls. "Next time I'll blow your brains out."

The noise from the corridor is much louder now and I can make out the shape of someone appearing through the darkness. Any second now and I'll be caught.

I look down. My eyes meet Silvio's. He turns away from me, swinging the gun backwards and forward between Ben and Greta.

The three of them are in a kind of triangle. Silvio in the centre of the arena. Ben down here, beneath me. Greta over on the platform. They both face Silvio.

I crane my head down a little further: look at where he's standing; look at what's above his head. A plan forms in my mind. It's risky, but it might just work.

BEN

I think I always really knew it would come down to this, that it would all be for nothing. All I can think about are Hoshiko and Greta. How do I get them out of this?

Silvio doesn't look like a bad guy. He's tiny really, with fine, chiselled features. There's something chilling about him though, and it's not just the fact that he's aiming a gun at my head. You just look at him and you know, somehow, that he's *evil*.

Greta stands above us, her chin thrust forward in defiance.

There's only one choice left for Hoshi to make now. Stay there and get caught by the police, or come down and get shot by this crazed ringmaster. Some choice.

"Look," I plead with Silvio. "I'm the one they want most of all. I'll come with you right now: you'll get all the glory. Please. Greta will give you back your chimp and you can let her and Hoshi go. No one will ever know."

He laughs, maniacally and then snarls.

"Bojo is not a chimp, you imbecile! You think I'd let Hoshiko go now, after everything she's done? This is my Cirque. Mine! The people in it are mine. They need to be taught that no one, *no one*, challenges my authority; no one even so much as breathes here without my say-so. Have you any idea what revenue you've cost me? What damage to my reputation?"

I realize with a shiver that the guy is completely insane. A – what's the word? – a megalomaniac. He's facing towards me, waving the gun, up to the hatch where we're all assuming

Hoshi still is, back to me, then to Greta, so he doesn't see the hatch to the left of him slowly move.

He doesn't see a girl on a trapeze drop down above his head.

Greta and I see though. We see her, and we see what she's holding in her mouth.

The grenade.

She catches my eye and fixes on me. She doesn't take it off me as she swings across. It's like it was that first night in the Cirque.

I don't want us to die here, tonight, like this.

She arcs across the arena, faster and faster, the grenade dangling precariously in her mouth. What was it that sergeant guy said? It will obliterate anything within five metres.

Like a light going on in my head, I realize suddenly what her plan is.

Silvio's over five metres from the door. If Greta and I can somehow get near enough to the exit before he sees her, maybe, just maybe, this could work.

Inch by inch, I begin edging across, really, really slowly, in the unlikely hope that Silvio won't notice me moving.

I take a deep breath.

"She's not up there any more," I tell him, trying to sound confident. "This whole time you've been worrying about your stupid monkey, she's gone."

His head snaps over to the open hatch. He laughs, but he's not certain.

"She can't go anywhere. She's trapped, you fool."

"She can and she did. I've just watched her head straight

out of that door. There's more than one hatch in the roof of this circus ring, you know."

He looks to where I'm pointing. It's as far away from the exit as I can get.

Greta catches on quickly. As quick as lightning, she jumps from the podium and runs across to stand next to me, holding on to Bojo the whole time.

"She's escaped, Silvio. You'll never find her now."

"Then she's sacrificed you!"

He fires the gun again, but this time, he doesn't miss. I feel an agony I never knew was possible in my leg. Everything swims. He's shot me.

HOSHIKO

As soon as he fires the gun, I know he's going to kill them. Ben's on the ground, holding his leg. He isn't dead though. His head's moving.

It's now or never.

I loop past the spot where Amina's body hung, just yesterday. I can feel her with me. It's like she's still here, alive, willing me on.

I bring one arm in and take the grenade out of my mouth.

Greta's not going to have the strength to move Ben on her own; I need to make sure I can reach them. Still swinging, I pull the pin out.

I swing towards the middle of the ring, towards Silvio. The instant I'm central, I drop the grenade. It lands with a clang at his feet.

He looks down at it, sizzling, then looks up and sees me for the first time. Our eyes meet. I see the realization hit him and I smile triumphantly before curling my legs up and somersaulting down, landing right next to Greta and Ben.

"Quick!"

We grab hold of Ben and pull him as hard and fast as we can, towards the exit.

We've nearly made it to the doorway when the blast hits us, shaking the whole building. My ears are deafened and we're all thrown forward about ten feet.

We're OK though, we're OK. I pull myself up, reach down and help Greta stand. She is clutching on to Bojo tightly, as he chatters in terror. Ben's just about conscious and he stumbles forward.

I look behind me.

The whole arena is a ball of fire, blazing at its hardest where Silvio stood, seconds ago. I can't make anything out through the inferno, but he can't have survived this; he must have been blown to pieces.

Greta and I drag ourselves to the door, Ben propped between us. It's locked, but Greta's got the keys, stuffed down the front of her leotard. The water from the overhead sprinklers doesn't stand a chance in this inferno, not against the ferocity of the flames and the smell of toxic burning metal.

I look at Greta. She's gasping for breath.

"Drop to the floor," I tell her, somewhere in my mind remembering that the smoke won't be as intense there. She drops down.

Ben's propped up against me as I fiddle with the keys, the heat of the fire getting ever more intense. My wounded feet respond to the heat, as if they're being burnt anew. I must keep focusing.

I fiddle with key after key, my hands shaking clumsily. Finally, finally, it's the right one. I unlock the door, breathing in the sweet night air. We're out.

The three of us. Alive. Not dead. Not yet.

BEN

We make our way into the night, sucking down huge lungfuls of air. Woozy with the pain from my leg, I hang uselessly between the two girls like a dead weight.

I look down. Big mistake; there's a great bloody mess where my thigh usually is. I think I'm going to throw up again.

What now? I look around. Every building, every metre of space around us: flashing lights. We're completely surrounded by the police.

In the centre of them, directly opposite me, stands my mother.

Our eyes meet.

She must be beyond furious with me: I'm not supposed to challenge her, not supposed to embarrass her. I'm supposed to be a puppet, we all are.

I'm not though, not any more. My strings have been cut. I can think for myself now, feel with my heart and my head, just like I promised Priya I would.

Mother turns to the police officer next to her and says something to him.

"Benedict," he calls through a megaphone. "Step forward now and we'll get you to hospital, son."

Every officer has a gun aimed at Hoshi and Greta. They're going to shoot them: shoot them and save me.

Not if I can help it. I move in front of them, a human shield, protecting them.

I can feel myself swaying. Everything's gone misty; I don't know how much longer I can hold on.

"Dregs, walk towards me with your hands up!"

Slowly, Hoshiko moves from behind me and raises her hands and Greta follows suit. Hoshi looks at me, she mouths something.

"I love you."

My heart leaps.

"I love you too."

I step forward. I'm wobbling against her.

The police have totally surrounded us, their cars forming a barrier. One of them calls out.

"Give it up, Ben, don't do anything stupid."

Yeah right, like there's even that option.

"Give it up!" the same guy calls again.

Something about his voice clicks with me the second time: I recognize it. I look over. It's difficult to focus but, somehow, I manage. The police officer on the far right lowers his torch for an instant, shining it on his own face, instead of mine. He's removed his helmet. It's Jack.

"This way," I say as quietly as I can to Hoshiko and Greta. It's hard to get the words out. "Follow my lead."

We move as one, edging forward and to the right so that we reach Jack's car.

"I've got this one, Ma'am," he calls. "Benedict, Hoshiko, Greta. Get in the car." He looks at me, gives an almost imperceptible wink.

"Do what he says," I tell Hoshiko.

We lower ourselves awkwardly into the car while Jack gets into the driver's seat. He turns around for a second, grins at me, then puts his sirens on and we speed away, leaving the circus burning behind us.

HOSHIKO

It turns out the policeman driving us away is the same one who helped Ben before.

As soon as we're out of the Cirque, he switches off his sirens and lights, and takes one of the side roads, away from the main highway.

"Lucky, I got there in time," he says. "You aren't easy people to second guess."

"Where are we going?" Greta asks. She's still holding Bojo, stroking him gently as he calms down in her lap. Silvio was right: she'd never have hurt him.

"There's a van, waiting for us at the top of the hill. We arranged it before, just in case we got you out of there alive." He laughs. "Didn't think we would though. Not for one second, if I'm honest."

"What about you? What are you going to do?" I ask him. His eyes meet mine in the rear-view mirror.

"I blew my cover the second I left that circus with you. You aren't the only ones running for your lives now; they'll be after all of us in about five seconds."

Another person who's sacrificed himself for us.

"I'm so sorry," I tell him.

"Hey, I couldn't stand being in the police anyway; only did it so I could help the cause." His jovial tone doesn't seem to fit the gravity of the situation. "I'd rather die like this than live like that."

"Where are we going?" Greta asks, again.

"Well now, there's a question. First, we switch vehicles.

Secondly, I think we might need some first aid; we've got people lined up who can help. Then, your guess is as good as mine. Out of the country quickly, I suppose, if we can make it in time. They'll be closing all the borders soon. Ben made a little speech earlier that's already changed things. They're rioting down in the city, Pures and Dregs together."

His eyes meet mine again.

"This isn't the end, Hoshiko, not by a long shot. It's the beginning."

Ben is slumped against me, unconscious now.

"It's OK," Jack must see the fear on my face. "He'll be fine. It's superficial. He wouldn't have made it out at all if it wasn't."

"What about the others? That blast? Did it get anyone else?"

I feel sick; dreading the answer to my question.

"No. They were all locked in their dorms once the show was cancelled. The impact won't have reached over there. Luckily the arena was empty; the whole place was a ball of flames."

I think of Silvio, the grenade at his feet; I picture him being blown to pieces. Maybe a better person than me would feel guilty, but I don't. Whatever happens now, at least *he* can't hurt me, or Greta, or any of the other Dregs, ever again.

We wind along the roads and make it to the top of the hill. There, just as Jack said there would be, is a van, hidden in a little thicket. He comes around, opens the door, and lifts Ben out. Greta and I follow. I'm limping, but I can make it.

I look down the hill. A stream of flashing blue lights

stretches in both directions, as far as the eye can see. The Powerhouse monument is still beaming its smile down on the city but, underneath its gaze, the arena burns. The place I've spent most of my life. It looks somehow beautiful, flaming in the night.

"Hoshiko?" Jack's voice breaks my daze.

Ben is already slumped on a pile of blankets in the back of the van. Greta gets in next and sits up close to me. I take her hand, and gently ease my other arm around Ben, cradling his head against me.

As we drive away, I watch the Cirque burn. It grows smaller and smaller, becoming just a speck on the horizon until, finally, I can see it no more.

ACKNOWLEDGEMENTS

Firstly, I would like to thank my two lovely sons, Will and Adam – you two will always be my very best creations.

Producing a book is a team effort and there are so many other people I would like to thank…

My mum and dad, who have always believed in me and supported me, practically and emotionally, right from when I was a little girl and Mum carried a story I wrote around in her handbag. Mum has read every draft of this book and has been such an invaluable proofreader.

My sisters, Katie and Gemma, my biggest cheerleaders and the providers of the greatest free childcare in the world.

Thérèse Coen, who was the first person in the industry to believe in *Show Stopper* and believe in me, and who championed me so wonderfully from the very beginning. Your enthusiastic response to my submission and all your efforts afterwards were the start of this book's journey and I cannot begin to tell you how much that means.

Everyone from the fantastic Madeleine Milburn agency, especially Maddy, Alice Sutherland-Hawes and Hayley Steed for representing me so well and for all of your hard work and commitment. It's good to know I am in such safe hands.

All the wonderful people at Scholastic for taking a chance on me and for helping me through this journey.

Thanks especially to Olivia Horrox and Roisin O'Shea for such brilliant publicity and marketing.

Emma Jobling and Peter Matthews for their patience and

attention to detail. (And sorry to both for my dodgy semi-colon use!)

Andrew Biscomb and his team for the wonderful artwork they have produced. I loved the sparkly purple awesomeness of the proof copy and was completely blown away by the intricate, original and beautiful final cover design.

And, of course, I owe so much to Lauren Fortune, my brilliant editor. You have shown such faith in me and such passion for my work, and have been such a source of inspiration and support. This book would not be here today without you.

The extremely talented Siân Schwar, the best writing friend a girl could ever wish for. I loved sharing the early stages of our journey together and I know that your time is coming soon – maybe once the baby/ies grow up a bit! You have been such an important part of all this and I don't think I could have done it without you.

My trusted friends and family who read the book early on, and gave me so much support and encouragement when all of this just seemed an unlikely dream. Joanna Large, Kat Parmley, Fiona Vickers, Nicola Heelam (my cheerleader in the north!), Auntie Janette, Laura Dockerill, Gill Barker, Sarah Martin, Lin Hurlock, Mary Callender, Olly Murley… I hope I haven't forgotten anyone and I'm so sorry if I have.

My brilliant English teacher, Mrs Morley, who lit the fire and fanned the flames.

The girls of 2CG at Brentwood School, for being a very talented and inspiring bunch of writers themselves, and because I promised them I'd give them a mention!

The reader for buying this book – I hope you like it.

And last, but not least, thank you to Mark – I could not have done any of this without your support. Thank you for putting up with a messy house and a slightly deranged wife for all these years and for giving me the time and space to write – not easy with a young family to entertain and care for. Thank you for reading *Show Stopper* time and time again for me and for giving me so much constructive and helpful advice that, by rights, you should be credited as a co-author. Thanks above all, for being the best friend and husband I could ever have, and the best daddy in the world to our boys. I love you.

Hayley Barker has a BA (hons) degree from Birmingham University and has taught secondary school English for eighteen years. She is a huge YA fiction fan and says being published is the most exciting thing that has ever happened to her. Hayley was inspired to write *Show Stopper* by her fears about the growing wave of crime and animosity against minority groups in England. She lives in Essex with her husband and two young sons.

Follow Hayley on Twitter: @HayleyABarker